W9-ATN-571

ALSO BY TONI MORRISON

The Bluest Eye (1970)

Sula (1974)

Song of Solomon (1977)

Tar Baby (1981)

Beloved (1987)

Jazz (1992)

Playing in the Dark (1992)

Race-ing Justice, En-Gendering Power (1992)
Editor

The Nobel Lecture in Literature (1994)

Birth of a Nation'hood (1996)
Coeditor with Claudia Brodsky Lacour

The Dancing Mind (1996)

PARADISE

PARADISE

TONI MORRISON

Alfred A. Knopf

NEW YORK · TORONTO

1998

THIS IS A BORZOI BOOK
PUBLISHED BY ALFRED A. KNOPF, INC.,
AND ALFRED A. KNOPF CANADA

Copyright © 1997 by Toni Morrison

All rights reserved under International and Pan-American
Copyright Conventions. Published in the United States
by Alfred A. Knopf, Inc., New York, and distributed by
Random House, Inc., New York. Published simultaneously
in Canada by Alfred A. Knopf Canada, a division of
Random House of Canada Limited, Toronto, and distributed
by Random House of Canada Limited, Toronto.

www.randomhouse.com

ISBN 0-679-43374-0
LC 97-80913

Canadian Cataloging in Publication Data
Morrison, Toni
Paradise
ISBN 0-676-97113-X
I. Title
PS3563.O8749P37   1998   813'.54   C97-932259-6

Manufactured in the United States of America

Published January 15, 1998
Reprinted Five Times
Seventh Printing, February 1998

Lois

For many are the pleasant forms which exist in
           numerous sins,
    and incontinencies,
    and disgraceful passions
    and fleeting pleasures,
        which (men) embrace until they become
        sober
        and go up to their resting place.
And they will find me there,
    and they will live,
    and they will not die again.

RUBY

They shoot the white girl first. With the rest they can take their time. No need to hurry out here. They are seventeen miles from a town which has ninety miles between it and any other. Hiding places will be plentiful in the Convent, but there is time and the day has just begun.

They are nine, over twice the number of the women they are obliged to stampede or kill and they have the paraphernalia for either requirement: rope, a palm leaf cross, handcuffs, Mace and sunglasses, along with clean, handsome guns.

They have never been this deep in the Convent. Some of them have parked Chevrolets near its porch to pick up a string of peppers or have gone into the kitchen for a gallon of barbecue sauce; but only a few have seen the halls, the chapel, the schoolroom, the bedrooms. Now they all will. And at last they will see the cellar and expose its filth to the light that is soon to scour the Oklahoma sky. Meantime they are startled by the clothes they are wearing—suddenly aware of being ill-dressed. For at the dawn of a July day how could they have guessed the cold that is inside this place? Their T-shirts, work shirts and dashikis soak up cold like fever. Those who have worn work shoes are unnerved by the thunder of their steps on marble floors; those in Pro-Keds by the silence. Then there is the grandeur. Only the two who are wearing ties seem to belong here and one by one each is reminded that before it was a Convent, this house was an embezzler's folly. A mansion where bisque and rose-tone marble floors segue into teak ones. Isinglass holds yesterday's light and patterns walls that were stripped and whitewashed fifty years ago. The ornate bathroom fixtures, which sickened the nuns, were replaced with good plain spigots, but the princely tubs and sinks, which could not be inexpensively removed, remain coolly corrupt. The embezzler's joy that could be demolished was, particularly in the dining room, which the nuns converted to a schoolroom, where stilled Arapaho girls once sat and learned to forget.

Now armed men search rooms where macramé baskets float next to Flemish candelabra; where Christ and His mother glow in niches trimmed in grapevines. The Sisters of the Sacred Cross chipped away all the nymphs, but curves of their marble hair still strangle grape leaves and tease the fruit. The chill intensifies as the men spread deeper into the mansion, taking their time, looking, listening, alert to the female malice that hides here and the yeast-and-butter smell of rising dough.

One of them, the youngest, looks back, forcing himself to see how the dream he is in might go. The shot woman, lying uncomfortably on marble, waves her fingers at him—or seems to. So his dream is doing okay, except for its color. He has never before dreamed in colors such as these: imperial black sporting a wild swipe of red, then thick, feverish yellow. Like the clothes of an easily had woman. The leading man pauses, raising his left hand to halt the silhouettes behind him. They stop, editing their breath, making friendly adjustments in the grip of rifles and handguns. The leading man turns and gestures the separations: you two over there to the kitchen; two more upstairs; two others into the chapel. He saves himself, his brother and the one who thinks he is dreaming for the cellar.

They part gracefully without words or haste. Earlier, when they blew open the Convent door, the nature of their mission made them giddy. But the target, after all, is detritus: throwaway people that sometimes blow back into the room after being swept out the door. So the venom is manageable now. Shooting the first woman (the white one) has clarified it like butter: the pure oil of hatred on top, its hardness stabilized below.

Outside, the mist is waist high. It will turn silver soon and make grass rainbows low enough for children's play before the sun burns it off, exposing acres of bluestem and maybe witch tracks as well.

Ruby

. . .

The kitchen is bigger than the house in which either man was born. The ceiling barn-rafter high. More shelving than Ace's Grocery Store. The table is fourteen feet long if an inch, and it's easy to tell that the women they are hunting have been taken by surprise. At one end a full pitcher of milk stands near four bowls of shredded wheat. At the other end vegetable chopping has been interrupted: scallion piled like a handful of green confetti nestles brilliant disks of carrot, and the potatoes, peeled and whole, are bone white, wet and crisp. Stock simmers on the stove. It is restaurant size with eight burners and on a shelf beneath the great steel hood a dozen loaves of bread swell. A stool is overturned. There are no windows.

One man signals the other to open the pantry while he goes to the back door. It is closed but unlocked. Peering out he sees an old hen, her puffed and bloody hind parts cherished, he supposes, for delivering freaks—double, triple yolks in outsize and misshapen shells. Soft stuttering comes from the coop beyond; fryers padding confidently into the yard's mist disappear, reappear and disappear again, each flat eye indifferent to anything but breakfast. No footprints disturb the mud around the stone steps. This man closes the door and joins his partner at the pantry. Together they scan dusty mason jars and what is left of last year's canning: tomatoes, green beans, peaches. Slack, they think. August just around the corner and these women have not even sorted, let alone washed, the jars.

He turns the fire off under the stockpot. His mother bathed him in a pot no bigger than that. A luxury in the sod house where she was born. The house he lives in is big, comfortable, and this town is resplendent compared to his birthplace, which had gone from feet to belly in fifty years. From Haven, a dreamtown in Oklahoma Territory, to Haven, a ghosttown in Oklahoma State. Freedmen who stood tall in 1889 dropped to their knees in 1934 and were stomach-crawling by 1948. That is why they are here in this Convent. To make sure it never happens again. That nothing inside or out rots the one all-black town worth the pain. All the others he knew about or heard tell of knuckled to or merged with white towns; otherwise, like Haven, they had shriveled into tracery: foundation outlines marked by the way grass grew there, wallpaper turned negative behind missing window-panes, schoolhouse floors moved aside by elder trees growing toward the bell housing. One thousand citizens in 1905 becoming five hundred by 1934. Then two hundred, then eighty as cotton collapsed or railroad companies laid their tracks elsewhere. Subsistence farming, once the only bounty a large family needed, became just scrap farming as each married son got his bit, which had to be broken up into more pieces for his children, until finally the owners of the bits and pieces who had not walked off in disgust welcomed any offer from a white speculator, so eager were they to get away and try someplace else. A big city this time, or a small town—anywhere that was already built.

But he and the others, veterans all, had a different idea. Loving what Haven had been—the idea of it and its reach—they carried that devotion, gentling and nursing it from Bataan to Guam, from Iwo Jima to Stuttgart, and they made up their minds to do it again. He touched the stove hood admiring its construction and power. It was the same length as the brick oven that once sat in the middle of his hometown. When they got back to the States, they took it apart, carrying the bricks, the hearthstone and its iron plate two hundred and forty miles west—far far from the old Creek Nation which once upon a time a witty government called "unassigned land." He remembers the ceremony they'd had when the Oven's iron lip was recemented into place and its worn letters polished for all to see. He himself had helped clean off sixty-two years of carbon and animal fat so the words shone as brightly as they did in 1890 when they were new. And if it hurt—pulling asunder what their grandfathers had put together—it was nothing compared to what they had endured and what they might become if they did not begin anew. As new fathers, who had fought the world, they could not (would not) be less than the Old Fathers who had outfoxed it; who had not let danger or natural evil keep them from cutting Haven out of mud and who knew enough to seal their triumph with that priority. An Oven. Round as a head, deep as desire. Living in or near their wagons, boiling meal in the open, cutting sod and mesquite for shelter, the Old Fathers did that first: put most of their strength into constructing the huge, flawlessly designed Oven that both nourished them and monumentalized what they had done. When it was finished—each pale brick perfectly pitched; the chimney wide, lofty; the pegs and grill secure; the draft pulling steadily from the tail hole; the fire door plumb—then the ironmonger did his work. From barrel staves and busted axles, from kettles and bent nails, he fashioned an iron plate five feet by two and set it at the base of the Oven's mouth. It is still not clear where the words came from. Something he heard, invented, or something whispered to him while he slept curled over his tools in a wagon bed. His name was Morgan and who knew if he invented or stole the half-dozen or so words he forged. Words that seemed at first to bless them; later to confound them; finally to announce that they had lost.

The man eyes the kitchen sink. He moves to the long table and lifts the pitcher of milk. He sniffs it first and then, the pistol in his right hand, he uses his left to raise the pitcher to his mouth, taking such long, measured swallows the milk is half gone by the time he smells the wintergreen.

On the floor above two men walk the hall and examine the four bedrooms, each with a name card taped on its door. The first name, written in lipstick, is Seneca. The next, Divine, is inked in capital letters. They exchange knowing looks when they learn that each woman sleeps not in a bed, like normal people, but in a hammock. Other than that, and except for a narrow desk or an end table, there is no additional furniture. No clothes in the closets, of course, since the women wore no-fit dirty dresses and nothing you could honestly call shoes. But there are strange things nailed or taped to the walls or propped in a corner. A 1968 calendar, large X's marking various dates (April 4, July 19); a letter written in blood so smeary its satanic message cannot be deciphered; an astrology chart; a fedora tilted on the plastic neck of a female torso, and, in a place that once housed Christians—well, Catholics anyway—not a cross of Jesus anywhere. But what alarms the two men most is the series of infant booties and shoes ribboned to a cord hanging from a crib in the last bedroom they enter. A teething ring, cracked and stiff, dangles among the tiny shoes. Signaling with

7

his eyes, one man directs his partner to four more bedrooms on the opposite side of the hall. He himself moves closer to the bouquet of baby shoes. Looking for what? More evidence? He isn't sure. Blood? A little toe, maybe, left in a white calfskin shoe? He slides the safety on his gun and joins the search across the hall.

These rooms are normal. Messy—the floor in one of them is covered with food-encrusted dishes, dirty cups, its bed invisible under a hill of clothes; another room sports two rocking chairs full of dolls; a third the debris and smell of a heavy drinker—but normal at least.

His saliva is bitter and although he knows this place is diseased, he is startled by the whip of pity flicking in his chest. What, he wonders, could do this to women? How can their plain brains think up such things: revolting sex, deceit and the sly torture of children? Out here in wide-open space tucked away in a mansion—no one to bother or insult them—they managed to call into question the value of almost every woman he knew. The winter coat money for which his father saved in secret for two harvests; the light in his mother's eyes when she stroked its seal collar. The surprise party he and his brothers threw for a sister's sixteenth birthday. Yet here, not twenty miles away from a quiet, orderly community, there were women like none he knew or ever heard tell of. In this place of all places. Unique and isolated, his was a town justifiably pleased with itself. It neither had nor needed a jail. No criminals had ever come from his town. And the one or two people who acted up, humiliated their families or threatened the town's view of itself were taken good care of. Certainly there wasn't a slack or sloven woman anywhere in town and the reasons, he thought, were clear. From the beginning its people were free and protected. A sleepless woman could always rise from her bed, wrap a shawl around her shoulders and sit on the steps in the moonlight. And if she felt like it she could walk out the yard and on down the road. No lamp and no fear. A hiss-crackle from the side of the road would never scare her because whatever it was that made the sound, it wasn't something creeping up on her. Nothing for ninety miles around thought she was prey. She could stroll as slowly as she liked, think of food preparations, war, of family things, or lift her eyes to stars and think of nothing at all. Lampless and without fear she could make her way. And if a light shone from a house up a ways and the cry of a colicky baby caught her attention, she might step over to the house and call out softly to the woman inside trying to soothe the baby. The two of them might take turns massaging the infant stomach, rocking, or trying to get a little soda water down. When the baby quieted they could sit together for a spell, gossiping, chuckling low so as not to wake anybody else.

The woman could decide to go back to her own house then, refreshed and ready to sleep, or she might keep her direction and walk further down the road, past other houses, past the three churches, past the feedlot. On out, beyond the limits of town, because nothing at the edge thought she was prey.

At each end of the hall is a bathroom. As each man enters one, neither is working his jaws because both believe they are prepared for anything. In one bathroom, the biggest, the taps are too small and dowdy for the wide sink. The bathtub rests on the backs of four mermaids—their tails split wide for the tub's security, their breasts arched for stability. The tile underfoot is bottle green. A Modess box is on the toilet tank and a bucket of soiled things stands nearby. There is no toilet paper. Only one mirror has not been covered with chalky paint and that one the man ignores. He does not want to see himself stalking females or their liquid. With relief he backs out and closes the door. With relief he lets his handgun point down.

Downstairs two men, a father and his son, are not smiling, although when they first enter the chapel they feel like it because it was true: graven idols were worshipped here. Tiny men and women in white dresses and capes of blue and gold stand on little shelves cut into niches in the wall. Holding a baby or gesturing, their blank faces fake innocence. Candles had obviously burned at their feet and, just as Reverend Pulliam said, food had probably been offered as well, since there were little bowls on either side of the doorway. When this was over they would tell Reverend Pulliam how right he was and laugh in Reverend Misner's face.

There were irreconcilable differences among the congregations in town, but members from all of them merged solidly on the necessity of this action: Do what you have to. Neither the Convent nor the women in it can continue.

Pity. Once, the Convent had been a true if aloof neighbor, surrounded by corn, buffalo grass, clover and approached by a dirt track barely seen from the road. The mansion-turned-Convent was there long before the town, and the last boarding Arapaho girls had already gone when the fifteen families arrived. That was twenty-five years ago, when all their dreams outstretched the men who had them. A road straight as a die had been cleared through the center of town and lined on one side by a paved walk. Seven of the families had more than five hundred acres, three had nearly a thousand. By and by, when the road became a named street, a man named Ossie organized a horse race to celebrate. From army-issue tents, half-finished houses and freshly cleared land people rode in, bringing what they had. Out came stored-away things and things got up on the spot: guitars and late melon, hazelnuts, rhubarb pies and a mouth organ, a washboard, roast lamb, pepper rice, Lil Green, "In the Dark," Louis Jordan and His Tympany Five; homemade beer and groundhog meat fried and simmered in gravy. The women tied bright scarves over their hair; the children made themselves hats of wild poppies and river vine. Ossie owned a two-year-old and a four, both fast and pretty as brides. The other horses were simply company: Ace's spotted horse, Miss Esther's ancient featherweight, all four of Nathan's plow horses plus his mare and a half-broke pony that, unclaimed, grazed the creekbank.

The riders quarreled so long over saddle or bareback, the mothers of nursing babies told them to mount or change roles. The men argued handicaps and placed quarter bets with abandon. When the gun went off only three horses leapt forward. The rest stepped sideways or cut out over lumber stacked near unfinished homes. When the race finally got under way, the women yelled from the meadow, while their children shrieked and danced in grass up to their shoulders. The pony finished first, but since it lost its rider two furlongs out, the winner was Nathan's auburn mare. The little girl with the most poppies on her head was chosen to present the first-place ribbon hung with Ossie's Purple Heart. The winner was seven years old then and grinning as though he'd won the Kentucky Derby. Now he was somewhere down in the cellar of a Convent watching out for awful women who, when they came, one by one, were obviously not nuns, real or even pretend, but members, it was thought, of some other cult. Nobody knew. But it wasn't important to know because all of them, each in her turn, and like the old Mother Superior and the servant who used to, still sold produce, barbecue sauce, good bread and the hottest peppers in the world. For a pricey price you could buy a string of the purply black peppers or a relish made from them. Either took the cake for pure burning power. The relish lasted years with proper attention, and though many customers tried planting the seeds, the pepper grew nowhere outside the Convent's garden.

Strange neighbors, most folks said, but harmless. More than harmless, helpful even on occasion. They took people in—lost folk or folks who needed a rest. Early reports were of kindness and very good food. But now everybody knew it was all a lie, a front, a carefully planned disguise for what was really going on. Once the emergency was plain, representatives from all three churches met at the Oven because they couldn't agree on which, if any, church should host a meeting to decide on what to do now that the women had ignored all warnings.

It was a secret meeting, but the rumors had been whispered for more than a year. Outrages that had been accumulating all along took shape as evidence. A mother was knocked down the stairs by her cold-eyed daughter. Four damaged infants were born in one family. Daughters refused to get out of bed. Brides disappeared on their honeymoons. Two brothers shot each other on New Year's Day. Trips to Demby for VD shots common. And what went on at the Oven these days was not to be believed. So when nine men decided to meet there, they had to run everybody off the place with shotguns before they could sit in the beams of their flashlights to take matters into their own hands. The proof they had been collecting since the terrible discovery in the spring could not be denied: the one thing that connected all these catastrophes was in the Convent. And in the Convent were those women.

The father walks the aisle checking the pews right and left. He runs a frond of light from his Black & Decker under each seat. The knee rests are turned up. At the altar he pauses. One window of pale yellow floats above him in the dimness. Things look uncleaned. He steps to a tray of small glasses positioned on the wall to see if any food offerings remain there. Except for grime and spider webbing, the red glasses are empty. Maybe they are not for food but for money. Or trash? There is a gum wrapper in the dirtiest one. Doublemint.

He shakes his head and joins his son back at the altar. The son points. The father beams the wall below the yellow window where, just barely, the sun announces. The outline of a huge cross comes into view. Clean as new paint is the space where there used to be a Jesus.

The brothers approaching the cellar were once identical. Although they are twins, their wives look more alike than they do. One is smooth, agile and smokes Te Amo cigars. The other is tougher, meaner, but hides his face when he prays. But both have wide innocent eyes and both are as single-minded now standing before a closed door as they were in 1942 when they enlisted. Then they were looking for an out—a break away from a life where all was owed, nothing owned. Now they want in. Then, in the forties, they had nothing to lose. Now everything requires their protection. From the beginning when the town was founded they knew isolation did not guarantee safety. Men strong and willing were needed when lost or aimless strangers did not just drive through, hardly glancing at a sleepy town with three churches within one mile of one another but nothing to serve a traveler: no diner, no police, no gas station, no public phone, no movie house, no hospital. Sometimes, if they were young and drunk or old and sober, the strangers might spot three or four colored girls walk-dawdling along the side of the road. Walking a few yards, stopping as their talk required; skipping on, pausing to laugh or slap another's arm in play. The strangers get interested in them, perhaps. Three cars, say, a '53 Bel Air, green with cream-colored interior, license number 085 B, six cylinders, double molding on rear fender pontoon, Powerglide two-speed automatic transmission; and say a '49 Dodge Wayfarer, black, cracked rear window, fender skirts, fluid drive, checkerboard grille; and a '53 Oldsmobile with Arkansas plates. The drivers slow down, put their heads out the windows and holler. Their eyes crinkled in mischief they drive around the girls, making U-turns and K's, churning up grass seed in front of the houses, flushing cats in front of Ace's Grocery Store. Circling. The girls' eyes freeze as they back into each other. Then, one at a time, the townsmen come out of the houses, the backyards, off the scaffold of the bank, out of the feed store. One of the passengers has opened the front of his trousers and hung himself out the window to scare the girls. The girls' little hearts stand up and they cannot close their eyes fast enough, so they jerk their heads aside. But the townsmen do look at it, see the wish in this most militant of gestures, and smile. Smile reluctantly and in spite of themselves because they know that from this moment on, if not before, this man, till his final illness, will do as much serious damage to colored folks as he can.

More men come out, and more. Their guns are not pointing at anything, just held slackly against their thighs. Twenty men; now twenty-five. Circling the circling cars. Ninety miles from the nearest O for operator and ninety from the nearest badge. If the day had been dry, the dust spuming behind the tires would have discolored them all. As it was, just a little gravel kicked up in the tread they left behind.

The twins have powerful memories. Between them they remember the details of everything that ever happened—things they witnessed and things they have not. The exact temperature of the weather when the cars circled the girls as well as the bushel yield of every farm in the county. And they have never forgotten the message or the specifics of any story, especially the controlling one told to them by their grandfather—the man who put the words in the Oven's black mouth. A story that explained why neither the founders of Haven nor their descendants could tolerate anybody but themselves. On the journey from Mississippi and two Louisiana parishes to Oklahoma, the one hundred and fifty-eight freedmen were unwelcome on each grain of soil from Yazoo to Fort Smith. Turned away by rich Choctaw and poor whites, chased by yard dogs, jeered at by camp prostitutes and their children, they were nevertheless unprepared for the aggressive discouragement they received from Negro towns already being built. The headline of a feature in the *Herald*, "Come Prepared or Not at All," could not mean them, could it? Smart, strong, and eager to work their own land, they believed they were more than prepared—they were destined. It stung them into confusion to learn they did not have enough money to satisfy the restrictions the "self-supporting" Negroes required. In short, they were too poor, too bedraggled-looking to enter, let alone reside in, the communities that were soliciting Negro homesteaders. This contemptuous dismissal by the lucky changed the temperature of their blood twice. First they boiled at being written up as "people who preferred saloons and crap games to homes, churches and schools." Then, remembering their spectacular history, they cooled. What began as overheated determination became cold-blooded obsession. "They don't know we or about we," said one man. "Us free like them; was slave like them. What for is this difference?"

Denied and guarded against, they altered their route and made their way west of the unassigned lands, south of Logan County, across the Canadian River into Arapaho territory. Becoming stiffer, prouder with each misfortune, the details of which were engraved into the twins' powerful memories. Unembellished stories told and retold in dark barns, near the Oven at sunset, in the Sunday afternoon light of prayer meetings. About the saddles of the four black-skinned bandits who fed them dried buffalo meat before robbing them of their rifles. About the soundlessness of the funnel that twisted through and around their camp; the sleeping children who woke sailing through the air. The glint of the horses on which watching Choctaw sat. At suppertime, when it was too dark for any work except that which could be done by firelight, the Old Fathers recited the stories of that journey: the signs God gave to guide them—to watering places, to Creek with whom they could barter their labor for wagons, horses and pasture; away from prairie-dog towns fifty miles wide and Satan's malefactions: abandoned women with no belongings, rumors of riverbed gold.

The twins believed it was when he discovered how narrow the path of righteousness could be that their grandfather chose the words for the Oven's lip. Furniture was held together by wooden dowels because nails were so expensive, but he sacrificed his treasure of three-inch and four, bent and straight, to say something important that would last.

Once the letters were in place, but before anyone had time to ponder the words they formed, a roof was raised next to where the Oven sat waiting to be seasoned. On crates and makeshift benches, Haven people gathered for talk, for society and the comfort of hot game. Later, when buffalo grass gave way to a nice little town with a street down the middle, wooden houses, one church, a school, a store, the citizens still gathered there. They pierced guinea hens and whole deer for the spit; they turned the ribs and rubbed extra salt into sides of cooling veal. Those were the days of slow cooking, when flames were kept so low a twenty-pound turkey roasted all night and a side could take two days to cook down to the bone. Whenever livestock was slaughtered, or when the taste for unsmoked game was high, Haven people brought the kill to the Oven and stayed sometimes to fuss and quarrel with the Morgan family about seasonings and the proper test for "done." They stayed to gossip, complain, roar with laughter and drink walking coffee in the shade of the eaves. And any child in earshot was subject to being ordered to fan flies, haul wood, clean the worktable or beat the earth with a tamping block.

In 1910 there were two churches in Haven and the All-Citizens Bank, four rooms in the schoolhouse, five stores selling dry goods, feed and foodstuffs—but the traffic to and from the Oven was greater than to all of those. No family needed more than a simple cookstove as long as the Oven was alive, and it always was. Even in 1934 when everything else about the town was dying; when it was clear as daylight that talk of electricity would remain just talk and when gas lines and sewers were Tulsa marvels, the Oven stayed alive. Until the Big Drought, running water was not missed because the well was deep. As boys, the twins had swung overhand from the cottonwood branches leaning near it and hung dangerously above the clear water to admire the reflection of their feet. Time after time they heard stories of the blue dresses and bonnets the men bought for the women with cash from the first harvest or the first cuts from the herd. The theatrical arrival of the Saint Louis piano, ordered soon as Zion's floor was laid. They imagined their mother as a ten-year-old among other young girls clustered quietly about the piano, sneaking a touch, a key stroke before the deaconess slapped their hands away. Their pure sopranos at rehearsal

15

singing "He will take care of you . . . ," which He did, safe to say, until He stopped.

The twins were born in 1924 and heard for twenty years what the previous forty had been like. They listened to, imagined and remembered every single thing because each detail was a jolt of pleasure, erotic as a dream, out-thrilling and more purposeful than even the war they had fought in.

In 1949, young and newly married, they were anything but fools. Long before the war, Haven residents were leaving and those who had not packed up were planning to. The twins stared at their dwindling postwar future and it was not hard to persuade other home boys to repeat what the Old Fathers had done in 1890. Ten generations had known what lay Out There: space, once beckoning and free, became unmonitored and seething; became a void where random and organized evil erupted when and where it chose—behind any standing tree, behind the door of any house, humble or grand. Out There where your children were sport, your women quarry, and where your very person could be annulled; where congregations carried arms to church and ropes coiled in every saddle. Out There where every cluster of whitemen looked like a posse, being alone was being dead. But lessons had been learned and relearned in the last three generations about how to protect a town. So, like the ex-slaves who knew what came first, the ex-soldiers broke up the Oven and loaded it into two trucks even before they took apart their own beds. Before first light in the middle of August, fifteen families moved out of Haven—headed not for Muskogee or California as some had, or Saint Louis, Houston, Langston or Chicago, but deeper into Oklahoma, as far as they could climb from the grovel contaminating the town their grandfathers had made.

"How long?" asked the children from the back seats of the cars. "How long will it be?"

"Soon," the parents replied. Hour after hour, the answer was the same. "Soon. Pretty soon." When they saw Beaver Creek sliding through the muzzle of a state shaped like a gun, on through the acres of grass (cheaper than cheap after the tornadoes of 1949) that their pooled discharge pay had bought, it was pretty, soon and right on time.

What they left behind was a town whose once proud streets were weed-choked, monitored now by eighteen stubborn people wondering how they could get to the post office where there might be a letter from long gone grandchildren. Where the Oven had been, small green snakes slept in the sun. Who could have imagined that twenty-five years later in a brand-new town a Convent would beat out the snakes, the Depression, the tax man and the railroad for sheer destructive power?

Now one brother, a leader in everything, smashes the cellar door with the butt of his rifle. The other waits a few feet back with their nephew. All three descend the steps ready and excited to know. They are not disappointed. What they see is the devil's bedroom, bathroom, and his nasty playpen.

The nephew always knew that his mother had tried as hard as she could to hang on. She had managed to see him ride the winning horse, but beyond that she had no strength. Not even enough to get interested in the debates about what to call this place she had traveled to with her brothers and her little boy. For three years New Haven had been the name most agreed to, although a few were loud in suggesting other names—names that did not speak, they said, of failure new or repeated. Pacific veterans liked Guam, others Inchon. Those who fought in Europe kept coming up with names only the children enjoyed pronouncing. The women had no firm opinion until the nephew's mother died. Her funeral—the town's first—stopped the schedule of discussion and its necessity. They named the town after one of their own and the men did not gainsay them. All right. Well. Ruby. Young Ruby.

It pleased his uncles who could then both mourn the sister and honor the friend and brother-in-law who didn't make it back. But the nephew, winner of Ossie's Purple Heart, heir to his father's dog tags, witness to his mother's name painted on signs and written on envelopes for the rest of his life, was displaced by these sad markings. The heart, the tags, the post office designation outsized him somehow. The women who had known and tended his mother spoiled Ruby's boy. The men who enlisted with his father favored Ruby's husband's boy. The uncles took him for granted. When the decision was taken at the Oven, he was there. But two hours ago, when they'd swallowed the last piece of red meat, an uncle simply tapped him on the shoulder and said, "We got coffee in the truck. Go get your rifle." Which he did, but he took the palm cross too.

It was four in the morning when they left; going on five when they arrived because, not wanting engine hum or headlights to ruin their cover of darkness, they walked the final miles. They parked the trucks in a copse of shin oak, for light could signal uninterrupted for mile upon mile in this country. When casing heads for fifty miles were invisible, a lit birthday cake could be spotted as soon as the match was struck. Half a mile from their destination fog surrounded them to their hips. They reached the Convent just seconds before the sun did and had a moment to see and register for all time how the mansion floated, dark and malevolently disconnected from God's earth.

In the schoolroom, which used to be a dining room and now has no function except storage of desks pushed to the wall, the view is clear. The men of Ruby bunch at its windows. Finding nothing but confirming evidence elsewhere in the Convent, they gather here. The New Fathers of Ruby, Oklahoma. The chill they first encountered is gone; so is the mist. They are animated—warm with perspiration and the nocturnal odor of righteousness. The view is clear.

Track. That's all the nephew can think of. Four-hundred-yard dashers or even the three-mile runners. The heads of two of them are thrown back as far as their necks will allow; fists tight as their arms pump and stretch for distance. One has her nappy head down, butting air and time wide open, one hand reaching for a winner's wire nowhere in her future. Their mouths are open, pulling in breath, giving up none. The legs of all are off the ground, split wide above the clover.

Bodacious black Eves unredeemed by Mary, they are like panicked does leaping toward a sun that has finished burning off the mist and now pours its holy oil over the hides of game.

God at their side, the men take aim. For Ruby.

MAVIS

The neighbors seemed pleased when the babies smothered. Probably because the mint green Cadillac in which they died had annoyed them for some time. They did all the right things, of course: brought food, telephoned their sorrow, got up a collection; but the shine of excitement in their eyes was clear.

When the journalist came, Mavis sat in the corner of the sofa, not sure whether to scrape the potato chip crumbs from the seams of the plastic cover or tuck them further in. But the journalist wanted the photo taken first, so the photographer ordered Mavis to the middle of the sofa, with the surviving children on either side of their distraught and grieving mother. She asked for the father too, of course. Jim? Is it Jim Albright? But Mavis said he wasn't feeling so good, couldn't come out, they'd have to go ahead without him. The journalist and the photographer exchanged looks, and Mavis thought they probably knew anyway that Frank—not Jim—was sitting on the edge of the bathtub drinking Seagram's without a glass.

Mavis moved to the center of the sofa and cleaned her fingernails of potato chip dust until the other children joined her. The "other children" is what they would always be now. Sal put her arm around her mother's waist. Frankie and Billy James were squished together on her right. Sal pinched her, hard. Mavis knew instantly that her daughter wasn't nervous before the camera and all, because the pinch grew long, pointed. Sal's fingernails were diving for blood.

"This must be terrible for you." Her name, she said, was June.

"Yes, m'am. It's terrible for all of us."

"Is there something you want to say? Something you want other mothers to know?"

"M'am?"

June crossed her knees and Mavis saw that this was the first time she had worn the white high-heeled shoes. The soles were barely smudged. "You know. Something to warn them, caution them, about negligence."

"Well." Mavis took a deep breath. "I can't think of any. I guess. I."

The photographer squatted, cocking his head as he examined the possibilities.

"So some good can come out of this awful tragedy?" June's smile was sad.

Mavis straightened against the success of Sal's fingernails. The camera clicked. June moved her felt-tipped pen into place. It was a fine thing. Mavis had never seen anything like it—made ink on the paper but dry, not all blotty. "I don't have nothing to say to strangers right now."

For the second time the photographer adjusted the front window shade and walked back to the sofa holding a black box to Mavis' face.

"I understand," said June. Her eyes went soft, but the shine was like that of the neighbors. "And I do hate to put you through this, but maybe you could just tell me what happened? Our readers are simply appalled. Twins and all. Oh, and they want you to know you are in their prayers every single day." She let her glance sweep the boys and Sal. "And you all too. They are praying for each and every one of you."

Frankie and Billy James looked down at their bare feet. Sal rested her head on her mother's shoulder while she clenched the flesh at Mavis' waist.

"So could you tell us?" June smiled a smile that meant "Do me this favor."

"Well." Mavis frowned. She wanted to get it right this time. "He didn't want the Spam. I mean the kids like it but he don't so. In this heat you can't keep much meat. I had a whole chuck steak go green on me once so I went and took the car, just some weenies, and I thought, well, Merle and Pearl. I was against it at first but he said—"

"M-e-r-l-e?"

22

"Yes, m'am."

"Go on."

"They wasn't crying or nothing but he said his head hurt. I understood. I did. You can't expect a man to come home from that kind of work and have to watch over babies while I go get something decent to put in front of him. I know that ain't right."

"So you took the twins. Why didn't you take the other children along?"

"It's a weasel out back," said Frankie.

"Groundhog," said Billy James.

"Shut!" Sal leaned over Mavis' stomach and pointed at her brothers.

June smiled. "Wouldn't it have been safer," she continued, "with the other children in the car? I mean, they're older."

Mavis slid her thumb under her bra strap, pulling it back over her shoulder. "I wasn't expecting no danger. Higgledy Piggledy is just yonder. I could of went to the Convenience but their stuff sits too long for me."

"So you left the newborns in the car and went in to buy some chuck steak—"

"No, m'am. Weenies."

"Right. Wieners." June was writing quickly but didn't seem to be crossing out anything. "But what I want to ask is, why did it take so long? To buy one item."

"It didn't. Take long. I couldn't of been in there more than five minutes, tops."

"Your babies suffocated, Mrs. Albright. In a hot car with the windows closed. No air. It's hard to see that happening in five minutes."

It could be sweat, but it hurt enough to be blood. She didn't dare swat Sal's hand away or acknowledge the pain even slightly. Instead she scratched the corner of her mouth and said, "I've punished myself over that, but that's pretty near the most it could of been. I walked in there straight to the dairy section and picked up two packs of Armours which is high you know but I didn't even look for the price. Some of them is cheaper but just as good. But I was hurrying so I didn't look."

"You were hurrying?"

"Oh, yes, m'am. He was fit to be tied. Spam ain't nothing for a working man to eat."

"And wieners are?"

"I thought about chops. I thought about chops."

"Didn't you know your husband was coming home for supper, Mrs. Albright? Doesn't he come home for supper every day?"

She's a really nice person, Mavis thought. Polite. She didn't look around the room or at the boys' feet, or jump at the crashing noise from the rear of the house, followed by a toilet flush.

The sound of the photographer snapping his cases was loud when the toilet stopped. "Got it," he said. "Real nice meeting you, m'am." He leaned in to shake Mavis' hand. His hair was the same color as the reporter's.

"Get enough of the Cadillac?" asked June.

"Plenty." He made an O with thumb and forefinger. "You all be nice, hear?" He touched his hat and was gone.

Sal left off squeezing her mother's waist. She leaned forward and concentrated on swinging her foot, only occasionally hitting Mavis' shin.

From where they sat no one in the room could see the Cadillac parked in front of the house. But it had been seen for months by everybody in the neighborhood and could now be seen by anybody in Maryland since the photographer had taken more shots of it than he had of them. Mint green. Lettuce green. Cool. But the color wouldn't show in the newspaper. What would show would be the size, the flashiness of the place where babies had died. Babies forever unseen now because the mother did not even have a snapshot of their trusting faces.

Sal jumped up and screamed, "Ow! Look! A beetle!" and stomped on her mother's foot.

Mavis had said, "Yes, m'am. He come home for supper every day," and wondered what that would be like: to have a husband who came home every day. For anything. After the reporter left, she wanted to go look at the damage Sal had done to her side, but Frank was still in the bathroom, asleep probably, and it wasn't a good idea to bother him. She thought to clean the potato chip crumbs from the seams of the plastic covers, but where she wanted to be was in the Cadillac. It wasn't hers; it was his, yet Mavis loved it maybe more than he did and lied to him about losing the second set of keys. It was what she talked about last as June left, saying, "It ain't new, though. It's three years old. A '65." If she could, she would have slept out there, in the back seat, snuggled in the place where the twins had been, the only ones who enjoyed her company and weren't a trial. She couldn't, of course. Frank told her she better not touch, let alone drive, the Cadillac as long as she lived. So she was as surprised as anybody when she stole it.

"You all right?" Frank was already under the sheet, and Mavis woke with a start of terror, which dissolved quickly into familiar fright.

"I'm okay." She searched the darkness for a sign, trying to feel, smell his mood in advance. But he was a blank, just the way he had been at supper the evening of the newspaper interview. The perfect meat loaf (not too loose, not too tight—two eggs made the difference) must have pleased him. Either that or he had reached balance: enough in, enough at hand. In any case, he'd been easy, even playful, at the table, while the other children were downright bold. Sal had Frank's old shaving razor unfolded by her plate and asked her father a series of questions, all starting with "Is it sharp enough to cut . . . ?" And Frank would answer, "Cut anything from chin hair to gristle," or "Cut the eyelashes off a bedbug," eliciting peals of laughter from Sal. When Billy James spit Kool-Aid into Mavis' plate, his father said, "Hand me that catsup, Frankie, and Billy you stop playing in your mother's food, you hear?"

She didn't think it would take them long, and seeing how they were at supper, enjoying each other's jokes and all, she knew Frank would let the children do it. The newspaper people would think of something catchy, and June, "the only lady journalist the *Courier* had," would do the human interest.

Mavis tried not to stiffen as Frank made settling-down noises on the mattress. Did he have his shorts on? If she knew that she would know whether he was looking to have sex, but she couldn't find out without touching him. As if to satisfy her curiosity, Frank snapped the waistband of his boxers. Mavis relaxed, permitted herself a sigh that she hoped sounded like a snore. The sheet was off before she could complete it. When he pulled her nightgown up, he threw it over her face, and she let that mercy be. She had misjudged. Again. He was going to do this first and then the rest. The other children would be behind the door, snickering, Sal's eyes as cold and unforgiving as they were when she was told of the accident. Before Frank came to bed, Mavis had been dreaming of something important she was supposed to do, but couldn't remember what it was. Just as it came to her, Frank had asked her was she all right. Now she supposed she really was all right because the important thing she'd forgotten would never need doing anymore.

Would it be quick like most always? or long, wandering, collapsing in wordless fatigue?

It was neither. He didn't penetrate—just rubbed himself to climax while chewing a clump of her hair through the nightgown that covered her face. She could have been a life-size Raggedy Ann.

Afterwards he spoke to her in the dark. "I don't know, Mave. I just don't know."

Should she say, What? What you mean? What don't you know? Or keep quiet? Mavis chose silence because suddenly she understood that he was talking not to her but to the other children, snickering behind the door.

"Maybe," he said. "Maybe we can fix it. Maybe not. I just don't know." He let out a deep yawn, then, "Don't see how, though."

It was, she knew, the signal—to Sal, to Frankie, to Billy James.

The rest of the night she waited, not closing her eyes for a second. Frank's sleep was sound and she would have slipped out of bed (as soon as he had not smothered or strangled her) and opened the door except for the breathing beyond it. She was sure Sal squatted there— ready to pounce or grab her legs. Her upper lip would be raised showing eleven-year-old teeth too big for her snarling mouth. Dawn, Mavis thought, would be critical. The trap would be agreed upon but maybe not laid yet. Her sharpest concentration would be needed to locate it before it sprung.

Mavis

At the first hint of gray light Mavis eased out of the bed. If Frank woke it was all over. Clutching a pair of red pedal pushers and a Daffy Duck sweatshirt, she made it to the bathroom. She took a soiled brassiere from the hamper and got dressed fast. No panties, and she couldn't go back in the bedroom for her shoes. The big thing was to get past the other children's room. The door stood open and, although there was no sound coming out, Mavis chilled at the thought of approaching it. Down the hall to the left was the little kitchen–dining room, the living room to the right. She would have to decide which way she was headed before she ran past that door. They would probably expect her to go straight to the kitchen as usual, so maybe she should shoot for the front door. Or maybe they counted on her changing a habit, and the trap was not in the kitchen at all.

Suddenly she remembered her purse was in the living room, perched on the television cabinet, which, when the set broke, had become a catchall. And the spare keys were pinned under a tear in the purse's lining. Holding her breath, eyes wide to the darkness, Mavis padded quickly past the other children's open door. With her back exposed to that much danger, she felt feverish—sweaty and cold together.

Not only was her purse where she remembered, Sal's galoshes were lying at the front door. Mavis grabbed the purse, stuck her feet in her daughter's yellow boots and escaped onto the front porch. She did not look toward the kitchen and never saw it again.

Getting out of the house had been so intense, she was pulling the Cadillac away from the curb when she realized she had no idea of what to do next. She drove toward Peg's; she didn't know the woman all that well, but her tears at the funeral impressed Mavis. She had always wanted to know her better, but Frank found ways to prevent acquaintance from becoming friendship.

The one streetlight seemed miles away and the sun reluctant to rise, so she had trouble finding Peg's house. When, finally, she did, she parked across the street to wait for stronger skylight before knocking on the door. Peg's house was dark, the shade of the picture window still down. Complete quiet. The wooden girl in the petunias, her face hidden by a fresh blue bonnet, tilted a watering can, a family of carved ducks lined at her heels. The lawn, edged and close-cut, looked like a carpet sample of expensive wool. Nothing moved, neither the tiny windmill nor the ivy surrounding it. At the side of the house, however, a rose of Sharon, taller than Peg's roof and older, was shaking. Stirred by the air conditioner's exhaust it danced, roughing blossoms and buds to the grass. Wild, it looked wild, and Mavis' pulse raced with it. According to the Cadillac's clock it wasn't five-thirty yet. Mavis decided to drive around for a while and return at a respectable hour. Six maybe. But they would be up, too, by then and Frank would see that the Caddy was gone. He would call the police for sure.

Mavis swung away from the curb, sad and frightened by how dumb she was. Not only was the whole neighborhood familiar with the car, a photograph of it would be in today's paper. When Frank bought it and drove it home the men on the street slapped the hood and grinned, leaned in to sniff the interior, hit the horn and laughed. Laughed and laughed some more because its owner had to borrow a lawn mower every couple of weeks; because its owner had no screens in his windows and no working television; because two of his six porch posts had been painted white three months earlier, the rest still flaking yellow; because its owner sometimes slept behind the wheel of the car he'd traded in—all night—in front of his own house. And the women, who saw Mavis driving the children to the White Castle wearing sunglasses on cloudy days, flat-out stared before shaking their heads. As though they knew from the start that the Cadillac would someday be notorious.

Creeping at twenty miles per hour, Mavis entered route 121, thankful for the shelter of darkness left. As she passed the County Hospital, a silent ambulance glided out of the driveway. A green cross in a field of white slid from brilliant emergency light into shadow. Fifteen times she had been a patient there—four times for childbirth. During the next-to-last admission, when the twins were due, Mavis' mother came from New Jersey to help out. She kept house and minded the other children for three days. When the twins were delivered, she went back to Paterson—a three-hour drive, thought Mavis. She could be there before *The Secret Storm*, which she had missed all summer long.

At a Fill 'n Go gas station, Mavis checked her wallet before she answered the attendant. Three ten-dollar bills were folded behind her driver's license.

"Ten," she said.

"Gallons or dollars, m'am?"

"Gallons."

In the adjacent lot, Mavis noticed the window of a breakfast diner reflecting coral in the early light.

"Is that there place open?" she shouted over highway truck roar.

"Yes, m'am."

Tripping occasionally on gravel, she walked toward the diner. Inside, the waitress was eating crab cakes and grits behind the counter. She covered her plate with a cloth and touched the corners of her mouth before wishing Mavis a good morning and taking her order. When Mavis left, carrying a paper cup of coffee and two honey dips in a napkin, she caught the waitress's broad smile in the Hires Root Beer mirror by the exit. The grin bothered her all the way back to the gas station until, stepping into the car, she saw her canary-yellow feet.

Away from the pump, parked behind the diner, she put her breakfast on the dashboard while rummaging in the glove compartment. She found an unopened pint of Early Times, another bottle with an inch or so of scotch whiskey, paper napkins, a teething ring, several rubber bands, a pair of dirty socks, a battery-dead flashlight, a tube of lipstick, a Florida map, rolls of breath mints and a few traffic tickets. She dropped the teething ring into her purse, twisted her hair into a sad little ponytail that stuck out from the rubber band like hen feathers, and smeared the stranger's lipstick on her mouth. Then she sat back and sipped the coffee. Too nervous to ask for milk or sugar, she'd ordered it black and could not force herself to take a third swallow. The stranger's lipstick smirked sloppily from the cardboard rim.

The Cadillac drank ten gallons of gasoline every ninety miles. Mavis wondered whether to call her mother or simply arrive. The latter seemed smarter. Frank may have called his mother-in-law by now or might do so any minute. Better if her mother could say truthfully, "I don't know where she is." Paterson took five hours, not three, and she had four dollars and seventy-six cents when she saw its sign. The fuel gauge touched E.

The streets looked narrower than she remembered, and the stores were different. The northern leaves were already starting to turn. Driving underneath them, in the dappled hall they made, she felt as though the pavement slid forward instead of retreating. The faster she traveled, the more road appeared ahead.

The Cadillac shut down a block from her mother's house, but Mavis managed to coast across the intersection and incline the automobile against the curb.

It was too soon. Her mother wouldn't be home from the preschool till the afternoon children had been picked up. The door key was no longer under the reindeer, so Mavis sat on the back porch and struggled out of the yellow boots. Her feet looked as though they belonged to somebody else.

Frank had already called at five-thirty a.m. when Mavis was staring at Peg's rose of Sharon. Birdie Goodroe told Mavis she had hung up on him after telling him she couldn't think what the hell he was talking about and who the hell did he think he was, dragging her out of her sleep? She was not pleased. Not then and not later when her daughter tapped on the kitchen window looking like a bat out of hell, which is what she said as soon as she opened the door. "Girl, you look like a bat out of hell what you doing up here in little kiddie boots?"

"Ma, just let me in, okay?"

Birdie Goodroe had barely enough calf liver for two. Mother and daughter ate in the kitchen, Mavis presentable now—washed, combed, aspirined and swimming a little in Birdie's housedress.

"Well, let me have it. Not that I need to be told."

Mavis wanted some more of the baby peas and tipped the bowl to see if any were left.

"I could see this coming, you know. Anybody could," Birdie continued. "Don't need more'n a mosquito's brain."

There were a few. A couple of tablespoons. Mavis scraped them onto her plate wondering if there was to be any dessert. Quite a bit of the fried potatoes were still in her mother's plate. "You going to eat those, Ma?"

Birdie pushed her plate toward Mavis. There was a tiny square of liver, too, and some onions. Mavis scraped it all onto her plate.

"You still have children. Children need a mother. I know what you've been through, honey, but you do have other children."

The liver was a miracle. Her mother always got every particle of the tight membrane off.

"Ma." Mavis wiped her lips with a paper napkin. "Why couldn't you make it to the funeral?"

Birdie straightened. "You didn't get the money order? And the flowers?"

"We got them."

"Then you know why. I had to choose—help bury them or pay for a trip. I couldn't afford to do both. I told you all that. I asked you all straight out which thing would be the best, and you both said the money. Both of you said so, both."

"They're going to kill me, Ma."

"Are you going to hold that over my head for the rest of my life? All I've done for you and those children?"

"They already tried but I got away."

"You're all I have, now your brothers gone and got themselves shot up like—" Birdie slapped the table.

"They got no right to kill me."

"What?"

"He's making the other children do it."

"What? Do what? Speak up so I can hear what you saying."

"I'm saying they are going to kill me."

"They? Who? Frank? What they?"

"All of them. The kids too."

"Kill you? Your children?"

Mavis nodded. Birdie Goodroe widened her eyes first, then looked into her lap as she held her forehead in the palm of her hand.

They didn't talk anymore for a while, but later, at the sink, Birdie asked, "Were the twins trying to kill you too?"

Mavis stared at her mother. "No! Oh, no, Ma! Are you crazy? They're babies!"

"All right. All right. Just asking. It's unusual, you know, to think little children . . ."

"Unusual? It's—it's evil! But they'll do what he says. And now they'll do anything. They already tried, Ma!"

"Tried how? What did they do?"

"Sal had a razor and they was laughing and watching me. Every minute watching me."

"What did Sal do with the razor?"

"She had it next to her plate and she was looking at me. They all was."

Neither woman spoke about it again, because Birdie told Mavis she could stay if and only if she never talked that way again. That she wouldn't tell Frank, if he called back, or anybody else that she was there, but if she said one more word about killing she would call him right away.

In a week Mavis was on the road, but this time she had a plan. Days before she heard her mother talking low into the mouthpiece of the telephone, saying, "You better get up here fast and I mean pronto," Mavis had walked around the house, while Birdie was at the Play-Skool, thinking: money, aspirin, paint, underwear; money, aspirin, paint, underwear. She took all she could find of the first two, the checks in two brown government envelopes propped against the photograph of one of her killed-in-action brothers, and both bottles of Bayer. She took a pair of rhinestone clips from Birdie's jewelry box and stole back the car keys her mother thought she had hidden so well; poured two gallons of lawn mower gasoline into the Cadillac's tank and drove away for more. In Newark she found an Earl Scheib paint shop and waited two days in the Y dormitory until it was sprayed magenta. The twenty-nine dollars advertised turned out to be for a standard-size car only. Sixty-nine dollars is what they made her pay for the Cadillac. The underwear and thong sandals she bought at Woolworth's. At a Goodwill she bought a light-blue pantsuit, drip dry, and a white cotton turtleneck. Just right, she thought, for California. Just right.

With a crisp new Mobil map beside her on the seat, she sped out of Newark heading for route 70. As more and more of the East was behind her, the happier she became. Only once had she felt this kind of happiness. On the Rocket ride she took as a kid. When the rocket zoomed on the downward swing, the rush made her giddy with pleasure; when it slowed just before turning her upside down through the high arc of its circle, the thrill was intense but calm. She squealed with the other passengers, but inside was the stable excitement of facing danger while safely strapped in strong metal. Sal hated it; so did the boys when, later on, she took them to the amusement park. Now, in flight to California, the memory of the Rocket ride and its rush were with her at will.

According to the map the way was straight. All she had to do was find 70, stay on it until Utah, make a left on down to Los Angeles. Later she remembered traveling like that—straight. One state, then the next, just as the map promised. When her funds dwindled to coins, she was forced to look for hitchhikers. But other than the first and the last, she could not remember the order of the girls. Picking up girls was easiest. They were safe company, she hoped, and they helped with gas and food and sometimes invited her to a place where they could crash. They graced primary routes, intersections, ramps to bridges, the verges of gas stations and motels, in jeans belted low on the hips and flared at the bottom. Flat hair swinging or hair picked out in Afros. The white ones were the friendliest; the colored girls slow to melt. But all of them told her about the world before California. Underneath the knowing talk, the bell-chime laughter, the pointed silences, the world they described was just like her own pre-California existence—sad, scary, all wrong. High schools were dumps, parents stupid, Johnson a creep, cops pigs, men rats, boys assholes.

The first girl was outside Zanesville. That's where sitting in a roadside diner, counting her money, the runaway appeared. Mavis had noticed her going into the ladies' room, then, quite a bit later, coming out dressed in different clothes: a long skirt this time, and a flowing blouse that touched her thighs. Outside in the parking lot, the girl ran to the Cadillac's passenger window and asked for a lift. Smiling happily, she jerked open the door when Mavis nodded. The girl said her name—Sandra but call me Dusty—and talked for thirty-two miles. Not interested in anything about Mavis, Dusty ate two Mallomars and chattered, mostly about the owners of the six dog tags that hung from her neck. Boys in her high school class or whom she had known in junior high. She'd got two from when they dated; the rest she begged from their families—souvenirs. All dead or missing.

Mavis agreed to drive through Columbus and drop Dusty at her girlfriend's house. They arrived in a soft rain. Someone had done the last mowing of the season. Dusty's hair matted in brown licks; the glorified scent of newly cut grass in rain, the clink of dog tags, half a Mallo. That was Mavis' memory of her first detour with a hitchhiker. Except for the last, the others were out of sequence. Was it in Colorado that she saw a man sitting on a bench under pines in a rest area? He ate slowly, very slowly while he read a newspaper. Or before? It was sunny, cold. Anyway somewhere around that place she picked up the girl who stole her rhinestone clips. But earlier—near Saint Louis, was it?—she opened the passenger door to two girls shivering on route 70. Wind beaten, their army jackets closed tight around their chins, leather clogs, thick gray socks—they wiped their noses while their hands were still pocketed.

Not far, they said. A place just a few miles out, they said. The place, a sparkling green cemetery, was as peopled as a park. Lines of cars necklaced the entrance. Groups of people, solitary strollers, all patient in the wind, mixed with boys from a military school. The girls thanked Mavis and got out, running a little to join a set of graveside mourners. Mavis lingered, amazed by the unnatural brightness of the green. What she thought were military students turned out to be real soldiers—but young, so young, and as fresh-looking as the headstones they stood before.

It must have been after that when Mavis picked up Bennie—the last one and the one she liked best and who stole her raincoat and Sal's boots. Bennie was glad to know that, like her, Mavis was going all the way to L.A. She, Bennie, was heading for San Diego. Not a talker, small or big, Bennie sang. Songs of true love, false love, redemption; songs of unreasonable joy. Some drew tears, others were deliberately silly. Mavis sang along once in a while, but mostly she listened and in one hundred and seventy-two miles never got tired of hearing her. Mile after mile rolled by urged and eased by the gorgeous ache in Bennie's voice.

She didn't like to eat at highway stops. If they were there, because Mavis insisted on it, Bennie drank water while Mavis wolfed down cheese melts and fries. Twice Bennie directed them through towns, searching for colored neighborhoods, where they could eat "healthy," she said. At those places Bennie ate slowly, steadily, with repeat orders, side dishes and always something to go. She was careful with her money but didn't seem worried about it, and shared the cost at every gas pump.

Mavis never learned what she planned to do or who meet in L.A. (well, San Diego). "To get it on," was her single answer to Mavis' inquiry. Nevertheless, somewhere between Topeka and Lawrence, Kansas, she disappeared along with Mavis' clear plastic raincoat and Sal's yellow boots. Odd, because Mavis' five-dollar bill was still attached to the gearshift with a rubber band. They had finished the barbecue and potato salad in a tacky restaurant named Hickey's. Bennie's "to go" order was wrapped and sitting on the table. "I'll take care of this," she said, nodding toward the check. "You go on to the toilet before we hit the road." When Mavis came out, Bennie and her ribs-to-go were gone.

"How the hell I know?" was what the waitress answered. "She didn't leave even a penny tip."

Mavis fished out a quarter and placed it on the counter. She waited a few minutes in the car before trying to find her way back to sweet 70.

The quiet Bennie left in the Cadillac was unbearable. Mavis kept the radio on, and if one of Bennie's songs came on, she sang too, mourning the inferior rendition.

Panic struck in an Esso station.

Returning the rest room key, Mavis looked through the window. Beyond, under the fluorescent lights sheltering the pump, Frank was leaning into the Cadillac window. Could he have grown that much hair in two weeks? And his clothes. Black leather jacket, shirt opened almost to his navel, gold chains. Mavis buckled and when the attendant stared at her she tried to make it look as though she'd stumbled. There was nowhere to run. She rummaged the Colorado maps in the rack. She looked again. He was gone. Parked close by, she thought, waiting for her to emerge.

I'll scream, she told herself, pretend I don't know him, fight him, call the police. The car was no longer mint green, but oh God—the license plate was the same. She had the reg. Suppose he brought the title papers. Was there a bulletin out? She could not stand still and there was no retreat. Mavis went forward. Not running. Not tripping. Head down, searching her purse for a twenty-dollar bill.

Back in the car, waiting for the attendant to collect the money, she examined her surroundings in the rear- and side-view windows. Nothing. She paid and turned on the ignition. Right then the black-jacketed, open shirt torso appeared in the right-hand mirror. Gold links catching fluorescent light. Hard as she tried to control it, the Cadillac lurched out of the gas lane. Scared now, she forgot what to look for. Junction what? Turn right to go south. No, west. Enter 70 at what? But this was east. Exit ramp goes where?

An hour later she was traveling a road already driven twice before. Exiting as soon as possible, she found herself on a narrow bridge and a street lined with warehouses. Secondary routes, she decided, would be better anyway. Fewer police, fewer streetlights. Trembling at every traffic light, she made it out of town. She was on route 18 when night came, and drove on and on until there was nothing but fumes to fuel the engine. The Cadillac neither sighed nor coughed. It simply stopped in a well of darkness, headlights picking out thirty feet of tarmac. Mavis switched off the lights and locked the doors. A little courage, she whispered. Like the girls running from, running toward. If they could roam around, jump in cars, hitchhike to burials, search strange neighborhoods for food, make their own way alone or with only each other for protection, certainly she could wait in darkness for morning to come. She had done it all her adult life, was able to sleep best in daylight. Besides and after all, she was not a teenager; she was a twenty-seven-year-old mother of . . .

Early Times didn't help. The tears wet her chin, crept down her neck anyway. What it did eventually was knock her out.

Mavis woke felt-mouthed, ugly, unfocused, and knew she was ravenous because the sun, watermelon red, looked edible. The screaming blue horizon that surrounded her was minus invitation or reproach and supported by a billion miles of not one thing.

There was no choice. She relieved herself as Dusty had taught her, got back in the car to wait for another one to pass by. Bennie was smart; she never left anywhere without a dripping box of food. Mavis felt her stupidity close in on her head like a dry sack. A grown woman who could not cross the country. Could not make a plan that accommodated more than twenty minutes. Had to be taught how to dry herself in the weeds. Too rattle-minded to open a car's window so babies could breathe. She did not know now why she had run from the gold links coming toward her. Frank was right. From the very beginning he had been absolutely right about her: she was the dumbest bitch on the planet.

During the wait, in which no car or truck or bus approached, she dozed, woke to awful thoughts, dozed again. Suddenly she sat up, wide awake, and decided not to starve. Would the road girls just sit there? Would Dusty? Bennie? Mavis looked closely at the surroundings. The billion miles of not one thing had trees in the distance. Was this grass or a crop of some kind? Every road went somewhere, didn't it? Mavis collected her purse, looked for her raincoat and discovered it was gone. "Christ!" she shouted and slammed the door.

The rest of the morning she stayed on the same road. When the sun was highest, she turned into a narrower one because it offered shade. Still tarmac, but not enough room for two automobiles to pass without using the shoulder. When the road ran out of trees, she saw ahead to the left a house. It looked small but close and it took a while for her to discover it was neither. She had to negotiate acres of corn to arrive. Either the house was backwards or it had no driveway. As she drew closer she saw it was stone—sandstone, maybe, but dark with age. At first there seemed to be no windows, but then she made out the beginning of a porch and saw the reflection of huge windows on the ground floor. Circling to the right, she glimpsed a driveway leading not to the front door but around to the side. Mavis turned left. The grass near the porch was tended. Claws gripped the finials on either side of the stone steps. Mavis climbed the stairs and knocked on the door. No answer. She walked around to the driveway side and saw a woman sitting in a red wooden chair at the edge of a vegetable garden.

"Excuse me," Mavis called, her hands funneling around her mouth.

The woman faced her, but Mavis couldn't tell where she was looking. She was wearing sunglasses.

"Excuse me." Mavis moved closer. No need to shout now. "I broke down a ways back. Can anybody help? Is there someplace I can call?"

The woman stood up, gathering the hem of her apron in both hands, and came forward. She wore a yellow cotton dress with tiny white flowers and fancy buttons under an apron of what looked like sailcloth. Her low-heeled shoes were unlaced. On her head a wide-brimmed straw hat. The sun was beating hard; a hot wind kicked up, turning back the brim of her hat.

"No telephone out here," she said. "Come inside."

Mavis followed her into the kitchen where the woman dumped pecans from her apron into a box by the stove and removed her hat. Two Hiawatha braids trailed down her shoulders. She slid out of her shoes, propped open the door with a brick and took off her sunglasses. The kitchen was big, full of fragrances and a woman's solitary mess. Her back turned to Mavis, she asked her, "You a drinking woman?"

Mavis didn't know if a drink was being offered or solicited.

"No, I'm not."

"Lies not allowed in this place. In this place every true thing is okay."

Startled, Mavis breathed into her palm. "Oh. I drank some of my husband's liquor a while back, but I'm not what you'd call a drinking woman. I was just, well, wrung out. Driving so long and then running out of gas."

The woman busied herself lighting the stove. Her braids fell forward.

"I forgot to ask your name. Mine's Mavis Albright."

"People call me Connie."

"I'd appreciate some coffee, Connie, if you got any."

Connie nodded without turning around.

"You work here?"

"I work here." Connie lifted her braids from her chest and dropped them behind her shoulders.

"Is any of the family here? Seem like I knocked for the longest time."

"No family. Just her upstairs. She couldn't answer the door if she wanted to and she don't want to."

"I'm headed out by California. You think you can help me get some gas back to my car? Show me the way out of here?"

The woman sighed at the stove but didn't reply.

"Connie?"

"I'm thinking."

Mavis looked around the kitchen that seemed to her as large as her junior high school cafeteria and that also had swinging wooden doors. She imagined rooms full of rooms beyond those doors.

"You all ain't scared out here by yourselves? Don't seem like there's nothing for miles outside."

Connie laughed. "Scary things not always outside. Most scary things is inside." She turned from the stove with a bowl and placed it before Mavis, who looked in despair at the steaming potatoes, over which a pat of butter melted. The Early Times drunk turned her hunger into nausea but she said thank you and accepted the fork in Connie's hand. Anyway, the smell of the coffee was promising.

Connie sat down next to her. "Maybe I go with you," she said.

Mavis looked up. It was the first time she saw the woman's face without the sunglasses. Quickly she looked back at the food and poked the fork into the bowl.

"What you say me and you go to California?"

Mavis felt, but could not face, the woman's smile. Had she washed her hands before warming up the potatoes? Her smell was walnuts, not pecans. "What about your job here?" Mavis forced herself to taste a tiny bit of potato. Salty.

"It's by the sea, California?"

"Yeah. Right on the coast."

"Be nice to see water again." Connie kept her eyes on Mavis' face. "Wave after wave after wave. Big water. Blue, blue, blue, yes?"

"That's what they say. Sunny California. Beaches, oranges . . ."

"Maybe too sunny for me." Connie got up abruptly and went to the stove.

"Can't be sunnier than here." The butter, salt and pepper mashed into the potatoes wasn't all that bad. Mavis was eating rapidly. "Go for miles and don't see a speck of shade."

"True," said Connie. She placed two cups of coffee and a pot of honey on the table. "Too much sunshine in the world. Vex me. Can't take it no more."

A breeze swept through the kitchen door, displacing the food smell with a sweeter one. Mavis had thought she would gulp the coffee when it arrived, but the satisfaction of the hot, salty potatoes made her patient. Following Connie's example she spooned honey into her cup, stirring slowly.

"Did you think up anything about how I can get me some gasoline?"

"Wait awhile. Today maybe, tomorrow maybe. People be out to buy."

"Buy? Buy what?"

"Garden things. Things I cook up. Things they don't want to grow themselves."

"And one of them can take me to get some gas?"

"Sure."

"Suppose nobody comes?"

"Always come. Somebody always come. Every day. This morning already I sold forty-eight ears of corn and a whole pound of peppers." She patted her apron pocket.

Blowing gently into her cup, Mavis went to the kitchen door and looked out. When she first arrived she was so happy to find someone at home she had not looked closely at the garden. Now, behind the red chair, she saw flowers mixed in with or parallel to rows of vegetables. In some places staked plants grew in a circle, not a line, in high mounds of soil. Chickens clucked out of sight. A part of the garden she originally thought gone to weed became, on closer inspection, a patch of melons. An empire of corn beyond.

"You didn't do all that by yourself, did you?" Mavis gestured toward the garden.

"Except the corn," said Connie.

"Wow."

Connie put the breakfast bowl in the sink. "You want to clean yourself up?"

The rooms full of rooms Mavis imagined to be lying through the swinging doors had kept her from asking to go to a bathroom. Here in the kitchen she felt safe; the thought of leaving it disturbed her. "I'll wait to see who comes by. Then I'll try to get myself together. I know I look a sight." She smiled, hoping the refusal did not signal her apprehension.

"Suit yourself," said Connie and, sunglasses in place, patted Mavis' shoulder as she stepped into her splayed shoes and on out to the yard.

Left alone Mavis expected the big kitchen to lose its comfort. It didn't. In fact she had an outer-rim sensation that the kitchen was crowded with children—laughing? singing?—two of whom were Merle and Pearl. Squeezing her eyes shut to dissipate the impression only strengthened it. When she opened her eyes, Connie was there, dragging a thirty-two-quart basket over the floor.

"Come on," she said. "Make yourself useful."

Mavis frowned at the pecans and shook her head at the nutcrackers, picks and bowls Connie was assembling. "No," she said. "Think of something else I can do to help. Shelling that stuff would make me crazy."

"No it wouldn't. Try it."

"Uh uh. Not me." Mavis watched as she organized the tools. "Shouldn't you put some newspaper down? Be easier to clean up."

"No newspapers in this house. No radio either. Any news we get have to be from somebody telling it face-to-face."

"Just as well," Mavis said. "All the news these days is bad as can be. Can't do nothing about it anyway."

"You give in too quick. Look at your nails. Strong, curved like a bird's—perfect pecan hands. Fingernails like that take the meat out whole every time. Beautiful hands, yet you say you can't. Make you crazy. Make me crazy to see good nails go to waste."

Later, watching her suddenly beautiful hands moving at the task, Mavis was reminded of her sixth-grade teacher opening a book: lifting the corner of the binding, stroking the edge to touch the bookmark, caressing the page, letting the tips of her fingers trail down the lines of print. The melty-thigh feeling she got watching her. Now, working pecans, she tried to economize her gestures without sacrificing their grace. Connie, having launched her into the chore, was gone, saying she had to "see about Mother." Sitting at the table, smelling the pleasure the wind brought through the door, Mavis wondered how old Connie's mother was. Judging by the age of her daughter, she would have to be in her nineties. Also, how long before a customer would come? Had anybody bothered the Cadillac yet? At whatever gas station she got to, would there be a map showing the way back to sweet 70, or even 287? She would go north then, to Denver, then scoot west. With luck she'd be on her way by suppertime. With no luck, she'd be ready to leave in the morning. She would be back on concrete, listening to the car radio that had got her through the silence Bennie left, hours of nonstop driving—two fingers impatiently twirling for the better song, the nicer voice. Now the radio was across a field, down one road, then another. Off. In the space where its sound ought to be was . . . nothing. Just an absence, which she did not think she could occupy properly without the framing bliss of the radio. From the table where she sat admiring her busy hands, the radio absence spread out. A quiet, secret fire breathing itself and exhaling the sounds of its increase: the crack of shells, the tick of nut meat tossed in the bowl, cooking utensils in eternal adjustment, insect whisper, the argue of long grass, the faraway cough of cornstalks.

It was peaceful, but she wished Connie would return lest she start up again—imagining babies singing. Just as the length of the woman's absence seemed much too long, Mavis heard a car crunching gravel. Then braking. A door slap.

"Hey, old lady." A woman's voice, light, loose.

Mavis turned and saw a dark-skinned woman, limber and moving quickly, mount the steps and halt when she didn't see what she expected.

"Oh, excuse me."

"That's okay," said Mavis. "She's upstairs. Connie."

"I see."

Mavis thought the woman was looking very carefully at her clothes.

"Oh, lovely," she said, coming to the table. "Just lovely." She stuck her fingers into the bowl of pecans and gathered a few. Mavis expected her to eat some, but she let them fall back to the heap. "What's Thanksgiving without pecan pie? Not a thing."

Neither one of them heard the bare feet plopping, and since the swinging doors had no sound, Connie's entrance was like an apparition.

"There you are!" The black woman opened her arms. Connie entered them for a long swaying hug. "I scared this girl to death. Never saw a stranger inside here before."

"Our first," said Connie. "Mavis Albright, this is Soane Morgan."

"Hi, hon."

"Morgan. Mrs. Morgan."

Mavis' face warmed, but she smiled anyway and said, "Sorry. Mrs. Morgan," while taking note of the woman's expensive oxford shoes, sheer stockings, wool cardigan and the cut of her dress: summer-weight crepe, pale blue with a white collar.

Soane opened a crocheted purse. "I brought some more," she said, and held up a pair of aviator-style sunglasses.

"Good. I got one pair left."

Soane glanced at Mavis. "She eats sunglasses."

"Not me. This house eats them." Fitting the stems behind her ears, Connie tested the dark lenses at the doorway. She turned her face directly to the sun and the "Hah!" she shouted was full of defiance.

"Somebody order shelled pecans, or is this your idea?"

"My idea."

43

"Make a lot of pies."

"Make more than pie." Connie rinsed the sunglasses under the sink tap and peeled away the sticker.

"I don't want to hear, so don't tell me. I came for the you-know-what."

Connie nodded. "Can you get this girl some gasoline for her automobile? Take her and bring her back?" She was drying and polishing the new glasses, checking for spots and lint from the towel.

"Where is your car?" asked Soane. There was wonder in her voice, as though she doubted anyone in thongs, wrinkled slacks and a child's dirty sweatshirt could have a car.

"Route eighteen," Mavis told her. "Took me hours to walk here, but in a car . . ."

Soane nodded. "Happy to. But I'll have to get somebody else to drive you back. I would, but I've got too much to do. Both my boys due on furlough." Proudly, she looked at Connie. "House'll be full before I know it." Then, "How's Mother?"

"Can't last."

"You sure Demby or Middleton's not a better idea?"

Connie slipped the aviator glasses into her apron pocket and headed for the pantry. "She wouldn't draw but one breath in a hospital. The second one would be her last."

The small pouch Connie placed on top of a basket of pecans could have been a grenade. Positioned on the seat of the Oldsmobile between Mavis and Soane Morgan, the cloth packet emanated tension. Soane kept touching it as though to remind herself that it was there. The easy talk in the kitchen had disappeared. Suddenly formal, Soane said very little, answered Mavis' questions with the least information and asked none of her own.

"Connie's nice, isn't she?"

Soane looked at her. "Yes. She is."

For twenty minutes they traveled, Soane cautious at every rise or turn of the road, however slight. She seemed to be on the lookout for something. They stopped at a one-pump gas station in the middle of nowhere and asked the man who limped to the window for five gallons to carry. There was an argument, peppered with long silences, about the five-gallon can. He wanted Mavis to pay for it; she said she would return it when she came back to fill her tank. He doubted it. Finally they settled for a two-dollar deposit. Soane and Mavis drove away, turned into another road, heading east for what seemed like an hour. Pointing toward a fancy wooden sign, Soane said, "Here we are." The sign read RUBY POP. 360 on top and LODGE 16 at the bottom.

Mavis' immediate impression of the little town was how still it was, as though no one lived there. Except for a feed store and a savings and loan bank, it had no recognizable business district. They drove down a wide street, past enormous lawns cut to dazzle in front of churches and pastel-colored houses. The air was scented. The trees young. Soane turned into a side street of flower gardens wider than the houses and snowed with butterflies.

The odor of the five-gallon can had been fierce in Soane's car. But in the boy's truck, propped between Mavis' feet, it was indistinguishable from the others. The gluey, oily, metally combination might have made her retch if he had not done voluntarily what Mavis had been unable to ask of Soane Morgan: turn on the radio. The disc jockey announced the tunes as though they were made by his family or best friends: King Solomon, Brother Otis, Dinah baby, Ike and Tina girl, Sister Dakota, the Temps.

As they bounced along, Mavis, cheerful now, enjoyed the music and the shaved part in the boy's hair. Although he was pleasanter than Soane, he didn't have much more to say. They were several miles away from Ruby pop. 360 and listening to the seventh of *Jet* magazine's top twenty when Mavis realized that, other than the gas station guy, she had not seen a single white.

"Any white people in your town?"

"Not to live, they ain't. Come on business sometime."

When they glimpsed the mansion in the distance on the way to the Cadillac, he asked, "What's it like in there?"

"I only been in the kitchen," Mavis answered.

"Two old women in that big of a place. Don't seem right."

The Cadillac was unmolested but so hot the boy licked his fingers before and after he unscrewed the gas cap. And he was nice enough to start the engine for her and tell her to leave the doors open for a while before she got in. Mavis did not have to struggle to get him to accept money—Soane had been horrified—and he drove off accompanying "Hey Jude" on his radio.

Behind the wheel, cooling in the air-conditioned air, Mavis regretted not having noticed the radio station's number on the dashboard of the boy's truck. She fiddled the dial uselessly as she drove the Cadillac back to Connie's house. She parked, and the Cadillac, dark as bruised blood, stayed there for two years.

It was already sunset when the boy started the engine. Also she had forgotten to ask him for directions. Also she couldn't remember where the gas station with her two-dollar deposit was and didn't want to search for it in the dark. Also Connie had stuffed and roasted a chicken. But her decision to spend the night was mostly because of Mother.

The whiteness at the center was blinding. It took a moment for Mavis to see the shape articulated among the pillows and the bone-white sheets, and she might have remained sightless longer had not an authoritative voice said, "Don't stare, child."

Connie bent over the foot of the bed and reached under the sheet. With her right hand she raised Mother's heels and with her left fluffed the pillows underneath them. Muttering "Toenails like razors," she resettled the feet gently.

When her eyes grew accustomed to dark and light, Mavis saw a bed shape far too small for a sick woman—almost a child's bed—and a variety of tables and chairs in the rim of black that surrounded it. Connie selected something from one of the tables and leaned into the light that ringed the patient. Mavis, following her movements, watched her apply Vaseline to lips in a face paler than the white cloth wrapped around the sick woman's head.

"There must be something that tastes better than this," said Mother, trailing the tip of her tongue over her oiled lips.

"Food," said Connie. "How about some of that?"

"No."

"Bit of chicken?"

"No. Who is this you brought in here? Why did you bring somebody in here?"

"I told you. Woman with a car need help."

"That was yesterday."

"No it wasn't. This morning I told you."

"Well, hours ago, then, but who invited her into my privacy? Who did that?"

"Guess. You, that's who. Want your scalp massaged?"

"Not now. What is your name, child?"

Mavis whispered it from the dark she stood in.

"Step closer. I can't see anything unless it's right up on me. Like living in an eggshell."

"Disregard her," Connie told Mavis. "She sees everything in the universe." Drawing a chair bedside, she sat down, took the woman's hand and one by one stroked back the cuticles on each crooked finger.

Mavis moved closer, into the circle of light, resting her hand on the metal foot of the bed.

"Are you all right now? Is your automobile working?"

"Yes, m'am. It's fine. Thank you."

"Where are your children?"

Mavis could not speak.

"There used to be a lot of children here. This was a school once. A beautiful school. For girls. Indian girls."

Mavis looked at Connie, but when she returned her glance, Mavis quickly lowered her eyes.

The woman in the bed laughed lightly. "It's hard, isn't it," she said, "looking in those eyes. When I brought her here they were green as grass."

"And yours was blue," said Connie.

"Still are."

"So you say."

"What color, then?"

"Same as me—old-lady wash-out color."

"Hand me a mirror, child."

47

"Give her nothing."

"I'm still in charge here."

"Sure. Sure."

All three watched the brown fingers gentling the white ones. The woman in the bed sighed. "Look at me. Can't sit up by myself and arrogant to the end. God must be laughing His head off."

"God don't laugh and He don't play."

"Yes, well, you know all about Him, I'm sure. Next time you see Him, tell Him to let the girls in. They bunch around the door, but they don't come in. I don't mind in the daytime, but they worry my sleep at night. You're feeding them properly? They're always so hungry. There's plenty, isn't there? Not those frycake things they like but good hot food the winters are so bad we need coal a sin to burn trees on the prairie yesterday the snow sifted in under the door quaesumus, da propitius pacem in diebus nostris Sister Roberta is peeling the onions et a peccato simus semper liberi can't you ab omni perturbatione securi . . ."

Connie folded Mother's hands on the sheet and stood, signaling Mavis to follow her. She closed the door and they stepped into the hall.

"I thought she was your mother. I mean the way you talked, I thought she was your own mother." They were descending the wide central stairs.

"She is my mother. Your mother too. Whose mother you?"

Mavis did not answer, partly because she couldn't speak of it but also because she was trying to remember where, in a house with no electricity, the light in Mother's room came from.

After the roast chicken supper, Connie showed Mavis to a large bedroom. From the four cots in it, she chose the one closest to the window, where she knelt looking out. Two milky moons, instead of the one hanging there, would have been just like Connie's eyes. Beneath them a swept world. Unjudgmental. Tidy. Ample. Forever.

California, which way?

Maryland, which way?

Merle? Pearl?

The lion cub that ate her up that night had blue eyes instead of brown, and he did not have to hold her down this time. When he circled her shoulders with his left paw, she willingly let her head fall back, clearing the way to her throat. Nor did she fight herself out of the dream. The bite was juicy, but she slept through that as well as other things until the singing woke her.

Mavis Albright left the Convent off and on, but she always returned, so she was there in 1976.

On that July morning she had been aware for months of the sourness between the Convent and the town and she might have anticipated the truckload of men prowling the mist. But she was thinking of other things: tattooed sailors and children bathing in emerald water. And exhausted by the pleasures of the night before, she let herself drift in and out of sleep. An hour later, shooing pullets out of the schoolroom, she smelled cigar smoke and the merest trace of Aqua Velva.

GRACE

Either the pavement was burning or she had sapphires hidden in her shoes. K.D., who had never seen a woman mince or switch like that, believed it was the walk that caused all the trouble. Neither he nor his friends lounging at the Oven saw her step off the bus, but when it pulled away there she was—across the street from them in pants so tight, heels so high, earrings so large they forgot to laugh at her hair. She crossed Central Avenue toward them, taking tiny steps on towering block heels not seen since 1949.

She walked fast, as though tripping through red coals or else in pain from something stuck in the toes of her shoes. Something valuable, K.D. thought, otherwise she would have removed it.

He carried the equipment box through the dining room. Narrow panels of lace spilled from a basket on the side table. Aunt Soane worked thread like a prisoner: daily, methodically, for free, producing more lace than could ever be practical. Out back the garden skirting to the left was weed-free and nicely tilled. K.D. turned right toward the shed and entered. The collies were thrilled to see him. He had to straddle Good to keep her down. Her ears were soft in his fingers and he was steady with the camphor-soaked cotton. The ticks came away like coffee grounds. He put his palm under her jaw; she licked his chin. Ben, the other collie, head on paws, looked on. Life at Steward Morgan's ranch loaded the dogs with mess. They needed a few days in Ruby under K.D.'s care twice a year. He took the bristle brush from the box. Dug deep in Good's hair, brushing it smooth and singing, softly in a Motown falsetto, the song he'd made up for her when she was a puppy. "Hey good dog; stay good dog; old good dog; my good dog. Everybody needs a good good good dog. Everybody needs a good a good a good good dog."

Good stretched her pleasure.

Just those concerned would be at the meeting tonight. Everybody, that is, except the one who started it all. His uncles Deek and Steward, Reverend Misner, Arnette's father and brother. They would discuss the slapping but not the pregnancy and certainly not the girl with sapphires hidden in her shoes.

Suppose she hadn't been there. Suppose her navel had not peeked over the waist of her jeans or her breasts had just hushed, hushed for a few seconds till they could figure out how to act—what attitude to strike. In public, without girls hanging around, they would have known. As a group they would have assumed the right tone immediately. But Arnette was there, whining, and so was Billie Delia.

K.D. and Arnette had separated themselves from the others. To talk. They stood near the dwarf oaks behind the picnic benches and tables for a conversation worse than he ever thought talking could be. What Arnette said was, "Well, what are you going to do about it?" What she meant was: I'm going to Langston in September and I don't want to be pregnant or to abort or get married or feel bad by myself or face my family. He said, "Well, what are *you* going to do about it?" thinking: You cornered me at more socials than I can remember and when I finally agreed I didn't have to take your drawers down you beat me to it so this ain't my problem.

They had just begun to veil threats and unveil mutual dislike when the bus pulled away. All heads, all, turned. First because they had never seen a bus in the town—Ruby was not a stop on the way to someplace else. Second to see why it stopped at all. The vision that appeared when the bus drove away, standing on the road shoulder between the schoolhouse and Holy Redeemer, riveted the attention of everybody lounging at the Oven. She didn't have on any lipstick but from one hundred and fifty feet, you could see her eyes. The silence that descended seemed permanent until Arnette broke it.

"If that's the kind of tramp you want, hop to it, nigger."

K.D. looked from Arnette's neat shirtwaist dress to the bangs across

her forehead and then into her face—sullen, nagging, accusatory—
and slapped it. The change in her expression well worth it.

Somebody said, "Ow!" but mostly his friends were assessing the
screaming tits closing in on them. Arnette fled; Billie Delia too, but,
like the good friend she was, looked back, to see them forcing themselves to look at the ground, the bright May sky or the length of their
fingernails.

Good was finished. Her belly hair could stand a light clipping—its
knots were otherwise impossible—but she was beautiful. K.D. started
on Ben's coat, rehearsing his line of defense to Arnette's family. When
he described the incident to his uncles they had frowned at the same
time. And like a mirror image in gestures if not in looks, Steward spit
fresh Blue Boy while Deek lit a cigar. However disgusted both were,
K.D. knew they would not negotiate a solution that would endanger
him or the future of Morgan money. His grandfather had named his
twins Deacon and Steward for a reason. And their family had not built
two towns, fought white law, Colored Creek, bandits and bad weather,
to see ranches and houses and a bank with mortgages on a feed store, a
drugstore and a furniture store end up in Arnold Fleetwood's pocket.
Since the loose bones of his cousins had been buried two years ago,
K.D., their hope and their despair, was the last male in a line that
included a lieutenant governor, a state auditor and two mayors. His
behavior, as always, required scrutiny and serious correction. Or
would the uncles see it another way? Maybe Arnette's baby would be a
boy, a Morgan grandnephew. Would her father, Arnold, have any
rights then that the Morgans had to respect?

Fondling Ben's coat, picking burrs from the silky strands of hair, K.D.
tried to think like his uncles—which was hard. So he stopped trying
and slipped off into his dream of choice. Only this time it included
Gigi and her screaming tits.

"Hi." She cracked her gum like a professional. "Is this Ruby? Bus
driver said this was it."

"Yep. Yeah. Uh huh. Sure is." The lounging boys spoke as one.

"Any motels around?"

They laughed at that and felt comfortable enough to ask her who she was looking for and from where she had come.

"Frisco," she said. "And rhubarb pie. Got a light?"

The dream, then, would be in Frisco.

The Morgan men conceded nothing but were uneasy at the choice of meeting place. Reverend Misner had thought it best to serve protocol and go to Fleetwood rather than season the raw insult done to the family by making the aggrieved come to the house of the aggressor.

K.D., Deek and Steward had sat in the parsonage living room all nods and conciliatory grunts, but K.D. knew what his uncles were thinking. He watched Steward shift tobacco and hold the juice. So far the credit union Misner had formed was no-profit—small emergency loans to church members; no-penalty payback schedules. Like a piggy bank, Deek had said. But Steward said, Yeah for now. The reputation of the church Misner had left to come to Ruby floated behind him: covert meetings to stir folks up; confrontations with rather than end runs around white law. He obviously had hope for a state that had once decided to build a whole new law school to accommodate one student—a Negro girl—and protect segregation at the same time. He clearly took seriously the possibility of change in a state that had also built an open closet right next to a classroom for another Negro student to sit in by himself. That was in the forties, when K.D. was a nursing infant, before his mother, her brothers, his cousins, and all the rest left Haven. Now, some twenty years later, his uncles listened weekly to Misner's sermons, but at the close of each of them they slid behind the steering wheel of their Oldsmobile and Impala and repeated the Old Fathers' refrain: "Oklahoma is Indians, Negroes and God mixed. All the rest is fodder." To their dismay, Reverend Misner often treated fodder like table food. A man like that could encourage strange behavior; side with a teenage girl; shift ground to Fleetwood. A man like that, willing to throw money away, could give customers ideas. Make them think there was a choice about interest rates.

Still, the Baptists were the largest congregation in town as well as the most powerful. So the Morgans sorted Reverend Misner's opinions carefully to judge which were recommendations easily ignored and which were orders they ought to obey.

In two cars they drove barely three miles from Misner's living room to Fleetwood's house.

Somewhere in an Oklahoma city, June voices are doubled by the sunlit water of a swimming pool. K.D. was there once. He had ridden the Missouri, Kansas, Texas line with his uncles and waited outside on the curb while they talked business inside a red-brick building. Excited voices sounded near, and he went to see. Behind a chain-link fence bordered by wide seamless concrete he saw green water. He knows now it was average size, but then it filled his horizon. It seemed to him as though hundreds of white children were bobbing in it, their voices a cascade of the world's purest happiness, a glee so sharply felt it had brought tears. Now, as the Oldsmobile U-turned at the Oven, where Gigi had popped her gum, K.D. felt again the yearning excitement of sparkly water and the June voices of swimmers. His uncles had not been pleased at having to search the city's business district for him and chastised him on the train and later in the automobile all the way back to Ruby. Small price then, and small price now. The eruptions of "How the hell you get in these messes? You should be with people your own age. Why you want to lay with a Fleetwood anyhow? You see that boy's children? Damn!"—all of them exploded without damage. Just as he had already seen the sparkly water, he had already seen Gigi. But unlike the swimming pool, this girl he would see again.

They parked bumper-to-bumper to the side of Fleetwood's house. When they knocked on the door each man, except for Reverend Misner, began to breathe through his mouth as a way of narrowing the house odor of illness.

Arnold Fleetwood never wanted to sleep in a pup tent, on a pallet or a floor ever again. So he put four bedrooms in the spacious house he built on Central Avenue. Sleeping arrangements for himself, his wife and each of their two children left a guest room they were proud of. When his son, Jefferson, came back from Vietnam and took Sweetie, his bride, into his own bed, there was still the guest room. It would have become a nursery had they not needed it as a hospital ward for Jeff and Sweetie's children. The way things turned out, Fleet now slept on a hideaway in the dining room.

The men sat on spotless upholstery waiting for Reverend Misner to finish seeing the women who were nowhere in sight. Both of the Mrs. Fleetwoods spent all their energy, time and affection on the four children still alive—so far. Fleet and Jeff, grateful for but infuriated by that devotion, turned their shame sideways. Being in their company, sitting near them, was hard. Conversation harder.

K.D. knew that Fleet owed his uncles money. And he knew that Jeff wanted very much to kill somebody. Since he couldn't kill the Veterans Administration others just might have to do. Everybody was relieved when Misner came back down the stairs, smiling.

"Yes. Well." Reverend Misner clasped his hands, gave them a little shake near his shoulder as though he'd already knocked the contestant out. "The ladies promise to bring us coffee and I believe they said rice pudding later. That's the best reason I know of to get started." He smiled again. He was very close to being too handsome for a preacher. Not just his face and head, but his body, extremely well made, called up admiring attention from practically everybody. A serious man, he took his obvious beauty as a brake on sloth—it forced him to deal carefully with his congregation, to take nothing for granted: not the adoration of the women or the envy of the men.

No one returned his smile concerning dessert. He pressed on.

"Let me lay out the situation as I know it. Correct me, you all, if I get it wrong or leave out something. My understanding is that K.D. here has done an injury, a serious injury, to Arnette. So right off we can say K.D. has a problem with his temper and an obligation—"

"Ain't he a little old to have his temper raised toward a young girl?" Jefferson Fleetwood, seething in a low chair farthest from the lamplight, interrupted. "I don't call that temper. I call it illegal."

"Well, at that particular moment, he was way out of line."

"Beg your pardon, Reverend. Arnette is fifteen." Jeff looked steadily into K.D.'s eyes.

"That's right," said Fleet. "She ain't been hit since she was two years old."

"That may be the problem." Steward, known for inflammatory speech, had been cautioned by Deek to keep his mouth shut and let him, the subtle one, do the talking. Now his words blew Jeff out of his chair.

"Don't you come in my house dirt-mouthing my family!"

"Your house?" Steward looked from Jeff to Arnold Fleetwood.

"You heard me! Papa, I think we better call this meeting off before somebody gets hurt!"

"You right," said Fleet. "This is my child we talking about. My child!"

Only Jeff was standing, but now Misner rose. "Gentlemen. Whoa!" He held up his hands and, towering over the seated men, put to good use his sermon-making voice. "We are men here; men of God. You going to put God's work in the gutter?"

K.D. saw Steward struggling with the need to spit and stood up also. "Look here," he said. "I'm sorry. I am. I'd take it back if I could."

"Done is done, friends." Misner lowered his hands.

K.D. continued. "I respect your daughter—"

"Since when?" Jeff asked him.

"I always respected her. From when she was that high." K.D. leveled his hand around his waist. "Ask anybody. Ask her girlfriend, Billie Delia. Billie Delia will tell you that."

The effect of the genius stroke was immediate. The Morgan uncles held in their smiles, while the Fleetwoods, father and son, bristled. Billie Delia was the fastest girl in town and speeding up by the second.

"This ain't about no Billie Delia," said Jeff. "This is about what you did to my baby sister."

"Wait a minute," said Misner. "Maybe we could get a better fix, K.D., if you could tell us why you did it. Why? What happened? Were you drinking? Did she aggravate you somehow?" He expected this forthright question to open up a space for honesty, where the men could stop playing bear and come to terms. The sudden quiet that followed surprised him. Steward and Deek both cleared their sinuses at the same time. Arnold Fleetwood stared at his shoes. Something, Misner guessed, was askew. In that awkward silence they could hear above their heads the light click of heels: the women pacing, servicing, fetching, feeding—whatever it took to save the children who could not save themselves.

"We don't care about why," said Jeff. "What I want to know is what you going to do about it?" He shot his forefinger into the chair arm on the word "do."

Deek leaned back and spread his thighs wider, as though to welcome territory that naturally belonged to him. "What you have in mind?" he asked.

"First off, apologize," said Fleet.

"I just did," said K.D.

"Not to me. To her. To her!"

"Yes, sir," said K.D. "I will."

"All right," Deek said. "That's first. What's second?"

Jeff answered. "You better never lay your hand on her again."

"I won't lay a thing on her, sir."

"Is there a third?" asked Deek.

"We need to know he means it," said Fleet. "Some sign it's meant."

"Sign?" Deek managed to look puzzled.

"My sister's reputation is messed up, ain't it?"

"Uh huh. I can see that."

"Nothing can fix that, can it?" Jeff's question combined defiance and inquiry.

Deek leaned forward. "Well, I don't know. Hear she's going to college. That'll put all this behind her. Maybe we can help out some."

Jeff grunted. "I don't know about that." He looked at his father. "What do you think, Papa? Would that . . . ?"

"Have to ask her mother. She's hit by this too, you know. Hit worse'n I am, maybe."

"Well," said Deek, "whyn't you talk it over with her, then? If she's agreeable, stop by the bank. Tomorrow."

Fleet scratched his jaw. "Can't make any promises. Mable is a mighty proud woman. Mighty proud."

Deek nodded. "Got a reason to be, daughter going to college and all. We don't want anything to stand in the way of that. Credit to the town."

"When that school start up, Fleet?" Steward cocked his head.

"August, I believe."

"She be ready then?"

"What do you mean?"

"Well," Steward answered. "August's a long way off. This here is May. She might change her mind. Decide to stay on."

"I'm her father. I'll arrange her mind."

"Right," said Steward.

"Settled then?" Deek asked.

"Like I say. Have to talk to her mother."

"Of course."

"She's the key. My wife's the key."

Deek smiled outright for the first time that evening. "Women always the key, God bless 'em."

Reverend Misner sighed as though breathable air were available again. "God's love is in this house," he said. "I feel it every time I come here. Every time." He looked toward the ceiling while Jefferson Fleetwood stared at him with stricken eyes. "We treasure His strength but we mustn't ignore His love. That's what keeps us strong. Gentlemen. Brothers. Let us pray."

They bowed their heads and listened obediently to Misner's beautifully put words and the tippy-tap steps of women who were nowhere in sight.

The next morning Reverend Misner was surprised by how well he had slept. The meeting with the Morgans and Fleetwoods the previous night had made him uneasy. There was a grizzly bear in Fleetwood's living room—quiet, invisible, but making deft movement impossible. Upstairs he'd made the women laugh—well, Mable anyway. Sweetie smiled but clearly didn't enjoy his banter. Her eye was ever on her children. A slide. A lean. A suck of air—she bent over a crib and made quick, practiced adjustments. But her expression was mildly patronizing as if to say what could there be to amuse her and why would he try? She acquiesced when he asked her to join him in prayer. Bowed her head, closed her eyes, but when she faced him with a quiet "Amen," he felt as though his relationship with the God he spoke to was vague or too new, while hers was superior, ancient and completely sealed.

He had better luck with Mable Fleetwood, who was delighted enough with his visit to prolong their conversation unnecessarily. Downstairs the men he had assembled, after learning what had happened at the Oven, waited—as did the grizzly.

Misner fought his pillow for a moment and convinced himself that the ending was satisfactory. Tempers banked, a resolution surfaced, peace declared. At least he hoped so. The Morgans always seemed to be having a second conversation—an unheard dialogue right next to the one they spoke aloud. They performed as one man, but something in Deek's manner made Misner wonder if he wasn't covering for his brother—propping him the way you would a slow-learning child. Arnold's air of affront was coy: a formula everyone expected but knew had no weight. Jefferson's skin was thin as gauze. But it was K.D. who irritated Misner most. Too quick to please. An oily apology. A devious smile. Misner despised males who hit women—and a fifteen-year-old? What did K.D. think he was doing? His relation to Deek and Steward protected him, of course, but it was hard to like a man who relied on that. Servile to his uncles; brutal with females. Then, later that evening, as Misner warmed up the fried steak and potatoes Anna Flood had brought him for his supper, he had looked out of his window and seen K.D. speeding down Central in Steward's Impala. Smiling—he'd bet on it—his devious smile.

Such nagging thoughts he believed would keep him awake most of the night, but in the morning he woke as if from the sweetest of sleeps. Anna's food, he supposed. Still, he wondered, what had K.D. been zooming to on the road out of town?

.   .   .

A man and a woman fucking forever. When the light changes every four hours they do something new. At the desert's edge they fuck to the sky tide of Arizona. Nothing can stop them. Nothing wants to. Moonlight arches his back; sunlight warms her tongue. There is no way to miss or mistake them if you know where they are: right outside Tucson on I-3, in a town called Wish. Pass through it; take the first left. Where the road ends and the serious desert begins, keep going. The tarantulas are poisonous but it is necessary to go on foot because no tires can manage the terrain. One hour, tops, you'll see loving to beat the sky. Sometimes tender. Other times rough. But they never stop. Not for dust storms or heat hovering at 108 degrees. And if you are patient and catch them in one of the desert's random rainfalls you will see the color of their bodies deepen. But they keep on doing it in the rare pure rain—the black couple of Wish, Arizona.

Over and over Mikey told Gigi how they looked and how to find them outside his hometown. They would have been, could have been, a tourist attraction, he said, except they embarrassed local people. A committee of concerned Methodists, organized to blow them up or disguise them with cement, got started, but it died after a few preliminary investigations. The committee members said their objections were not antisex at all but antiperversion, since it was believed by some, who had looked very carefully, that the couple was two women making love in the dirt. Others, after an equally careful examination (close up and with binoculars), said no, they were two males—bold as Gomorrah.

Mikey, however, had touched the body parts and knew for a fact one was a woman, the other a man. "So what?" he said. "They weren't doing it on a highway, after all. You had to go way out of the way to find them." Mikey said the Methodists wanted to get rid of them but they wanted them to be there too. That even a bunch of repressed rednecks, too scared to have wet dreams, knew they needed the couple. Even if they never went near them, he said, they needed to know they were out there. At sunrise, he said, they turned copper and you knew they'd been at it all night. At noon they were silvery gray. Then afternoon blue, then evening black. Moving, moving, all the time moving.

Gigi loved to hear him say that part: "Moving, moving, all the time moving."

When they got split up, Mikey got ninety days. Gigi was released from the emergency room with an Ace bandage on her wrist. Everything happened so fast they had no time to plan where to meet. The court-appointed lawyer came out saying no bail, no probation. His client had to do the whole three months. After calculating the sentence, minus the three weeks spent in jail, Gigi sent Mikey a message through the CA lawyer. The message was "Wish April fifteenth."

"What?" asked the lawyer.

"Just say it. 'Wish April fifteenth.' "

What did Mikey say to her message?

" 'Right on,' " he said. " 'Right on.' "

There was no Mikey, there was no Wish, there was no I-3 and nobody was fucking in the desert. Everybody she spoke to in Tucson thought she was crazy.

"Maybe the town I'm looking for is too small for a map," she offered.

"Then ask the troopers. No town so small they don't know it."

"The rock formation is off the road. Looks like a couple making love."

"Well, I seen some lizards do it in the desert, miss."

"Cactus, mebbe?"

"Now there's a possibility."

They laughed themselves weak.

After running her finger down columns in the telephone directory and finding no one in the area with Mikey's last name, Rood, Gigi gave him up. Reluctantly. The eternal desert coupling, however, she held on to for dear and precious life. Underneath gripping dreams of social justice, of an honest people's guard—more powerful than her memory of the boy spitting blood into his hands—the desert lovers broke her heart. Mikey did not invent them. He may have put them in the wrong place, but he had only summoned to the surface what she had known all her life existed . . . somewhere. Maybe Mexico, which is where she headed.

The dope was heavy, the men always ready, but ten days later she woke up crying. She called Alcorn, Mississippi, collect.

"Bring your butt home, girl. World change enough to suit you? Everybody dead anyway. King, another one of them Kennedys, Medgar Evers, a nigger name of X, Lord I can't think who all since you left not to speak of right here remember L.J. used to work down at the route two mall somebody walked in there broad daylight with a pistol shaped like nothing nobody ever seen before . . ."

Gigi let her head fall back on the plaster wall near the telephone. Outside the bodega a clerk swung a broom at some children. Girls. Without underwear.

"I'm coming, Granddaddy. I'm heading home right now."

Most of the time she had both seats to herself. Space to spread out. Sleep. Read back issues of *Ramparts* rolled in her knapsack. When she boarded the Santa Fe, the train pulled out crowded with air force men in blue. Soon 4-H'ers crowded the cars. But when she transferred to the MKT, the cars were never full again.

The man with the earring didn't come looking for her. She sought him out. Just to talk to somebody who wasn't encased in polyester and who looked like he might smoke something other than Chesterfields.

He was short, almost a dwarf, but his clothes were East Coast hip. His Afro was neat, not ragged, and he wore seeds of gold around his neck, one matching stud in his ear.

They stood next to each other at the snack bar, which the attendant insisted on calling the dining car. She ordered a Coke without ice and a brownie. He was paying for a large cup of ice only.

"That ought to be free," Gigi said to the man behind the counter. "He shouldn't have to pay for the cup."

"Excuse me, m'am. I just follow rules."

"I ordered no ice. Did you deduct anything?"

"Course not."

"Don't trouble yourself," the short man said.

"I ain't troubled," Gigi told him, and then, to the counterman:

"Listen, you. Give him the ice you weren't going to charge me for, okay?"

"Miss, do I have to call the conductor?"

"If you don't, I will. This is train robbery, all right—trains robbing people."

"It's all right," said the man. "Just a nickel."

"It's the principle," said Gigi.

"A five-cent principle ain't no principle at all. The man needs a nickel. Needs it real bad." The short man smiled.

"I don't need nothing," said the attendant. "It's the rules."

"Have two," said the man, and flicked a second nickel into the saucer.

Gigi glaring, the earring man smiling, they left the snack bar together. She sat down across the aisle from him to expand on the incident, while the man crunched ice.

"Gigi." She held out her hand. "You?"

"Dice," he said.

"Like chopping small?"

"Like pair of."

He touched her with a cool, cool hand and they made up stories for each other for miles. Gigi even got comfortable enough to ask him had he ever seen or heard tell of a rock formation that looked like a man and a woman making out. He laughed and said no, but that he once heard about a place where there was a lake in the middle of a wheat field. And that near this lake two trees grew in each other's arms. And if you squeezed in between them in just the right way, well, you would feel an ecstasy no human could invent or duplicate. "They say after that can't nobody turn you down."

"Nobody turns me down now."

"Nobody? I mean no-o-body!"

"Where is this place?"

"Ruby. Ruby, Oklahoma. Way out in the middle of nowhere."

"You been there?"

"Not yet. But I plan to check it out. Say they got the best rhubarb pie in the nation."

"I hate rhubarb."

"Hate it? Girl, you ain't lived. You ain't lived at all."

"I'm going home. See my folks."

"Where's home for you?"

"Frisco. All my folks live in Frisco. I just talked to my grandfather. They're waiting on me."

Dice nodded but said nothing.

Gigi stuffed the brownie wrapper in her empty paper cup. I am not lost, she thought. Not lost at all. I can go see Granddaddy or go back to the Bay or . . .

The train slowed. Dice rose to collect his luggage from the overhead rack. He was so short he had to stand on tiptoe. Gigi helped him and he didn't seem to mind.

"Well, I get off here. Nice talking with you."

"You too."

"Good luck. Watch out, now. Don't get wet."

If the boys standing in front of a kind of barbecue grill had said, No, this is Alcorn, Mississippi, she probably would have believed them. Same haircuts, same stares, same loose hick smiles. What her granddaddy called "country's country." Some girls were there too, arguing, it seemed, with one of them. In any case, they weren't much help, but she enjoyed the waves of raw horniness slapping her back as she walked off down the street.

First dust, fine as flour, sifted into her eyes, her mouth. Then the wind wrecked her hair. Suddenly she was out of town. What the locals called Central Avenue just stopped, and Gigi was at Ruby's edge at the same time she had reached its center. The wind, soundless, came from the ground rather than the sky. One minute her heels clicked, the next they were mute in swirling dirt. On either side of her, tall grass rolled like water.

She had stopped five minutes ago in a so-called drugstore, bought cigarettes and learned that the boys at the barbecue grill were telling the truth: there was no motel. And if there was any pie it wasn't served at a restaurant because there wasn't one of those either. Other than the picnic benches at the barbecue thing, there was no public place to sit down. All around her were closed doors and shut windows where parted curtains were swiftly replaced.

So much for Ruby, she thought. Mikey must have sent her that lying freak on the train. She just wanted to see. Not just the thing in the wheat field, but whether there was anything at all the world had to say for itself (in rock, tree or water) that wasn't body bags or little boys spitting blood into their hands so as not to ruin their shoes. So. Alcorn. She might as well start over in Alcorn, Mississippi. Sooner or later one of those trucks parked by the Seed and Feed store would have to start up and she would hitch the hell out of there.

Holding on to her hair and squinting against the wind, Gigi considered walking back toward the feed store. Her backpack felt heavy in high heels and if she didn't move, the wind might topple her. As suddenly as it had begun the wind quit; in its absence she heard an engine coming toward her.

"You headed out to the Convent?" A man in a wide-brimmed hat opened the door of his van.

Gigi tossed her backpack on the seat and climbed in. "Convent? You kidding? Anything but. Can you put me near a *real* bus stop or train station or something?"

"You in luck. Take you right to the track."

"Great!" Gigi dug around in the pack between her knees. "Smells new."

"Brand-new. You all my first trip."

"You all?"

"Have to make a stop. Another passenger going to take a train ride too." He smiled. "My name's Roger. Roger Best."

"Gigi."

"But you free. The other one I charge," he said, cutting his eyes away from the road. Pretending to examine the scenery through the passenger window, he looked at her navel first, then further down, then up.

Gigi pulled out a mirror and, as best she could, repaired the wind damage to her hair, thinking, Yeah. I'm free, all right.

And she was. Just as Roger Best said, there was no charge to the living, but the dead cost twenty-five dollars.

Every now and then the woman sitting on the porch steps lifted her aviator's glasses to wipe her eyes. One braid from under her straw hat fell down her back. Roger leaned on his knee and spoke to her for what seemed to Gigi a long time, then they both went inside. When Roger came out, he was closing his wallet and frowning.

"Ain't no help out here. You may's well wait inside. Going to take me a while to get the body down."

Gigi turned to look behind her but couldn't see through the partition.

"Jesus! Shit! This here's a hearse?"

"Sometimes. Sometimes it's a ambulance. Today it's a hearse." He was all business now. No quick glances at her breasts. "Got to get it on board the MKT at eight-twenty p.m. And I got to be there not *in* time but *on* time."

Gigi was quick but clumsy stepping out of the van, now hearse, but she made it around the house, up the wide wooden stairs and through the front doors in no time at all. He had said "Convent," so she thought sweet but stern women floating in sailboat hats above long black sleeves. But there was nobody, and the woman in the straw hat had disappeared. Gigi walked through a marble foyer into another one, twice the size. In the dimness she could see a hallway extending to the right and to the left. In front of her more wide stairs. Before she could decide which way to go, Roger was behind her carrying a metal something with wheels. He moved toward the stairs, mumbling, "Not a bit of help, not a bit." Gigi turned right, rushing toward light coming from under a pair of swing doors. Inside was the longest table she had ever seen, in the biggest kitchen. She sat there, chewing her thumbnail, wondering just how bad could it be riding with a dead person? There was some herb in her pack. Not much but enough, she thought, to keep her from freaking. She reached out and pinched off a bit of crust from a pie sitting before her and noticed for the first time the place was loaded with food, mostly untouched. Several cakes, more pies, potato salad, a ham, a large dish of baked beans. There must be nuns, she thought. Or maybe all this was from the funeral. Suddenly, like a legitimate mourner, she was ravenous.

Gigi was gobbling, piling more food onto her plate even while she scooped from it, when the woman entered without her straw hat or her glasses and lay down on the stone-cold floor.

Her mouth was full of baked beans and chocolate cake so Gigi could not speak. Outside Roger's horn blasted. Gigi put her spoon down but held on to the cake as she walked over to where the woman lay. Squatting down, she wiped her mouth and said, "Can I help you?" The woman's eyes were closed but she shook her head no.

"Is it anybody else here I can call?"

She opened her eyes then, and Gigi saw nothing—just a faint circle where the edge of the iris used to be.

"Hey, girl. You coming?" Roger's voice was puny and distant over the throb of his engine. "I got a train to meet. On time! I got to be on time!"

Gigi leaned down closer, gazing into eyes with nothing to recommend them.

"I said is anybody else here?"

"You," she murmured. "You here." Each word sailed toward Gigi on a wave of alcohol breath.

"You hear me? I can't wait all day!" Roger warned.

Gigi waved her free hand across the woman's face to make sure she was blind as well as drunk.

"Stop that," said the woman, whispering but annoyed.

"Oh," said Gigi, "I thought. Why don't you let me get you a chair?"

"I'm gone, hear? Gone!" Gigi heard the engine rev and the hearse shift from neutral into reverse.

"I'm missing my ride. What you want me to do?"

The woman turned over on her side and folded her hands under her cheek. "Be a darling. Just watch. I haven't closed my eyes in seventeen days."

"Wouldn't a bed do the trick?"

"Be a darling. Be a darling. I don't want to sleep when nobody there to watch."

"On the floor?"

But she was asleep. Breathing like a child.

Gigi stood up and looked around the kitchen, slowly swallowing cake. At least there were no dead people here now. The sound of the hearse grew fainter and then slipped away.

Fright, not triumph, spoke in every foot of the embezzler's mansion. Shaped like a live cartridge, it curved to a deadly point at the north end where, originally, the living and dining rooms lay. He must have believed his persecutors would come from the north because all the first-floor windows huddled in those two rooms. Like lookouts. The southern end contained signs of his desire in two rooms: an outsize kitchen and a room where he could play rich men's games. Neither room had a view, but the kitchen had one of the mansion's two entrances. A veranda curved from the north around the bullet's tip, continued along its wall past the main entrance, and ended at the flat end of the ammunition—its southern exposure. Except from the bedrooms no one in the house could see the sun rise, and there was no vantage point to see it set. The light, therefore, was always misleading.

He must have planned to have a lot of good-time company in his fortress: eight bedrooms, two giant bathrooms, a cellar of storerooms that occupied as much space as the first floor. And he wanted to amuse his guests so completely they would not think of leaving for days on end. His efforts to entertain were no more sophisticated or interesting than he was—mostly food, sex and toys. After two years of semi-covert construction, he managed one voluptuous party before he was arrested, just as he feared, by northern lawmen, one of whom attended his first and only party.

The four teaching sisters who moved into his house when it was offered for sale at a pittance diligently canceled the obvious echoes of his delight but could do nothing to hide his terror. The closed-off, protected "back," the poised and watchful "tip," an entrance door guarded by the remaining claws of some monstrous statuary, which the sisters had removed at once. A rickety, ill-hanging kitchen door the only vulnerability.

Gigi, as high as possible on her limited supply, and roaming through the mansion while the drunken woman slept on the kitchen floor, immediately recognized the conversion of the dining room into a schoolroom; the living room into a chapel; and the game room alteration to an office—cue sticks and balls, but no pool table. Then she discovered the traces of the sisters' failed industry. The female-torso candleholders in the candelabra hanging from the hall ceiling. The curls of hair winding through vines that once touched faces now chipped away. The nursing cherubim emerging from layers of paint in the foyer. The nipple-tipped doorknobs. Layabouts half naked in old-timey clothes, drinking and fondling each other in prints stacked in closets. A Venus or two among several pieces of nude statuary beneath the cellar stairs. She even found the brass male genitalia that had been ripped from sinks and tubs, packed away in a chest of sawdust as if, however repelled by the hardware's demands, the sisters valued nevertheless its metal. Gigi toyed with the fixtures, turning the testicles designed to release water from the penis. She sucked the last bit of joint—Ming One—and laid the roach on one of the alabaster vaginas in the game room. She imagined men contentedly knocking their cigars against those ashtrays. Or perhaps just resting them there, knowing without looking that the glowing tip was slowly building a delicate head.

She avoided the bedrooms because she didn't know which one had belonged to the dead person, but when she went to use one of the bathrooms, she saw that no toilet activity was not meant to be reflected in a mirror that reflected in another. Most, set firmly into wall tile, had been painted. Bending to examine the mermaids holding up the tub, she noticed a handle fastened to a slab of wood surrounded by floor tile. She was able to reach and lift the handle, but not able to budge it.

Suddenly she was fiercely hungry again and returned to the kitchen, to eat and do as the woman had asked: be a darling and watch while she slept—like an antique tripper afraid to come down alone. She was finished with the macaroni, some ham and another slice of cake when the woman on the floor stirred and sat up. She held her face in both hands for a moment, then rubbed her eyes.

"Feel better?" asked Gigi.

She took a pair of sunglasses from an apron pocket and put them on. "No. But rested."

"Well that *is* better."

The woman got up. "I suppose. Thank you—for staying."

"Sure. Hangover's a bitch. I'm Gigi. Who died?"

"A love," said the woman. "I had two; she was the first and the last."

"Aw, I'm sorry," Gigi said. "Where's he taking her? The dude in the hearse."

"Far. To a lake named for her. Superior. That's how she wanted it."

"Who else lives here? You didn't cook all this food, did you?"

The woman filled a saucepan with water and shook her head.

"What you gonna do now?"

"Gigi Gigi Gigi Gigi Gigi. That's what frogs sing. What did your mother name you?"

"Her? She gave me her own name."

"Well?"

"Grace."

"Grace. What could be better?"

Nothing. Nothing at all. If ever there came a morning when mercy and simple good fortune took to their heels and fled, grace alone might have to do. But from where would it come and how fast? In that holy hollow between sighting and following through, could grace slip through at all?

It was the I-give woman serving up her breasts like two baked Alaskas on a platter that took all the kick out of looking in the boy's eyes. Gigi watched him battle his stare and lose every time. He said his name was K.D. and tried hard to enjoy her face as much as her cleavage while he talked. It was a struggle she expected, rose to and took pleasure in—normally. But the picture she had wakened to an hour earlier spoiled it.

Unwilling to sleep on the second floor where a person had just died, Gigi had chosen the leather sofa in the used-to-be-game-room office. Windowless, dependent on no longer available electricity for light, the room encouraged her to sleep deeply and long. She missed the morning entirely and woke in the afternoon, in a darkness hardly less than she'd fallen asleep in. Hanging on the wall in front of her was the etching she had barely glanced at when poking around the day before. Now it loomed into her line of vision in the skinny light from the hall. A woman. On her knees. A knocked-down look, cast-up begging eyes, arms outstretched holding up her present on a platter to a lord. Gigi tiptoed over and leaned close to see who was the woman with the I-give-up face. "Saint Catherine of Siena" was engraved on a small plaque in the gilt frame. Gigi laughed—brass dicks hidden in a box; pudding tits exposed on a plate—but in fact it didn't feel funny. So when the boy she had seen in town the day before parked his car near the kitchen door and blew his horn, her interest in him had an edge of annoyance. Propped in the doorway she ate jam-covered bread while she listened to him and watched the war waged in his eyes.

His smile was lovely and his voice attractive. "Been riding around looking all over for you. Heard you was out here. Thought you might be still."

"Who told you that?"

"A friend. Well, a friend of a friend."

"You mean that hearse dude?"

"Uh huh. Said you changed your mind about getting to the train station."

"News sure travels fast out here, even if nothing else does."

"We get around. Wanna go for a ride? Go as fast as you want."

Gigi licked jam from her thumb and forefinger. She looked to the left toward the garden and thought she saw in the distance a glint of metal or maybe a mirror reflecting light. As from a state trooper's sunglasses.

"Gimme a minute," she said. "Change my clothes."

In the game room she put on a yellow skirt and a dark red top. Then she consulted her astrology chart before stuffing her belongings (and a few souvenirs) in her backpack which she slung into the car's rear seat.

"Hey," said K.D. "We just going for a little ride."

"Yeah," she answered, "but who knows? I might change my mind again."

They drove through mile after mile of sky-blue sky. Gigi had not really looked at the scenery from the train windows or the bus. As far as she was concerned, there was nothing out there. But speeding along in the Impala was more like cruising on a DC-10, and the nothing turned out to be sky—unignorable, custom-made, designer sky. Not empty either but full of breath and all the eye was meant for.

"That's the shortest skirt I ever saw." He smiled his lovely smile.

"Minis," said Gigi. "In the real world they're called miniskirts."

"Don't they make people stare at you?"

"Stare. Drive for miles. Have car wrecks. Talk stupid."

"You must like it. Reckon that's what they're for, though."

"You explain your clothes; I'll explain mine. Where'd you get those pants, for instance?"

"What's wrong with them?"

"Nothing. Listen, you want to argue, take me back."

"No. No, I don't want to argue; I just want to . . . ride."

"Yeah? How fast?"

"Told you. Fast as I can."

"How long?"

"Long as you want."

"How far?"

"All the way."

The desert couple was big, Mikey said. From any angle you looked, he said, they took up the sky, moving, moving. Liar, thought Gigi; not this sky. This here sky was bigger than everything, including a woman with her breasts on a tray.

When Mavis pulled into the driveway, near the kitchen door, she slammed the brakes so hard her packages slid from the seat and fell beneath the dashboard. The figure sitting in the garden's red chair was totally naked. She could not see the face under the hat's brim but she knew it wore no sunglasses. A mere month she'd been away, and for three weeks of that time couldn't wait to get back. Something must have happened, she thought. To Mother. To Connie. At the squeal of the brakes, the sunning figure did not move. Only when she slammed the Cadillac door did the person sit up and push back the hat. Calling out, "Connie! Connie?" Mavis hurried toward the garden's edge. "Who the hell are you? Where's Connie?"

The naked girl yawned and scratched her pubic hair. "Mavis?" she asked.

Relieved to learn she was known, spoken of, at least, Mavis lowered her voice. "What are you doing out here like that? Where's Connie?"

"Like what? She's inside."

"You're naked!"

"Yeah. So? You want the cigar?"

"Do they know?" Mavis glanced toward the house.

"Lady," said Gigi, "are you looking at something you never saw before or something you don't have or you a clothes freak or what?"

"There you are." Connie came down the steps, her arms wide, toward Mavis. "I missed you." They hugged and Mavis surrendered to the thump of the woman's heart against her own.

"Who is she, Connie, and where are her clothes?"

"Oh, that's little Grace. She came the day after Mother died."

"Died? When?"

"Seven days now. Seven."

"But I brought the things. I have it all in the car."

"No use. Not for her anyway. My heart's all scrunched, but now you back I feel like cooking."

"You haven't been eating?" Mavis shot a cold glance at Gigi.

"A bit. Funeral foods. But now I'll cook fresh."

"There's plenty," said Gigi. "We haven't even touched the—"

"You put some clothes on!"

"You kiss my ass!"

"Do it, Grace," said Connie. "Go, like a good girl. Cover yourself we love you just the same."

"She ever hear of sunbathing?"

"Go on now."

Gigi went, exaggerating the switch of both the cheeks she had offered Mavis.

"What rock did she crawl out from under?" Mavis asked.

"Hush," said Connie. "Soon you'll like her."

No way, Mavis thought. No way at all. Mother's gone, but Connie's okay. I've been here almost three years, and this house is where we are. Us. Not her.

They did everything but slap each other, and finally they did that. What postponed the inevitable were loves forlorn and a very young girl in too tight clothes tapping on the screen door.

"You have to help me," she said. "You have to. I've been raped and it's almost August."

Only part of that was true.

SENECA

Something was scratching on the pane. Again. Dovey turned over on her stomach, refusing to look out of the window each time she heard it. He wasn't there. He never came at night. Deliberately she drove her mind onto everyday things. What would she fix for supper tomorrow?

Not much point to garden peas. May as well use canned. Not a taste bud in Steward's mouth could tell the difference. Blue Boy packed in his cheek for twenty years first narrowed his taste to a craving for spices, then reduced it altogether to a single demand for hot pepper.

When they got married, Dovey was sure she could never cook well enough to suit the twin known to be pickier than his brother, Deek. Back from the war, both men were hungry for down-home food, but dreaming of it for three years had raised their expectations, exaggerated the possibilities of lard making biscuits lighter than snow, the responsibility sharp cheese took on in hominy. When they were discharged and back home, Deek hummed with pleasure as he sucked sweet marrow from hocks or crunched chicken bones to powder. But Steward remembered everything differently. Shouldn't the clove be down in the tissue, not just sitting on top of the ham? And the chicken-fried steak—Vidalia onions or Spanish?

On her wedding day, Dovey had stood facing the flowered wall-paper, her back to the window so her sister, Soane, could see better. Dovey held up the hem of her slip while Soane drew the seams. The little brush tickled the backs of her legs, but she stood perfectly still.

81

There were no silk stockings in Haven or the world in 1949, but to get married obviously bare-legged mocked God and the ceremony.

"I don't expect he'll be satisfied at table," Dovey told her sister.

"Why not?"

"I don't know. He compliments my cooking, then suggests how to improve it next time."

"Hold still, Dovey."

"Deek doesn't do that to you, does he?"

"Not that. He's picky other ways. But I wouldn't worry about it if I was you. If he's satisfied in bed, the table won't mean a thing."

They laughed then, and Soane had to do a whole seam over.

Now the difficulty that loomed in 1949 had been solved by tobacco. It didn't matter whether her peas were garden fresh or canned. Convent peppers, hot as hellfire, did all the cooking for her. The trouble it took to cultivate peas was wasted. A teaspoon of sugar and a plop of butter in canned ones would do nicely, since the bits of purple-black pepper he would sprinkle over them bombed away any quiet flavor. Take late squash, for example.

Almost always, these nights, when Dovey Morgan thought about her husband it was in terms of what he had lost. His sense of taste one example of the many she counted. Contrary to his (and all of Ruby's) assessment, the more Steward acquired, the more visible his losses. The sale of his herd at 1958's top dollar accompanied his defeat in the statewide election for church Secretary because of his outspoken contempt for the schoolchildren sitting in in that drugstore in Oklahoma City. He had even written a hateful letter to the women who organized the students. His position had not surprised her, since ten years earlier he'd called Thurgood Marshall a "stir-up Negro" for handling the NAACP's segregation suit in Norman. In 1962 the natural gas drilled to ten thousand feet on the ranch filled his pockets but shrunk their land to a toy ranch, and he lost the trees that had made it so beautiful to behold. His hairline and his taste buds faltered over time. Small losses that culminated with the big one: in 1964, when he was forty, Fairy's curse came true: they learned neither could ever have children.

Now, almost ten years later, he had "cleaned up," as he put it, in a real estate deal in Muskogee, and Dovey didn't have to wonder what else he would lose now because he was already in a losing battle with Reverend Misner over words attached to the lip of the Oven. An argument fueled in part, Dovey thought, by what nobody talked about: young people in trouble or acting up behind every door. Arnette, home from college, wouldn't leave her bed. Harper Jury's boy, Menus, drunk every weekend since he got back from Vietnam. Roger's granddaughter, Billie Delia, disappeared into thin air. Jeff's wife, Sweetie, laughing, laughing at jokes no one made. K.D.'s mess with that girl living out at the Convent. Not to speak of the sass, the pout, the outright defiance of some of the others—the ones who wanted to name the Oven "such-and-such place" and who had decided that the original words on it were something that enraged Steward and Deek. Dovey had talked to her sister (and sister-in-law) about it; to Mable Fleetwood; to Anna Flood; to a couple of women in the Club. Opinions were varied, confusing, even incoherent, because feelings ran so high over the matter. Also because some young people, by snickering at Miss Esther's finger memory, had insulted entire generations preceding them. They had not suggested, politely, that Miss Esther may have been mistaken; they howled at the notion of remembering invisible words you couldn't even read by tracing letters you couldn't pronounce.

"Did she see them?" asked the sons.

"Better than that!" shouted the fathers. "She felt them, touched them, put her finger on them!"

"If she was blind, sir, we could believe her. That'd be like braille. But some five-year-old kid who couldn't read her own tombstone if she climbed out of her grave and stood in front of it?"

The twins frowned. Fleet, thinking of his mother-in-law's famous generosity, leapt out of the pew and had to be held back.

The Methodists, early on, had smiled at the dissension among the Baptists. The Pentecostals laughed out loud. But not for long. Young members in their own churches began to voice opinions about the words. Each congregation had people who were among or related to the fifteen families to leave Haven and start over. The Oven didn't belong to any one denomination; it belonged to all, and all were asked to show up at Calvary. To discuss it, Reverend Misner said. The weather was cool, garden scents strong, and when they assembled at seven-thirty the atmosphere was pleasant, people simply curious. And it remained so right through Misner's opening remarks. Maybe the young folks were nervous, but when they spoke, starting with Luther Beauchamp's sons, Royal and Destry, their voices were so strident the women, embarrassed, looked down at their pocketbooks; shocked, the men forgot to blink.

It would have been better for everyone if the young people had spoken softly, acknowledged their upbringing as they presented their views. But they didn't want to discuss; they wanted to instruct.

"No ex-slave would tell us to be scared all the time. To 'beware' God. To always be ducking and diving, trying to look out every minute in case He's getting ready to throw something at us, keep us down."

"You say 'sir' when you speak to men," said Sargeant Person.

"Sorry, sir. But what kind of message is that? No ex-slave who had the guts to make his own way, build a town out of nothing, could think like that. No ex-slave—"

Deacon Morgan cut him off. "That's my grandfather you're talking about. Quit calling him an ex-slave like that's all he was. He was also an ex–lieutenant governor, an ex-banker, an ex-deacon and a whole lot of other exes, and he wasn't making his own way; he was part of a whole group making their own way."

Having caught Reverend Misner's eyes, the boy was firm. "He was born in slavery times, sir; he was a slave, wasn't he?"

"Everybody born in slavery time wasn't a slave. Not the way you mean it."

"There's just one way to mean it, sir," said Destry.

"You don't know *what* you're talking about!"

"None of them do! Don't know jackshit!" shouted Harper Jury.

"Whoa, whoa!" Reverend Misner interrupted. "Brothers. Sisters. We called this meeting in God's own house to try and find—"

"One of His houses," snarled Sargeant.

"All right, one of His houses. But whichever one, He demands respect from those who are in it. Am I right or am I right?"

Harper sat down. "I apologize for the language. To Him," he said, pointing upward.

"That might please Him," said Misner. "Might not. Don't limit your respect to Him, Brother Jury. He cautions every which way against it."

"Reverend." The Reverend Pulliam stood up. He was a dark, wiry man—white-haired and impressive. "We have a problem here. You, me. Everybody. The problem is with the way some of us talk. The grown-ups, of course, should use proper language. But the young people—what they say is more like backtalk than talk. What we're here for is—"

Royal Beauchamp actually interrupted him, the Reverend! "What is talk if it's not 'back'? You all just don't want us to talk at all. Any talk is 'backtalk' if you don't agree with what's being said. . . . Sir."

Everybody was so stunned by the boy's brazenness, they hardly heard what he said.

Pulliam, dismissing the possibility that Roy's parents—Luther and Helen Beauchamp—were there, turned slowly to Misner. "Reverend, can't you keep that boy still?"

"Why would I want to?" asked Misner. "We're here not just to talk but to listen too."

The gasps were more felt than heard.

Pulliam narrowed his eyes and was about to answer when Deek Morgan left the row and stood in the aisle. "Well, sir, I have listened, and I believe I have heard as much as I need to. Now, you all listen to me. Real close. Nobody, I mean nobody, is going to change the Oven or call it something strange. Nobody is going to mess with a thing our grandfathers built. They made each and every brick one at a time with their own hands." Deek looked steadily at Roy. "They dug the clay—not you. They carried the hod—not you." He turned his head to include Destry, Hurston and Caline Poole, Lorcas and Linda Sands. "They mixed the mortar—not a one of you. They made good strong brick for that oven when their own shelter was sticks and sod. You understand what I'm telling you? And we respected what they had gone through to do it. Nothing was handled more gently than the bricks those men—men, hear me? not slaves, ex or otherwise— the bricks those men made. Tell, them, Sargeant, how delicate was the separation, how careful we were, how we wrapped them, each and every one. Tell them, Fleet. You, Seawright, you, Harper, you tell him if I'm lying. Me and my brother lifted that iron. The two of us. And if some letters fell off, it wasn't due to us because we packed it in straw like it was a mewing lamb. So understand me when I tell you nobody is going to come along some eighty years later claiming to know better what men who went through hell to learn knew. Act short with me all you want, you in long trouble if you think you can disrespect a row you never hoed."

Twenty varieties of "amen" italicized Deek's pronouncement. The point he'd made would have closed off further argument if Misner had not said:

"Seems to me, Deek, they are respecting it. It's because they do know the Oven's value that they want to give it new life."

The mutter unleashed by this second shift to the young people's position rose to a roar, which subsided only to hear how the antagonists responded.

"They don't want to give it nothing. They want to kill it, change it into something they made up."

"It's our history too, sir. Not just yours," said Roy.

"Then act like it. I just told you. That Oven already has a history. It doesn't need you to fix it."

"Wait now, Deek," said Richard Misner. "Think what's been said. Forget naming—naming the Oven. What's at issue is clarifying the motto."

"Motto? Motto? We talking command!" Reverend Pulliam pointed an elegant finger at the ceiling. " 'Beware the Furrow of His Brow.' That's what it says clear as daylight. That's not a suggestion; that's an order!"

"Well, no. It's not clear as daylight," said Misner. "It says '. . . the Furrow of His Brow.' There is no 'Beware' on it."

"You weren't there! Esther was! And you weren't here, either, at the beginning! Esther was!" Arnold Fleetwood's right hand shook with warning.

"She was a baby. She could have been mistaken," said Misner.

Now Fleet joined Deek in the aisle. "Esther never made a mistake of that nature in her life. She knew all there was to know about Haven and Ruby too. She visited us before we had a road. She named this town, dammit. 'Scuse me, ladies."

Destry, looking strained and close to tears, held up his hand and asked, "Excuse me, sir. What's so wrong about 'Be the Furrow'? 'Be the Furrow of His Brow'?"

"You can't be God, boy." Nathan DuPres spoke kindly as he shook his head.

"It's not being Him, sir; it's being His instrument, His justice. As a race—"

"God's justice is His alone. How you going to be His instrument if you don't do what He says?" asked Reverend Pulliam. "You have to obey Him."

"Yes, sir, but we *are* obeying Him," said Destry. "If we follow His commandments, we'll be His voice, His retribution. As a people—"

Harper Jury silenced him. "It says 'Beware.' Not 'Be.' Beware means 'Look out. The power is mine. Get used to it.' "

" 'Be' means you putting Him aside and you the power," said Sargeant.

"We *are* the power if we just—"

"See what I mean? See what I mean? Listen to that! You hear that, Reverend? That boy needs a strap. Blasphemy!"

As could have been predicted, Steward had the last word—or at least the words they all remembered as last because they broke the meeting up. "Listen here," he said, his voice thick and shapely with Blue Boy. "If you, any one of you, ignore, change, take away, or add to the words in the mouth of that Oven, I will blow your head off just like you was a hood-eye snake."

Dovey Morgan, chilled by her husband's threat, could only look at the floorboards and wonder what visible shape his loss would take now.

Days later she still hadn't made up her mind about who or which side was right. And in discussion with others, including Steward, she tended to agree with whomever she was listening to. This matter was one she would bring to her Friend—when he came back to her.

Driving away from the meeting at Calvary, Steward and Dovey had a small but familiar disagreement about where to go. He was headed out to the ranch. It was reduced to a show ranch now that gas rights had been sold, but in Steward's mind it was home—where his American flag flew on holidays; where his honorable discharge papers were framed; where Ben and Good could be counted on to bang their tails maniacally when he appeared. But the little house they kept on St. Matthew Street—a foreclosure the twins never resold—was becoming more and more home to Dovey. It was close to her sister, to Mount Calvary, the Women's Club. It was also where her Friend chose to pay his calls.

"Drop me right here, Steward. I'll walk the rest of the way."

"You going to catch your death."

"No I won't. Night chill feels good right now."

"Girl, you a torment," he said, but he patted her thigh before she got out.

Dovey walked slowly down Central Avenue. In the distance she could see lanterns from the Juneteenth picnic hanging near the Oven. Four months now, and no one had taken them down to store for next year. Now they provided light—just a little, just enough—for other kinds of freedom celebrations going on in its shadows. On her left was the bank, not as tall as any of the churches but seeming nevertheless to hog the street. Neither brother had wanted a second floor like the Haven bank had, where the Lodge kept its quarters. They didn't want traffic into their building for any reason other than bank business. The Haven bank their father owned collapsed for a whole lot of reasons, and one of them, Steward maintained, was having Lodge meetings on the premises. "Ravels the concentration," he'd said. Three streets beyond, on her right, next to Patricia Best's house, was the school where Dovey had taught while the ranch house was being completed but Soane had taught longer since she lived so close. Pat ran the school by herself now, with Reverend Misner and Anna Flood filling in for Negro History classes and after-school typing lessons. The flowers and vegetables on one side of the school were an extension of the garden in front of Pat's own house.

Dovey turned left into St. Matthew Street. The moon's light glittered white fences gone slant in an effort to hold back chrysanthemums, foxglove, sunflowers, cosmos, daylilies, while mint and silver king pressed through the spaces at the bottom of the slats. The night sky, like a handsome lid, held the perfume down, saving it, intensifying it, refusing it the slightest breeze on which to escape.

The garden battles—won, lost, still at bay—were mostly over. They had raged for ten years, having begun suddenly in 1963, when there was time. The women who were in their twenties when Ruby was founded, in 1950, watched for thirteen years an increase in bounty that had never entered their dreams. They bought soft toilet paper, used washcloths instead of rags, soap for the face alone or diapers only. In every Ruby household appliances pumped, hummed, sucked, purred, whispered and flowed. And there was time: fifteen minutes when no firewood needed tending in a kitchen stove; one whole hour when no sheets or overalls needed slapping or scrubbing on a washboard; ten minutes gained because no rug needed to be beaten, no curtains pinned on a stretcher; two hours because food lasted and therefore could be picked or purchased in greater quantity. Their husbands and sons, tickled to death and no less proud than the women, translated a five-time markup, a price per pound, bale or live weight, into Kelvinators as well as John Deere; into Philco as well as Body by Fisher. The white porcelain layered over steel, the belts, valves and Bakelite parts gave them deep satisfaction. The humming, throbbing and softly purring gave the women time.

The dirt yards, carefully swept and sprinkled in Haven, became lawns in Ruby until, finally, front yards were given over completely to flowers for no good reason except there was time in which to do it. The habit, the interest in cultivating plants that could not be eaten, spread, and so did the ground surrendered to it. Exchanging, sharing a cutting here, a root there, a bulb or two became so frenetic a land grab, husbands complained of neglect and the disappointingly small harvest of radishes, or the too short rows of collards, beets. The women kept on with their vegetable gardens in back, but little by little its produce became like the flowers—driven by desire, not necessity. Iris, phlox, rose and peonies took up more and more time, quiet boasting and so much space new butterflies journeyed miles to brood in Ruby. Their chrysalises hung in secret under acacias, and from there they joined blues and sulphurs that had been feeding for decades in buckwheat and clover. The red bands drinking from sumac competed with the newly arrived creams and whites that loved jewel flowers and nasturtiums. Giant orange wings covered in black lace hovered in pansies and violets. Like the years of garden rivalry, the butterflies were gone that cool October evening, but the consequence remained—fat, overwrought yards; clumps and chains of eggs. Hiding. Until spring.

Touching the pickets lining the path, Dovey climbed the steps. There on the porch she hesitated and thought of turning back to call on Soane, who had left the meeting early. Soane worried her; seemed to have periods of frailty not related to the death of her sons five years ago. Maybe Soane felt what Dovey did—the weight of having two husbands, not one. Dovey paused, then changed her mind and opened the door. Or tried to. It was locked—again. Something Steward had recently begun that made her furious: bolting the house as though it were a bank too. Dovey was sure theirs was the only locked door in Ruby. What was he afraid of? She patted the dish under a pot of dracaena and picked up the skeleton key.

Before that first time, but never again, there was a sign. She had been upstairs, tidying the little foreclosed house, and paused to look through a bedroom window. Down below the leaf-heavy trees were immobile as a painting. July. Dry. One hundred one degrees. Still, opening the windows would freshen the room that had been empty for a year. It took her a moment—a tap here, a yank or two—but she managed finally to raise the window all the way up and lean forward to see what was left of the garden. From her position in the window the trees hid most of the backyard and she stretched a bit to see beyond their spread. Then a mighty hand dug deep into a giant sack and threw fistfuls of petals into the air. Or so it seemed. Butterflies. A trembling highway of persimmon-colored wings cut across the green tree-tops forever—then vanished.

Later, as she sat in a rocker under those trees, he came by. She had never seen him before and did not recognize any local family in his features. At first she thought it was Menus, Harper's son, who drank and who once had owned the house. But this man was walking straight and quickly, as though late for an appointment, using this yard as a shortcut to someplace else. Perhaps he heard the light cry of her rocker. Perhaps he wondered whether his trespass was safe. In any case, when he turned and saw her he smiled, raising a palm in greeting.

"Afternoon," she called.

He changed his direction and came near to where she sat.

"You from around here?"

"Close," he said, but he did not move his lips to say so.

He needed a haircut.

"I saw some butterflies a while back. Up there." Dovey pointed. "Orangy red, they were. Just as bright. Never saw that color before. Like what we used to call coral when I was a girl. Pumpkin color, but stronger." She wondered, at the time, what on earth she was talking about and would have stuttered to a polite close—something about the heat, probably, the relief evening would bring—except he looked so interested in what she was describing. His overalls were clean and freshly ironed. The sleeves of his white shirt were rolled above the elbows. His forearms, smoothly muscled, made her reconsider the impression she got from his face: that he was underfed.

"You ever see butterflies like that?"

He shook his head but evidently thought the question serious enough for him to sit on his heels before her.

"Don't let me keep you from where you're going. It was just, well, my Lord, such a sight."

He smiled sympathetically and looked toward the place she had pointed to. Then he stood up, brushing the seat of his overalls, although he had not sat down in the grass, and said, "Is it all right if I pass through here?"

"Of course. Anytime. Nobody lives here now. The man who

owned it lost it. Nice, though, isn't it? We're thinking about maybe using it from time to time. My husband . . ." She was babbling, she knew, but he seemed to be listening earnestly, carefully to every word. At last she stopped—too ashamed of her silliness to go on—and repeated her invitation to use the shortcut whenever he wanted.

He thanked her and left the yard, moving quickly between the trees. Dovey watched his figure melt in the shadow lace veiling the houses beyond.

She never saw the persimmon wings again. He, however, did return. About a month later, then off and on every month or two. Dovey kept forgetting to ask Steward, or anybody else, who he might be. Young people were getting harder to identify and when friends or relatives visited Ruby, they did not always attend services, as people used to do, and get introduced to the congregation. She could not ask his age but supposed he was at least twenty years younger than she, and perhaps that alone made her keep his visits secret.

Thing was, when he came, she talked nonsense. Things she didn't know were on her mind. Pleasures, worries, things unrelated to the world's serious issues. Yet he listened intently to whatever she said. By a divining she could not explain, she knew that once she asked him his name, he would never come again.

Once, she fed him a slice of bread loaded with apple butter and he ate it all.

More and more frequently she found reasons to remain on St. Matthew Street. Not hoping or looking for him, but content to know he had and would come by there—for a chat, a bite, cool water on a parched afternoon. Her only fear was that someone else would mention him, appear in his company, or announce a prior claim to his friendship. No one did. He seemed hers alone.

So on the evening of the argument with the young people at Mount Calvary, Dovey stuck the key in the lock of the foreclosed house, annoyed with Steward for making it necessary and agitated by the nasty turn the meeting had taken. She hoped to sit with a cup of hot tea, read some verses or a few psalms and collect her thoughts on the matter that was angering everybody, in case her Friend passed by in the morning. If he did, she would ask his opinion. But she had decided against tea or reading and, after saying her prayers, climbed into bed, where an unanswerable question blocked sleep: aside from giving up his wealth, can a rich man be a good one? She would ask her Friend about that too.

Now, at least, at last, the backyard was lovely enough to receive him. At the first visit it had been a mess, untended, trashy—home to cats, garden snakes, straying chickens—with only the coral-colored wings to recommend it. She had to fix it up herself. K.D. balked and gave unimaginative excuses. And it was hard getting young people interested. Billie Delia used to be her helper, which was surprising since boys dominated her brain otherwise. But something was wrong there too. No one had seen her for some time and the girl's mother, Pat Best, foreclosed all questions. Still angry, thought Dovey, at the town's treatment of her father. Although Billie Delia was not at the meeting, her attitude was. Even as a little girl, with that odd rosy-tan skin and wayward brown hair, she pushed out her lips at everything—everything but gardening. Dovey missed her and wondered what Billie Delia thought of changing the Oven's message.

"Beware the Furrow of His Brow"? "Be the Furrow of His Brow"? Her own opinion was that "Furrow of His Brow" alone was enough for any age or generation. Specifying it, particularizing it, nailing its meaning down, was futile. The only nailing needing to be done had already taken place. On the Cross. Wasn't that so? She'd ask her Friend. And then tell Soane. Meantime the scratching sound was gone and on the cusp of sleep she knew canned peas would do just fine.

Steward rolled down the window and spit. Carefully so the wind would not return it to his face. He was disgusted. "Cut me some slack." That was the slogan those young simpletons really wanted to paint on the Oven. Like his nephew, K.D., they had no notion of what it took to build this town. What they were protected from. What humiliations they did not have to face. Driving, as always, as fast as the car would go once he was back on the county road heading for his ranch, Steward mulled over the difference between "Beware" and "Be" and how Big

Papa would have explained it. Personally he didn't give a damn. The point was not why it should or should not be changed, but what Reverend Misner gained by instigating the idea. He spat again, thinking how much of a fool Misner turned out to be. Foolish and maybe even dangerous. He wondered if that generation—Misner's and K.D.'s— would have to be sacrificed to get to the next one. The grand- and great-grandchildren who could be trained, honed as his own father and grandfather had done for Steward's generation. No breaks there; no slack cut then. Expectations were high and met. Nobody took more responsibility for their behavior than those good men. He remembered his brother's, Elder Morgan's, account of disembarking from Liverpool at a New Jersey port. Hoboken. In 1919. Taking a walk around New York City before catching his train, he saw two men arguing with a woman. From her clothes, Elder said, he guessed she was a streetwalking woman, and registering contempt for her trade, he felt at first a connection with the shouting men. Suddenly one of the men smashed the woman in her face with his fist. She fell. Just as suddenly the scene slid from everyday color to black and white. Elder said his mouth went dry. The two whitemen turned away from the unconscious Negro woman sprawled on the pavement. Before Elder could think, one of them changed his mind and came back to kick her in the stomach. Elder did not know he was running until he got there and pulled the man away. He had been running and fighting for ten straight months, still unweaned from spontaneous violence. Elder hit the whiteman in the jaw and kept hitting until attacked by the second man. Nobody won. All were bruised. The woman was still lying on the pavement when a small crowd began yelling for the police. Frightened, Elder ran and wore his army overcoat all the way back to Oklahoma for fear an officer would see the condition of his uniform. Later, when his wife, Susannah, cleaned, pressed and mended it, he told her to remove the stitches, to let the jacket pocket flap, the shirt collar stay ripped, the buttons hang or remain missing. It was too late to save the bloodstains, so he tucked the bloody handkerchief into the pants pocket along with his two medals. He never got the sight of that whiteman's fist in that colored woman's face out of his mind. Whatever he felt about her trade, he thought about her, prayed for her till the end of his life. Susannah put up a protracted argument, but the Morgan men won. Elder was buried as he demanded to be: in the uniform with its rips on display. He didn't excuse himself for running, abandoning the woman, and didn't expect God to cut him any slack for it. And he was prepared for Him to ask how it happened. Steward liked that story, but it unnerved him to know it was based on the defense of and prayers for a whore. He did not sympathize with the whitemen, but he could see their point, could even feel the adrenaline, imagining the fist was his own.

Steward parked and entered the house. He did not look forward to any bed without Dovey in it and tried again to think of an argument to keep her from staying in town so often. It would be futile; he could deny her nothing. He met the collies and took them along to see how well the hands had done their work. They were local men, whose wives and fathers he knew; who attended the same or a nearby church and who hated as he did the notion of "cut me some slack." Again the bitterness rose. Had he any sons, they would have been sterling examples of rectitude, laughing at Misner's notions of manhood: backtalk, name changes—as if word magic had anything to do with the courage it took to be a man.

Steward leashed the dogs and unlatched the horse barn. His preference was to mount around four a.m. and ride Night till sunrise. He loved to roam the pastures, where everything was in the open. Saddled on Night, he rediscovered every time the fresh wonder of knowing that on one's own land you could never be lost the way Big Papa and Big Daddy and all seventy-nine were after leaving Fairly, Oklahoma. On foot and completely lost, they were. And angry. But not afraid of anything except the condition of the children's feet. By and large they were healthy. But the pregnant women needed more and more rest. Drum Blackhorse's wife, Celeste; his grandmother, Miss Mindy; and Beck, his own mother, were all with child. It was the shame of seeing one's pregnant wife or sister or daughter refused shelter that had rocked them, and changed them for all time. The humiliation did more than rankle; it threatened to crack open their bones.

Steward remembered every detail of the story his father and grandfather told, and had no trouble imagining the shame for himself.

Dovey, for instance, before each miscarriage, her hand resting on the small of her back, her eyes narrowed, looking inward, always inward at the baby inside her. How would he have felt if some highfalutin men in collars and good shoes had told her, "Get away from here," and he, Steward, couldn't do a thing about it? Even now, in 1973, riding his own land with free wind blowing Night's mane, the thought of that level of helplessness made him want to shoot somebody. Seventy-nine. All their belongings strapped to their backs or riding on their heads. Young ones time-sharing shoes. Stopping only to relieve themselves, sleep and eat trash. Trash and boiled meal, trash and meal cake, trash and game, trash and dandelion greens. Dreaming of a roof, fish, rice, syrup. Raggedy as sauerkraut, they dreamed of clean clothes with buttons, shirts with both sleeves. They walked in a line: Drum and Thomas Blackhorse at the head, Big Papa, lame now, carried sitting up on a plank at the tail. After Fairly they didn't know which way to go and didn't want to meet anybody who might tell them or have something else in mind. They kept away from wagon trails, tried to stay closer to pinewoods and streambeds, heading northwest for no particular reason other than it seemed farthest away from Fairly.

The third night Big Papa woke his son, Rector, and motioned for him to get up. Leaning heavily on two sticks, he moved a ways off from the campsite and whispered, "Follow me, you."

Rector went back for his hat and followed his father's slow, painful steps. He thought, with alarm, that the old man was going to try to get to a town in the middle of the night, or apply to one of the farms where dark sod houses nestled up against a hillock. But Big Papa took him deeper into the piney wood where the odor of resin, lovely at first, soon gave him a headache. The sky was brilliant with stars that dwarfed the crescent moon, turning it into a shed feather. Big Papa stopped and with groaning effort knelt down.

"My Father," he said. "Zechariah here." Then, after a few seconds of total silence, he began to hum the sweetest, saddest sounds Rector ever heard. Rector joined Big Papa on his knees and stayed that way all night. He dared not touch the old man or interfere with his humming prayer, but he couldn't keep up and sat back on his haunches to relieve the pain in his knees. After a while he sat all the way down, holding his hat in his hand, his head bowed, trying to listen, stay awake, understand. Finally he lay on his back and watched the star trail above the trees. The heartbreaking music swallowed him, and he felt himself floating inches aboveground. He swore later that he did not fall asleep. That during the whole night he listened and watched. Surrounded by pine trees, he felt rather than saw the sky fading at groundline. It was then he heard the footsteps—loud like a giant's tread. Big Papa, who had not moved a muscle or paused in his song, was quickly silent. Rector sat up and looked around. The footsteps were thundering, but he couldn't tell from which direction they came. As the hem of skylight widened, he could make out the silhouettes of tree trunks.

They saw him at the same time. A small man, seemlike, too small for the sound of his steps. He was walking away from them. Dressed in a black suit, the jacket held over his shoulder with the forefinger of his right hand. His shirt glistening white between broad suspenders. Without help of stick and with nary a groan, Big Papa stood up. Together they watched the man walking away from the palest part of the sky. Once, he lingered to turn around and look at them, but they could not see the features of his face. When he began walking again, they noticed he had a satchel in his left hand.

"Run," said Big Papa. "Gather the people."

"You can't stay here by yourself," said Rector.

"Run!"

And Rector did.

When everyone was roused, Rector led them to where he and Big Papa had spent the night. They found him right there, standing straighter than the pines, his sticks tossed away, his back to the rising sun. No walking man was in sight, but the peace that washed Zechariah's face spread to their own spirits, calming them.

"He is with us," said Zechariah. "He is leading the way."

From then on, the journey was purposeful, free of the slightest complaints. Every now and then the walking man reappeared: along a riverbed, at the crest of a hill, leaning against a rock formation. Only once did someone gather courage to ask Big Papa how long it might take.

"This is God's time," he answered. "You can't start it and you can't stop it. And another thing: He's not going to do your work for you, so step lively."

If the loud footsteps continued, they did not hear them. Nobody saw the walking man but Zechariah and sometimes a child. Rector never saw him again—until the end. Until twenty-nine days later. After being warned away by gunshot; offered food by some black women in a field; robbed of their rifles by two cowboys—none of which disturbed their determined peace—Rector and his father both saw him.

It was September by then. Any other travelers would be cautious going into Indian country with no destination and winter on the way. But if they were uneasy, it didn't show. Rector was lying in tall grass, waiting for a crude trap to spring—rabbit, he hoped, groundhog, gopher, even—when just ahead, through a parting in the grass, he saw the walking man standing, looking around. Then the man squatted, opened his satchel and began rummaging in it. Rector watched for a while, then crawled backward through the grass before jumping up and running back to the campsite where Big Papa was finishing a cold breakfast. Rector described what he had seen and the two headed toward the place where the trap had been set. The walking man was still there, removing items from his satchel and putting others back. Even as they watched, the man began to fade. When he was completely dissolved, they heard the footsteps again, pounding in a direction they could not determine: in back, to the left, now to the right. Or was it overhead? Then, suddenly, it was quiet. Rector crept forward; Big Papa was crawling too, to see what the walker had left behind. Before they had gone three yards they heard a thrashing in the grass. There in the trap, bait and pull string undisturbed, was a guinea fowl. Male, with plumage to beat the band. Exchanging looks, they left it there and moved to the spot where they believed the walker had spread the items from his satchel. Not a thing in sight. Only a depression in the grass. Big Papa leaned down to touch it. Pressing his hand into the flattened grass, he closed his eyes.

"Here," he said. "This is our place."

Well, it wasn't, of course. Not yet anyway. It belonged to a family of State Indians, and it took a year and four months of negotiation, of

labor for land, to finally have it free and clear. Coming from lush vege-
tation to extravagant space could have made them feel small when
they saw more sky than earth, grass to their hips. To the Old Fathers it
signaled luxury—an amplitude of soul and stature that was freedom
without borders and without deep menacing woods where enemies
could hide. Here freedom was not entertainment, like a carnival or a
hoedown that you can count on once a year. Nor was it the table droppings from the entitled. Here freedom was a test administered by the
natural world that a man had to take for himself every day. And if he
passed enough tests long enough, he was king.

Maybe Zechariah never wanted to eat another stick-roasted rabbit, or cold buffalo meat. Maybe, having been routed from office by
whites, refused a homestead by coloreds, he wanted to make a permanent feature in that open land so different from Louisiana. Anyway,
while they set up temporary quarters—lean-tos, dugouts—and hauled
wood in a wagon with two horses the State Indians lent them,
Zechariah corralled some of the men into building a cook oven. They
were proud that none of their women had ever worked in a whiteman's kitchen or nursed a white child. Although field labor was harder
and carried no status, they believed the rape of women who worked in
white kitchens was if not a certainty a distinct possibility—neither of
which they could bear to contemplate. So they exchanged that danger
for the relative safety of brutal work. It was that thinking that made a
community "kitchen" so agreeable. They were extraordinary. They
had served, picked, plowed and traded in Louisiana since 1755, when
it included Mississippi; and when it was divided into states they had
helped govern both from 1868 to 1875, after which they had been
reduced to field labor. They had kept the issue of their loins fruitful for
more than two hundred years. They had denied each other nothing,
bowed to no one, knelt only to their Maker. Now, remembering their
lives and works, Steward was steadied, his resolve cemented. Imagine,
he thought, what Big Papa or Drum Blackhorse or Juvenal DuPres
would think of those puppies who wanted to alter words of beaten iron.

The sun wasn't due to rise for some time and Steward couldn't
ride that long anymore. So he urged Night around and headed toward
home, thinking up another thing he would say, or do, to keep Dovey

from spending nights in town. Sleep without the fragrance of her hair next to him was impossible.

At the same moment, before morning light, Soane was standing in the kitchen of the biggest house in Ruby, whispering to the darkness outside the window.

"Look out, quail. Deek's gunning for you. And when he comes back he'll throw a sackful of you on my clean floor and say something like: 'This ought to take care of supper.' Proud. Like he's giving me a present. Like you were already plucked, cleaned and cooked."

Because the kitchen was flooded with newly installed fluorescent light, Soane could not see into the darkness outside as she waited for the kettle to boil. She wanted to get her tonic properly steeped before her husband returned. One of Connie's preparations lay at her fingertips, a tiny cloth bag folded into a waxed paper packet. Its contents representing the second time Connie had saved her. The first time was a terrible mistake. No, not a mistake, a sin.

She thought it was midnight when Deek eased out of bed and dressed in hunting clothes. But when he crept downstairs in sock feet, she'd looked at the clock glow: 3:30. Two hours more of sleep, she thought, but it was six a.m. when she woke, and she had to hurry. Get breakfast, lay out his business clothes. Before that, however, her tonic—very much needed now, because the air was thinning again. It had started thinning out, as if from too much wear, not when Scout was killed but two weeks later—even before Scout's body had been shipped—when they were informed that Easter was dead too. Babies. One nineteen, the other twenty-one. How proud and happy she was when they enlisted; she had actively encouraged them to do so. Their father had served in the forties. Uncles too. Jeff Fleetwood was back from Vietnam none the worse. And although he did seem a little shook up, Menus Jury got back alive. Like a fool she believed her sons would be safe. Safer than anywhere in Oklahoma outside Ruby. Safer in the army than in Chicago, where Easter wanted to go. Safer than Birmingham, than Montgomery, Selma, than Watts. Safer than Money, Mississippi, in 1955 and Jackson, Mississippi, in 1963. Safer than Newark,

Detroit, Washington, D.C. She had thought war was safer than any city in the United States. Now she had four unopened letters mailed in 1968 and delivered to the Demby post office four days after she buried the last of her sons. She had never been able to open them. Both had been home on furlough that Thanksgiving, 1968. Seven months after King's murder, and Soane had sobbed like the redeemed to see both her boys alive. Her sweet colored boys unshot, unlynched, unmolested, unimprisoned. "Prayer works!" she shouted when they piled out of the car. It was the last time she had seen them whole. Connie had sold her shelled pecans enough for two Thanksgiving pies. A girl with a broke-down car was out there that day, and although Soane drove her to buy the gasoline she needed to go where she was headed, the girl had stayed on. Still, she must have gone off somewhere before the Mother died, otherwise Connie would not have needed to light a fire in the fields. Nobody would have known except for the plume of black smoke. Anna Flood saw it, drove out and got the news.

Soane had to hurry then too. Speak to Roger, go to the bank to telephone strangers up north, collect food from neighbor women and cook some things herself. She, Dovey and Anna carried it out there, knowing full well there was no one to eat it but themselves. Hurry, hurry, then too, because the body had to be shipped quickly up north. In ice. Connie seemed strange, broken somehow and Soane added her to the list of people who worried her life. K.D., for example. And Arnette. And Sweetie. And now the Oven site was on her mind. A few young men had taken to congregating there with 3.2 beer, people said, and the small children who liked to play there had been told to go home. Or so their mothers said. Then a few girls (who Soane thought needed slapping) found reason to be there. The way Arnette and Billie Delia used to.

Folks said these young men needed something to do. But Soane, knowing there was so much to do, didn't believe that was it. Something was going on. Something besides the fist, jet black with red fingernails, painted on the back wall of the Oven. Nobody claimed responsibility—but more shocking than collective denial was the refusal to remove it. The loungers said no, they hadn't put it there, and no, they wouldn't take it off. Although Kate Golightly and Anna

Flood, with Brillo, paint thinner and a bucket of hot soapy water, eventually got it off, five days passed, during which the town leaders in a hot rage forbade anyone but the loungers to erase it. The clenched fingers, red-tipped and thrust sideways, not up, hurt more than a blow and lasted longer. It produced a nagging, hateful pain that Kate's and Anna's scrubbing could not erase. Soane couldn't understand it. There were no whites (moral or malevolent) around to agitate or incense them, make them ugly-up the Oven and defy the adults. In fact local citizens were prospering, had been on a roll for more than a decade: good dollars for beef, for wheat, gas rights sold, oil fueling purchases and backing speculation. But during the war, while Ruby thrived, anger smallpoxed other places. Evil Times, said Reverend Pulliam from New Zion's pulpit. Last Days, said Pastor Cary at Holy Redeemer. Nothing was said at Calvary right away because that congregation was still waiting for the new preacher, who, when he did come in 1970, said Good News: "I will vanquish thine enemies before thine eyes," saith the Lord, Lord, Lord.

That was three years ago. This was 1973. Her little girl—was it?—would be nineteen years old now if Soane had not gone to the Convent for the help sin always needed. Shortly afterwards standing at the clothesline, struggling with the wind to pin sheets, Soane had looked up to see a lady in the yard smiling. She wore a brown wool gown and a white linen old-timey bonnet and carried a peck basket. When the lady waved, Soane returned the stranger's greeting as best she could with a mouthful of clothespins—a nod she hoped was polite. The lady turned and moved on. Soane noticed two things: the basket was empty but the lady carried it with two hands as though it were full, which, as she knew now, was a sign of what was to come—an emptiness that would weigh her down, an absence too heavy to carry. And she knew who sent the lady to tell her so.

Steam hiss interrupted her menu of regret and Soane poured hot water into a cup over the little muslin bag. She placed a saucer over the cup and let the medicine steep.

Maybe they ought to go back to the way they did things when her babies were new. When everybody was too busy building, stocking, harvesting to quarrel or think up devilment. The way it was before Mount Calvary was completed. When baptisms were held in sweet water. Beautiful baptisms. Baptisms to break the heart, full of major chords and weeping and the thrill of being safe at last. When the pastor held the girls in his arms, lowering them one by one into newly hallowed water, never letting go. Breathless, the others watched. Breathless, the girls rose, each in her turn. Their wet, white robes billow in sunlit water. Hair and face streaming they looked to heaven before bowing their heads for the command: "Go, now." Then the reassurance: "Daughter, thou art saved." The softest note, when it hit sanctified water, doubled, trebled itself; then other notes from other throats came and traveled along with the first. Tree birds hushed and tried to learn. Slowly, then, hand in hand, heads on supporting shoulders, the blessed and saved waded to the banks and made their way to the Oven. To dry, embrace, congratulate one another.

Now Calvary had an inside pool; New Zion and Holy Redeemer had special vessels for dribbling a little water on an upright head.

Minus the baptisms the Oven had no real value. What was needed back in Haven's early days had never been needed in Ruby. The trucks they came in brought cookstoves as well. The meat they ate clucked in the yard, or fell on its knees under a hammer, or squealed through a slice in its throat. Unlike at Haven's beginning, when Ruby was founded hunting game was a game. The women nodded when the men took the Oven apart, packed, moved and reassembled it. But privately they resented the truck space given over to it—rather than a few more sacks of seed, rather than shoats or even a child's crib. Resented also the hours spent putting it back together—hours that could have been spent getting the privy door on sooner. If the plaque was so important—and judging from the part of the meeting she had witnessed, she supposed it was—why hadn't they just taken it by itself, left the bricks where they had stood for fifty years?

Oh, how the men loved putting it back together; how proud it had made them, how devoted. A good thing, she thought, as far as it went, but it went too far. A utility became a shrine (cautioned against not only in scary Deuteronomy but in lovely Corinthians II as well) and, like anything that offended Him, destroyed its own self. Nobody better to make the point than the wayward young who turned it into a different kind of oven. One where the warming flesh was human.

When Royal and the other two, Destry and one of Pious DuPres' daughters, asked for a meeting, it was quickly agreed upon. No one had called a town meeting in years. Everybody, including Soane and Dovey, thought the young people would first apologize for their behavior and then pledge to clean up and maintain the site. Instead they came with a plan of their own. A plan that completed what the fist had begun. Royal, called Roy, took the floor and, without notes, gave a speech perfect in every way but intelligibility. Nobody knew what he was talking about and the parts that could be understood were plumb foolish. He said they were way out-of-date; that things had changed everywhere but in Ruby. He wanted to give the Oven a name, to have meetings there to talk about how handsome they were while giving themselves ugly names. Like not American. Like African. All Soane knew about Africa was the seventy-five cents she gave to the missionary society collection. She had the same level of interest in Africans as they had in her: none. But Roy talked about them like they were neighbors or, worse, family. And he talked about white people as though he had just discovered them and seemed to think what he'd learned was news.

Yet there was something more and else in his speech. Not so much what could be agreed or disagreed with, but a kind of winged accusation. Against whites, yes, but also against them—the townspeople listening, their own parents, grandparents, the Ruby grownfolk. As though there was a new and more manly way to deal with whites. Not the Blackhorse or Morgan way, but some African-type thing full of new words, new color combinations and new haircuts. Suggesting that outsmarting whites was craven. That they had to be told, rejected, confronted. Because the old way was slow, limited to just a few, and weak. This last accusation swole Deek's neck and, on a weekday, had him blowing out the brains of quail to keep his own from exploding.

He would be pulling in with a bag of them any minute now, and later on Soane would serve up a platter of their tender, browned halves. So she contemplated rice or sweet potatoes as the contents of her cup steeped. When she swallowed the last drop, the back door opened.

"What's that?"

She liked the smell of him. Windy-wet and grassy. "Nothing."

Deek tossed his sack on the floor. "Give me some of it, then."

"Go on, Deek. How many?"

"Twelve. Gave six to Sargeant." Deek sat down and before taking off his jacket unlaced his boots. "Enough to take care of two suppers."

"K.D. go with you?"

"No. Why?" He grunted with the effort of debooting.

Soane picked up the boots and put them on the back porch. "He's hard to find these days. Up to something, I bet."

"You put coffee on? Like what?"

Soane sniffed the dark air, testing its weight, before closing the door. "Can't tell, exactly. But he has too many reasons for wearing thin shoes."

"Chasing tail, I expect. 'Member that gal dragged herself in town some time back and was staying out to that Convent?"

Soane turned to him, coffee tin at her breast as she eased off the lid. "Why you say 'dragged'? Why you have to say 'dragged' like that? You see her?"

"No, but other folks did."

"And?"

Deek yawned. "And nothing. Coffee, baby. Coffee, coffee."

"So don't say 'dragged.' "

"Okay, okay. She didn't drag in." Deek laughed, dropping his outer clothes on the floor. "She floated in."

"What's wrong with the closet, Deek?" Soane looked at the water-proof pants, the black and red jacket, the flannel shirt. "And what's that supposed to mean?"

"Heard her shoes had six-inch heels."

"You lying."

"And flying."

"Well. If she's still at the Convent, she must be all right."

Deek massaged his toes. "You just partial to those women out there. I'd be careful if I was you. How many of them now? Four?"

"Three. The old lady died, remember?"

Deek stared at her, then looked away. "What old lady?"

"The Reverend Mother. Who'd you think?"

"Oh, right. Yeah." Deek continued stirring the blood in his feet. Then he laughed. "First time Roger got to use his big new van."

"Ambulance," said Soane, gathering up his clothes.

"Brought three payments in the next day. Hope he can keep up the rest. Not enough hospital or mortuary business around here justify that overpriced buggy he got."

The coffee smell was starting, and Deek rubbed his palms.

"Is he hurting?" Soane asked.

"Not yet. But since his profit depends on the sick and the dead, I'd just as soon he went bankrupt."

"Deek!"

"Couldn't do a damn thing for my boys. Buried in a bag like kittens."

"They had lovely coffins! Lovely!"

"Yeah, but inside. . . ."

"Quit, Deek. Why don't you just quit." Soane touched her throat.

"I 'spect he'll make out. If I go before he does. In which case, well, you know what to do. I don't feature riding in that van nohow, but I want a top-of-the-line box, so he'll make out just fine. Fleet's the one in trouble." He stood at the sink and lathered his hands.

"You keep saying that. How come?"

"Mail order."

"What?" Soane poured coffee into the big blue cup her husband preferred.

"You all go to Demby, don't you? When you want a toaster or an electric iron you order out of a catalogue and go all the way out there to pick it up. Where's that put him?"

"Fleet never has much on hand. And what he does have has been there too long. That lounge chair changed colors three times sitting in the window."

"That's why," said Deek. "If he can't move old inventory, he can't buy new."

"He used to do all right."

Deek tipped a little coffee into the saucer. "Ten years ago. Five." The dark pool rippled under his breath. "Boys coming out of Veetnam, getting married, setting up. War money. Farms doing okay, everybody doing okay." He sucked at the saucer rim and sighed his pleasure. "Now, well. . . ."

"I don't understand, Deek."

"I do." He smiled up at her. "You don't need to."

She had not meant that she didn't understand what he was talking about. She'd meant she didn't understand why he wasn't worried enough by their friends' money problems to help them out. Why, for instance, couldn't Menus have kept the house he bought? But Soane didn't try to explain; she just looked closely at his face. Smooth, still handsome after twenty-six years and beaming, now, with satisfaction. Shooting well that morning had settled him and returned things to the way they ought to be. Coffee the right color; the right temperature. And later today, quail without their brains would melt in his mouth.

Every day the weather permitted, Deacon Morgan drove his brilliant black sedan three-fourths of a mile. From his own house on St. John Street, he turned right at the corner onto Central, passed Luke, Mark and Matthew, then parked neatly in front of the bank. The silliness of driving to where he could walk in less time than it took to smoke a cigar was eliminated, in his view, by the weight of the gesture. His car was big and whatever he did in it was horsepower and worthy of com-ment: how he washed and waxed it himself—never letting K.D. or any enterprising youngster touch it; how he chewed but did not light cigars in it; how he never leaned on it, but if you had a conversation with him, standing near it, he combed the hood with his fingernails, scrap-ing flecks he alone could see, and buffing invisible stains with his pocket handkerchief. He laughed along with friends at his vanity, because he knew their delight at his weakness went hand in hand with their awe: the magical way he (and his twin) accumulated money. His prophetic wisdom. His total memory. The most powerful of which was one of his earliest.

Forty-two years ago he had fought for hand room in the rear win-

dow of Big Daddy Morgan's Model T, space in which to wave goodbye
to his mother and baby sister, Ruby. The rest of the family—Daddy,
Uncle Pryor, his older brother Elder, and Steward, his twin—were
packed tight against two peck baskets of food. The journey they were
about to begin would take days, maybe two weeks. The Second Grand
Tour, Daddy said. The Last Grand Tour, laughed Uncle Pryor.

The first one had been in 1910, before the twins had been born,
while Haven was still struggling to come alive. Big Daddy drove his
brother Pryor and his firstborn son, Elder, all over the state and beyond
to examine, review and judge other Colored towns. They planned to
visit two outside Oklahoma and five within: Boley, Langston City,
Rentiesville, Taft, Clearview, Mound Bayou, Nicodemus. In the end,
they made it to only four. Big Daddy, Uncle Pryor and Elder spoke
endlessly of that trip, how they matched wits with and debated preach-
ers, pharmacists, dry-goods store owners, doctors, newspaper publish-
ers, schoolteachers, bankers. They discussed malaria, the booze bill,
the threat of white immigrants, the problems with Creek freedmen,
the trustworthiness of boosters, the practicality of high book learning, the need for technical training, the consequences of statehood,
lodges and the violence of whites, random and organized, that swirled
around them. They stood at the edge of cornfields, walked rows of
cotton. They visited print shops, elocution classes, church services,
sawmills; they observed irrigation methods and storage systems. Mostly
they looked at land, houses, roads.

Eleven years later Tulsa was bombed, and several of the towns Big
Daddy, Pryor and Elder had visited were gone. But against all odds,
in 1932 Haven was thriving. The crash had not touched it: personal
savings were substantial, Big Daddy Morgan's bank had taken no risks
(partly because white bankers locked him out, partly because the sub-
scription shares had been well protected) and families shared everything, made sure no one was short. Cotton crop ruined? The sorghum
growers split their profit with the cotton growers. A barn burned? The
pine sappers made sure lumber "accidentally" rolled off wagons at certain places to be picked up later that night. Pigs rooted up a neighbor's
patch? The neighbor was offered replacements by everybody and was
assured ham at slaughter. The man whose hand was healing from a

chopping block mistake would not get to the second clean bandage before a fresh cord was finished and stacked. Having been refused by the world in 1890 on their journey to Oklahoma, Haven residents refused each other nothing, were vigilant to any need or shortage.

The Morgans did not admit to taking pleasure in the failure of some of those Colored towns—they carried the rejection of 1890 like a bullet in the brain. They simply remarked on the mystery of God's justice and decided to take the young twins and go on a second tour to see for themselves.

What they saw was sometimes nothing, sometimes sad, and Deek remembered everything. Towns that looked like slave quarters, picked up and moved. Towns intoxicated with wealth. Other towns affecting sleep—squirreling away money, certificates, deeds in unpainted houses on unpaved streets.

In one of the prosperous ones he and Steward watched nineteen Negro ladies arrange themselves on the steps of the town hall. They wore summer dresses of material the lightness, the delicacy of which neither of them had ever seen. Most of the dresses were white, but two were lemon yellow and one a salmon color. They wore small, pale hats of beige, dusty rose, powdery blue: hats that called attention to the wide, sparkly eyes of the wearers. Their waists were not much bigger than their necks. Laughing and teasing, they preened for a photographer lifting his head from beneath a black cloth only to hide under it again. Following a successful pose, the ladies broke apart in small groups, bending their tiny waists with rippling laughter, walking arm in arm. One adjusted another's brooch; one exchanged her pocketbook with another. Slender feet turned and tipped in thin leather shoes. Their skin, creamy and luminous in the afternoon sun, took away his breath. A few of the younger ones crossed the street and walked past the rail fence, close, so close, to where he and Steward sat. They were on their way to a restaurant just beyond. Deek heard musical voices, low, full of delight and secret information, and in their tow a gust of verbena. The twins did not even look at each other. Without a word they agreed to fall off the railing. While they wrestled on the ground, ruining their pants and shirts, the Negro ladies turned around to see. Deek and Steward got the smiles they wanted before Big Daddy interrupted his conversation and stepped off the porch to pick each son up by his pants waist, haul them both onto the porch and crack butt with his walking stick.

Even now the verbena scent was clear; even now the summer dresses, the creamy, sunlit skin excited him. If he and Steward had not thrown themselves off the railing they would have burst into tears. So, among the vivid details of that journey—the sorrow, the stubbornness, the cunning, the wealth—Deek's image of the nineteen summertime ladies was unlike the photographer's. His remembrance was pastel colored and eternal.

The morning after the meeting at Calvary, pleased with his bird quota and fired, not tired, from no sleep, he decided to check out the Oven before opening up the bank. So he turned left instead of right on Central and drove past the school on the west side, Ace's Grocery, Fleetwood's Furniture and Appliance and several houses on the east. When he arrived at the site he circled it. Except for a few soda cans and some paper that had escaped the trash barrel, the place was blank. No fists. No loungers. He should speak to Anna Flood who owned Ace's store now—get her to clean up the pop cans and mess that came from purchases made at her store. That's what Ace, her father, used to do. Swept that place like it was his own kitchen, inside, out and if you'd let him he'd sweep all across the road. Pulling back onto Central, Deek noticed Misner's beat-up Ford parked at Anna's. Beyond, to his left, he could hear schoolchildren group-reciting a poem he'd learned by rote too, except he had had to hear Dunbar's lines only once to memorize them completely and forever. When he and Steward had enlisted there was a lot to learn—from how to tie an army tie to how to pack a bag. And just as they had in Haven's schoolhouse, they had been first to understand everything, remember everything. But none of it was as good as what they learned at home, sitting on the floor in a firelit room, listening to war stories; to stories of great migrations—those who made it and those who did not; to the failures and triumphs of intelligent men—their fear, their bravery, their confusion; to tales of love deep and permanent. All there in the one book they owned then.

Black leather covers with gold lettering; the pages thinner than young leaves, than petals. The spine frayed into webbing at the top, the corners fingered down to skin. The strong words, strange at first, becoming familiar, gaining weight and hypnotic beauty the more they heard them, made them their own.

As Deek drove north on Central, it and the side streets seemed to him as satisfactory as ever. Quiet white and yellow houses full of industry; and in them were elegant black women at useful tasks; orderly cupboards minus surfeit or miserliness; linen laundered and ironed to perfection; good meat seasoned and ready for roasting. It was a view he would be damned if K.D. or the idleness of the young would disturb.

It was a far cry from the early days of Haven and his grandfather would have scoffed at the ease of it—buying property with dollars ready to hand instead of trading years of labor for it. He would have been embarrassed by grandsons who worked twelve hours five days a week instead of the eighteen-to-twenty-hour days Haven people once needed just to keep alive, and who could hunt quail for pleasure rather than the desperate need to meet a wife and eight children at table without shame. And his cold, rheumy eyes would have narrowed at the sight of the Oven. No longer the meeting place to report on what done or what needed; on illness, births, deaths, comings and goings. The Oven that had witnessed the baptized entering sanctified life was now reduced to watching the lazy young. Two of Sargeant's boys, three of Poole's, two Seawrights, two Beauchamps, a couple of DuPres children—Sut's and Pious' girls. Even Arnette and Pat Best's only child used to dawdle there. All of whom ought to be somewhere chopping, canning, mending, fetching. The Oven whose every brick had heard live chords praising His name was now subject to radio music, record music—music already dead when it filtered through a black wire trailing from Anna's store to the Oven like a snake. But his grandfather would have been pleased too. Instead of children and adults convening at night in those early days to scratch letters and figures with pebbles on scraps of shale, learning to read from those who could, there was a schoolhouse here too. Not as big as the one they'd built in Haven, but it was open eight months a year and no begging the state for money to run it. Not one cent.

And just as Big Papa foretold, if they stayed together, worked, prayed and defended together, they would never be like Downs, Lexington, Sapulpa, Gans where Colored were run out of town overnight. Nor would they be among the dead and maimed of Tulsa, Norman, Oklahoma City, not to mention victims of spontaneous whippings, murders and depopulation by arson. Except for a crack here, a chink there everything in Ruby was intact. There was no need to wonder if moving the Oven had been a mistake; whether it needed its original soil as foundation for the respect and wholesome utility that was its due. No. No, Big Papa. No, Big Daddy. We did right.

Deek reassured himself with more force than confidence, for he was increasingly uneasy about Soane. Nothing he could put his fingernail under, just a steady sense of losing ground. He shared her sadness, believed he felt the loss of sons precisely and keenly as she did, except he knew more about it than she did. He, like most of the Morgans, had seen action, which is to say live death. Watched it when it was visited on others; watched it when he visited it on others. He knew that bodies did not lie down; that most often they flew apart and that what had been shipped to them in those boxes, what they pulled off the train platform in Middleton, was a collection of parts that weighed half of what a nineteen-year-old would. Easter and Scout were in integrated units and if Soane thought about it, she might consider herself lucky to know that whatever was missing, the parts were all of black men— which was a courtesy and a rule the medics tried hard to apply for fear of adding white thighs and feet to a black head. If Soane suspected what was likely—oh, man. He regretted having slipped up over coffee and mentioned what Roger was unable to do. He did not want her even to imagine the single question he put to Roger—first with Scout then with Easter: Are all the parts black? Meaning, if not, get rid of the white pieces. Roger swore to their racial consistency and the regal coffins were a sign of Morgan gratitude and a source of balm for Soane. Still, the residue of that loss seemed to be accumulating in a way he could not control. He did not trust the medicine she took and he certainly did not trust its source. But there was nothing in her behavior he could fault. She was as beautiful as it was possible for a good woman to be; she kept a good home and did good works everywhere. Was, in fact, more generous than he would have liked, but that was hardly a complaint. There was nothing to do about it. Soane was burdened with the loss of two sons; he was burdened with the loss of all sons. Since his twin had no children the Morgans had arrived at the end of the line. Well, yes, there were Elder's children—a flock of them roosting everywhere except at home, some of whom visited Ruby for a week only to cut it short, so eager were they to get away from the peace they found dull, the industry they found tedious and the heat they found insulting. So it was useless even to think of them as part of the legitimate line of Morgans. He and Steward were truer heirs, proof of which was Ruby itself. Who, other than the rightful heirs, would have repeated exactly what Zechariah and Rector had done? But since part of the charge had been to multiply, it was a heavy hurt to know that K.D. was the only means by which they could. K.D., son of a sister and the army buddy they gave her to. The knot that formed in Deek's chest whenever he thought about her was familiar. Ruby. That sweet, modest laughing girl whom he and Steward had protected all their lives. She had gotten sick on the trip; seemed to heal, but failed rapidly again. When it became clear she needed serious medical help, there was no way to provide it. They drove her to Demby, then further to Middleton. No colored people were allowed in the wards. No regular doctor would attend them. She had lost control, then consciousness by the time they got to the second hospital. She died on the waiting room bench while the nurse tried to find a doctor to examine her. When the brothers learned the nurse had been trying to reach a veterinarian, and they gathered their dead sister in their arms, their shoulders shook all the way home. Ruby was buried, without benefit of a mortuary, in a pretty spot on Steward's ranch, and it was then that the bargain was struck. A prayer in the form of a deal, no less, with God, no less, which He seemed to honor until 1969, when Easter and Scout were shipped home. After that they understood the terms and conditions of the deal much better.

Perhaps they had made a mistake in 1970, discouraging K.D. and Fleet's daughter. She was pregnant but, after a short stay at that Convent, if she had it, she sure didn't have it. The uncles had been worried about the shape Fleetwood's offspring took, and besides, there were other suitable candidates around. But K.D. was still messing around with one of the strays living out there where the entrance to hell is wide, and it was time to give him the news: every brothel don't hang a red light in the window.

He was braking in front of the bank when he noticed a solitary figure ahead. He recognized her right away but watched her carefully because first of all she had no coat, and because second, he had not seen her out of her house in six years.

Central Avenue, three wide graded miles of tarmac, began at the Oven and ended at Sargeant's Feed and Seed. The four side streets east of Central were named after the Gospels. When a fifth street was needed it was named St. Peter. Later on, as Ruby grew, streets were laid on the west side of Central, and although these newer streets were continuations of those on the east—situated right across from them— they acquired secondary names. So St. John Street on the east become Cross John on the west. St. Luke became Cross Luke. The sanity of this pleased most everybody, Deek especially, and there was always room for additional houses (financed, if need be, by the Morgan brothers' bank) in the plots and acres behind and beyond those already built. The woman Deek was watching seemed to be leaving Cross Peter Street and heading toward Sargeant's Feed and Seed. But she did not stop there. Instead she was moving resolutely north, where Deek knew there was nothing for seventeen miles. What could the sweetest girl, named for her nature, be doing coatless on a chilly October morning that far from the home she had not stepped out of since 1967?

A movement in his rearview mirror took his attention, and he recognized the small red truck coming in from south country. Its driver would be Aaron Poole, late, as Deek knew he would be, since he was bringing in the final payment on his loan. After considering letting Poole wait and driving on to catch up with Sweetie, Deek cut off his motor. July, his clerk and secretary, was not due until ten. There should be no occasion when the bank of a good and serious town did not open on time.

.   .   .

Anna Flood said, "See. Just look at him."

She was watching Deek's sedan circle the Oven and then cruise slowly past her store. "Why does he have to hover like that?"

Richard Misner looked up from the woodstove. "He's just checking on things," he said, and went back to laying the fire. "Got a right, doesn't he? It's sort of his town, wouldn't you say? His and Steward's?"

"I would not. They may act like they own it, but they don't."

Misner liked a tight fire, and the one he was preparing would be just that. "Well, they founded it, didn't they?"

"Who've you been talking to?" Anna left the window and walked to the back stairs, leading to her apartment. There she slid a pan of meat leavings and cereal under the stairwell. The cat, turned vicious by motherhood, stared at her with warning eyes. "Fifteen families founded this town. Fifteen, not two. One was my father, another my uncle—"

"You know what I mean," Misner interrupted her.

Anna peeped into the darkness trying to see inside the box where the litter lay. "I do not."

"The money," said Misner. "The Morgans had the money. I guess I should say they financed the town—not founded it."

The cat would not eat while being watched, so Anna forfeited a peep at the kittens and turned back to Richard Misner. "You wrong there too. Everybody pitched in. The bank idea was just a way of doing it. Families bought shares in it, you know, instead of just making deposits they could run through any old time. This way their money was safe."

Misner nodded and wiped his hands. He didn't want another argument. Anna refused to understand the difference between investing and cooperating. Just as she refused to believe the woodstove gave more warmth than her little electric heater.

"The Morgans had the resources, that's all," she said. "From their father's bank back in Haven. My grandfather, Able Flood, was his partner. Everybody called him Big Daddy, but his real name was—"

"I know, I know. Rector. Rector Morgan, also known as Big Daddy. Son of Zechariah Morgan, known throughout Christendom as Big

115

Papa." And then he quoted a refrain the citizens of Ruby loved to recite. " 'Rector's bank failed, but he didn't.' "

"It's true. The bank had to close down—in the early forties—but it didn't close out. I mean they had enough so we could start over. I know what you're thinking, but you can't honestly say it didn't work. People prosper here. Everybody."

"Everybody's prospering on credit, Anna. That's not the same thing."

"So?"

"So what if the credit's gone?"

"It can't be gone. We own the bank; the bank doesn't own us."

"Aw, Anna. You don't get it, do you? You don't understand."

She enjoyed his face even when he was putting down people she liked. Steward, for example, he seemed to despise, but it was Steward who had taught her the scorpion lesson. When Anna was four, she was sitting on the new porch of her father's store—back in 1954—when everybody was building something while a group of men including Steward were helping Ace Flood finish the shelving. They were inside, resting after a quick lunch, while Anna derailed ants on the steps: introducing obstacles into their routes, watching them climb over the leaf's edge and go on as though a brand-new green mountain were an inevitable part of their journey. Suddenly a scorpion shot out near her bare foot, and she ran wide-eyed into the store. The talk stopped while the men weighed this infantile interruption, and it was Steward who picked her up in his arms, asked, What's bothering you, good-lookin'? and relieved her fears. Anna clung to him while he explained that the scorpion's tail was up because it was just as scared of her as she was of it. In Detroit, watching baby-faced police handling guns, she remembered the scorpion's rigid tail. Once, she had asked Steward what it felt like to be a twin. "Can't say," he answered, "since I was never not one. But I guess it feels more complete."

"Like you can never be lonely?" Anna asked.

"Well, yes. Like that. But more like . . . superior."

When Ace died she came back to Ruby and was about to sell out—the store, the apartment, the car, everything—and return to

Detroit, when he came riding into town, alone, in a beat-up Ford. Calvary's new minister.

Anna folded her arms on the wooden counter. "I own this store. My daddy died—it's mine. No rent. No mortgage. Just taxes, town fees. I buy things; I sell things; the markup is mine."

"You're lucky. What about the farms? Suppose a crop fails, say, two years in a row. Does old Mrs. Sands or Nathan DuPres get to take out their share? Borrow on it? Sell it to the bank? What?"

"I don't know what they do, but I do know it's no gain to the bank for them to lose it. So they'd give them money to buy more seed, guano, whatever."

"You mean *lend* them the money."

"You're making my head ache. Where you come from, all that might be true. Ruby's different."

"Hope so."

"Is so. Any problem brewing sure ain't money."

"Well, what is it then?"

"Hard to figure, but I don't like the way Deek's face looks when he's checking the Oven. He does it every day God sends now. More like hunting than checking. They're just kids."

"That fist painting scared a lot of people."

"Why? It was a picture! You'd think somebody had burned a cross!" Annoyed, she started wiping things—jars, case fronts, the soda pop cooler. "He should talk to the parents, not go hunting for the kids like he's a sheriff. Kids need more than what's here."

Misner couldn't agree more. Since the murder of Martin Luther King, new commitments had been sworn, laws introduced but most of it was decorative: statues, street names, speeches. It was as though something valuable had been pawned and the claim ticket lost. That was what Destry, Roy, Little Mirth and the rest were looking for. Maybe the fist painter was looking for it too. In any case, if they couldn't find the ticket, they might break into the pawnshop. Question was, who pawned it in the first place and why.

"You told me that's why you left—nothing to do—but you never said why you came back."

Anna wasn't about to explain all of that, so she elaborated on what he already knew. "Yeah. Well. Thought I could do something up north. Something real that wouldn't break my heart. But it was all, I don't know, talk, running around. I got confused. Still, I don't regret going one bit—even though it didn't work out."

"Well, I'm glad it didn't, whatever the reason." He stroked her hand.

Anna returned his touch. "I'm worried," she said. "About Billie Delia. We have to come up with something, Richard. Something more than choir competitions and Bible class and ribbons for fat vegetables and baby showers . . ."

"What about her?"

"Oh, I don't know. She came in here a while back, and I knew right away she had something on her mind, but the truck was late with my goods, so I was short with her."

"Which is to say what?"

"She's gone off. At least I think so. Nobody's seen her."

"What does her mother say?"

Anna shrugged. "Pat's hard to talk to. Kate asked her about Billie Delia—hadn't seen her at choir practice. Know what she did? Answered Kate's question with another." Anna mimicked Pat Best's soft, cold voice. " 'Why do you need to know that?' She and Kate are close, too."

"You think she's courting harm? She couldn't just disappear without anybody knowing where to."

"I don't know what I think."

"Talk to Roger. He should know. He's her grandfather."

"*You* ask him. Not me."

"Say, what is all this feeling about Roger? I've been here three years, almost, and I can't make out why folks freeze around him. Is it his mortuary business?"

"Probably. That and, well, he 'prepared,' if you get my meaning, his own wife."

"Oh."

"That's something to think about, ain't it?"

"Still."

They were quiet for a moment, thinking about it. Then Anna walked around the counter and stood at the window. "You know, you right smart about weather. This is the third time I disbelieved you and was proved wrong."

Misner joined her. Just touching the pane they could tell the temperature had dropped suddenly into the teens.

"Go ahead. Light it," she said, laughing and happy to be wrong if it made this man she adored right. There were church women who disapproved of his obvious interest in her—her and nobody else. And Pat Best was skilled at hiding her own interest in him. But Anna thought there was more to it than perhaps their own plans for this handsome, intelligent man and their various daughters and nieces. She was certain the disapproval was mostly because of her unstraightened hair. My God, the conversations she had been forced to have when she came back from Detroit. Strange, silly, invasive probings. She felt as though they were discussing her pubic hair, her underarm hair. That if she had walked completely naked down the street they would have commented only on the hair on her head. The subject summoned more passion, invited more opinions, solicited more anger than that prostitute Menus brought home from Virginia. She probably would have straightened it again, eventually—it wasn't a permanent change or a statement—except it clarified so much for her in the days when she was confused about so much else. Instantly she could identify friends and those who were not; recognize the well-brought-up, the ill-raised, the threatened, the insecure. Dovey Morgan liked it; Pat Best hated it; Deek and Steward shook their heads; Kate Golightly loved it and helped her keep it shaped; Reverend Pulliam preached a whole sermon about it; K.D. laughed at it; most of the young people admired it, except Arnette. Like a Geiger counter, her hair registered, she believed, tranquillity or the intensity of a rumbling, deep-down disorder.

The fire, smelling wonderfully, attracted the mother cat. She curled up behind the stove, though her eyes remained alert to predators—human or otherwise.

"Let me make some coffee," Anna said, eyeing the clouds above Holy Redeemer. "This might get serious."

119

Ace Flood's faith had been the mountain-moving kind, so he built his store to last. Sandstone. Sturdier than some churches. Four rooms for his family above; below, a spacious storeroom, a tiny bedroom, and a fifteen-foot-high selling area crammed with shelves, bins, cases and drawers. The windows were regular house type—he didn't want or need display; no big, wasteful "looking-in" plate glass for him. Let folks come inside to see what he had. He didn't have many things but he had a lot of what he stocked. Before he died, he saw his store change from a necessary service in Ruby to a business patronized by the loyal for certain items, though they balked at his prices and more and more drove their trucks to Demby for cheaper (and better) supplies. Anna changed all that. What Ace's Grocery now lacked in size of inventory it gained in variety and style. She offered free coffee on cold days, iced tea when it was hot. She put out two chairs and a small table for the elderly and those who drove in from farms and wanted to rest awhile. And since adults, nowadays, never frequented the Oven next to her store—except for special events—she catered to the appetites of the young who liked to gather there. She sold her own pies, made her own candy along with the lots she picked up in Demby. She kept three kinds of soda pop instead of one. Sometimes she sold the black-as-eight-rock peppers the Convent grew. She kept hog's head cheese in the cooler, as her father had, along with local butter and salted pork. But canned goods, dried beans, coffee, sugar, syrup, baking soda, flour, salt, catsup, paper products—all the items nobody could or wanted to make at home—took up the space Ace Flood once used for cloth, work shoes, light tools, kerosene. Now Sargeant's Feed and Seed sold the shoes, the tools, the kerosene, and Harper's drugstore sold the needles, thread, counter medicine, prescriptions, sanitary napkins, stationery and tobacco. Except for Blue Boy. Steward had relied on Ace for that and wasn't about to change his habits.

In Anna's hands, Ace's Grocery blossomed through variety, comfort and flexibility. Because she let Menus cut hair in the back on Saturdays, incidental purchases rose. Because she had a nice toilet downstairs, casual users felt obliged to become customers before they left. Farming women came in for peppermint after church; the men for sacks of raisins. Invariably they picked up a little something more from the shelves.

The contentment she drew from Richard's fire made her smile. But she couldn't be a minister's wife. Never. Could she? Well, he had not asked her to be one—so enjoy the stove heat, the nape of his neck and the invisible presence of kittens.

After a while, a station wagon drove up and parked so close to the store, both Misner and Anna could see the fever in the baby's blue eyes. The mother held the child over her shoulder and stroked its yellow hair. The driver, a city-dressed man in his forties, got out and pushed open Anna's door.

"How you all doing?" He smiled.

"Fine, and you?"

"Look like I'm lost. Been trying to find eighteen west for more'n an hour." He looked at Misner and grinned an apology for having violated the male rule of never asking for directions. "Wife made me stop. Said she's had it."

"It's a ways back the way you come from," said Misner, looking at the Arkansas plates, "but I can tell you how to find it."

"'Preciate it. 'Preciate it," said the man. "Don't expect there's a doctor around here, is there?"

"Not around these parts. You have to get to Demby for that."

"What's wrong with the baby?" Anna asked.

"Sort of pukey. Hot too. We're fairly well supplied, but who'd pack aspirin or cough medicine on a little old trip like this? Can't think of every damn thing, can you? Jesus."

"Your baby coughing? I don't believe you need cough medicine." Anna squinted through the window. "Ask your wife to come in out the cold."

"Drugstore'll have aspirin," said Misner.

"I didn't see no drugstore. Where 'bouts is it?"

"You passed it, but it doesn't look like a drugstore—looks like a regular house."

"How am I going to find it then? Houses round here don't seem to have numbers."

"Tell me what all you want and I'll get it for you. Then tell your wife to bring that baby inside." Misner reached for his coat.

"Just some aspirin and some cough medicine. 'Preciate it. I'll get my wife."

The blast from the open door rattled the coffee cups. The man got back in the station wagon; Misner took off in his ratty Ford. Anna thought about making some cinnamon toast. The pumpkin bread would be stale now. Be nice if she had an overripe banana—the baby looked constipated. Mush it up with a little apple butter.

The man came back shaking his head. "I'll just keep the motor running. She says she'll stay put."

Anna nodded. "You got far to go?"

"Lubbock. Say, is that coffee hot?"

"Uh huh. How you like it?"

"Black and sweet."

He'd taken two sips when the station wagon horn sounded. "Shit. Excuse me," he said. When he came back he bought licorice, peanut butter, crackers and three Royal Crowns and carried them out to his wife. Then he returned to finish his coffee, sipping it in silence while Anna poked the fire.

"You better gas up when you get on eighteen. Blizzard's coming."

He laughed. "Blizzard? In Lubbock, Texas?"

"You ain't in Texas yet," said Anna. She looked toward the window and saw two figures approach, then Misner shouldered open the door, with Steward close on his heels.

"Here you go," said Misner, handing over the bottles. The man took them and rushed out to the station wagon. Misner followed to give him directions.

"Who all is that?" asked Steward.

"Just some lost folks." Anna handed him a thirty-two-ounce tin of Blue Boy.

"Lost folks or lost whites?"

"Oh, Steward, please."

"Big difference, Anna girl. Big. Right, Reverend?" Misner was just stepping back in.

"They get lost like everybody else," said Anna.

"Born lost. Take over the world and still lost. Right, Reverend?"

"You just contradicted yourself." Anna laughed.

"God has one people, Steward. You know that." Misner rubbed his hands, then blew on them.

"Reverend," said Steward, "I've heard you say things *out* of ignorance, but this is the first time I heard you say something *based* on ignorance."

Misner smiled and was about to answer when the lost man entered again to pay Misner for the medicine.

"Blizzard's heading in." Steward looked at the man's light clothing and thin shoes. "You might want to ride it out somewhere. Gas station on eighteen. Wouldn't go no further than that if I was you."

"I'll beat it." The man closed his wallet. "I'll gas up on eighteen, but we crossing that state line today. Thank you. You all been a big help. 'Preciate it."

"They never listen," said Steward as the station wagon drove away. He himself, having been around in 1958 when whole herds froze, had been pumping water, nailing down, forking alfalfa and storing up since Wednesday. He was in town for tobacco and syrup and to pick up Dovey.

"Say, Steward," Misner said. "You seen Roger's granddaughter, Billie Delia?"

"What should I see her for?"

"Anna says nobody has. Of course, we haven't asked her mother."

Steward, picking up on the "we," put a crisp five-dollar bill on the counter. "You won't get nothing there," he said, thinking, No major loss if she did run off. Serve Pat right, he thought. She noses about in everybody's business but clams up if you get near hers. "That reminds me, Deek told me he saw Sweetie this morning—just walking on down the road. No overcoat. Nothing."

"Sweetie? Out of her house?" Anna stressed her disbelief.

"Down what road?" asked Misner.

"Not Sweetie."

"Deek swears it was her."

"Must have been," said Misner. "I saw her too. Right outside my house. I thought she was going to knock, but she turned around and headed back toward Central. Look to me like she was going on home."

"Didn't. Deek said she was way past Sargeant's—marching out of town like a soldier."

"Didn't he stop her?"

Steward stared at Anna as though he couldn't believe her words. "He was opening up the bank, girl."

Misner frowned. Anna cut off anything he might have been about to say with, "You all want some coffee? Maybe some pumpkin bread?"

Both men accepted.

"Somebody better speak to Jeff." It was Anna's voice but all three glanced at a wall of shelves beyond which was Fleetwood's Furniture and Appliance.

Despite the predictions—from Richard Misner's gaze, Steward Morgan's watchfulness—a tiny piece of the sky flashed a watercolor palette: orange-peach, minty green, seashore blue. The rest of the sky, pewter, served to brighten this odd, picture-book sun break. It lasted a full hour and thrilled everybody who saw it. Then it faded, and a leaden sky solidified over the relentless wind. By noon the first snow came. Stinging pellets, popping, not melting, before the wind. The second snow, two hours later, didn't pop. It lay down quietly and covered everything there was.

Sweetie had said, "Be back directly, Miss Mable." "Won't be gone but a minute, Miss Mable."

Meant to say it. Maybe she did say it. Anyway it was in her head to say. But she had to hurry quick before one of them gurgled.

On the porch, the walkway, Sweetie's stride was purposeful—as though there were somewhere important she had to be. Something important she had to do and it would take just a few minutes and she would be right back. In time to massage a little bottom to keep the sores away; or to siphon phlegm or grind food or clean teeth or trim nails or launder out urine or cradle in her arms or sing but mostly in time to watch. To never take her eyes off unless her mother-in-law was there, and to watch then as well, because Miss Mable's eyes weren't as sharp as they once had been. Others offered help, repeatedly at first, irregularly now, but she always declined. Sweetie was the best at watching. Her mother-in-law second best. Arnette used to be good, but not anymore. Jeff and her father-in-law couldn't look, let alone watch.

The problem had never been watching while she was awake. It was watching while asleep. For six years she slept on the pallet near the cribs, or in bed with Jeff, her breath threaded, her ear tunnel ready, every muscle braced to spring. She knew she slept because she dreamed a little, although she couldn't remember what about. But it was getting harder and harder to watch and sleep at the same time.

When dawn broke and Mable came into the dim room with a cup of coffee, Sweetie stood to take it. She knew Mable had already run her bathwater and folded a towel and fresh nightgown over the chair in the bedroom. And she knew she would offer to do her hair—braid it, wash it, roll it or just scratch her scalp. The coffee would be wonderful, dark and loaded with sugar. But she also knew that if she drank it this one time and went to bed in morning sun this one time she would never wake up, and who would watch her babies then?

So she took the coffee and said, or meant to, "Be back in a minute, Miss Mable."

Downstairs, she put the cup and saucer on the dining table, then, unwashed, coatless and with uncombed hair, she opened the front door and left. Quickly.

She was not hoping to walk until she dropped or fainted or froze and then slipped into nothingness for a while. The small thing she wanted was not to have that dawn coffee, the already drawn bath, the folded nightgown and then the watchful sleep in that order, forever, every day and in particular this here particular day. The only way to change the order, she thought, was not to do something differently but to do a different thing. Only one possibility arose—to leave her house and step into a street she had not entered in six years.

Sweetie traveled the length of Central Avenue—past the Gospel-named streets, past New Zion, Harper's Drugstore, the bank, Mount Calvary. She detoured into Cross Peter, left it and walked past Sargeant's Feed and Seed. North of Ruby, where the quality of the road changed twice, her legs were doing brilliantly. So was her skin, for she didn't feel the cold. The fresh outside air, to which she was unaccustomed, hurt her nostrils, and she set her face to bear it. She did not know she was smiling, nor did the girl staring at her from the bed of a brand-new '73 pickup. The girl thought Sweetie was crying, and a black woman weeping on a country road broke her heart all over again.

She peered at Sweetie from her hiding place among empty crates. The Ford truck, heading south, slowed as it passed Sweetie, then stopped. In the cab, the driver and his wife exchanged looks. Then the driver leaned out the window, twisting his head to holler at Sweetie's back, "You need some help?"

Sweetie did not turn her head or acknowledge the offer. The couple looked at each other and sucked teeth as the husband shifted into drive. Fortunately, the road inclined at that point, otherwise the brokenhearted hitchhiker would have hurt herself when she jumped from the back of the truck. The couple could see in the rearview mirror a passenger they didn't know they had, running to join the pitiful, ill-raised creature who had not even said No, thank you.

When the girl whose heart was breaking caught up with the woman, she knew enough not to touch or speak or insert herself into the determined bubble the crying woman had become. She walked ten or so paces behind, studying the shapely dark ankles above worn white loafers. The wrinkled shirtwaist dress, pale blue with sagging pockets. The sleeper's hair—pressed flat on one side, disheveled on the other. And every now and then a sob that sounded like a giggle.

They moved this way for more than a mile. The walker going somewhere; the hitcher going anywhere. The wraith and her shadow.

The morning was cold, cloudy. Wind streamed the tall grasses on either side of the road.

Fifteen years ago, when the brokenhearted hitcher was five years old, she had spent four nights and five days knocking on every door in her building.

"Is my sister in here?"

Some said no; some said who?; some said what's your name, little girl? Most didn't open the door at all. That was 1958, when a child could play all over brand-new government housing in safety.

The first two days, after making her rounds on floors ever higher, higher, and making sure she had not missed a single door, she waited. Jean, her sister, would be coming back anytime now, because dinner food was on the table—meat loaf, string beans, catsup, white bread— and a full pitcher of Kool-Aid was in the refrigerator. She occupied herself with two coloring books, a deck of cards and a wetting baby doll. She drank milk, ate potato chips, saltines with apple jelly and, little by little, the whole meat loaf. By the time the hated string beans were all that was left of the dinner, they were too shriveled and mushy to bear.

The third day, she began to understand why Jean was gone and how to get her back. She cleaned her teeth and washed her ears carefully. She also flushed the toilet right away, as soon as she used it, and folded her socks inside her shoes. She spent a long time wiping up the Kool-Aid and picking up the pieces of glass from the pitcher that crashed when she tried to lift it from the refrigerator. She remembered the Lorna Doones that were in the bread box but dared not climb up on a chair to open it. Those were her prayers: if she did everything right without being told, either Jean would walk in or when she knocked on one of the apartment doors, there'd she be! Smiling and holding out her arms.

Meantime the nights were terrible.

On the fourth day, having brushed her eighteen milk teeth until the toothbrush was pink with blood, she stared out of the window through warm rain-sprinkle at morning people going to work, children to school. Then for a long time no one passed. Then an old woman with a man's jacket roofed above her head against the fine rain. Then a man tossing seed on bare places in the grass. Then a tall woman walked past the window. No coat and nothing on her head, she touched her eyes with the back of her arm, the inside of her wrist. She was crying.

Later, the sixth day, when the caseworker came, she thought about the crying woman who looked nothing at all like Jean—was not even the same color. But before that, on the fifth day, she found—or rather saw—something that had been right there for her all along. Demoralized by unanswered prayers, bleeding gums and hunger she gave up goodness, climbed up on a chair and opened the bread box. Leaning against the box of Lorna Doones was an envelope with a word she recognized instantly: her own name printed in lipstick. She opened it, even before she tore into the cookie box, and pulled out a single sheet of paper with more lipstick words. She could not understand any except her own name again at the top, "Jean" at the bottom, loud red marks in between.

Soaking in happiness, she folded the letter back in the envelope, put it in her shoe and carried it for the rest of her life. Hiding it, fighting for the right to keep it, rescuing it from wastebaskets. She was six years old, an ardent first-grade student, before she could read the whole page. Over time, it became simply a sheet of paper smeared firecracker red, not one decipherable word left. But it was the letter, safe in her shoe, that made leaving with the caseworker for the first of two foster homes possible. She thought about the crying woman briefly then, more later, until the sight of her became an occasional heartbreaking dream.

The wind that had been stirring the grass was carrying snow now—scarce, sandy and biting like glass. The hitcher stopped to pull a serape from her duffel, then ran to catch up and wrap it around the walker's shoulders.

Sweetie flailed her hands until she understood that she was being warmed, not prevented. Not once, while the wool cloth was being wrapped around her shoulders, did she stop walking. She kept on moving, chuckling—or was it sobbing?

The hitcher remembered passing a large house less than a half hour earlier as she hid among the crates. What took twenty minutes in a truck would take pedestrians hours, but she thought they ought to be able to reach the place before dark. The question was the cold; another was how to stop the crying woman, get her to rest and, once they reached shelter, get her inside it. Eyes like those were not uncommon. In hospitals they belonged to patients who paced day and night; on the road, unconfined, people with eyes like that would walk forever. The hitcher decided to spend the time talking and started out by introducing herself.

Sweetie heard what she said and, for the first time since she'd left her house, stumbled as she turned her smiling—or crying—face toward the uninvited companion. Sin, she thought. I am walking next to sin and wrapped in its cloak. "Have mercy," she murmured, and gave a little laugh—or whimper.

By the time they saw the Convent, Sweetie was cozy. Although she had felt none of the biting cold sweeping the road, she was comforted by the warm snow covering her hair, filling her shoes. And grateful to be so clearly protected from and unassociated with the sin shape walking next to her. The sign of Sweetie's state of grace was how badly the warm snow whipped the shape, silenced it, froze it and left it breathing heavily, barely able to hang on, while she, Sweetie, marched unbowed through the cutting wind.

Of her own accord, Sweetie slogged up the driveway. But she let the demon do the rest.

The woman who opened the door to the banging said "Ooh!" and yanked them both inside.

They seemed like birds, hawks, to Sweetie. Pecking at her, flapping. They made her sweat. Had she been stronger, not so tired from the night shift of tending her babies, she would have fought them off. As it was, other than pray, there was nothing she could do. They put her in a bed under so many blankets perspiration ran into her ears. Nothing they offered would she eat or drink. Her lips were shut, her teeth clenched. Silently, fervently, she prayed for deliverance, and don't you know she got it: they left her alone. In the quiet room Sweetie thanked her Lord and drifted into a staticky, troubled sleep. It was the baby cry that woke her, not the shivering. Weak as she was, she got up, or tried to. Her head hurt and her mouth was dry. She noticed that she was not in a bed but on a leather couch in a dark room. Sweetie's teeth were rattling when one of the hawks, with a blood-red mouth, came into the room carrying a kerosene lamp. It spoke to her in the sweetest voice, the way a demon would, but Sweetie called on her Savior, and it left. Somewhere in the house the child continued to cry, filling Sweetie with rapture—she had never heard that sound from her own. Never heard that clear yearning call, sustained, rhythmic. It was like an anthem, a lullaby, or the bracing chords of the decalogue. All of her children were silent. Suddenly, in the midst of joy, she was angry. Babies cry here among these demons but not in her house?

When two of the hawks came back, one carrying a tray of food, she asked them, "Why is that child crying here?"

They denied it, of course. Lied straight through the weeping that sifted through the room. One of them even tried to distract her, saying:

"I've heard children laughing. Singing sometimes. But never crying."

The other one cackled.

"Let me out of here." Sweetie struggled to make her voice shout. "I have to get home."

"I'm going to take you. Soon as the car warms up." Same sly demon tones.

"Now," said Sweetie.

"Take some aspirin and eat some of this."

"You let me out of this place now."

"What a bitch," said one.

"It's just fever," said the other. "And keep your mouth shut, can't you?"

It was patience, and blocking out every sound except the admonitions of her Lord, that got her out of there. First into a rusty red car that stalled in the snow at the foot of the driveway, and finally, praise, praise His holy name, into her husband's arms.

He was with Anna Flood. They had been on their way from the minute she'd called on her Savior. Sweetie literally fell into Jeff's arms.

"What you doing way out here? We couldn't get through all night. Where is your mind? Lord, girl. Sweetheart. What happened?"

"They made me, snatched me," Sweetie cried. "Oh God, take me home. I'm sick, Anna, and I have to look after the babies."

"Shh. Don't worry about that."

"I have to. I have to."

"It's going to be all right now. Arnette's coming home."

"Turn the heater up. I'm so cold. How come I'm so cold?"

. . .

Seneca stared at the ceiling. The cot's mattress was thin and hard. The wool blanket scratched her chin, and her palms hurt from shoveling snow in the driveway. She had slept on floors, on cardboard, on nightmare-producing water beds and, for weeks at a time, in the back seat of Eddie's car. But she could not fall asleep on this clean, narrow childish bed.

The crying woman had flipped — in the night and the next morning as well. Seneca had spent the whole night up, listening to Mavis and Gigi. The house seemed to belong to them, although they referred to somebody named Connie. They cooked for her and didn't pry. Other than discussing her name — where'd she get it? — they behaved as though they knew all about her and were happy for her to stay. Later, in the afternoon, when she thought she would drop from exhaustion, they showed her to a bedroom with two cots.

"Nap awhile," said Mavis. "I'll call you when dinner's ready. You like fried chicken?" Seneca thought she would throw up.

They didn't like each other at all, so Seneca had equalized her smiles and agreeableness. If one cursed and joked nastily about the other, Seneca laughed. When the other rolled her eyes in disgust, Seneca shot her an understanding look. Always the peacemaker. The one who said yes or I don't mind or I'll go. Otherwise — what? They might not like her. Might cry. Might leave. So she had done her best to please, even if the Bible turned out to be heavier than the shoes. Like all first offenders, he wanted both right away. Seneca had no trouble with the size eleven Adidas, but Preston, Indiana, didn't sport bookstores, religious or regular. She detoured to Bloomington and found something called *The Living Bible*, and one without color pictures but with lots of lined pages for recording dates of births, deaths, marriages, baptisms. It seemed a marvelous thing — a list of whole families' activities over the years — so she chose it. He was angry, of course; so much that it dimmed his pleasure in the extravagant black and white running shoes.

"Can't you get anything right? Just a *small* Bible! Not a goddamn encyclopedia!"

He was guilty as charged and she had known him for only six months, but already he knew how hopeless she was. He accepted the enormous Bible nonetheless and told her to leave it and the shoes at the desk with his name and his number. Made her write it down as though she might have trouble remembering five numbers in a row. She had brought ham sandwiches too (his letter said they could have a picnic-type lunch in the visitors' quarters) but he was too nervous and irritated to eat.

The other visitors seemed to be having a lovely time with their prisoners. Children teased each other; curled up in the arms of their fathers, playing with their faces, hair, fingers. Women and girls touched the men, whispered, laughed out loud. They were the regulars—familiar with the bus drivers, the guards and coffee wagon personnel. The prisoners' eyes were soft with pleasure. They noticed everything, commented on everything. The report cards little boys brought to them in fat brown envelopes; the barrettes in the little girls' hair; the state of the women's coats. They listened carefully to details of friends and family not there; had advice and instruction for every piece of domestic news. They seemed terribly manly to Seneca— leaderlike in their management of the visit. From where to sit, where to put the paper wrappings, to medical advice and books to send. What they never spoke of was what was going on inside, and they did not ever acknowledge the presence of the guards. Perhaps Attica was on their minds.

Maybe, she thought, as his sentence wore on, Eddie would be like that. Not furious, victimized, as he was on this their first visit since he was arraigned. Whining. Blaming. The Bible so big it embarrassed him. Mustard instead of mayo on the sandwiches. He didn't want to hear anything about her new job at a school cafeteria. Only Sophie and Bernard interested him: their diets. Was she letting them out at night? They needed a good long run. Use their muzzles only when they are outside.

She left Eddie Turtle in the visitors' hall promising him four things. To send pictures of the dogs. To sell the stereo. To get his mother to cash the savings bonds. To call the lawyer. Send, sell, get, call. That's how she would remember.

Heading for the bus shelter, Seneca tripped and fell on one knee. A guard stepped forward and helped her up.

"Watch it, there, miss."

"Sorry. Thanks."

"How you girls expect to walk in those things, I don't know."

"Supposed to be good for you," she said, smiling.

"Where? In Holland?" He laughed pleasantly, showing two rows of gold fillings.

Seneca adjusted her string bag and asked him, "How far is Wichita from here?"

"Depends on how you traveling. In a car it'd be—oh—ten, twelve hours. Bus, longer."

"Oh."

"You got family in Wichita?"

"Yes. No. Well, my boyfriend does. I'm going to pay his mother a visit."

The guard removed his cap to smooth his crew cut. "That's nice," he said. "Good barbecue in Wichita. Make sure you get you some."

Somewhere in Wichita there probably was very good barbecue, but not in Mrs. Turtle's house. Her house was strictly vegetarian. Nothing with hooves, feathers, shell or scales appeared on her table. Seven grains and seven greens—eat one of each (and only one) each day, and you lived forever. Which she planned to do, and no, she wasn't about to cash in the savings bonds her husband left her for anybody, let alone somebody who drove a car over a child and left it there, even if that somebody was her only son.

"Oh, no, Mrs. Turtle. He didn't know it was a little kid. Eddie thought it was a . . . a . . ."

"What?" asked Mrs. Turtle. "What did he think it was?"

"I forgot what he told me, but I know he wouldn't do that. Eddie loves kids. He really does. He's really very sweet. He asked me to bring him a Bible."

"He's sold it by now."

Seneca looked away. The television screen flickered. On it, grave-faced men lied softly, courteously to each other.

"Little girl, you've known him less than a growing season. I've known him all his life."

"Yes, m'am."

"You think I'm going to let him put me in the poorhouse so a slick lawyer can stay rich?"

"No, m'am."

"You been watching those Watergate lawyers?"

"No, m'am. Yes, m'am."

"Well, then. Don't say another word about it. You want some supper or not?"

The grain was wheat bread; the green was kale. Strong iced tea helped wash them both down.

Mrs. Turtle did not offer a bed for the night, so Seneca hoisted her bag and walked down the quiet street in Wichita's soft evening air. She had not quit her job to make this trip, but the supervisor made it clear that an absence this soon was not to a new employee's advantage. Perhaps she was already fired. Maybe Mrs. Turtle would let her telephone her housemates to see if anyone had called to say "Don't bother coming back." Seneca turned around, retracing her steps.

At the door, her knuckles lifted for the knock, she heard sobbing. A flat-out helpless mothercry—a sound like no other in the world. Seneca stepped back, then went to the window, pressing her left hand to her chest to keep her heart down. She kept it there—imagining its small red valves stuttering, faltering, trying to get back on line—as she fled down the brick steps out to the sidewalk, skirting dirt streets, then macadam, then concrete all the way to the bus station. Only when she was sitting frog-legged on a molded plastic bench did she surrender to the wails that continued to careen in her head. Alone, without witness, Mrs. Turtle had let go her reason, her personality, and shrieked for all the world like the feathered, finned and hoofed whose flesh she never ate—the way a gull, a cow whale, a mother wolf might if her young had been snatched away. Her hands had been in her hair; her mouth wide open in a drenched face.

Short-breathed and dry-mouthed, Seneca escaped from the sobs. Rushing down broad streets and narrow, slowing when near the business part of town. Upon entering the station she bought peanuts and ginger ale from the vending machines and was immediately sorry, since she really wanted sweet, not salt. Ankles crossed, knees spread, she sat on a bench in the waiting room, pocketed the nuts and sipped the ginger ale. Finally her panic subsided and the screams of a hurt woman were indistinguishable from everyday traffic.

Nighttime coming, and the station was as crowded as a morning commuter stop. The warm September day had not cooled when the sun set. There was no worthy difference between the thick air of the waiting room and the air outside. Passengers and their companions appeared calm, hardly interested in the journey or the farewell. Most of the children were asleep, on laps, luggage and seats. Those who were not tortured anyone they could. Adults fingered tickets, blotted dampness from their necks, patted babies and murmured to each other. Soldiers and sweethearts examined the schedules posted behind glass. Four teenaged boys with stocking caps on their heads sang softly near the vending machines. A man in a gray chauffeur's uniform strolled the floor as though looking for his passenger. A handsome man in a wheelchair navigated himself gracefully through the entrance, only slightly annoyed by the inconvenient design of the door.

There were two hours and twenty minutes before Seneca's bus departed, so she wondered if she should spend it at one of the movies she'd passed. *Serpico, The Exorcist, The Sting,* were the hot choices, but it felt like betrayal to see any one of them without Eddie's arm around her shoulder. Thinking of his predicament and her bumbling efforts to help him, Seneca sighed heavily, but there was no danger of tears. She had not shed one even when she found Jean's letter next to the Lorna Doones. Well cared for, loved, perhaps, by the mothers in both of the foster homes, she knew it was not her self that the mothers had approved of but the fact that she took reprimand quietly, ate what given, shared what she had and never ever cried.

The ginger ale was rattling through the straw when the chauffeur stood before her and smiled.

"Excuse me, miss. May I speak to you for a moment?"

"Sure. I mean. Sure." Seneca scooted over to make room on the bench, but he did not sit down.

"I'm authorized to offer you five hundred dollars for some complicated but quite easy work, if you're interested."

Seneca opened her mouth to say: complicated *and* easy? His eyes were cloudy gray and the buttons on his uniform glimmered like ancient gold.

"Oh, no. Thanks, but I'm on my way out of here," she said. "My bus leaves in two hours."

"I understand. But the work won't take long. Perhaps if you'd talk to my employer—she's right outside—she can describe it to you. Unless, of course, you have to be somewhere in a hurry?"

"She?"

"Yes. Mrs. Fox. Step this way. It'll take just a minute."

A limousine throbbed under bright streetlights a few yards from the station entrance. When the chauffeur opened the door, the head of a very pretty woman turned toward Seneca.

"Hello. I'm Norma. Norma Keene Fox. I'm looking for some help." She didn't hold out her hand, but her smile made Seneca want her to. "Can I talk to you about it?"

The white linen blouse she wore was sleeveless, cut low. Her beige skirt was long. When she uncrossed her legs, Seneca saw bright sandals, coral-painted toenails. Champagne-colored hair rushed back behind ears with no earrings.

"What kind of help?" Seneca asked.

"Come inside so I can explain. It's hard talking through an open car door."

Seneca hesitated.

Mrs. Fox's laugh was a warm tumble of bells. "It's okay, dear. You don't have to take the job if you don't want it."

"I didn't say I didn't."

"Well, then. Come. It's cooler in here."

The door click was soft but profound and Mrs. Fox's Bal à Versailles was irresistible.

Something confidential, she said. Nothing illegal, of course, just private. You type? A little? I want somebody not from around here. I hope five hundred is enough. I could go a little higher for a really intelligent girl. David will drive you back to the bus station, even if you decide not to take the job.

136

Only then did Seneca realize the limousine was no longer parked. The interior lights were still on. The air was cooled. The limousine floated.

This is a lovely part of the world, Norma continued. But narrow-minded, if you know what I mean. Still, I wouldn't live anywhere else. My husband doesn't believe me, neither do my friends, because I'm from back East. When I go back there, they say *Wichita?* Like that. But I love it here. Where are you from? I thought so. They don't wear jeans like that around here. They should, though, if they've got the bottom, I mean. Like you do. Yes. My son's at Rice. Lots of people work for us, but it's only when Leon is away—that's my husband—that I can get anything accomplished. That's where you come in, if you agree, I mean. Married? Well, what I need done only an intelligent female can do. You don't wear lipstick, do you? Good. Your lips are lovely like that. I told David, find an intelligent girl, please. No farmgirls. No dairy queens. He's very good. He found you. Our place is out of town a ways. No, thank you. I can't digest peanuts. Oh dear, you must be starving. We'll have a very good supper and I'll explain what I want done. Really simple if you can follow directions. It's confidential work so I prefer to hire a stranger rather than someone local. Are those your own lashes? Gracious. David? Do you know if Mattie cooked a real supper tonight? No fish, I hope, or do you like fish? Trout's wonderful in Kansas. I think some chicken, fried, might do the trick. We have beautifully fed poultry here—they eat better than most people do. No, don't put them away. Give them to me. Who knows? They might come in handy.

Seneca spent the following three weeks in gorgeous rooms, with gorgeous Norma and food too pretty to eat. Norma called her many sweet things but not once asked what her name was. The front door was never locked and she could leave anytime she wanted to. She didn't have to stay there, moving from peacock feathers to abject humiliation; from coddling to playful abuse; from caviar tartlets to filth. But the pain framed the pleasure, gave it edge. The humiliation made surrender deep, tender. Long-lasting.

When Leon Fox telephoned his imminent return, Norma gave

her the five hundred dollars and some clothes, including a cashmere serape. As promised, David drove her to the bus station, his buttons extra gleamy in the sunlight. They did not speak during the drive.

Seneca wandered Wichita for hours, stopping in a coffee shop, resting in a city park. At a loss as to where to go or what to do. Get a job near the prison and stand by him? Meaning follow his instructions, apologize for not getting his mother's savings. Go back to Chicago? Pick up her life-before-Eddie? Instant friends. Catch-quick jobs. Temporary housing. Stolen food. Eddie Turtle had been settled life to her for six months, and now he was gone. Or should she just move on? The chauffeur had picked her up for Norma like a stray puppy. No, not even that. But like a pet you wanted to play with for a while—a little while—but not keep. Not love. Not name it. Just feed it, play with it, then return it to its own habitat. She had five hundred dollars, and other than Eddie, no one knew where she was. Maybe she ought to keep it that way.

Seneca hadn't decided much of anything when she saw the first place to hide—a flatbed loaded with cement sacks. When she was discovered the driver held her against a tire, splicing his questions, curses and threats with mild flirtations. Seneca said nothing at first, then suddenly begged permission to go to the bathroom. "I have to go. Bad," she said. The driver sighed and released her, shouting a final warning at her back. She hitched a few times after that but so disliked the necessary talk she accepted the risk of stowing away in trucks. She preferred traveling resolutely nowhere, closed off from society, hidden among quiet cargo—no one knowing she was there. When she found herself among crates in a brand-new '73 pickup, jumping out of it to follow a coatless woman was the first pointedly uninstructed thing she had ever done.

The sobbing—or was she giggling?—woman was gone now. The snow had stopped. Downstairs, someone was calling her name.

"Seneca? Seneca? Come on, baby. We're waiting for you."

DIVINE

"Let me tell you about love, that silly word you believe is about whether you like somebody or whether somebody likes you or whether you can put up with somebody in order to get something or someplace you want or you believe it has to do with how your body responds to another body like robins or bison or maybe you believe love is how forces or nature or luck is benign to you in particular not maiming or killing you but if so doing it for your own good.

"Love is none of that. There is nothing in nature like it. Not in robins or bison or in the banging tails of your hunting dogs and not in blossoms or suckling foal. Love is divine only and difficult always. If you think it is easy you are a fool. If you think it is natural you are blind. It is a learned application without reason or motive except that it is God.

"You do not deserve love regardless of the suffering you have endured. You do not deserve love because somebody did you wrong. You do not deserve love just because you want it. You can only earn—by practice and careful contemplation—the right to express it and you have to learn how to accept it. Which is to say you have to earn God. You have to practice God. You have to think God—carefully. And if you are a good and diligent student you may secure the right to show love. Love is not a gift. It is a diploma. A diploma conferring certain privileges: the privilege of expressing love and the privilege of receiving it.

"How do you know you have graduated? You don't. What you do know is that you are human and therefore educable, and therefore

141

capable of learning how to learn, and therefore interesting to God, who is interested only in Himself which is to say He is interested only in love. Do you understand me? God is not interested in you. He is interested in love and the bliss it brings to those who understand and share that interest.

"Couples that enter the sacrament of marriage and are not prepared to go the distance or are not willing to get right with the real love of God cannot thrive. They may cleave together like robins or gulls or anything else that mates for life. But if they eschew this mighty course, at the moment when all are judged for the disposition of their eternal lives, their cleaving won't mean a thing. God bless the pure and holy. Amen."

Some of the amens that accompanied and followed Reverend Senior Pulliam's words were loud, others withholding; some people did not open their mouths at all. The question, thought Anna, was not why but who. Who was Pulliam blasting? Was he directing his remarks to the young people, warning them to shape up their selfish lives? Or was he aiming at their parents for allowing the juvenile restlessness and defiance that had been rankling him even before that fist appeared on the Oven? Most likely, she thought, he was bringing the weight of his large and long Methodist education to bear down on Richard. A stone to crush his colleague's message of God as a permanent interior engine that, once ignited, roared, purred and moved you to do your own work as well as His—but, if idle, rusted, immobilizing the soul like a frozen clutch.

That must be it, she thought. Pulliam was targeting Misner. Because surely he would not stand before the bride and groom—a guest preacher asked to make a few (few!) remarks before the ceremony to a congregation made up of almost everybody in Ruby, only a third of whom were members of Pulliam's church—and frighten them to death on their wedding day. Because surely he would not insult the bride's mother and sister-in-law, who wore like a coat the melancholy of tending broken babies and who not only had not chastised God for that knockout blow to everything they dreamed of but seemed to increase in steadfastness as each year passed. And although the groom had no living parents, surely Pulliam did not intend to embarrass his aunts—to put the feet of those devout women to the fire for caring (too much, perhaps?) for the sole "son" the family would ever have, now that Soane's boys were dead, Dovey having had none, and not allowing mourning for either of those losses to tear them up or close their hearts. Surely not. And surely Pulliam was not trying to rile the groom's uncles, Deacon and Steward, who behaved as if God were their silent business partner. Pulliam had always seemed to admire them, hinting repeatedly that they belonged in Zion, not Calvary, where they had to listen to the namby-pamby sermons of a man who thought teaching was letting children talk as if they had something important to say that the world had not heard and dealt with already.

Who else would feel the sting of "God is not interested in you." Or wince from the burn in "if you think love is natural you are blind." Who else but Richard Misner who now had to stand up and preside, over the most anticipated wedding anyone could remember, under the boiling breath of Senior "Take No Prisoners" Pulliam? Unless, of course, he was talking to her, telling her: Cleave unto another if you want, but if you are not cleaving to God (Pulliam's God, that is) your marriage will not be worth the license. Because he knew she and Richard were talking marriage, and he knew she helped him organize the young disobedients. "Be the Furrow."

Rogue mint overwhelmed the flower arrangements around the altar. Clumps of it, along with a phlox called wild sweet william, grew beneath the church windows that at eleven o'clock were opened to a climbing sun. The light falling from the April sky was a gift. Inside the church the maplewood pews, burnished to a military glow, set off the spring-white walls, the understated pulpit, the comfortable almost picket-fence look of the railing, where communicants could kneel to welcome the spirit one more time. Above the altar, high into its clean, clear space, hung a three-foot oak cross. Uncluttered. Unencumbered. No gold competed with its perfection or troubled its poise. No writhe or swoon of the body of Christ bloated its lyric thunder.

The women of Ruby did not powder their faces and they wore no harlot's perfume. So the voluptuous odor of mint and sweet william disturbed the congregation, made it reel in anticipation of a good time with plenty good food at Soane Morgan's house. There would be

143

music by anyone: July on the upright piano; the Male Chorus; a Kate Golightly solo; the Holy Redeemer Quartet; a dreamy-eyed boy named Brood on the steps with a mouth organ. There would be the press of good clothing; silk dresses and starched shirts forgotten as folks leaned against trees, sat on the grass, mishandled second helpings of cream peas. There would be the shouts of sugar-drunk children; the crackle of wedding gift paper snatched from the floor and folded so neatly it seemed more valuable than the gift it had enclosed. Farmers, ranchers and wheat-growing women would let themselves be yanked from chairs and clapped into repeating dance steps from long ago. Teenagers would laugh and blink their eyes in an effort to hide their want.

But more than joy and children high on wedding cake, they were looking forward to the union of two families and an end to the animus that had soaked the members and friends of those families for four years. Animus that centered on the maybe-baby the bride had not acknowledged, announced or delivered.

Now they sat, as did Anna Flood, wondering what on earth Reverend Pulliam thought he was doing. Why cast a pall now? Why diminish the odor of rogue mint and phlox; blunt the taste of the roast lamb and lemon pies awaiting them. Why fray the harmony, derail the peace this marriage brought?

Richard Misner rose from his seat. Annoyed; no, angry. So angry he could not look at his fellow preacher and let him see how deep the cut. Throughout Pulliam's remarks he had gazed expressionless at the Easter hats of the women in the pews. Earlier that morning he had planned five or six opening sentences to launch the sacred rite of matrimony, crafted them carefully around Revelation 19:7,9, sharpening the "marriage supper of the Lamb" image, coring it to reveal the reconciliation this wedding promised. He had segued from Revelation to Matthew 19:6, "Wherefore they are no more twain, but one flesh," to seal not only the couple's fidelity to each other but the renewed responsibilities of all Morgans and Fleetwoods.

Now he looked at the couple standing patiently before the altar and wondered whether they had understood or even heard what had been laid on them. He, however, did understand. Knew this lethal view of his chosen work was a deliberate assault on all he believed. Suddenly he understood and shared Augustine's rage at the "proud minister" whom he ranked with the devil. Augustine had gone on to say that God's message was not corrupted by the messenger; "if [the light] should pass through defiled beings, it is not itself defiled." Although Augustine had not met Senior Pulliam, he must have known ministers like him. But his dismissal of them to Satan's company did not acknowledge the damage words spoken from a pulpit could wreak. What would Augustine say as anodyne to the poison Pulliam had just sprayed over everything? Over the heads of men finding it so hard to fight their instincts to control what they could and crunch what they could not; in the hearts of women tirelessly taming the predator; in the faces of children not yet recovered from the blow to their esteem upon learning that adults would not regard them as humans until they mated; of the bride and groom frozen there, desperate for this public bonding to dilute their private shame. Misner knew that Pulliam's words were a widening of the war he had declared on Misner's activities: tempting the young to step outside the wall, outside the town limits, shepherding them, forcing them to transgress, to think of themselves as civil warriors. He knew also that a public secret about a never-born baby poked through the grounds of the quarrel like a fang.

Suitable language came to mind but, not trusting himself to deliver it without revealing his deep personal hurt, Misner walked away from the pulpit, to the rear wall of the church. There he stretched, reaching up until he was able to unhook the cross that hung there. He carried it then, past the empty choir stall, past the organ where Kate sat, the chair where Pulliam was, on to the podium and held it before him for all to see—if only they would. See what was certainly the first sign any human anywhere had made: the vertical line; the horizontal one. Even as children, they drew it with their fingers in snow, sand or mud; they laid it down as sticks in dirt; arranged it from bones on frozen tundra and broad savannas; as pebbles on riverbanks; scratched it on cave walls and outcroppings from Nome to South Africa. Algonquin and Laplanders, Zulu and Druids—all had a finger memory of this original mark. The circle was not first, nor was the parallel or the triangle. It was this mark, this, that lay underneath every other. This mark, rendered in the placement of facial features. This mark of a standing human figure poised to embrace. Remove it, as Pulliam had done, and Christianity was like any and every religion in the world: a population of supplicants begging respite from begrudging authority; harried believers ducking fate or dodging everyday evil; the weak negotiating a doomed trek through the wilderness; the sighted ripped of light and thrown into the perpetual dark of choicelessness. Without this sign, the believer's life was confined to praising God and taking the hits. The praise was credit; the hits were interest due on a debt that could never be paid. Or, as Pulliam put it, no one knew when he had "graduated." But with it, in the religion in which this sign was paramount and foundational, well, life was a whole other matter.

See? The execution of this one solitary black man propped up on these two intersecting lines to which he was attached in a parody of human embrace, fastened to two big sticks that were so convenient, so recognizable, so embedded in consciousness *as consciousness*, being both ordinary and sublime. See? His woolly head alternately rising on his neck and falling toward his chest, the glow of his midnight skin dimmed by dust, streaked by gall, fouled by spit and urine, gone pewter in the hot, dry wind and, finally, as the sun dimmed in shame, as his flesh matched the odd lessening of afternoon light as though it were evening, always sudden in that climate, swallowing him and the other death row felons, and the silhouette of this original sign merged with a false night sky. See how this official murder out of hundreds marked the difference; moved the relationship between God and man from CEO and supplicant to one on one? The cross he held was abstract; the absent body was real, but both combined to pull humans from backstage to the spotlight, from muttering in the wings to the principal role in the story of their lives. This execution made it possible to respect—freely, not in fear—one's self and one another. Which was what love was: unmotivated respect. All of which testified not to a peevish Lord who was His own love but to one who enabled human love. Not for His own glory—never. God loved the way humans loved one another; loved the way humans loved themselves; loved the genius on the cross who managed to do both and die knowing it.

But Richard Misner could not speak calmly of these things. So he stood there and let the minutes tick by as he held the crossed oak in his hands, urging it to say what he could not: that not only is God interested in you; He *is* you.

Would they see? Would they?

For those who could see it, the groom's face was a study. He looked up at the cross Reverend Misner was holding holding holding. Saying nothing, just holding it there in locked time while the unendurable silence was sprinkled with coughs and soft, encouraging grunts. People were already nervous about his wedding because buzzards had been seen flying north over the town. The question in their minds was whether that was an omen for harm (they circled the town) or for good (none landed). Simpletons, he thought. If this marriage was doomed, it had nothing to do with birds.

Suddenly the open windows were not enough. The groom began to perspire in his beautifully cut black suit. Anger shot through him like a .32. Why was everybody using his wedding, messing up his ceremony, to extend a quarrel he could care less about? He wanted it over. Over and done with so his uncles would shut up; so Jeff and Fleet would stop spreading lies about him, so he could take his place among the married and propertied men of Ruby, so he could burn all those letters from Arnette. But especially so he could flush that Gigi bitch out of his life completely. Like sugar turning from unreasonable delight to the body's mortal enemy, his craving for her had poisoned him, rendered him diabetic, stupid, helpless. Following months of risky sweetness, she had become indifferent, bored, even hateful. In tall corn he had waited for her; in moonlight he had crept behind hen-houses to meet her; spent money that was not his to entertain her; lied to get something other than a truck to drive her; planted a marijuana crop for her; carried ice in August heat to cool the inside of her thighs; bought her a battery-powered radio she adored, a chenille robe she laughed at. Most of all he had loved her for years, an aching, humiliating, self-loathing love that drifted from pining to stealth.

He had read the first letter he got from Arnette but put the others in a shoe box in his aunt's attic; he was in a hurry to destroy them (or maybe even read them) before anybody discovered the eleven unopened envelopes posted from Langston, Oklahoma. He assumed they were all about love and grief, love in spite of grief. Whatever. But what could Arnette know of either the way he did? Had she sat through the night in a copse of shin oak to catch a glimpse? Had she trailed a beat-up Cadillac all the way to Demby just to see? Had she been thrown out of a house by women? Cursed by women? And still, still been unable to stay away? Not, that is, until his uncles sat him down and gave him the law and its consequences.

So here he was, standing at the altar, his elbow supporting the thin wrist of his bride, in his pocket the fold of Easter palm she had given him for protection. He was aware of the heavy breathing of his soon-to-be brother-in-law at his right; and the animosity of Billie Delia burrowing into the back of his head. He was certain it would go on forever, this blocked rage, because Misner seemed to be struck dumb by the cross he held.

A cross the bride gazed at in terror. And she had been so happy. At last so very very happy. Free of the bleak sadness that encased her as soon as she was home from college: the unrelenting suffocation in her parents' house; the brand-new disgust that accompanied the care of her broken nieces and nephews; the need for sleep that alarmed her mother, annoyed her sister-in-law and infuriated her brother and father; the flat-out nothing-to-doness, interrupted only by wonder and worry about K.D. Although he had never answered her first twelve letters, she'd kept on writing, but not mailing, forty more. One a week for the whole first year she was away. She believed she loved him absolutely because he was all she knew about her self—which was to say, everything she knew of her body was connected to him. Except for Billie Delia, no one had told her there was any other way to think of herself. Not her mother; not her sister-in-law. Last year, when she was a senior she came home for Easter break and he asked to see her, came twice for dinner, took her to Nathan DuPres' ranch to help with the Children's Day picnic, and then suggested they get married. It was a miracle that lasted all the way down to this brilliant day in April. Everything perfect: her period had come and gone; her gown, made entirely of Soane Morgan's lace, was heavenly; the gold band tucked into her brother's vest was engraved with both their initials entwined. The hole in her heart had closed finally, and now, at the last minute, the preacher was rocking strange, trying to hold up the marriage, distort, maybe even destroy it. Standing there, his face like granite, holding a cross as though nobody had ever seen one before. She pressed her fingers into the arm that held hers, willing Misner to get on with it. Say it, say it! "Dearly Beloved, we are gathered here . . . we are gathered here." Suddenly, soundlessly, in the muffled silence that Misner imposed, a tiny rent opened in exactly the place where her heart's hole had been. She held her breath and felt the increase, like a run in a stocking. Soon the little tear would yawn, stretch wide, wider, sapping all her strength until it got what it needed to seal itself and permit the heart to go on beating. She was acquainted with it, had thought marrying K.D. would permanently heal it, but now, waiting for "We are gathered here . . . ," anxious for "Do you take this . . . ," she knew better. Knew exactly what was and would always be missing.

Say it, please, she urged. Please. And hurry. Hurry. I've got things to do.

Billie Delia shifted her bouquet from her left hand to her right. Tiny thorns pricked through her white cotton gloves and the freesia blossoms were closing as she'd known they would. Only the tea roses remained sturdy with promises you could count on to be kept. She had suggested baby's breath to flatter the yellow buds but was astonished to find that not one garden had any. No baby's breath anywhere. Then yarrow, she said, but the bride refused to carry to her wedding a weed that cattle ate. So there they were, both of them, holding water-hungry freesia and tea roses improperly dethorned. Other than the damage being done to her palms, the wait Reverend Misner was forcing on everybody did not bother or surprise her. It was just one more piece of foolishness that made up this foolish wedding that everybody thought was a cease-fire. But the war was not between the Morgans, the Fleetwoods and those who sided with either. It was true that Jeff had taken to carrying a handgun; that Steward Morgan and Arnold Fleetwood had shouted at each other in the street; that people wandered into Anna Flood's back room to lounge in Menus' barbershop not for haircuts but to grunt and sigh over the rumor of an outrage that had taken place out at the Convent; that based on this gossip Reverend Pulliam had preached a sermon taken from Jeremiah 1:5: "Before I formed thee in the belly I knew thee, and before thou camest forth out of the womb I sanctified thee." Reverend Misner countered with Paul's words to the Corinthians: ". . . the greatest of these is love." But to Billie Delia the real battle was not about infant life or a bride's reputation but about disobedience, which meant, of course, the stallions were fighting about who controlled the mares and their foals. Senior Pulliam had scripture and history on his side. Misner had scripture and the future on his. Now, she supposed, he was making the world wait until it understood his position.

Billie Delia lowered her gaze from Misner's searching eyes to the heavy lace on the bride's head to the back of the groom's neck and thought immediately of a horse she once loved. Although it was the groom who held in his name the memory of a legendary horse race, it was she whose life had been maimed by it. Hard Goods, the winning horse that K.D. had ridden when Ruby was founded, belonged to Mr. Nathan DuPres. Years after that race but before she could walk, Mr. Nathan had hoisted her on Hard Goods' bare back, which she rode with such glee it made everybody laugh. From then on, every month or so, when he came into town on errands, he unsaddled the horse and led it around the schoolyard next to her house, holding her waist with the palm of his hand. "Mount up these children," he would say. "Need more horsewomen in this land. Everybody crying for a motorcar better mount up their children early! Hard Goods ain't never had a flat!" It continued until Billie Delia was three years old—too little, still, for everyday underwear, and nobody noticed or cared how perfect her skin felt against that wide expanse of rhythmically moving animal flesh. While she struggled to grip Hard Goods with her ankles and endure the rub of his spine, the grown-ups smiled, taking pleasure in her pleasure while calling Mr. Nathan a retrograde Negro who needed to learn how to shift gears so he could get somewhere on time. Then one day. A Sunday. Hard Goods came loping down the street with Mr.

Nathan astride. Billie Delia, who hadn't seen horse or rider for a long while, ran toward them, begging for a lift. Mr. Nathan promised to stop by after service. Still in her Sunday clothes, she waited in her yard. When she saw him coming, negotiating space among the after-church crowd, she ran out into the middle of Central Avenue, where she pulled down her Sunday panties before raising her arms to be lifted onto Hard Goods' back.

Things seemed to crumple after that. She got an unintelligible whipping from her mother and a dose of shame it took her years to understand. That's when the teasing began, more merciless because her mother was the teacher. Suddenly there was a dark light in the eyes of boys who felt comfortable staring at her. Suddenly a curious bracing in the women, a looking-away look in the men. And a permanent watchfulness in her mother. Nathan DuPres did not make her another offer. Hard Goods was lost to her forever, remembered publicly as the horse that won the race with K.D. on his back, privately as the recipient of a little girl's shame. Only Mrs. Dovey Morgan and her sister, Soane, treated her with easy kindness—stopping her in the street to adjust the bow in her braids, praising her work in their kitchen gardens; and once when Mrs. Dovey Morgan stopped her to wipe what she thought was makeup from Billie Delia's rosy lips, she did it with a smile and no hateful lecture. Even apologized when her handkerchief came away clean. If it had not been for them and Anna Flood's return her teens would have been unlivable. Nor did Anna or the Morgan ladies make her feel the freakishness of being an only child—perhaps because they had few or no children themselves. Most families boasted nine, eleven, even fifteen children. And it was inevitable that she and Arnette, who had no sisters and just one brother, become best friends.

She knew people took her for the wild one, the one who from the beginning not only had no qualms about pressing her nakedness on a horse's back but preferred it, would drop her drawers in public on Sunday just to get to the thrill of it. Although it was Arnette who had sex at fourteen (with the groom), Billie Delia carried the burden. She quickly learned the cautionary look in the eyes of girls whose mothers had warned them away from Billie Delia. In fact she was untouched. So far. Since she was helplessly in love with a pair of brothers, her virginity, which no one believed existed, had become as mute as the cross Reverend Misner was holding aloft.

Now his eyes were closed. His jaw muscles working overtime. He held the cross as though it were a hammer he was trying not to bring down lest it hurt somebody. Billie Delia wished he would open his eyes again, look at the groom and bust him over the head with it. But no. That would embarrass the bride who had won, finally, the husband her maid of honor despised. A husband who had propositioned Billie Delia before and after his thing with Arnette. A husband who, while Arnette was away, had forgotten all about her and chased any dress whose wearer was under fifty. A husband who had left his future bride pregnant and on her own, knowing that it was the unmarried mother-to-be (not the father-to-be) who would have to ask her church's forgiveness. Billie Delia had heard of such things, but any girl who got pregnant in Ruby could count on marriage, whether the boy was eager or not, because he still had to live near her family and with his own. Still had to meet her in church or anywhere else he turned. But not this groom. This groom let the bride suffer for four years and consented to a wedding only when he was kicked out of another woman's bed. Kicked so hard he couldn't get to the altar fast enough. She remembered vividly the day the kicker had arrived in shoes already designed for the groom's behind. Billie Delia's hatred of the strange-looking girl was instant and would have been eternal had she not taken refuge in the Convent herself one chilly October day after a quarrel with her mother turned ugly. Her mother fought her like a man that day. She had run to Anna Flood, who told her to wait upstairs while she dealt with some deliveryman business. Billie Delia cried alone for what seemed like hours, licking her split lip and touching the swelling under her eye. When she spied Apollo's truck, she slipped down the back stairs, and while he was buying soda pop, she got into the cab. Neither of them knew what to do. Apollo offered to take her out to his family's place. But ashamed of having to explain her face to his parents and put up with the stares of any one of his twelve brothers and sisters, she asked him to drive her out to the Convent. That was the fall of 1973. What she saw and learned there changed her forever.

Agreeing to be Arnette's maid of honor was the last sentimental thing she would ever do in Ruby. She got a job in Demby, bought a car and probably would have driven it to Saint Louis, except for her helpless double love.

With or without chaw in his mouth, Steward was not a patient man. So he was surprised to find himself calm watching Misner's behavior. All around him the congregation had begun to murmur, exchange looks, but Steward, believing he was less confounded than they were, did neither in spite of no soothing wad of tobacco. As a small boy, he had listened to Big Daddy describe a sixty-five-mile journey he'd taken to bring supplies back to Haven. It was 1920. State prohibition was now national. A sickness called rocking pneumonia gripped Haven and Big Daddy was one of the few able bodies able to go. He went alone. On horseback. He got what he needed in Logan County, and with the medicines bundled under his coat, the other supplies tied to the horse, he lost his way and found himself after sunset unsure of which way to go. He smelled, but could not see, a campfire that seemed to be fairly close by on his left. Then suddenly, to his right, he heard whoops, music and gunshots. But he saw no lights in that direction. Stuck in darkness with invisible strangers on both sides, he had to decide whether to ride toward the smoke and meat smells or toward the music and guns. Or neither. The campfire might be warming robbers; the music might be amusing lynchers. His horse decided. Smelling others of its kind it trotted toward the campfire. There Big Daddy found three Sac and Fox men sitting near a fire hidden in a hole. He dismounted, approached carefully, hat in hand, and said, "Evening." The men welcomed him and, learning of his destination, warned him against entering the town. The women there fight with their fists, they said; the children are drunk; the men don't argue or debate but speak only with firearms; liquor laws don't apply. They had come to rescue a family member, who had been drinking in there for twelve days. Already one of them was in there, searching for him. What's the name of the town? Big Daddy asked. Pura Sangre, they answered. At its northern edge was a sign: No Niggers. At its southern edge a cross. Big Daddy spent several hours with them and, before light, thanked them and left—backtracking to find his way home.

When Steward heard the story the first time, he could not close his mouth, thinking of that moment when his father was all alone in the dark, guns to the right, strangers to the left. But the grown-ups laughed and thought of something else. "No niggers at one end, a cross at the other and the devil loose in between." Steward didn't get it. How could the devil be anywhere near a cross? What was the connection between the two signs? Since that time, however, he had seen crosses between the titties of whores; military crosses spread for miles; crosses on fire in Negroes' yards, crosses tattooed on the forearms of dedicated killers. He had seen a cross dangling from the rearview mirror of a car full of whites come to insult the little girls of Ruby. Whatever Reverend Misner was thinking, he was wrong. A cross was no better than the bearer. Now Steward fingered his mustache aware of his twin shifting his feet, getting ready to grab the pew in front of him and put a stop to Misner's behavior.

Soane, sitting next to Deek, listening to his heavy breathing, understood how grave her mistake. She was about to touch her husband on the arm to caution him from rising, when Misner lowered the cross at last and spoke the opening words of the ceremony. Deek sat back and cleared his sinuses, but the damage was done. They were right back where they'd started when Jefferson Fleetwood pulled a gun on K.D.; when Menus had to interrupt a pushing match between Steward and Arnold. And when Mable had sent no cake to the All Church Bake Sale. The peace and goodwill summoned by the announcement of the marriage were now shattered. The reception at her house would be a further digest of the problem, and most disturbing, Soane, unbeknownst to others, had made the mistake of inviting Connie and the Convent girls to the wedding reception. Having misread the warning, she was about to hostess one of the biggest messes Ruby had ever seen. Both of her dead sons were leaning against the Kelvinator, cracking the shells of Spanish peanuts. "What's that in the sink?" Easter asked her. She looked and saw feathers—brightly colored but small like chicken feathers—lying in a heap in her sink. It made her wonder: she hadn't killed or plucked any fowl and would never have put feathers there. "I don't know," she answered. "You should gather them up, Mama," Scout told her. "That's no place for them, you know." They both laughed and crunched the nuts. She woke wondering what kind of bird was colored that way. When pairs and pairs of buzzards flew over the town, she thought that was the significance of the dream: that no matter what, this marriage would fix nothing. Now she believed her sons had tried to tell her something else: she'd been concentrating on the colors, while the point was the sink. "That's no place for them, you know." The strange feathers she had invited did not belong in her house.

When finally Kate Golightly touched the organ keys and the couple turned around to face the congregation, Soane cried. Partly at the sad bright smiles of the bride and groom, partly in dread of the malice, set roaming now, and on its way to her house.

It had long been noticed that the Morgan brothers seldom spoke to or looked at each other. Some believed it was because they were jealous of one another; that their views only seemed to be uniform; that down deep was a mutual resentment which surfaced in small ways. In their automobile arguments, for example: one's fierce preference for Chevrolets, the other's stubborn defense of Oldsmobiles. In fact the brothers not only agreed on almost everything; they were in eternal if silent conversation. Each knew the other's thoughts as well as he knew his face and only once in a while needed the confirmation of a glance.

Now they stood in different rooms of Deek's house, thinking the same thing. Fortunately, Misner was late, Menus sober, Pulliam triumphant and Jeff preoccupied with Sweetie. Mable, who had attended the ceremony, had relieved her daughter-in-law for the reception. The wedding couple were in line—glazed smiles in place, but in line nevertheless. Pastor Cary—soothing and jovial—was the best bet for keeping things steady. He and his wife, Lily, were treasured for their duets, and if they could get some music going . . .

Steward opened the piano while Deek moved through the guests. As he passed Reverend Pulliam, nodding and smiling with Sweetie and Jeff, Deek gave him a reassuring pat on the shoulder. In the dining room the food table drew appreciative murmurs but as yet no takers except children. The coos over the gift table seemed strained, excessive. Steward waited at the piano, his steel-gray hair and innocent eyes in perfect balance. The children around him shone like agate; the women were brilliant but quiet in their still fresh Easter clothes; the men's squeaky new shoes glistened like melon seeds. Everyone was stiff, overly polite. Deek must be having trouble persuading the Carys, he thought. Steward reached for tobacco, silently urging his twin to try somebody else—the Male Chorus, Kate Golightly—quick before Pulliam took it in his head to pray them back into battle stations or, Lord help us, Jeff began reciting his VA grievances. Once that started his next target would be K.D. who had never served in the military. Where is Soane? he wondered. Steward could see Dovey unpinning the veil from the bride's hair and his innocent eyes enjoyed his wife's figure once more. In anything—Sunday dress, white church uniform or even his own bathrobe—the look of her body made him smile with satisfaction. But Deek was cautioning him now about distraction, so Steward left off admiring Dovey and saw the success of his brother's efforts. Kate came toward the piano and sat down. She flexed her fingers and began to play. First a preparatory trill, accompanied by friendly coughs and murmurs of anticipation. Then Simon and Lily Cary arrived, humming, humming, while they considered what to begin with. They were a third of the way into "Precious Lord, take my hand," smiles had turned toward the direction of the music, when they heard the horn blast of an ancient Cadillac.

Connie did not come, but her boarders did. Mavis drove the Cadillac, with Gigi and Seneca in the back and a somebody new in the passenger seat. None of them was dressed for a wedding. They piled out of the car looking like go-go girls: pink shorts, skimpy tops, see-through skirts; painted eyes, no lipstick; obviously no underwear, no stockings. Jezebel's storehouse raided to decorate arms, earlobes, necks, ankles

156

and even a nostril. Mavis and Soane, greeting each other on the lawn, were uncomfortable. Two other women sauntered into the dining room and surveyed the food tables. They said "Hi" and wondered aloud if there was anything other than lemonade and punch to drink. There wasn't, so they did what a few other young people had already done: drifted out of the Morgans' yard and strolled past Anna Flood's store to the Oven. The few local girls already there clumped together and withdrew, leaving the territory to the Poole boys: Apollo, Brood and Hurston. To the Seawrights: Timothy Jr. and Spider. To Destry, Vane and Royal. Menus joined them, but Jeff, to whom he had been speaking, did not. Neither did the watching groom. Dovey was removing the fat from a lamb slice when the music hit. She cut her finger in the blare and sucked it when Otis Redding screamed "Awwwww, lil girl . . . ," obliterating the hymn's quiet plea. Inside, outside and on down the road the beat and the heat were ruthless.

"Oh, they're just having fun," a voice behind Reverend Pulliam whispered. He turned to look but could not locate the speaker, so he continued glaring out of the window. He knew about such women. Like children, always on the lookout for fun, devoted to it but always needing a break in order to have it. A lift, a hand, a five-dollar bill. Somebody to excuse or coddle them. Somebody to look down at the ground and say nothing when they disturbed the peace. He exchanged glances with his wife who nodded and left the window. She knew, as he did, that fun-obsessed adults were clear signs of already advanced decay. Soon the whole country would be awash in toys, tone-deaf from raucous music and hollow laughter. But not here. Not in Ruby. Not while Senior Pulliam was alive.

The Convent girls are dancing; throwing their arms over their heads, they do this and that and then the other. They grin and yip but look at no one. Just their own rocking bodies. The local girls look over their shoulders and snort. Brood, Apollo and Spider, steel-muscled farm boys with sophisticated eyes, sway and snap their fingers. Hurston sings accompaniment. Two small girls ride their bikes over; wide-eyed, they watch the dancing women. One of them, with amazing hair, asks can she borrow a bike. Then another. They ride the bikes down Central Avenue with no regard for what the breeze does to their long flowered skirts or how pumping pedals plumped their breasts. One coasts with her ankles on the handlebars. Another rides the handlebars with Brood on the seat behind her. One, in the world's shortest pink shorts, is seated on a bench, arms wrapped around herself. She looks drunk. Are they all? The boys laugh.

Anna and Kate carried their plates to the edge of Soane's garden.

"Which one?" whispered Anna.

"That one there," said Kate. "The one with the rag for a blouse."

"That's a halter," said Anna.

"Halter? Looks like a starter to me."

"She the one K.D. was messing with?"

"Yep."

"I know that one there. She comes in the store. Who the other two?"

"Beats me."

"Look. There goes Billie Delia."

"Naturally."

"Oh, come on, Kate. Leave Billie alone."

They spooned potato salad into their mouths. Behind them came Alice Pulliam, murmuring, "My, my, my-my-my."

"Hello, Aunt Alice," said Kate.

"Have you ever in your life seen such carrying on? Bet you can't locate one brassiere in the whole bunch." Alice held the crown of her hat in the breeze. "Why're you all smiling? I don't think this is the least bit funny."

"No. Course not," said Kate.

"This is a wedding, remember?"

"You're right, Aunt Alice. I said you right."

"How would you like to have somebody dancing nasty at your wedding?" Alice's bright black eyes searched Anna's hair.

Kate nodded sympathetically while pressing her lips tight so no smile could seep through them. Anna tried to look seriously affronted before this stern preacher's wife, thinking: Dear Jesus, I wouldn't last an hour in this town if I married Richard.

"I'm going to have to get Pastor himself to stop this," Alice said, and moved resolutely off toward Soane's house.

Anna and Kate waited several beats before setting their laughter free. Whatever else, thought Anna, the Convent women had saved the day. Nothing like other folks' sins for distraction. The young people were wrong. Be the Furrow of *Her* Brow. Speaking of which, where was Richard anyway?

Down on his knees, Richard Misner was angry at his anger, and at his mishandling of it. Used to obstacles, adept at disagreement, he could not reconcile the level of his present fury with what seemed to be its source. He loved God so much it hurt, although that same love sometimes made him laugh out loud. And he deeply respected his colleagues. For centuries they had held on. Preaching, shouting, dancing, singing, absorbing, arguing, counseling, pleading, commanding. Their passion burned or smoldered like lava over a land that had waged war against them and their flock without surcease. A lily-livered war without honor as either its point or reward; an unprincipled war that thrived as much on the victor's cowardice as on his mendacity. On stage and in print he and his brethren had been the heart of comedy, the chosen backs for parody's knife. They were cursed by death row inmates, derided by pimps. Begrudged even miserly collection plates. Yet through all of that, if the Spirit seemed to be slipping away they had held on to it with their teeth if they had to, grabbed it in their fists if need be. They took it to buildings ready to be condemned, to churches from which white congregations had fled, to quilt tents, to ravines and logs in clearings. Whispered it in cabins lit by moonlight lest the Law see. Prayed for it behind trees and in sod houses, their voices undaunted by roaring winds. From Abyssinian to storefronts, from Pilgrim Baptist to abandoned movie houses; in polished shoes, worn boots, beat-up cars and Lincoln Continentals, well fed or malnourished, they let their light, flickering low or blazing like a comet, pierce the darkness of days. They wiped white folks' spit from the faces of black children, hid strangers from posses and police, relayed life-preserving information faster than the newspaper and better than the radio. At sickbeds they looked death in the eye and mouth. They pressed the heads of weeping mothers to their shoulders before conducting their life-gouged daughters to the cemetery. They wept for chain gangs, reasoned with magistrates. Made whole congregations scream. In ecstasy. In belief. That death was *life*, don't you know, and *every* life, don't you know, was holy, don't you know, in His eyesight. Rocked as they were by the sight of evil, its snout was familiar to them. Real wonder, however, lay in the amazing shapes and substances God's grace took: gospel in times of persecution; the exquisite wins of people forbidden to compete; the upright righteousness of those who let no boot hold them down—people who made Job's patience look like restlessness. Elegance when all around was shabby.

Richard Misner knew all that. Yet, however intact his knowledge and respect, the tremor inside him now was ungovernable. Pulliam had fingered a membrane enclosing a ravenous appetite for vengeance, an appetite he needed to understand in order to subdue. Had the times finally gotten to him? Was the desolation that rose after King's murder, a desolation that climbed like a tidal wave in slow motion, just now washing over him? Or was it the calamity of watching the drawn-out abasement of a noxious President? Had the long, unintelligible war infected him? Behaving like a dormant virus in blossom now that it was coming to a raggedy close? Everybody on his high school football team died in that war. Eleven broad-backed boys. They were the ones he had looked up to, wanted to be like. Was he just now gagging at their futile death? Was that the origin of this incipient hunger for violence?

Or was it Ruby?

What was it about this town, these people, that enraged him? They were different from other communities in only a couple of ways: beauty and isolation. All of them were handsome, some exceptionally so. Except for three or four, they were coal black, athletic, with noncommittal eyes. All of them maintained an icy suspicion of outsiders. Otherwise they were like all small black communities: protective, God-loving, thrifty but not miserly. They saved and spent; liked money in the bank and nice things too. When he arrived he thought their flaws were normal; their disagreements ordinary. They were pleased by the accomplishments of their neighbors and their mockery of the lazy and the loose was full of laughter. Or used to be. Now, it seemed, the glacial wariness they once confined to strangers more and more was directed toward each other. Had he contributed to it? He could not help admitting that without his presence there would probably be no contention, no painted fists, no quarrels about missing language on an oven's lip. No warnings about meetings he held with a dozen or so young people. Certainly no public, let alone physical, antagonism between businessmen. And absolutely no runaways. No drinking. Even acknowledging his part in the town's unraveling, Misner was dissatisfied. Why such stubbornness, such venom against asserting rights, claiming a wider role in the affairs of black people? They, of all people, knew the necessity of unalloyed will; the rewards of courage and single-mindedness. Of all people, they understood the mechanisms of wresting power. Didn't they?

Over and over and with the least provocation, they pulled from their stock of stories tales about the old folks, their grands and great-grands; their fathers and mothers. Dangerous confrontations, clever maneuvers. Testimonies to endurance, wit, skill and strength. Tales of luck and outrage. But why were there no stories to tell of themselves? About their own lives they shut up. Had nothing to say, pass on. As though past heroism was enough of a future to live by. As though, rather than children, they wanted duplicates.

Misner was hoping for answers down there on his knees. Not a growing catalogue of questions. So he did what he was accustomed to doing: asked Him to come along as he struck out, late and agitated, for the wedding reception. Being in His company quieted anger. As he left the parsonage and turned into Central Avenue, he could hear the light breathing of his companion, but no word of advice or consolation. He was passing Harper's drugstore when he saw a crowd gathered near the Oven. From it, in a burst of tuneup-needy engine roar, shot a Cadillac. In less than a minute it passed him, and he recognized two Convent women among the passengers. By the time he got to the Morgans' yard, the crowd had dispersed. The sugar-drunk children were racing and tumbling with Steward's collies. The Oven was deserted. The instant he stepped inside Soane and Deek's house, he could see that all was aglow. Menus came forward to embrace him. Pulliam, Arnold and Deek interrupted their deep conversation to shake his hand. The Carys were singing a duet, a chorus backing them. So he was not startled to see Jeff Fleetwood laughing pleasantly with the very man he had drawn a gun on some weeks ago—the freshly married groom. Only the bride looked askew.

The silence in the Cadillac was not an embarrassed one. None of the passengers had high expectations of men in suits, so they were not surprised to be asked to leave the premises. "Give these little girls their bicycles back," said one. "Get on out of here," said another, through a mouthful of tobacco. The younger men who had laughed and cheered them on were ordered away without words. Just a look and a head movement from a man seven feet tall. Nor were they angry about the dismissal—slightly put out, maybe, but not seriously. One, the driver, had never seen a man who didn't look like an unlit explosion. Another, in the front passenger seat, considered the boring sexual images she had probably incited and recommitted herself to making tracks to somewhere else. A third, who had really been having fun, sat in the back seat thinking that although she knew what anger looked like, she had no idea what it might feel like. She always did what she was told, so when the man said, "Give these little girls . . . ," she did it with a smile. The fourth passenger was grateful for the expulsion. This was her second day at the Convent and the third day of having said not one word to anybody. Except today when the girl, Billie something, came to stand near her.

"You all right?" She wore a shell-pink gown and instead of the shower cap had tiny yellow roses pinned into her hair. "Pallas? You okay?"

She nodded and tried not to shiver.

"You're safe out there, but I'll come by to see if you need anything, all right?"

"Yes," Pallas whispered. Then, "Thanks."

So there. She had opened her lips a tiny bit to say two words, and no black water had seeped in. The cold still shook her bones, but the dark water had receded. For now. At night, of course, it would return and she would be back in it—trying not to think about what swam below her neck. It was the top of the water she concentrated on and the flashlight licking the edge, then darting farther out over the black glimmer. Hoping, hoping the things touching below were sweet little goldfish like the ones in the bowl her father bought her when she was five. Or guppies, angels. Not alligators or snakes. This was a lake not a swamp or the aquarium at the San Diego zoo. Floating over the water, the whispers were closer than their calls. "Here, pussy. Here, pussy. Kitty, kitty, kitty," sounded far away; but "Gimme the flash, dickface, izzat her, let go, maybe she drowned, no way," slid into the skin behind her ears.

Pallas stared out of the window at a sky so steady, landscape so featureless she had no sense of being in a moving car. The smell of Gigi's bubble gum mixed with her cigarette smoke was nauseating.

"Here, pussy. Here." Pallas had heard that before. A lifetime ago on the happiest day of her life. On the escalator. Last Christmas. Spoken by the crazy woman, whom she could see now in greater detail than when first sighted.

The hair at the top of her head, sectioned off with a red plastic barrette, would have been a small pompadour or a curl had it been longer than two or three inches. In the event, it was neither. Just a tuft held rigid by a child's barrette. Two other hair clips, one yellow, one neon purple, held fingerfuls of hair at her temples. Her dark velvet face was on display and rendered completely unseen by the biscuit-size disks of scarlet rouge, the fuchsia lipstick drawn crookedly beyond the rim of her lips, the black eyebrow pencil that trailed down toward her cheekbones. Everything else about her was dazzle and clunk: white plastic earrings, copper bracelets, pastel beads at her throat, and much, much more where all that came from in the bags she carried: two BOAC carrier bags and a woven metal purse shaped like a cigar box. She wore a white cotton halter and a little-bitty red skirt. The hose on her short legs, a cinnamon color thought agreeable to black women's legs, were as much a study in running as her high heels were in run over. Inner arm skin and a small, sturdy paunch suggested she was about forty years old, but she could have been fifty or twenty. The dance she danced on the up escalator, the rolling hips, the sway of her head, called to mind a bygone era of slow grind in a badly lit room of couples. Not the electric go-go pace of 1974. The teeth could have been done anywhere: Kingston, Jamaica, or Pass Christian, Mississippi; Addis Ababa or Warsaw. Stunning gold, they dated her smile while giving it the seriousness the rest of her clothing withheld.

Most eyes looked away from her—down at the floating metal steps underfoot or out at the Christmas decorations enlivening the department store. Children, however, and Pallas Truelove stared.

California Christmases are always a treat and this one promised to be a marvel. Brilliant skies and heat turned up the gloss of artificial snow, plumped the green-and-gold, pink-and-silver wreaths. Pallas, laden with packages, just managed to avoid tripping off the down escalator. She didn't understand why the woman with the rouge and gold teeth fascinated her. They had nothing in common. The earrings that hung from Pallas' lobes were eighteen carat; the boots on her feet were handmade, her jeans custom-made, and the buckle on her leather belt was handsomely worked silver.

Pallas had stumbled off the escalator in a light panic, rushing to the doors, outside which Carlos was waiting for her. The revolting woman's singsong merged with the carols piping throughout the store: "Here's pussy. Want some pussy, pussy."

"Ma-a-a-vis!"

Mavis wouldn't look at her. Gigi always uglied up her name, pulling it out like a string of her sticky bubble gum.

"Can't you go over ten miles an hour? Cha-rist!"

"Car needs a new fan belt. And I'm not going to take it over forty," said Mavis.

"Ten. Forty. It's like walking." Gigi sighed.

"Maybe I'll just pull over here and let you see what walking's like. Want me to?"

"Don't fuck with me. Drag me out to that bummer . . . Did you see that guy, Sen? Menus. The one who shit himself when he stayed with us?"

Seneca nodded. "He didn't say anything mean, though."

"He didn't stop them either," said Gigi. "All that puke, that shit I cleaned up."

"Connie said he could stay. And we all cleaned it," said Mavis, "not just you. And nobody dragged you. You didn't have to go."

"He had the d.t.'s, for crying out loud."

"Close your window, please, Mavis?" Seneca asked.

"Too much wind back there?"

"She's shaking again. I think she's cold."

"It's ninety degrees! What the hell is the matter with her?" Gigi scanned the trembling girl.

"Should I stop?" asked Mavis. "She might throw up again."

"No, don't stop. I'll hold her." Seneca arranged Pallas in her arms, rubbing the goose-bumpy arms. "Maybe she's carsick. I thought the party would cheer her up some. Looks like it made her worse."

"That stupid, fucked-up town make anybody puke. I can't believe that's what they call a party. Hymns, for crying out loud!" Gigi laughed.

"It was a wedding party, not a disco." Mavis wiped the perspiration forming under her neck. "Besides, you just wanted to see your love pony again."

"That asshole?"

"Yeah. Him." Mavis smiled. "Now he's married, you want him back."

"If I want him back I can get him back. What I want is to leave this fucking place."

"You've been saying that for four years—right, Sen?"

Gigi opened her mouth, then paused. Was it four? She thought two. But at least two were spent fooling around with K.D., the prick. Had she let him keep her that long promising to get enough money to take her away? Or was it some other promise that kept her there? Of trees entwined near cold water. "Yeah, well, now I'm for real," she told Mavis, and hoped she really was.

After a grunt of disbelief from Mavis, the car was silent again. Pallas let her head rest on Seneca's breasts, wishing they were gone and that instead Carlos' hard, smooth chest supported her cheek as it had whenever she wanted for seven hundred miles. Her sixteenth-birthday gift, a red Toyota with a built-in eight-track tape deck, was crammed with Christmas presents. Things anybody's mother would like, but in a variety of colors and styles because she couldn't take a chance on having nothing that would please a woman she had not seen in thirteen years. Driving off with Carlos at the wheel just before Christmas was a holiday trip to see her mother. Not running away from her father; not eloping with the coolest, most gorgeous man in the world.

Everything had been carefully planned: items were hidden, movements camouflaged, lest Providence, the eagle-eyed housekeeper, or her brother, Jerome, see. Her father wasn't around enough to notice anything. He was a lawyer with a small client list, but two were big-time crossover black entertainers. As long as Milton Truelove kept them on top, he didn't need to acquire more, although he kept a lookout eye for other young performers who might hit the charts and stay there.

With Carlos' help it was as easy as it was exciting: the lies told to her girlfriends had to be cemented; the items left behind had to signal return, not escape (driver's license—a duplicate—her teddy bears, watch, toiletries, jewelry, credit cards). This last made it necessary to do massive check cashing and shopping on the very day they drove away. She wanted to buy more, much more, for Carlos, but he insisted otherwise. He never took presents from her in all the time she knew him—four months. Wouldn't even let her buy meals. He would close his beautiful eyes and shake his head as though her offer saddened him. Pallas had met him in the school parking lot the day her Toyota wouldn't start. Actually met him that day but had seen him many times. He was the movie-star-looking maintenance man at her high school. All the girls went creamy over him. The day he pressed the accelerator to the floor, telling Pallas her gas line was flooded, was the beginning. He offered to follow her home in his Ford to make sure she didn't stall out again. She didn't and he waved goodbye. Pallas brought him a present—an album—the next day and had trouble making him accept it. "Only if you let me buy you a chili dog," he said.

Pallas' mouth had gone felt with the thrill of it all. They saw each other every weekend after that. She did everything she could think of to get him to make love to her. He responded passionately to their necking but for weeks never allowed more. He was the one who said, "When we are married."

Carlos was not a janitor, really. He sculpted, and when Pallas told him about her painter mother and where she lived, he smiled and said it was a perfect place for an artist. The whole thing fell into place. Carlos could leave his job with little outcry during the holidays. Milton Truelove would be extra busy with clients' parties, showcase concerts and television deals. Pallas searched through years of birthday and Christmas cards from her mother for the most recent address, and the lovers were off without a hitch or a cloud. Except for the crazy black woman ruining the Christmas carols.

Pallas snuggled Seneca's breasts, which, although uncomfortable, diluted the chill racking her. The women in the front seat were quarreling again, in high-pitched voices that hurt her head.

"Exhibitionist bitch! Soane is a friend of ours. What do I tell her now?"

"She's Connie's friend. Nothing to do with you."

"I'm the one sell her the peppers, make up her tonic. . . ."

"Whazzat make you, a chemist? It's just rosemary, a little bran mixed with aspirin."

"Whatever it is, it's my responsibility."

"Only when Connie's drunk."

"Keep your nasty mouth off her. She never drank till you came."

"That's what you say. She even sleeps in the wine cellar."

"Her bedroom is down there! You're such a fool."

"She's not a maid anymore. She could sleep upstairs if she wanted. She just wants to be close to that liquor is all."

"God, I hate your guts."

Seneca intervened in a soft voice designed for harmony. "Connie's not drunk. She's unhappy. She should have come with us, though. It would have been different."

"It was fine. Just fine!" said Gigi. "Till those fucking preacher types came over." She lit a fresh cigarette from a dying one.

"Can't you stop smoking for two minutes?" Mavis asked.

"No!"

"Don't see what that nigger ever saw in you," Mavis continued. "Or maybe I do, since you can't seem to keep it covered."

"Jealous?"

"Like hell."

"Like hell, like hell. Nobody's fucked you in ten years, you dried-up husk."

"Get out!" Mavis screamed, braking the car. "Get the hell out of my car!"

"You gonna make me? Touch me, I'll tear your face off. You fucking felon!" and she rammed her cigarette into Mavis' arm.

They couldn't fight really well in the space available, but they tried. Seneca held Pallas in her arms and watched. Once upon a time she would try to separate them, but now she knew better. When they were exhausted they'd stop, and peace would reign longer than if she interfered. Gigi knew Mavis' touchy parts: anything insulting to Connie and any reference to her fugitive state. On her last trip Mavis learned from her mother of the warrant posted for her arrest for grand larceny, abandonment and suspicion of murdering two of her children.

The Cadillac rocked. Gigi was scrappy but vain—she didn't want bruises or scratches to mar her lovely face and she worried constantly about her hair. Mavis was slow but a steady, joyful hitter. When Gigi saw blood she assumed it was her own and scrambled from the car, Mavis scooting after her. Under a metal-hot sky void of even one arrow of birds they fought on the road and its shoulder.

Pallas sat up, mesmerized by the bodies roiling dust and crushing weeds. Intent bodies unaware of any watcher under a blank sky in Oklahoma or a painted one in Mehita, New Mexico. Months after Dee Dee Truelove's excited hugs and kisses: months of marveling at the spectacular scenery outside her mother's windows; months of eating wonderful food; months of artist talk among Dee Dee's friends—all kinds of artists: Indians, New Yorkers, old people, hippies, Mexicans, blacks—and months of talk among the three of them at night under stars Pallas thought only Disney made. After all those months, Carlos said, "This is where I belong," sighing deeply. "This is the home I've been looking for." His face, moon-drenched, made Pallas' heart stand. Her mother yawned. "Of course it is," said Dee Dee Truelove. Carlos yawned too, and right then she should have seen it— the simultaneous yawns, the settling-in voices. She should have calculated the arithmetic—Carlos was closer in age to Dee Dee than to her. Had she noticed, perhaps she could have prevented the grappling bodies exchanging moans in the grass, unmindful of any watcher. Then there would have been no stupefied run to the Toyota, no blind drive on roads without destinations, no bumping, sideswiping trucks. No water with soft things touching beneath.

Feeling again the repulsive tickle and stroke of tentacles, of invisible scales, Pallas turned away from the fighting-women scene and lifted her arm to circle Seneca's neck and press her face deeper into that tiny bosom.

Seneca alone saw the truck approach. The driver slowed, maybe to get around the Cadillac hogging the road, maybe to offer help, but he stayed long enough to see outlaw women rolling on the ground, dresses torn, secret flesh on display. And see also two other women embracing in the back seat. For long moments his eyes were wide. Then he shook his head and gunned the motor of his truck.

Finally Gigi and Mavis lay gasping. One, then the other, sat up to touch herself, to inventory her wounds. Gigi searched for the shoe she had lost; Mavis for the elastic that had held her hair. Wordlessly they returned to the car. Mavis drove with one hand. Gigi stuck a cigarette in the good side of her mouth.

In 1922 the white laborers had laughed among themselves—a big stone house in the middle of nothing. The Indians had not. In mean weather, with firewood a sacrilege in tree-scarce country, coal expensive, cow chips foul, the mansion seemed to them a demented notion. The embezzler had ordered tons of coal—none of which he got to use. The nuns who took the property over had endurance, kerosene and layers of exquisitely made habits. But in spring, summer and during some warm autumns, the stone walls of the house were a cool blessing.

Gigi raced up the stairs beating Mavis to available bathwater. While the plumbing coughed she stripped and looked at herself in the one unpainted mirror. Other than a knee and both elbows, the damage wasn't too bad. Nails broken, of course, but no puffed eye or broken nose. More bruises might show up tomorrow, though. It was the lip swelling around its split that troubled her. With pressure it oozed a trickle of blood and suddenly everybody was running through the streets of Oakland, California. Sirens—police? ambulance? fire trucks?—shook the eardrums. A wall of advancing police cut off passage east and west. The runners threw what they had brought or could find and fled. She and Mikey were holding hands at first, running down a side street behind a splinter crowd. A street of small houses, lawns. There were no shots—no gunfire at all. Just the musical screams of girls and the steady roar of men in fight-face. Sirens, yes, and distant bullhorns, but no breaking glass, no body slams, no gunfire. So why did a map of red grow on the little boy's white shirt? She wasn't seeing clearly. The crowd thickened and then stopped, prevented by something ahead. Mikey was several shoulders beyond her, pushing through. Gigi looked again at the boy on the fresh green lawn. He was so well dressed: bow tie, white shirt, glossy laced-up shoes. But the shirt was dirty now, covered with red peonies. He jerked, and blood flowed from his mouth. He held his hands out, carefully, to catch it lest it ruin his shoes the way it had already ruined his shirt.

Over a hundred injured, the newspaper said, but no mention of gunfire or a shot kid. No mention of a neat little colored boy carrying his blood in his hands.

The water trickled into the tub. Gigi put rollers in her hair. Then she got down on her stomach to examine again the progress she had made with the box hidden under the tub. The tile above it was completely dislodged, but the metal box seemed to be cemented in place. Reaching under the tub was the problem. If she'd told K.D., he would have helped her, but then she would have had to share the contents: gold, maybe, diamonds, great packets of cash. Whatever it was, it was hers—and Connie's if she wanted some. But no one else's. Never Mavis. Seneca wouldn't want any, and this latest girl, with the splintered-glass eyes and a head thick with curly hair—who knew who or what she was? Gigi stood up, brushed away dust and soil from her skin then stepped into the tub. She sat there going over her options. Connie, she thought. Connie.

Then, lying back so the bubbles reached her chin, she thought of Seneca's nose, the way her nostrils moved when she slept. Of the tilt of her lips whether smiling or not; her thick, perfectly winged eyebrows. And her voice—soft, mildly hungry. Like a kiss.

In the bathroom at the other end of the hall, an elated Mavis cleaned up at the sink. Then she changed clothes before going down to the kitchen to make supper. Leftover chicken, chopped with peppers and onions, tarragon, a sauce of some kind, cheese, maybe, and wrapped in that pancake thing Connie had taught her to make. That would please her. She would take a plate of it down to Connie and tell her what had happened. Not the fight. That wasn't important. In fact she had enjoyed it. Pounding, pounding, even biting Gigi was exhilarating, just as cooking was. It was more proof that the old Mavis was dead. The one who couldn't defend herself from an eleven-year-old girl, let alone her husband. The one who couldn't figure out or manage a simple meal, who relied on delis and drive-throughs, now created crepe-like delicacies without shopping every day.

But she was stung by Gigi's reference to her sexlessness—which was funny in a way. When she and Frank married she did like it. Sort of. Then it became required torture, longer but not much different from being slapped out of her chair. These years at the Convent were free of all that. Still, when the thing came at night she didn't fight it anymore. Once upon a time it had been an occasional nightmare—a lion cub that gnawed her throat. Recently it had taken another form—human—and lay on top or approached from the rear. "Incubus," Connie had said. "Fight it," she said. But Mavis couldn't or wouldn't. Now she needed to know if what Gigi said about her was the reason she welcomed it. She still heard Merle and Pearl, felt their flutter in every room of the Convent. Perhaps she ought to admit, confess, to Connie that adding the night visits to laughing children and a "mother" who loved her shaped up like a happy family. Better: when she took Connie her supper, she would tell her about the reception, how Gigi had embarrassed everybody, especially Soane, then ask her what to do about the night visits. Connie would know. Connie.

Norma Fox's cashmere serape came in handy once more. Seneca wrapped it around Pallas and asked if she wanted anything. Water? Something to eat? Pallas signaled no. She can't cry yet, thought Seneca. The pain was down too far. When it came up, tears would follow, and Seneca wanted Connie to be there when it happened. So she warmed the girl up as best she could, tried to smooth the heavy hair and, carrying a candle, led her down to Connie.

Part of the cellar, a huge cold room with a domed ceiling, was lined with racks of bottles. Wine as old as Connie. The nuns seldom touched it, Connie told her, only when they could get a priest out there to say the mass they were starved for. And on some Christmases they made a moist cake soaked in a 1915 Veuve Clicquot instead of rum. All around in shadow lurked the shapes of trunks, wooden boxes, furniture, disused and broken. Nude women in polished marble; men in rough stone. At the farthest end was the door to Connie's room. Although it was not built for a maid, as Mavis said, its original purpose was unclear. Connie used it, liked it, for its darkness. Sunlight was not a menace to her there.

Seneca knocked, got no answer and pushed open the door. Connie was sitting in a wicker rocking chair snoring lightly. When Seneca entered she woke instantly.

"Who's carrying that light?"

"It's me—Seneca. And a friend."

"Set it down over there." She motioned to a chest of drawers behind her.

"This is Pallas. She came a couple days ago. She said she wants to meet you."

"Did she?" asked Connie.

Candle flame made it difficult to see, but Seneca recognized the Virgin Mary, the pair of shiny nun shoes, the rosary and, on the dresser, something taking root in a jar of water.

"Who hurt you, little one?" asked Connie.

Seneca sat down on the floor. She had scant hope that Pallas would say much if anything at all. But Connie was magic. She just stretched out her hand and Pallas went to her, sat on her lap, talk-crying at first, then just crying, while Connie said, "Drink a little of this," and "What pretty earrings," and "Poor little one, poor, poor little one. They hurt my poor little one."

It was wine-soaked and took an hour; it was backward and punctured and incomplete, but it came out—little one's story of who had hurt her.

She lost her shoes, she said, so at first nobody would stop for her. Then, she said, the Indian woman in a fedora. Or rather a truckful of Indians stopped for her at dawn as she limped barefoot in shorts by the side of the road. A man drove. Next to him the woman, with a child on her lap. Pallas couldn't tell if it was a boy child or a girl. Six young men sat in the back. It was the woman who made it possible to accept the offer of a lift. Under the brim of her hat the sleet-gray eyes were expressionless but her presence among the men civilized them—as did the child in her lap.

"Where you headed?" she asked.

That was when Pallas discovered that her vocal cords didn't work. That for soundmaking power she couldn't rival the solitary windmill creaking in the field behind her. So she pointed in the direction the truck was going.

"Get in back, then," said the woman.

Pallas climbed among the males—her age mostly—and sat as far away from them as she could, praying that the woman was their mother sister aunt—or any restraining influence.

The Indian boys stared at her but said nothing at all. Arms on knees, they looked without a smile at her pink shorts, Day-Glo T-shirt. After a while, they opened paper bags and began to eat. They offered her a thick baloney sandwich and one of the onions they ate like apples. Afraid a refusal would insult them, Pallas accepted, then found herself eating all of it like a dog, gulping, surprised by her hunger. The truck's sway and rock put her to sleep for a few minutes off and on; each time it happened she woke fighting out of a dream of black water seeping into her mouth, her nose. They passed places with scattered houses, Agways, a gas station, but did not stop until they reached a sizable town. By then it was late afternoon. The truck moved down an empty street, slowing in front of a Baptist church that had "Primitive" in its sign.

"You wait there," the woman said. "Somebody'll come and take care of you."

The boys helped her climb down, and the truck drove off.

Pallas waited on the church steps. There were no houses that she could see and no one was in the street. As the sun dipped, the air turned chilly. Only the soles of her feet, raw and burning, distracted her from the cold overtaking her marrow. Finally she heard an engine and looked up to see the Indian woman again — but alone this time — driving the same truck.

"Get in," she said, and drove Pallas several blocks to a low building with a corrugated roof. "Go in there," she said. "It's a clinic. I don't know if you was bothered or what. You look like it to me. Like a bothered girl. But don't tell them in there. I don't know if it's true, but don't mention it, you hear? Better not to. Just say you was beat up or throwed out or something."

She smiled then, though her eyes were very grave. "Your hair's full of algae." She took off her hat and placed it on Pallas' head. "Go on," she said.

Pallas sat in the reception room along with patients as silent as she. Two elderly women with head scarves, a feverish baby in the arms of its sleeping mother. The receptionist looked at her with unwholesome curiosity but didn't say anything. It was threatening to get dark when two men came in, one with a partially severed hand. Pallas and the sleeping mother were yet to be attended to, but the man seeping blood into a towel took precedence. As the receptionist led him away, Pallas ran out of the entrance and around to the side of the building, where she lost every bit of the onion and baloney. Retching violently, she heard, before she saw, two women approach. Both wore shower caps and blue uniforms.

"Look at that," one said.

They came toward Pallas and stood, heads cocked, watching her heave.

"You on your way in or out?"

"Must be pregnant."

"You trying to see the nurse, honey?"

"She better hurry up."

"Let's take her to Rita."

"You take her, Billie. I got to go."

"She got a hat on but no shoes. Okay, go 'head. See you tomorrow."

Pallas straightened up, clutching her stomach, breathing hard through her mouth.

"Listen to me. Clinic's closing less you an emergency. You sure you ain't pregnant?"

Pallas, trying to control another retch, shuddered.

Billie turned to watch her friend's car leave the lot then looked down at the vomit. Without making a face she kicked dirt until it was out of sight.

"Where your pocketbook?" she asked, moving Pallas away from the buried sick. "Where you live? What they call you?"

Pallas touched her throat and made a sound like a key trying to turn in the wrong lock. All she could do was shake her head. Then, like a child alone in a deserted playground, she drew her name in the dirt with her toe. Then slowly, imitating the girl's earlier erasure with the vomit, she kicked her name away, covering it completely with red dirt.

Billie took off her shower cap. She was much taller than Pallas and had to bend to see into the downcast eyes.

"You come with me, girl," said Billie. "You a pitiful case if ever I see one. And I've seen some."

She drove through blue evening air speaking quietly, reassuringly. "This is a place where you can stay for a while. No questions. I did it once and they were nice to me. Nicer than—well, very nice. Don't be afraid. I used to be. Afraid of them, I mean. Don't see many girls like them out here." She laughed then. "A little nuts, maybe, but loose, relaxed, kind of. Don't be surprised if they don't have on any clothes. I was, at first, but then it was, I don't know, nothing. My mother would have knocked me into next week if I walked around like that. Anyway you can collect yourself there, think things through, with nothing or nobody bothering you all the time. They'll take care of you or leave you alone—whichever way you want it."

The blue darkened around them except for a trim of silver in the distance. The fields rippled in a warm wind but Pallas was shivering by the time they reached the Convent.

After handing her over to Mavis, the girl said, "I'll come back to check on you, okay? Name's Billie Cato."

The candle had burned down to an inch but its flame was high. Pallas wiped her mouth with the back of her hand. The rocking chair rocked. Connie's breathing was so deep Pallas thought she was sleeping. She could see Seneca, hand on chin, elbow on knee, looking up at her, but candle flame, like moonlight in Mehita, distorted faces.

Connie stirred.

"I asked who hurt you. You telling me who helped you. Want to keep that other part secret for a little longer?"

Pallas said nothing.

"How old are you?"

Eighteen, she started to answer, but then chose the truth. "Sixteen," she said. "I would have been a senior next year."

She would have cried again for her lost junior year, but Connie nudged her roughly. "Get up. You breaking my lap." Then, in a softer voice, "Go on and get some sleep now. Stay as long as you like and tell me the rest when you want to."

Pallas stood and wobbled a bit from the rocking and the wine.

"Thanks. But. I better call my father. I guess."

"We'll take you," said Seneca. "I know where there's a telephone. But you have to stop crying, hear?"

They left then, stepping carefully through the darkness, eyes trained on the low light the candle flame shed. Pallas, bred in the overlight of Los Angeles, in houses without basements, associated them with movie evil or trash or crawly things. She gripped Seneca's hand and breathed through her mouth. But the gestures were expressions of anticipated, not genuine, alarm. In fact, as they climbed the stairs, images of a grandmother rocking peacefully, of arms, a lap, a singing voice soothed her. The whole house felt permeated with a blessed malelessness, like a protected domain, free of hunters but exciting too. As though she might meet herself here—an unbridled, authentic self, but which she thought of as a "cool" self—in one of this house's many rooms.

A platter of tortilla-looking things sat on the table. Gigi, spruced up and quiet, with only a lopsided lip to mar her makeup, was fooling with her wide-band radio, trying to find the one station that played what she wanted to hear—not the agricultural news; country music or Bible stuff. Mavis, muttering cooking instructions to herself, was at the stove.

"Connie okay?" Mavis asked when she saw them enter.

"Sure. She was good for Pallas. Right, Pallas?"

"Yes. She's nice. I feel better now."

"Wow. It talks," said Gigi.

Pallas smiled.

"But is it going to puke some more? That's the question."

"Gigi. Shut the hell up." Mavis looked eagerly at Pallas. "You like crepes?"

"Um. Starved," Pallas answered.

"There's plenty. I put Connie's aside, and I can make even more if you want."

"It needs some clothes." Gigi was scanning Pallas closely. "Nothing I got will fit."

"Stop calling her 'it.' "

"All it's got worth having is a hat. Where'd you put it?"

"I've got jeans she can have," said Seneca.

Gigi snorted. "Make sure you wash them first."

"Sure."

"Sure? Why you say 'sure'? I haven't seen you wash one thing since you came here, including yourself."

"Cut it out, Gigi!" Mavis spoke from behind closed teeth.

"Well, I haven't!" Gigi leaned over the table toward Seneca. "We don't have much, but soap we do have."

"I said I'd wash them, didn't I?" Seneca wiped perspiration from under her chin.

"Why don't you roll up your sleeves? You look like a junkie," said Gigi.

"Look who's talking." Mavis chuckled.

"I'm talking junk, girl. Not a little boo."

Seneca looked at Gigi. "I don't put chemicals in my body."

"But you used to, didn't you?"

"No, I didn't used to."

"Let me see your arms, then."

"Get off!"

"Gigi!" Mavis shouted. Seneca looked hurt.

"Okay, okay," said Gigi.

"Why are you like that?" asked Seneca.

"I'm sorry. Okay?" It was a rare admission, but apparently sincere.

"I never took drugs. Never!"

"Said I was sorry. Christ, Seneca."

"She's a needler, Sen. Always sticking it in." Mavis cleaned her plate. "Don't let her get under your skin. That's where the blood is."

"Shut the fuck up!"

Mavis laughed. "There she goes again. So much for 'sorry.' "

"I apologized to Seneca, not you."

"Let's just drop it." Seneca sighed. "Is it okay to open the bottle, Mavis?"

"Not just okay; it's an order. We got to celebrate Pallas, don't we?"

"And her voice." Seneca smiled.

"And her appetite. *Look* at her."

Carlos had killed Pallas' appetite. While he loved her (or seemed to), food, other than that first chili dog, was a nuisance to her, an excuse to drink Cokes or a reason to go out. The pounds she had struggled with since elementary school melted away. Carlos had never commented on her weight, but the fact that from the first, when she was a butterball, he liked her anyway—chose her, made love to her— sealed her confidence in him. His betrayal when she was at her thinnest sharpened her shame. The nightmare event that forced her to hide in a lake had displaced for a while the betrayal, the hurt, that had driven her from her mother's house. She had not been able even to whisper it in the darkness of a candlelit room. Her voice had returned, but the words to say her shame clung like polyps in her throat.

The melted cheese covering the crepe-tortilla thing was tangy; the pieces of chicken had real flavor, like meat; the pale, almost white butter dripping from early corn was nothing like what she was accustomed to; it had a creamy, sweetish taste. There was a warm sugary sauce poured over the bread pudding. And glass after glass of wine. The fear, the bickering, the nausea, the awful dirt fight, the tears in the dark—all of the day's unruly drama dissipated in the pleasure of chewing food. When Mavis returned from taking Connie her supper, Gigi had found her station and was dancing the radio over to the open back door for better reception. She danced back to the table then and poured herself more wine. Eyes closed, hips grinding, she circled her arms to enclose the neck of a magic dancer. The other women watched her as they finished the meal. When last year's top tune, "Killing Me Softly," came on, it was not long before they all followed suit. Even Mavis. First apart, imagining partners. Then partnered, imagining each other.

Wine-soothed, they slept deep as death that night. Gigi and Seneca in one bedroom. Mavis alone in another. So it was Pallas, asleep on the sofa in the office/game room who heard the knocking.

The girl was wearing white silk shoes and a cotton sundress. She carried a piece of wedding cake on a brand-new china plate. And her smile was regal.

"I'm married now," she said. "Where is he? Or was it a she?"

Later that night, Mavis said, "We should have given her one of those dolls. Something."

"She's crazy," said Gigi. "I know everything about her. K.D. told me everything about her, and she's the whole nuthouse. Boy, is his ass in trouble."

"Why'd she come here on her wedding night?" asked Pallas.

"Long story." Mavis dabbed alcohol on her arm, comparing the bloody scratches to the ones Gigi had put there earlier. "Came here years back. Connie delivered her baby for her. She didn't want it, though."

"So where is it?"

"With Merle and Pearl, I think."

"Who?"

Gigi cut her eyes at Mavis. "It died."

"Doesn't she know that?" asked Seneca. "She said you all killed it."

"I told you she's the whole house of nuts."

"She left right after," Mavis said. "I don't know what she knows. She wouldn't even look at it."

They paused then, seeing it: the turned-away face, hands covering ears so as not to hear that fresh but mournful cry. There would be no nipple, then. Nothing to put in the little mouth. No mother shoulder to snuggle against. None of them wanted to remember or know what had taken place afterward.

"Maybe it wasn't his. K.D.'s," said Gigi. "Maybe she was cutting out on him."

"So? So what if it wasn't his? It was *hers*." Seneca sounded hurt.

"I don't understand." Pallas moved toward the stove, where the leftover bread pudding sat.

"I do. In a way." Mavis sighed. "I'll make us some coffee."

"Not for me. I'm going back to bed." Gigi yawned.

"She was really mad. You think she'll get back all right?"

"Saint Seneca. Please."

"She was screaming," Seneca said, staring at Gigi.

"So were we." Mavis measured coffee into the percolator basket.

"Yeah, but we didn't call her names."

Gigi sucked her teeth. "How do you know what to call a psycho who's got nothing better to do on her wedding night but hunt down a dead baby?"

"Call her sorry?"

"Sorry, my ass," Gigi answered. "She just wants to hang on to that little dick she married."

"Didn't you say you were going to bed?"

"I am. Come on, Seneca."

Seneca ignored her roommate. "Should we tell Connie?"

"What for?" snapped Mavis. "Look. I don't want that girl anywhere near Connie."

"I think she bit me." Pallas appeared surprised. "Look. Is that teeth marks?"

"What do you want, a rabies shot?" Gigi yawned. "Come on, Sen. Hey, Pallas. Lighten up."

Pallas stared. "I don't want to sleep down here by myself."

"Who said you had to? That was your idea."

"Ther're no more beds upstairs."

"Oh, Christ." Gigi started toward the hall, Seneca following. "What a baby."

"I told you. The others are stored in the cellar. I'll put one up tomorrow. You can sleep with me tonight," said Mavis. "Don't worry. She won't be back." She locked the back door then stood watching the coffee percolate. "By the way, what's your name? Last name, I mean."

"Truelove."

"No kidding. And your mother named you Pallas?"

"No. My father."

"What's her name? Your mother."

"Dee Dee. Short for Divine."

"Oooo. I love it. Gigi! Gigi! You hear that? Her name's Divine. Divine Truelove."

Gigi ran back to stick her head in the doorway. Seneca too.

"It is not! That's my mother's name."

"She a stripper?" Gigi was grinning.

"An artist."

"They all are, honey."

"Don't tease her," murmured Seneca. "She's had a long day."

"Okay, okay, okay. Good night . . . Divine." Gigi vanished back through the door.

"Don't pay her any attention," Seneca said, then, whispering quickly as she left, "She has a small mind."

Mavis, still smiling, poured coffee and cut bread pudding. She served Pallas and sat down next to her, blowing into the coffee steam. Pallas picked at a third helping of dessert.

"Show me the tooth marks," said Mavis.

Pallas turned her head and pulled at the neck of her T-shirt, exposing her shoulder.

"Oooo," Mavis groaned.

"Is every day like this here?" Pallas asked her.

"Oh, no." Mavis stroked the wounded skin. "This is the most peaceful place on earth."

"You'll take me to call my father tomorrow?"

"Yep. First thing." Mavis stopped her stroking. "I love your hair."

They finished the nighttime snack in silence. Mavis picked up the lamp, and they abandoned the kitchen to darkness. When they were in front of Mavis' bedroom door she didn't open it. She froze.

"Hear that? They're happy," she said, covering her laughing lips. "I knew it. They love that baby. Absolutely love it." She turned to Pallas. "They like you too. They think you're divine."

PATRICIA

Bells and pine trees, cut from green and red construction paper, were piled neatly on the dining room table. All done. Just the glitter was left for the trim. Last year she had made a mistake letting the smaller ones do it. After cleaning their fingers and elbows of glue, after picking specks of silver from their hair and cheeks, she had to do most of the decorations over anyway. This time she would hand out the bells and trees while monitoring each dot of glue herself. In staging the school's Christmas play the whole town helped or meddled: older men repaired the platform, assembled the crib; young ones fashioned new innkeepers and freshened the masks with paint. Women made doll babies, and children drew colored pictures of Christmas dinner food, mostly desserts—cakes, pies, candy canes, fruit—because roast turkeys were too much of a challenge for small fingers. When the little ones had silvered the bells and pine trees, Patricia herself would thread loops at their tops. The Eastern star was Harper's department. He checked it for repair each year making sure its points were sharp and that it would glow properly in the dark cloth sky. And she supposed old Nathan DuPres would deliver the opening remarks once again. A sweet man, but couldn't stay the point to save him. The church programs were more formal—sermons, choirs, recitations by the children and prizes for the ones who managed to get through them without stuttering, crying or freezing up—but the school program, featuring the Nativity and involving the whole town, was older, having started before the churches were even built.

Unlike recent years, the December days of 1974 were warm and windy. The sky was behaving like a showgirl: exchanging its pale, melancholy mornings for sporty ribbons of color in the evening. A mineral scent was in the air, sweeping down from some Genesis time when volcanoes stirred and lava cooled quickly under relentless wind. Wind that scoured cold stone, then sculpted it and, finally, crumbled it to the bits rock hounds loved. The same wind that once lifted streams of Cheyenne/Arapaho hair also parted clumps of it from the shoulders of bison, telling each when the other was near.

She had noticed the mineral smell all day and now, finished with grading papers and making decorations, she checked the showgirl sky for a repeat performance. But it was over. Just some lilac shapes running after a Day-Glo sun.

Her father had gone to bed early, exhausted from the monologue he had delivered at the supper table about the gas station he was planning. Eagle Oil was encouraging him—no use to talk to the big oil companies. Deek and Steward were interested in approving the loan, provided he could persuade somebody to sell him the property. So the question was where. Across from Anna's store? Good spot, but Holy Redeemer might not think so. North, then? Next to Sargeant's Feed and Seed? There would be plenty of customers—nobody would have to travel ninety miles for gasoline or keep tanks of it where they lived. The roads? Something might be done to the two dirt ones that extended south and north of Ruby's paved road to meet the county route. If he secured the franchise, the county might tarmac them both. It would be a problem, though, trying to get local people to agree to petition for it—the old ones would put up a fight. They liked being off the county road, accessible only to the lost and the knowledgeable. "But think on it, Patsy, just think on it. I could fix cars, engines; sell tires, batteries, fan belts. Soda pop too. Something Anna don't stock. No point in getting her riled up."

Patricia nodded. A very good idea, she thought, like all of his ideas. His veterinary practice (illegal—he had no license—but who knew or cared enough to drive a hundred miles to help Wisdom Poole yank on a foal stuck in its mother?); his butcher business (bring him the slaughtered steer—he'd skin, butcher, carve and refrigerate it for you); and of course the ambulance/mortuary business. Because he had wanted to be, studied to be, a doctor, most of his enterprises had to do with operating on the sick or dead. The gas station idea was the first nonsurgical proposal she could remember (though his eyes did fire when he spoke of taking apart engines). She wished he had been a doctor, had been accepted in a medical school. Chances are her mother would be alive today. Maybe not. Maybe he would have been away at Meharry instead of the mortuary school when Delia died.

Pat climbed the stairs to her bedroom and decided to while away the rest of the evening on her history project, or rather what used to be a history project but was nothing of the sort now. It began as a gift to the citizens of Ruby—a collection of family trees; the genealogies of each of the fifteen families. Upside-down trees, the trunks sticking in the air, the branches sloping down. When the trees were completed, she had begun to supplement the branches of who begat whom with notes: what work they did, for example, where they lived, to what church they belonged. Some of the nicer touches ("Was Missy Rivers, wife of Thomas Blackhorse, born near the Mississippi River? Her name seems to suggest . . .") she had gleaned from her students' autobiographical compositions. Not anymore. Parents complained about their children being asked to gossip, to divulge what could be private information, secrets, even. After that, most of her notes came from talking to people, asking to see Bibles and examining church records. Things got out of hand when she asked to see letters and marriage certificates. The women narrowed their eyes before smiling and offering to freshen her coffee. Invisible doors closed, and the conversation turned to weather. But she didn't want or need any further research. The trees still required occasional alterations—births, marriages, deaths—but her interest in the supplementary notes increased as the notes did, and she gave up all pretense to objective comment. The project became unfit for any eyes except her own. It had reached the point where the small *m* period was a joke, a dream, a violation of law that had her biting her thumbnail in frustration. Who were these women who, like her mother, had only one name? Celeste, Olive, Sorrow, Ivlin, Pansy. Who were these women with generalized last names? Brown, Smith, Rivers, Stone, Jones. Women whose identity rested on the men they married—if marriage applied: a Morgan, a Flood, a

Blackhorse, a Poole, a Fleetwood. Dovey had let her have the Morgan Bible for weeks, but it was the twenty minutes she spent looking at the Blackhorse Bible that convinced her that a new species of tree would be needed to go further, to record accurately the relationships among the fifteen families of Ruby, their ancestors in Haven and, further back, in Mississippi and Louisiana. A voluntary act to fill empty hours had become intensive labor streaked with the bad feelings that ride the skin like pollen when too much about one's neighbors is known. The town's official story, elaborated from pulpits, in Sunday school classes and ceremonial speeches, had a sturdy public life. Any footnotes, crevices or questions to be put took keen imagination and the persistence of a mind uncomfortable with oral histories. Pat had wanted proof in documents where possible to match the stories, and where proof was not available she interpreted—freely but, she thought, insightfully because she alone had the required emotional distance. She alone would figure out why a line was drawn through Ethan Blackhorse's name in the Blackhorse Bible and what the heavy ink blot hid next to Zechariah's name in the Morgan Bible. Her father told her some things, but he refused to talk about other things. Girlfriends like Kate and Anna were open, but older women—Dovey, Soane and Lone DuPres—hinted the most while saying the least. "Oh, I think those brothers had a disagreement of some kind." That's all Soane would say about the crossed-out name of her great-uncle. And not another word.

There were nine large intact families who made the original journey, who were thrown out and cast away in Fairly, Oklahoma, and went on to found Haven. Their names were legend: Blackhorse, Morgan, Poole, Fleetwood, Beauchamp, Cato, Flood and both DuPres families. With their siblings, wives and children, they were seventy-nine or eighty-one in all (depending on whether the two stolen children were counted). Along with them came fragments of other families: a sister and a brother, four cousins, a river of aunts and great-aunts shepherding the children of their dead sisters, brothers, nieces, nephews. Stories about these fragments, which made up some fifty more, surfaced in the writing compositions of Pat's students, the gossip and recollections at picnics, church dinners and woman talk over chores and hair preparation. Grandmothers sitting on the floor while a granddaughter scratched their scalps liked to reminisce aloud. Then bits of tales emerged like sparks lighting the absences that hovered over their childhoods and the shadows that dimmed their maturity. Anecdotes marked the spaces that had sat with them at the camp-fire. Jokes limned the mementos—a ring, a pocket watch—they had clamped in their fists while they slept and the descriptions of the clothes they had worn: too big shoes that belonged to a brother; the shawl of a great-aunt; the lace-trimmed bonnet of a younger sister. They talked about the orphans, males and females aged twelve to six-teen, who spotted the travelers and asked to join, and the two toddlers they simply snatched up because the circumstances in which the chil-dren were found wouldn't let them do otherwise. Another eight. So about one hundred and fifty-eight total completed the journey.

When they got to the outskirts of Fairly, it was agreed that Drum Blackhorse, Rector Morgan and his brothers, Pryor and Shepherd, would announce themselves, while the others waited with Zechariah, who was too lame by then to stand unaided and straight in front of unknown men whose respect he would have demanded and whose pity would have broken him in two. His foot was shot through—by whom or why nobody knew or admitted, for the point of the story seemed to be that when the bullet entered he neither cried out nor limped away. It was that wound that forced him to stay behind and let his friend and his sons speak in his stead. It proved, however, to be a blessing because he missed witnessing the actual Disallowing; and missed hearing disbelievable words formed in the mouths of men to other men, men like them in all ways but one. Afterwards the people were no longer nine families and some more. They became a tight band of wayfarers bound by the enormity of what had happened to them. Their horror of whites was convulsive but abstract. They saved the clarity of their hatred for the men who had insulted them in ways too confounding for language: first by excluding them, then by offer-ing them staples to exist in that very exclusion. Everything anybody wanted to know about the citizens of Haven or Ruby lay in the ramifi-cations of that one rebuff out of many. But the ramifications of those ramifications were another story.

Pat went to the window and raised it. Her mother's grave lay at the edge of the yard. The wind soughed as though trying to dislodge sequins from the black crepe sky. Lilac bushes swished the side of the house. The mineral trace was overcome by the smell of supper food in the air. Pat closed the window, returned to her desk to prepare for another entry in her log.

Arnette and K.D., married last April, were expecting a child next March. Or so said Lone DuPres, who ought to know. Lone was one of the stolen babies. Fairy DuPres had noticed her sitting quiet as a rock outside the door of a sod house. The sight of the silent child in a filthy shift could have remained just one more lonely picture they came across, except that the desolation about the place was unforgiving. Fairy was fifteen then and bullheaded. She and Missy Rivers went to investigate. Inside was the dead mother and not a piece of bread in sight. Missy groaned before she spit. Fairy said, "God damn it. 'Scuse me, Lord," and picked the baby up. When they told the others what they'd found, seven men reached for their shovels: Drum Blackhorse, his sons Thomas and Peter, Rector Morgan, Able Flood, Brood Poole, Sr., and Nathan DuPres' father, Juvenal. While they dug, Fairy fed the baby water-soaked meal cake. Praise Compton tore her underskirt to wrap around it. Fulton Best fashioned a sturdy cross. Zechariah, flanked by two of his boys, Shepherd and Pryor, and resting his ruined foot on its heel, delivered a burial prayer. His daughters Loving, Ella and Selanie gathered pink yarrow for the grave. There was a serious discussion about what to do with the child—where to place her— because the men seemed adamant about not adding a half-starved baby to their own quarter-starved ones. Fairy put up such a fight she wore them down and then argued with Bitty Cato over the name. Fairy won that, too, and named the baby Lone because that's how they found her. And Lone she still was for she never married, and when Fairy, who raised her and taught her everything she came to know about midwifery, died, Lone slipped right in and took over the birthing for everybody except now Arnette was insisting on going to the hospital in Demby to give birth. It cut Lone to the quick (she still believed that decent women had their babies at home and saloon women de-livered in hospitals), but she knew the Fleetwoods hadn't given up on thinking she was partly responsible for Sweetie and Jeff's children, in spite of the fact that she had delivered thirty-two healthy babies to doing-just-fine mothers since the last broken Fleetwood baby was delivered. So she said nothing except that Arnette's time would be March of '75.

Pat located the Morgan file and went to the limb that, so far, contained one line:

Coffee Smith (aka K.D. [as in Kentucky Derby]) m. Arnette Fleetwood

She wondered again who was that boy Ruby Morgan married? An army buddy of her brothers, it was said. But from where? His first name, Coffee, was the same as Zechariah's before he changed it to run for lieutenant governor; his last name was as generic as you could get. He was killed in Europe, so nobody got to know him well, not even his wife. You could tell from his photograph there wasn't a brush of Private Smith in his son. K.D. was a mirror of Blackhorse and Morgan blood.

There wasn't much space beneath the K.D.–Arnette entry, but she thought they probably wouldn't need more. If it lived, the baby they were expecting would certainly be an only child. Arnette's mother had only two children, one of whom had fathered only defectives. In addition, these later Morgans were not as prolific as the earlier ones. They were not like

Zechariah Morgan (aka Big Papa, né Coffee) m. Mindy Flood [nota bene: Anna Flood's great-aunt]

who had nine of fourteen children survive. Pat ran her finger over their names: Pryor Morgan, Rector Morgan, Shepherd Morgan, Ella Morgan, Loving Morgan, Selanie Morgan, Governor Morgan, Queen Morgan and Scout Morgan. Scooting up the margin in Skrip black ink, one of her earlier notes read: "It took seven births for them to get around to giving a female child an administrative, authoritative-sounding name, and I bet they called her 'Queenie.' " Another comment, threaded out from Zechariah's name and led by arrows, spread to the back of the page: "He renamed himself. Coffee was his birth name—a misspelling of Kofi, probably. And since no Louisiana Morgans or any of the Haven people had worked for any whites named Morgan, he must have chosen his last name as well as his first from something or someplace he liked. Zacharias, father of John the Baptist? or the Zechariah who had visions? The one who saw scrolls of curses and women in baskets; the one who saw Joshua's filthy clothes changed into rich ones; who saw the result of disobedience. The punishment for not showing mercy or compassion was a scattering among all nations, and pleasant land made desolate. All of that would fit nicely for Zechariah Morgan: the curse, the women stuffed into a basket with a lid of lead and hidden away in a house, but especially the scattering. The scattering would have frightened him. The breakup of the group or tribe or consortium of families or, in Coffee's case, the splitting up of a contingent of families who had lived with or near each other since before Bunker Hill. He would not have had trouble imagining the scariness of having everybody he knew thrown apart, thrown into different places in a foreign land and becoming alien to each other. He would have been frightened of not knowing a jawline that signified one family, a cast of eye or a walk that identified another. Of not being able to see yourself re-formed in a third- or fourth-generation grandchild. Of not knowing where the generations before him were buried or how to get in touch with them if you didn't know. That would be the Zechariah Coffee would have chosen for himself. That would have appealed to him if he had heard some mighty preacher tell the story of Joshua crowned. He would not name himself after Joshua, the king, but after the witness to whom God and angels spoke on a regular basis about things Coffee knew something about."

When she asked Steward where his grandfather got his last name, he'd grunted and said he thought it was Moyne originally, not Morgan. Or Le Moyne or something, but, "Some folks called him Black Coffee. We called him Big Papa. Called my daddy Big Daddy," as though that ended it. Insulted like, because he himself wasn't a papa or a daddy, big or otherwise. Because the Morgan line was crop feeble. One of Zechariah's (Big Papa's) sons, Rector, had seven children with his wife, Beck, but only four survived: Elder, the twins Deacon and

Steward, and K.D.'s mother, Ruby. Elder died leaving his wife, Susannah (Smith) Morgan, with six children—all of whom moved from Haven to northern states. Zechariah would have hated that. Moving would have been "scattering" to him. And he was right, for sure enough, from then on the fertility shriveled, even while the bounty multiplied. The more money, the fewer children; the fewer children, the more money to give the fewer children. Assuming you amassed enough of it, which was why the richest ones—Deek and Steward— were so keen on the issue of K.D.'s marriage. Or so Pat supposed.

All of them, however, each and every one of the intact nine families, had the little mark she had chosen to put after their names: 8-R. An abbreviation for eight-rock, a deep deep level in the coal mines. Blue-black people, tall and graceful, whose clear, wide eyes gave no sign of what they really felt about those who weren't 8-rock like them. Descendants of those who had been in Louisiana Territory when it was French, when it was Spanish, when it was French again, when it was sold to Jefferson and when it became a state in 1812. Who spoke a patois part Spanish, part French, part English, and all their own. Descendants of those who, after the Civil War, had defied or hidden from whites doing all they could to force them to stay and work as sharecroppers in Louisiana. Descendants of those whose worthiness was so endemic it got three of their children elected to rule in state legislatures and county offices: who, when thrown out of office without ceremony or proof of wrongdoing, refused to believe what they guessed was the real reason that made it impossible for them to find other mental labor. Almost all of the Negro men chased or invited out of office (in Mississippi, in Louisiana, in Georgia) got less influential but still white-collar work following the purges of 1875. One from South Carolina ended his days as a street sweeper. But they alone (Zechariah Morgan and Juvenal DuPres in Louisiana, Drum Blackhorse in Mississippi) were reduced to penury and/or field labor. Fifteen years of begging for sweatwork in cotton, lumber or rice after five glorious years remaking a country. They must have suspected yet dared not say that their misfortune's misfortune was due to the one and only feature that distinguished them from their Negro peers. Eight-rock. In 1890 they had been in the country for one hundred and twenty years.

So they took that history, those years, each other and their uncorruptible worthiness and walked to the "Run." Walked from Mississippi and Louisiana to Oklahoma and got to the place described in advertisements carefully folded into their shoes or creased into the brims of their hats only to be shooed away. This time the clarity was clear: for ten generations they had believed the division they fought to close was free against slave and rich against poor. Usually, but not always, white against black. Now they saw a new separation: light-skinned against black. Oh, they knew there was a difference in the minds of whites, but it had not struck them before that it was of consequence, serious consequence, to Negroes themselves. Serious enough that their daughters would be shunned as brides; their sons chosen last; that colored men would be embarrassed to be seen socially with their sisters. The sign of racial purity they had taken for granted had become a stain. The scattering that alarmed Zechariah because he believed it would deplete them was now an even more dangerous level of evil, for if they broke apart and were disvalued by the impure, then, certain as death, those ten generations would disturb their children's peace throughout eternity.

Pat was convinced that when the subsequent generations of 8-rock males did scatter, just as Zechariah feared, into the army, it could have been over and done with. Should have been over and done with. The rejection, which they called the Disallowing, was a burn whose scar tissue was numb by 1949, wasn't it? Oh, no. Those that survived that particular war came right back home, saw what had become of Haven, heard about the missing testicles of other colored soldiers; about medals being torn off by gangs of rednecks and Sons of the Confederacy—and recognized the Disallowing, Part Two. It would have been like watching a parade banner that said WAR-WEARY SOLDIERS! NOT WELCOME HOME! So they did it again. And just as the original wayfarers never sought another colored townsite after being cold-shouldered at the first, this generation joined no organization, fought no civil battle. They consolidated the 8-rock blood and, haughty as ever, moved farther west. The New Fathers: Deacon Morgan, Steward Morgan, William Cato, Ace Flood, Aaron Poole, Nathan DuPres, Moss DuPres, Arnold Fleetwood, Ossie Beauchamp, Harper

Jury, Sargeant Person, John Seawright, Edward Sands and Pat's father, Roger Best, who was the first to violate the blood rule. The one nobody admitted existed. The one established when the Mississippi flock noticed and remembered that the Disallowing came from fair-skinned colored men. Blue-eyed, gray-eyed yellowmen in good suits. They were kind, though, as the story went. Gave them food and blankets; took up a collection for them; but were unmoving in their refusal to let the 8-rocks stay longer than a night's rest. The story went that Zechariah Morgan and Drum Blackhorse forbade the women to eat the food. That Jupe Cato left the blankets in the tent, with the collected offering of three dollars and nine cents neatly stacked on top. But Soane said her grandmother, Celeste Blackhorse, sneaked back and got the food (but not the money), secretly passing it to her sister Sally Blackhorse, to Bitty Cato and Praise Compton, to distribute to the children.

So the rule was set and lived a quietly throbbing life because it was never spoken of, except for the hint in words Zechariah forged for the Oven. More than a rule. A conundrum: "Beware the Furrow of His Brow," in which the "You" (understood), vocative case, was not a command to the believers but a threat to those who had disallowed them. It must have taken him months to think up those words—just so—to have multiple meanings: to appear stern, urging obedience to God, but slyly not identifying the understood proper noun or specifying what the Furrow might cause to happen or to whom. So the teenagers Misner organized who wanted to change it to "Be the Furrow of His Brow" were more insightful than they knew. Look what they did to Menus, forcing him to give back or return the woman he brought home to marry. The pretty sandy-haired girl from Virginia. Menus lost (or was forced to give up) the house he'd bought for her and hadn't been sober since. And though they attributed his weekend drunks to his Vietnam memories, and although they laughed with him as he clipped their hair, Pat knew love in its desperate state when she saw it. She believed she had seen it in Menus' eyes as well as in her father's, poorly veiled by his business ventures.

Before she put away the K.D. pages, Pat scribbled in the margin: "Somebody beat up Arnette. The Convent women, as folks say? Or, quiet as it's kept, K.D.?" Then she picked up the file for Best, Roger. On the back of the title page, labeled:

Roger Best m. Delia

she wrote: "Daddy, they don't hate us because Mama was your first customer. They hate us because she looked like a cracker and was bound to have cracker-looking children like me, and although I married Billy Cato, who was an 8-rock like you, like them, I passed the skin on to my daughter, as you and everybody knew I would. Notice how a lot of those Sands who married Seawrights are careful to make sure that their children marry into other 8-rock families. We were the first visible glitch, but there was an invisible one that had nothing to do with skin color. I know all of the couples wanted preacher-attended marriages, and many had them. But there were many others that practiced what Fairy DuPres called 'takeovers.' A young widow might take over a single man's house. A widower might ask a friend or a distant relative if he could take over a young girl who had no prospects. Like Billy's family. His mother, Fawn, born a Blackhorse, was taken over by his grandmother's uncle, August Cato. Or, to put it another way, Billy's mother was wife to her own great-uncle. Or another way: my husband's father, August Cato, is also his grandmother's (Bitty Cato Blackhorse's) uncle and therefore Billy's great-granduncle as well. (Bitty Cato's father, Sterl Cato, took over a woman named Honesty Jones. It must have been she who insisted on naming her daughter Friendship, and she was probably riled at hearing the child called Bitty for the rest of her life.) Since Bitty Cato married Peter Blackhorse, and since her daughter, Fawn Blackhorse, was wife to Bitty's uncle, and since Peter Blackhorse is Billy Cato's grandfather—well, you can see the problem with blood rules. It's distant, I know, and August Cato was an old man when he took over little Fawn Blackhorse. And he never would have done it without Blackhorse permission. And he never would have received permission if he had a loose reputation because coupling outside marriage or takeovers was not only frowned upon, it could get you ostracized so completely it behooved the fornicators to pack up and leave. As may have been the case (it would explain the line through his name) with Ethan Blackhorse—Drum's youngest brother—and a woman named Solace, and certainly was believed to be the case with Martha Stone, Menus' mother (although Harper Jury couldn't settle on whom he thought his wife betrayed him with). So August Cato shunned temptation or any thought of looking outside the families and asked Thomas and Peter Blackhorse for Peter's daughter, Fawn. And maybe his advanced age was why she had just the one child, my husband, Billy. Still, the Blackhorse blood is there, and that makes my daughter, Billie Delia, a fifth? cousin to Soane and Dovey, because Peter Blackhorse was brother to Thomas Blackhorse and Sally Blackhorse, and Thomas Blackhorse was Soane's and Dovey's father. Now, Sally Blackhorse married Aaron Poole and had thirteen children. One of whom Aaron was going to name Deep, but Sally pitched a fit, so Aaron, with a humor more grim than anybody would have thought, named him Deeper. But two others of those thirteen children Billie Delia is in love with, and there is something wrong with that but other than number and the blood rules I can't figure out what."

Pat underscored the last five words then wrote down her mother's name, drew a line under it, enclosed it in a heart and continued:

"The women really tried, Mama. They really did. Kate's mother, Catherine Jury, you remember her, and Fairy DuPres (she's dead now), along with Lone and Dovey Morgan and Charity Flood. But none of them could drive then. You must have believed that deep down they hated you, but not all of them, maybe none of them, because they begged the men to go to the Convent to get help. I heard them. Dovey Morgan was crying as she left to find somebody, going from house to house: to Harper Jury, Catherine's own husband, to Charity's husband, Ace Flood, and to Sargeant Person's (how come that ignorant Negro doesn't know his name is Pierson?). All of the excuses were valid, reasonable. Even with their wives begging they came up with excuses because they looked down on you, Mama, I know it, and despised Daddy for marrying a wife with no last name, a wife without people, a wife of sunlight skin, a wife of racial tampering. Both midwives were in trouble (it was coming too soon, legs folded underneath) and all they wanted was to get one of the nuns at the Convent. Miss Fairy said one of them used to work in a hospital. Catherine

Jury went to Soane's to see if Deek was there. He wasn't, but Dovey was. It was Dovey who went to Seawright's, then Fleetwood's. Went to every house in walking distance. The Moss DuPreses lived way way out. So did Nathan (who would have hitched Hard Goods and galloped to Jesus for help). So did Steward, the Pooles, the Sands and the rest. Finally they got Senior Pulliam to agree. But by the time he got his shoes tied it was too late. Miss Fairy rushed from your bedside to Pulliam's house and hollered through his door—too exhausted to knock, too angry to step inside—and said, 'You can take your shoes back off, Senior! Might as well get your preacher clothes ready so you'll be in time for the funeral!' Then she was gone from there.

"When Daddy got back everybody was worried sick about what to do and how long the bodies could last before, father or no father, husband or no husband, you both had to go in the ground. But Daddy came back the second day. No time for a decent wake. So you were his first job. And a wonderful job he did too. You were beautiful. With the baby in the crook of your arm. You would have been so proud of him.

"He doesn't blame anybody except himself for being at mortuary graduation. We have quarreled about it and he doesn't agree with me that those 8-rock men didn't want to go and bring a white into town; or else didn't want to drive out to a white's house begging for help; or else they just despised your pale skin so much they thought of reasons why they could not go. Daddy says more than one woman has died in childbirth and I say, who? So the mother without one died and the baby whom you planned to name Faustine, if a girl, or Richard, after Daddy's oldest brother, if a boy, died too. It was a girl, Mama. Faustine. My baby sister. We would have grown up together. Patricia and Faustine. Too light, maybe, but together it would not have mattered to us. We'd be a team. I have no aunts or uncles, remember, because all of Daddy's sisters and brothers died of what they called walking pneumonia but what must have been the 1919 influenza epidemic. So I married Billy Cato partly because he was beautiful, partly because he made me laugh, and partly (mostly?) because he had the midnight skin of the Catos and the Blackhorses, along with that Blackhorse feature of stick-straight hair. Like Soane's and Dovey's hair, and like

Easter and Scout had. But he died, Billy did, and I took my lightish but not whiteish baby and moved back in your pretty little house with the mortuary and your headstone in back and have been drylongso teaching the children who call me Miss Best using Daddy's last name as everybody else does, so short was the time I was Pat Cato."

The words had long ago covered the back of the page, so she was using fresh sheets to continue:

"I may as well tell you that except for you and K.D.'s mother, nobody in Ruby has ever died. Please note I said *in* Ruby and they are real proud about that believing they are blessed and all because after 1953 anybody who died did it in Europe or Korea or someplace outside this town. Even Sweetie's children are still alive and God knows there is no reason they should be. Well, crazy as it sounds, I believe the claim of immortality is this town's rebuke against Daddy's mortuary business, since he has to wait for our killed-in-actions or somebody out at the Convent or an accident someplace else, otherwise his ambulance is never a hearse. (When Billy died there was nothing left to bury except some "effects," including a gold ring too twisted to poke a finger through.) They think Daddy deserves rebuke because he broke the blood rule first, and I wouldn't put it past them to refuse to die just to keep Daddy from success. As it turned out, war dead and accidents in other towns (Miss Fairy died on a trip back to Haven; Ace Flood died in the Demby hospital but was buried in Haven) were all the work Daddy has had and it is hardly enough. Neither is the ambulance business, so I work hard to convince him that the money the town pays me for teaching is just household money and he doesn't have to borrow anymore on his shares in Deek's bank and should forget gasoline stations and what all."

Leaning back in the chair, Pat folded her hands behind her head, wondering what was going to happen when more people got as old as Nathan or Lone. Then would her father's craft be required or would they do what they did on the way out of Louisiana? Bury them where they fell. Or were they right? Was death blocked from entering Ruby? Patricia was tired now and ready for sleep, but she couldn't let Delia go just yet.

"That was some ride, Mama, from Haven to here. You and me, Mama, among those skinny blue-black giants, neither they nor their wives staring at your long brown hair, your honey-speckled eyes. Did Daddy tell you, Don't worry your head; it was going to be all right? Remember how they needed you, used you to go into a store to get supplies or a can of milk while they parked around the corner? That was the only thing your skin was good for. Otherwise it bothered them. Reminded them of why Haven existed, of why a new town had to take its place. The one-drop law the whites made up was hard to live by if nobody could tell it was there. When we drove through a town, or when a sheriff's car was near, Daddy told us to get down, to lie on the floor of the car, because it would have been no use telling a stranger that you were colored and worse to say you were his wife. Did Soane or Dovey, new brides too, talk woman-talk with you? You thought you were pregnant again and so did they. So did you talk together about how you all felt? Make tea for hemorrhoids, give one another salt to lick or copper dirt to eat in secret? I craved baking soda when I carried Billie Delia. Did you when you carried me? Did the older women with children too advise you, like Aaron's wife, Sally, with four children already? What about Alice Pulliam—her husband wasn't a reverend yet but he had already heard the Call and decided to become one so they must have had some charitable, some godly feelings then when they were young. Did they make you welcome right away, or did they all wait for the Oven to be reassembled or, the following year, when the stream came back, baptize you just so they could speak to you directly, look you in the eyes?

"What did Daddy say to you at that AME Zion picnic? The one held for colored soldiers stationed at the base in Tennessee. How could either of you tell what the other was saying? He talking Louisiana, you speaking Tennessee. The music so different, the sound coming from a different part of the body. It must have been like hearing lyrics set to scores by two different composers. But when you made love he must have said I love you and you understood that and it was true, too, because I have seen the desperation in his eyes ever since—no matter what business venture he thinks up."

Patricia

Pat stopped and rubbed the callus on her middle finger. Her elbow and shoulder ached from gripping the pen so hard. Across the hall, through the bedroom door, she could hear her father snoring. As always she wished him pleasant dreams—something to assuage the unhappiness of his days, days spent trying to please, to make up for. Except for marrying her mother, she couldn't think what rule he had broken that made him so eager for the approval of those who disrespected him. He had described to her once what Haven looked like when he got out of the army. He said he sat on his father's porch coughing, so nobody would know he was weeping for us. His father, Fulton Best, and his mother, Olive, were inside, reading with great sorrow the applications he had filled out for the G.I. Bill funding. He wanted a college education so he could go to medical school, but he was also their only surviving child, all the others having died in the flu epidemic. His parents could not bear the thought of either his leaving again or his staying in a town slipping into erasure forever in every place except the heart. He was looking up and down the cracked concrete of Main Street when Ace Flood and Harper Jury walked up to him, saying there was a plan. Deek and Steward Morgan had a plan. When he heard what it was, the first thing he did was write to the hazel-eyed girl with light-brown hair who'd had his child during the war. Good thing he didn't tell them about us. They would have dissuaded him from marriage the way, later on, they did Menus. Maybe he knew they would, which is why he just sent for us. "Darling Delia, Come on. Right now. Here is the money order. I am going to have a lot of trouble keeping my heart quiet. Until you all get here I will be a crazy man. . . ." Their jaws must have dropped when we arrived, but other than Steward, nobody said anything directly. They didn't have to. Olive took to her bed. Fulton kept grunting and rubbing his knees. Only Steward had the gall to say out loud, "He's bringing along the dung we leaving behind." Dovey shushed him. Soane too. But Fairy DuPres cursed him, saying, "God don't love ugly ways. Watch out He don't deny you what you love too." A remark Dovey must have thought about a lot until 1964, when the curse was completed. But they were just women, and what they said was easily ignored by good brave men on their way to Paradise. They got there, too, and eventually had the satisfaction of seeing the dung buried. Most of it anyway. Some of it is still aboveground, instructing their grandchildren in a level of intelligence their elders will never acquire.

Pat sucked her teeth and pushed aside the Best file. She selected a composition notebook and without label or introduction continued to write.

"She won't listen to me. Not one word. She works in Demby at a clinic—cleaning up, I think, but she makes out like she's a nurse's aide because of the uniform she has to wear. I don't know how she lives. I mean she has a room, she says, in the house of a nice family. I don't believe it. Not all of it anyway. One of those Poole boys—both of them, probably—is visiting her. I know because the littlest one, Dina, told the class about her big brother showing her a house with a Santa Claus and Christmas lights all over the porch. Well, that was someplace other than Ruby, for sure. She is lying and I would rather be bit by the serpent himself than have a lying child. I didn't mean to hit her so hard. I didn't know I had. I just meant to stop her lying mouth telling me she didn't do anything. I saw them. All three of them back behind the Oven and she was in the middle. Plus I am the one who washes sheets around here."

Pat stopped, put down her pen and, covering her eyes with her hand, tried to separate what she had seen from what she feared to see. And what did the sheets have to do with it? Was there blood where there should not have been or no blood where there should have been? It was more than a year ago, and she thought everything was seared in her memory. The fight took place in October of 1973. Afterwards Billie Delia ran off and stayed at the Convent for two weeks and one day. She came back during the morning session, while Pat was teaching the under twelves, and stayed long enough to say she wasn't going to. They'd had ugly, hateful words, but both were afraid to get near the other lest the quarrel get physical as it had before. She left with one of those Poole boys and didn't come back till early this year to describe her job and write down her address. Since then Pat had seen her twice: once in March and then at Arnette's wedding, where she was bridesmaid and maid of honor both, since Arnette would not have anybody else, and no other girl wanted the honor anyway if it meant walking down the aisle with Billie Delia. Or so Pat thought. She had gone to the wedding, not the reception, but she hadn't missed a thing since she had a perfect view of the goings-on at the Oven with those girls from the Convent. She saw them. She saw those Poole boys. And she saw Billie Delia sit down and talk to one of the girls like they were old friends. She saw Reverend Pulliam and Steward Morgan argue with the girls, and when they drove off she saw Billie Delia throw her bouquet in Anna's trash can before she strolled off, Apollo and Brood Poole in tow.

Billie Delia left the next day in her very own car and never said a word to her about the wedding, the reception, the Convent girl or anything. Pat tried to remember how that pressing iron got into her hand, what had been said that had her running up the stairs with a 1950s GE electric iron called Royal Ease clutched in her fingers to slam against her daughter's head. She, the gentlest of souls, missed killing her own daughter by inches. She who loved children and protected them not only from each other but from too stern parents lunged after her own daughter. She who had trained herself to reasoning and soft manners and discretion and dignity, falling down the stairs and bruising herself so badly she had to cancel two days of class. Educated but self-taught also to make sure that everybody knew that the bastard-born daughter of the woman with sunlight skin and no last name was not only lovely but of great worth and inestimable value. Trying to understand how she could have picked up that pressing iron, Pat realized that ever since Billie Delia was an infant, she thought of her as a liability somehow. Vulnerable to the possibility of not being quite as much of a lady as Patricia Cato would like. Was it that business of pulling down her panties in the street? Billie Delia was only three then. Pat knew that had her daughter been an 8-rock, they would not have held it against her. They would have seen it for what it was—only an innocent child would have done that, surely. Have I missed something? Was there something else? But the question for her now in the silence of this here night was whether she had defended Billie Delia or sacrificed her. And was she sacrificing her still? The Royal Ease in her hand as she ran up the stairs was there to smash the young girl that lived in the minds of the 8-rocks, not the girl her daughter was.

Pat licked her bottom lip, tasted salt and wondered who exactly the tears were for.

Nathan DuPres, believed to be the oldest male in Ruby, welcomed the audience. He disputed the claim of seniority every year, pointing to his cousin Moss, then saying Reverend Simon Cary was a more suitable choice. But he let the town persuade him in the end because Reverend Cary talked too long, besides which he was not among the first families, so his arrival was associated not with World War II but with Korea. A stalwart man of such loving-kindness even Steward Morgan admired him, Nathan had married Elder Morgan's daughter, Mirth. Because they had no surviving children, he deeply cherished other people's: hosting the annual Children's Day picnic, fine-tuning the rehearsals, keeping cough drops and fireballs in his pockets to pass out.

Now, smelling slightly of the horse he'd just dismounted, he climbed the platform and surveyed the audience. Nathan cleared his throat and surprised himself. Whatever he'd prepared to say had left him and the words he did say seemed appropriate to some other event.

"I was five," he said, "when we left Louisiana and sixty-five when I hopped in the truck leaving Haven behind for this here new place. I know I wouldn't have done it if Mirth was alive or any of our children was still aboveground. You all know my babies — all of them — was took by a tornado in 1922. Me and Mirth found them in a stranger's wheat field. But I never regretted coming here. Never. There is honey in this land sweeter than any I know of, and I have cut cane in places where the dirt itself tasted like sugar, so that's saying a heap. No, I never had a gnat-minute's worth of regret. But there's a sadness in me now. Maybe in this season of my Lord's birth I'll learn what it is. This parch in my throat. The water that stays in my eyes. I know I've seen more years than God usually allows a man, but this dryness is new. The eye water too. When I run my mind over it, all I can come up with is a dream I had a while back."

In the next-to-last row, Lone DuPres sat next to Richard Misner, Anna on his other side. She leaned forward to glance at Anna and learn whether she, too, was losing her mind. Anna smiled but did not return her look, so she sat back to endure another one of old Nathan's incoherent dreams.

Nathan ran his fingers over his head, closed his eyes as if to get the details straight.

"Was an Indian come up to me in a bean row. Cheyenne, I believe. The vines were green, tender. The blossoms coming out all over. He looked at the row and shook his head, sorrowful-like. Then he told me too bad the water was bad; said there was plenty of it but it was foul. I said, But look here, look at all the flowers. Looks like a top crop to me. He said, The tallest cotton don't yield the best crop; besides, those flowers the wrong color. They's red. And I looked and sure enough they was turning pink, then red. Like blood drops. Scared me some. But when I looked back he was gone. And the petals was white again. I reckon that sighting is like this here story we going to tell again this evening. It shows the strength of our crop if we understand it. But it can break us if we don't. And bloody us too. May God bless the pure and holy and may nothing keep us apart from each other nor from the One who does the blessing. Amen."

When Nathan left the platform, amidst murmurs of kindness if not gratitude, Richard Misner took advantage of the pause to whisper something to Anna and leave his seat. He was hoping to relieve nascent waves of the claustrophobia that had not plagued him since he was jailed with thirty-eight others in a tiny cell in Alabama. He had embarrassed himself then, because the sweat and nausea signaled fear to his companions. And it was a hard lesson knowing that whatever risks he took, however eager he was for the dangerous confrontation, a crowded cell could humiliate him before teenagers without pity. Now, feeling the onslaught of suffocation in this tightly packed schoolhouse, he joined Pat Best, standing in the hall watching the play and the audience through the door. A long table of cakes, cookies and punch lined the wall behind her.

"Hello, Reverend." Pat did not look at him but adjusted her body to accommodate him in the doorway.

"Evening, Pat," he said, blotting moisture from his neck with his handkerchief. "Out here is better for me."

"Me too. See everything from here without stretching or peeping between two hats."

They looked over the heads of the audience as the curtains, made of percale sheets—laundered and carefully ironed—wavered. Children in white surplices filed through the parting, the perfection of their serious faces and flawless hair undone occasionally by a knee sock sliding down to an ankle or a bow tie twisted to the right. After a glance at Kate Golightly they took a uniform breath for O holy night, the stars are brightly shining . . .

At the second verse Richard Misner leaned over to Pat. "Mind if I ask you something?"

"No. Go ahead." She thought he was going to ask for a donation, because he had been having difficulty raising money (in the quantities he hoped for) to aid the legal defense of four teenagers arrested in Norman and charged with possession, resisting, arson, disorderly, inciting and whatever else the prosecution could ferret out of its statutes to level against black boys who said No or thought about it. They had been in jail, Richard Misner told his congregation, for almost two years. When arraigned, they'd been behind bars for twenty months. The trial date was about to be set, and lawyers needed to be paid for services already rendered and more to come. So far Richard had collected only what the women had given. Women who thought more about the pain felt by the boys' mothers than of the injustice of their sons' situation. The men, however, Fleetwoods, Pulliam, Sargeant Person and the Morgans, had been adamant in their refusal. Clearly Richard had not carefully enough shaped his plea. He should have built a prodigal sons foundation rather than a political one. Then, as he stood outside Calvary, continuing his requests, he would not have had to listen to "I don't hold with violence," from men who had handled guns all their lives. Or "Little illegal niggers with guns and no home training need to be in jail." This from Steward, of course. However much Richard insisted they had no guns, that demonstrations were not illegal, the men kept their wallets closed. Pat decided, if asked directly, to donate as much as she could. It was pleasant to think of his needing her generosity, so she was annoyed to learn that that was not at all what was on Richard Misner's mind.

"I'm trying to smooth a situation out at the Pooles', and I think I'd do well to talk to Billie Delia, if you don't mind. Is she here tonight?"

Pat held on to her elbows and turned to look at him. "Can't help you, Reverend."

"You sure?"

"I'm sure that whatever's going on out there has nothing to do with Billie Delia. Besides, she doesn't live here anymore. Moved to Demby." She would have liked to stop being so hostile to him, but with the mention of her daughter's relationship with those Poole boys, she couldn't control it.

"Her name's come up once or twice. But Wisdom Poole won't give me anything to go on. Something's tearing that family apart."

"They don't like prying, Reverend. It's a thing about Ruby."

"I understand that but something like this has a way of spreading, touching more than one family. When I first came here it was plain: if there was a problem brewing, a delegation was formed to see about it. Keep people from falling out with one another. Seen it with my own eyes and been a party to it too."

"I know."

"This community used to be tight as wax."

"It still is. In a crisis. But they keep to themselves otherwise."

"Don't you mean 'we'? 'We keep to ourselves'?"

"If I did, would you be asking me to explain things?"

"Pat, please. Don't take anything I say amiss. I just remembered that the young people in Bible class say 'they' too when talking about their parents."

"Bible class? More like a war class. Kind of military, from what I hear."

"Militant, maybe. Not military."

"No budding Panthers?"

"Is that what you think?"

"I don't know what to think."

"Well, let me tell you. Unlike most of the folks here, we read newspapers and different kinds of books. We keep up. And yes, we discuss strategies of defense. Not aggression. Defense."

"They know the difference?"

He didn't have to reply right away because applause began and lasted until the final member of the children's choir disappeared behind the curtain.

Someone turns off the ceiling lights. Quiet coughing domesticates the dark. Slowly, on a well-oiled pulley, the curtains part. Under lights positioned in the wings, throwing large shadows behind them, four figures in felt hats and too big suits stand at a table, counting giant dollar bills. The face of each one is hidden by a yellow and white mask featuring gleaming eyes and snarling lips, red as a fresh wound. Above a sign tacked to the table front, which reads INN, they count money, make slurping noises and do not stop when a parade of holy families dressed in torn clothes and moving in a slow two-step approaches them. Seven couples line up before the table of money. The boys carry staffs; the girls cuddle baby dolls.

Misner looked at them and, giving himself more time to think of a reply to Pat's question, concentrated on identifying the children onstage. The four youngest Cary girls: Hope, Chaste, Lovely and Pure; Dina Poole; and one of Pious DuPres' daughters—Linda. Then the boys, manfully grasping staffs while they two-stepped toward the money counters. Peace and Solarine Jury's two grandsons, Ansel and one they called Fruit; Joe-Thomas Poole paired with his sister Dina; Drew and Harriet Person's son, James; Payne Sands' boy, Lorcas, and two of Timothy Seawright's grandsons, Steven and Michael. Two of the masked ones were obviously Beauchamps—Royal and Destry, fifteen- and sixteen-year-olds who were already over six feet tall—but he wasn't sure of the other two. This was the first time he had attended the play. It was held two weeks before Christmas, when he returned to Georgia for his annual visit to his family. This year the trip was postponed because an all-family reunion was scheduled for New Year's. He would take Anna, if she agreed, let the folks look her over and, he supposed, let her look them over. He had hinted to the bishops that he was up for a new parish. Nothing urgent. But he was not sure he was well used in Ruby. He had thought any place was fine as long as there were young people to be taught, to be told, that Christ was judge and warrior too. That whites not only had no patent on Christianity; they were often its obstacle. That Jesus had been freed from white religion, and he wanted these kids to know that they did not have to beg for respect; it was already in them, and they needed only to display it. But the resistance he'd found in Ruby was wearing him out. More and more his students were being chastised about the beliefs he helped instill. Now Pat Best—with whom he'd taught Negro History every Thursday afternoon—was chipping away at his Bible class, confusing self-respect for arrogance, preparedness for disobedience. Did she think education was knowing just enough to get a job? She didn't seem to trust these Ruby hardheads with the future any more than he did, but neither did she encourage change. Negro history and lists of old-time achievements were enough for her but not for this generation. Somebody had to talk to them, and somebody had to listen to them. Otherwise . . .

"You know better than anybody how smart these young people are. Better than anybody . . ." His voice trailed off under "Silent Night."

"You think what I teach them isn't good enough?"

Had she read his mind? "Of course it's good. It's just not enough. The world is big, and we're part of that bigness. They want to know about Africa—"

"Oh, please, Reverend. Don't go sentimental on me."

"If you cut yourself off from the roots, you'll wither."

"Roots that ignore the branches turn into termite dust."

"Pat," he said with mild surprise. "You despise Africa."

"No, I don't. It just doesn't mean anything to me."

"What does, Pat? What does mean something to you?"

"The periodic chart of elements and valences."

"Sad," he said. "Sad and cold." Richard Misner turned away.

Lorcas Sands leaves the group of families and in a loud but breaking voice addresses the masks: "Is there room?"

The masks turn toward each other, then back to the supplicant, then back to each other, after which they roar, shaking their heads like angry lions. "Get on way from here! Get! There's no room for you!"

"But our wives are pregnant!" Lorcas points with the staff.

"Our children going to die of thirst!" Pure Cary holds a doll aloft.

The masked ones wag their heads and roar.

"That was not a nice thing to say to me, Richard."

"I'm sorry?"

"I am not sad or cold."

"I meant the chart, not you. Limiting your faith to molecules as if—"

"I don't limit anything. I just don't believe some stupid devotion to a foreign country—and Africa is a foreign country, in fact it's fifty foreign countries—is a solution for these kids."

"Africa is our home, Pat, whether you like it or not."

"I'm really not interested, Richard. You want some foreign Negroes to identify with, why not South America? Or Germany, for that matter. They have some brown babies over there you could have a good time connecting with. Or is it just some kind of past with no slavery in it you're looking for?"

"Why not? There was a whole lot of life before slavery. And we ought to know what it is. If we're going to get rid of the slave mentality, that is."

"You're wrong, and if that's your field you're plowing wet. Slavery *is* our past. Nothing can change that, certainly not Africa."

"We live in the world, Pat. The whole world. Separating us, isolating us—that's always been their weapon. Isolation kills generations. It has no future."

"You think they don't love their children?"

Misner stroked his upper lip and heaved a long sigh. "I think they love them to death."

. . .

Bobbing and bowing, the masked ones reach under the table and lift up big floppy cardboard squares pasted with pictures of food. "Here. Take this and get on out of here." Throwing the food pictures on the floor, they laugh and jump about. The holy families rear back as though snakes were being tossed at them. Pointing forefingers and waving fists, they chant: "God will crumble you. God will crumble you." The audience hums agreement: "Yes He will. Yes He will."

"Into dust!" That was Lone DuPres.

"Don't you dare to mistake Him. Don't you dare."

"Finer than flour he'll grind you."

"Say it, Lone."

"Strike you in the moment of His choosing!"

And sure enough, the masked figures wobble and collapse to the floor, while the seven families turn away. Something within me that banishes pain; something within me I cannot explain. Their frail voices are accompanied by stronger ones in the audience, and at the last note more than a few are wiping their eyes. The families cluster campfire style to the right of the stage. The girls rock the dolls. Away in the manger, no crib for His head. Slowly from the wings a boy enters. He wears a wide hat and carries a leather bag. The families make a half circle behind him. The big-hat boy kneels and draws bottles and packages from the satchel, which he arranges on the floor. The little Lord Jesus lay down His sweet head.

What's the point? Richard asked himself. Just enjoy the show and let Pat alone. He wanted to discuss, not argue. He watched the children's movements with mild affection at first, then with growing interest. He had assumed it was in order to please as many children as possible that there were four innkeepers, seven Marys and Josephs. But perhaps there were other reasons. Seven holy families? Richard tapped Pat on the shoulder. "Who put this together? I thought you told me there were nine original families. Where the other two? And why only one Wise Man? And why is he putting the gifts back in the satchel?"

"You don't know where you are, do you?"

211

"Well help me figure this place out. I know I'm an outsider, but I'm not an enemy."

"No, you're not. But in this town those two words mean the same thing."

Amazing grace, how sweet the sound. In a shower of gold paper stars, the families lay down the dolls, the staffs and form a ring. The voices from the audience peal as one. I once was lost but now am found.

Richard felt bitterness take the place of the nausea that had driven him from his seat. Twenty, thirty years from now, he thought, all sorts of people will claim pivotal, controlling, defining positions in the rights movement. A few would be justified. Most would be frauds. What could not be gainsaid, but would remain invisible in the newspapers and the books he bought for his students, were the ordinary folk. The janitor who turned off the switch so the police couldn't see; the grandmother who kept all the babies so the mothers could march; the backwoods women with fresh towels in one hand and a shotgun in the other; the little children who carried batteries and food to secret meetings; the ministers who kept whole churchfuls of hunted protesters calm till help came; the old who gathered up the broken bodies of the young; the young who spread their arms wide to protect the old from batons they could not possibly survive; parents who wiped the spit and tears from their children's faces and said, "Never mind, honey. Never you mind. You are not and never will be a nigger, a coon, a jig, a jungle bunny nor any other thing white folks teach their children to say. What you are is God's." Yes, twenty, thirty years from now, those people will be dead or forgotten, their small stories part of no grand record or even its footnotes, although they were the ones who formed the spine on which the televised ones stood. Now, seven years after the murder of the man in whose stead he would happily have taken the sword, he was herding a flock which believed not only that it had created the pasture it grazed but that grass from any other meadow was toxic. In their view Booker T. solutions trumped Du Bois problems every time. No matter who they are, he thought, or how special they think they are, a community with no politics is doomed to pop like Georgia fatwood. Was blind but now I see.

"Do they?" It was phrased as a question but it sounded like a conclusion to Pat.

"They are better than you think," she said.

"They are better than *they* think," he told her. "Why are they satisfied with so little?"

"This is their home; mine too. Home is not a little thing."

"I'm not saying it is. But can't you even imagine what it must feel like to have a true home? I don't mean heaven. I mean a real earthly home. Not some fortress you bought and built up and have to keep everybody locked in or out. A real home. Not some place you went to and invaded and slaughtered people to get. Not some place you claimed, snatched because you got the guns. Not some place you stole from the people living there, but your own home, where if you go back past your great-great-grandparents, past theirs, and theirs, past the whole of Western history, past the beginning of organized knowledge, past pyramids and poison bows, on back to when rain was new, before plants forgot they could sing and birds thought they were fish, back when God said Good! Good!—there, right there where you know your own people were born and lived and died. Imagine that, Pat. That place. Who was God talking to if not to my people living in my home?"

"You preaching, Reverend."

"No, I'm talking to you, Pat. I'm talking to you."

The final clapping began when the children broke the circle and lined up for their bows. Anna Flood rose when the audience did, pushing her way through to where Pat and Richard stood, animated, eyes locked. Both women had been subjected to speculation about which one the new and young and single and handsome preacher would favor. Anna and Pat were the only single women of a certain age available. Unless the new preacher liked them much younger, he'd have to choose between these two. Two years ago, Anna had won—she was

213

sure of it—hands down. So far. Now she moved toward Richard smiling broadly, hoping to freeze the tongues of anyone who might think otherwise seeing him prefer Pat's company to hers during the Christmas play. They were careful in their courtship, never touching in public. When she cooked supper for him they made sure the parsonage blazed with light, and he drove or walked her home by seven-thirty for all Ruby to see. Still, no date having been set, tongues might get restive. More than seemly behavior, however, was on her mind: Richard's eye light. It seemed dulled to her lately. As though he'd lost a battle on which his life depended.

She got to him just before the crowd surged out, pressing toward the food tables, chatting, laughing.

"Hi, Pat. What happened to you, Richard?"

"Sick as a dog there for a minute," he said. "Come on. Let's stand outside before it starts up again."

They said goodbye and left Pat to decide whether she wanted to talk to happy parents, mind the food table or leave. She had decided on the last when Carter Seawright stepped on her foot.

"Oh. Excuse me, Miss Best. I'm sorry."

"It's all right, Carter, but please calm yourself down."

"Yes, m'am."

"And don't forget. Right after the holidays, you and I have a make-up lesson. January sixth, you hear?"

"I be there, Miss Best."

"Is that 'I'll'? 'I'll be there'?"

"Yes, m'am, Miss Best. I will."

In the kitchen heating water for tea, Pat banged the cupboard door so hard the cups rattled. It was a toss-up as to whose behavior had annoyed her most, Anna's or her own. At least she could understand Anna: protecting her stake. But why had she defended people and things and ideas with a passion she did not feel? The deep weeping pleasure the audience took from the play disgusted her. All that nonsense she had grown up with seemed to her like an excuse to be hateful. Richard was right to ask, why seven and not nine? Pat had seen the play all her life, although she had never been chosen for any part other than the choir. That was when Soane taught school—before she even noticed the singularity of the numbers. It was some time later that she saw there were only eight. By the time she understood that the Cato line was cut, there was another erasure. Who? There were only two families who were not part of the original nine but had come to Haven early enough to have a kind of associate status: the Jurys (although their grandson, Harper, had married a Blackhorse original—good for him) and her father's father: Fulton Best. They didn't count as originals, so it had to be—who? Surely not the Floods if Anna married Richard Misner. Wouldn't that count? Could Richard save the Flood line? Or was it the Pooles, because of Billie Delia? No. There were shiploads of males in that family. It would be proof of Apollo's or Brood's dalliance, but if that were a deterrent, the Morgans themselves had been in grave danger until K.D. married Arnette. And if Arnette had a son rather than a daughter, how much safer their position would be. The Fleetwoods' too. Since Jeff and Sweetie had not measured up, Arnette was critical to both families.

The tea was ready, and Pat leaned over it, frowning, and so intent on puzzling the problem out that she did not hear Roger enter until he stood in the doorframe.

"You left too early," he said. "We caroled some."

"Yes? Oh. Well." Pat dredged up a smile.

"Missed some good cake too." He yawned. "Took up a good collection for Lone afterwards. Lord, that's a crazy woman." Too tired to laugh, Roger shook his head and smiled. "But she was good in her day." He turned to leave, saying, "Well, good night, baby. I have to squeal tires early tomorrow."

"Daddy." Pat spoke to his back.

"Uh huh?"

"Why do they change it? There used to be nine families in the play. Then eight for years and years. Now seven."

"What're you talking about?"

"You know."

"No. I don't know."

"The play. How the holy families get fewer and fewer."

"Kate does all that. And Nathan. Picking the children, I mean. Maybe they didn't have enough for the usual size."

"Daddy." He must have heard the doubt in her tone.

"What?" If he did, it didn't show.

"It was skin color, wasn't it?"

"What?"

"The way people get chosen and ranked in this town."

"Aw, no. Well, there might have been a little offense taken—long ago. But nothing hard."

"No? What about what Steward said when you got married?"

"Steward? Oh, well, the Morgans are very serious about themselves. Too serious sometimes."

Pat blew in her cup.

Roger met her silence and then returned to a less uncomfortable topic.

"I thought the play was pretty nice, myself. We have to do something about Nathan, though. He ain't the sharpest knife in the drawer anymore." Then, as an afterthought, "What Reverend Misner have to say for himself? Looked awful serious back there."

She didn't look up. "Just . . . talk."

"Anything happening with you two?"

"Daddy, please."

"No harm in asking, is there?" He paused for an answer, and when there was none he left, murmuring something about the furnace.

Yes there is. Harm. Pat sipped carefully from a spoon. Ask Richard Misner. Ask him what I just did to him. Or what everyone else does. When he asks questions, they close him out to anything but the obvious, the superficial. And I of all people know exactly what it feels like. Not good enough to be represented by eight-year-olds on a stage.

Fifteen minutes later Pat stood in the garden, seventy yards from Delia's tombstone. The evening had turned chilly but still not cold enough for snow. The lemon mint had shriveled, but lavender and sage bushes were full and fragrant. No wind to speak of, so the fire in the oil barrel was easily contained. One by one she dropped cardboard files, sheets of paper—both stapled and loose—into the flames. She had to tear the covers off the composition notebooks and hold them slant with a stick so they would not smother the fire. The smoke was bitter. She stepped back and gathered clumps of lavender and threw it in as well. It took some time, but finally she turned her back on the ashes and walked into her house trailing along the odor of burnt lavender. At the kitchen sink she washed her hands and dashed water on her face. She felt clean. Perhaps that was why she began to laugh. Lightly at first and then heavily, her head thrown back as she sat at the table. Did they really think they could keep this up? The numbers, the bloodlines, the who fucks who? All those generations of 8-rocks kept going, just to end up narrow as bale wire? Well, to stay alive maybe they could, maybe they should, since nobody dies in Ruby.

She wiped her eyes and lifted the cup from its saucer. Tea leaves clustered in its well. More boiling water, a little steeping, and the black leaves would yield more. Even more. Ever more. Until. Well, now. What do you know? It was clear as water. The generations had to be not only racially untampered with but free of adultery too. "God bless the pure and holy" indeed. That was their purity. That was their holiness. That was the deal Zechariah had made during his humming prayer. It wasn't God's brow to be feared. It was his own, their own. Is that why "Be the Furrow of His Brow" drove them crazy? But the bargain must have been broken or changed, because there were only seven now. By whom? The Morgans, probably. They ran everything, controlled everything. What new bargain had the twins struck? Did they really believe that no one died in Ruby? Suddenly Pat thought she knew all of it. Unadulterated and unadulteried 8-rock blood held its magic as long as it resided in Ruby. That was their recipe. That was their deal. For Immortality.

Pat's smile was crooked. In that case, she thought, everything that worries them must come from women.

"Dear God," she murmured. "Dear, dear God. I burned the papers."

CONSOLATA

In the good clean darkness of the cellar, Consolata woke to the wrenching disappointment of not having died the night before. Each morning, her hopes dashed, she lay on a cot belowground, repelled by her sluglike existence, each hour of which she managed to get through by sipping from black bottles with handsome names. Each night she sank into sleep determined it would be the final one, and hoped that a great hovering foot would descend and crush her like a garden pest.

Already in a space tight enough for a coffin, already devoted to the dark, long removed from appetites, craving only oblivion, she struggled to understand the delay. "What for?" she asked, and her voice was one among many that packed the cellar from rafter to stone floor. Several times a week, at night or in the shadowy part of the day, she rose aboveground. Then she would stand outside in the garden, walk around, look up at the sky to see the only light it had that she could bear. One of the women, Mavis usually, would insist on joining her. Talking, talking, always talking. Or a couple of others would come. Sipping from the dusty bottles with handsome names—Jarnac, Médoc, Haut-Brion and Saint-Émilion—made it possible to listen to them, even answer sometimes. Other than Mavis, who had been there the longest, it was getting harder and harder to tell one from another. What she knew of them she had mostly forgotten, and it seemed less and less important to remember any of it, because the timbre of each of their voices told the same tale: disorder, deception and, what Sister

221

Roberta warned the Indian girls against, drift. The three *d*'s that paved the road to perdition, and the greatest of these was drift.

Over the past eight years they had come. The first one, Mavis, during Mother's long illness; the second right after she died. Then two more. Each one asking permission to linger a few days but never actually leaving. Now and then one or another packed a scruffy little bag, said goodbye and seemed to disappear for a while—but only a while. They always came back to stay on, living like mice in a house no one, not even the tax collector, wanted, with a woman in love with the cemetery. Consolata looked at them through the bronze or gray or blue of her various sunglasses and saw broken girls, frightened girls, weak and lying. When she was sipping Saint-Émilion or the smoky Jarnac, she could tolerate them, but more and more she wanted to snap their necks. Anything to stop the badly cooked indigestible food, the greedy hammering music, the fights, the raucous empty laughter, the claims. But especially the drift. Sister Roberta would have pulped their hands. Not only did they do nothing except the absolutely necessary, they had no plans to do anything. Instead of plans they had wishes—foolish babygirl wishes. Mavis talked endlessly of surefire moneymaking ventures: beehives; something called "bed and breakfast"; a catering company; an orphanage. One thought she had found a treasure chest of money or jewels or something and wanted help to cheat the others of its contents. Another was secretly slicing her thighs, her arms. Wishing to be the queen of scars, she made thin red slits in her skin with whatever came to hand: razor, safety pin, paring knife. One other longed for what sounded like a sort of cabaret life, a crowded place where she could sing sorrow-filled songs with her eyes closed. Consolata listened to these babygirl dreams with padded, wine-dampened indulgence, for they did not infuriate her as much as their whispers of love which lingered long after the women had gone. One by one they would float down the stairs, carrying a kerosene lamp or a candle, like maidens entering a temple or a crypt, to sit on the floor and talk of love as if they knew anything at all about it. They spoke of men who came to caress them in their sleep; of men waiting for them in the desert or by cool water; of men who once had desperately loved them; or men who should have loved them, might have loved, would have.

On her worst days, when the maw of depression soiled the clean darkness, she wanted to kill them all. Maybe that was what her slug life was being prolonged for. That and the cold serenity of God's wrath. To die without His forgiveness condemned her soul. But to die without Mary Magna's fouled it per omnia saecula saeculorum. She might have given it freely if Consolata had told her in time, confessed before the old woman's mind faded to singsong. On that last day, Consolata had climbed into the bed behind her and, tossing the pillows on the floor, raised up the feathery body and held it in her arms and between her legs. The small white head nestled between Consolata's breasts, and so the lady had entered death like a birthing, rocked and prayed for by the woman she had kidnapped as a child. Kidnapped three children, actually; the easiest thing in the world in 1925. Mary Magna, a sister, not a mother, then, flatly refused to leave two children in the street garbage they sat in. She simply picked them up, took them to the hospital where she worked and cleaned them in a sequence of Ordorno's Baking Soda, Glover's Mange, soap, alcohol, Blue Ointment, soap, alcohol and then iodine carefully placed on their sores. She dressed them and, with the complicity of the other mission sisters, took them with her to the ship. They were six American nuns on their way back to the States after twelve years of being upstaged by older, sterner Portuguese Orders. Nobody questioned Sisters Devoted to Indian and Colored People paying cut-rate passage for three certainly not white urchins in their charge. For there were three now, Consolata being a last-minute decision because she was already nine years old. By anyone's standard the snatching was a rescue, because whatever life the exasperated, headstrong nun was dragging them to, it would be superior to what lay before them in the shit-strewn paths of that city. When they arrived in Puerto Limón, Sister Mary Magna placed two of them in an orphanage, for by then she had fallen in love with Consolata. The green eyes? the tea-colored hair? maybe her docility? Perhaps her smoky, sundown skin? She took her along as a ward to the post to which the difficult nun was now assigned—an asylum/boarding school for Indian girls in some desolate part of the North American West.

In white letters on a field of blue, a sign near the access road read CHRIST THE KING SCHOOL FOR NATIVE GIRLS. Maybe that was what everybody meant to call it, but in Consolata's living memory only the nuns used its proper name—mostly in prayer. Against all reason, the students, the state officials and those they encountered in town called it the Convent.

For thirty years Consolata worked hard to become and remain Mary Magna's pride, one of her singular accomplishments in a lifetime of teaching, nurturing and tending in places with names the nun's own parents had never heard of and could not repeat until their daughter pronounced them. Consolata worshipped her. When she was stolen and taken to the hospital, they stuck needles in her arms to protect her, they said, from diseases. The violent illness that followed she remembered as pleasant, because while she lay in the children's ward a beautiful framed face watched her. It had lake-blue eyes, steady, clear but with a hint of panic behind them, a worry that Consolata had never seen. It was worth getting sick, dying, even, to see that kind of concern in an adult's eyes. Every now and then the woman with the framed face would reach over and touch Consolata's forehead with the backs of her knuckles or smooth her wet, tangled hair. The glass beads hanging from her waist or from her fingers winked. Consolata loved those hands: the flat fingernails, the smooth tough skin of the palm. And she loved the unsmiling mouth, which never needed to show its teeth to radiate happiness or welcome. Consolata could see a cool blue light beaming softly under the habit. It came, she thought, from the heart of her.

Straight from the hospital, Consolata, in a clean brown dress that reached her ankles, accompanied the nuns to a ship called *Atenas*. After the Panama call they disembarked in New Orleans and from there traveled in an automobile, a train, a bus, another automobile. And the magic that started with the hospital needles piled up and up: toilets that swirled water clear enough to drink; soft white bread already sliced in its wrapper; milk in glass bottles; and all through the day every day the gorgeous language made especially for talking to heaven. Ora pro nobis gratia plena sanctificetur nomen tuum fiat voluntas tua, sicut in caelo, et in terra sed libera nos a malo a malo a malo. Only when they arrived at the school did the magic slow. Although the land had nothing to recommend it, the house was like a castle, full of a beauty Mary Magna said had to be eliminated at once. Consolata's first tasks were to smash offending marble figures and tend bonfires of books, crossing herself when naked lovers blew out of the fire and had to be chased back to the flame. Consolata slept in the pantry, scrubbed tile, fed chickens, prayed, peeled, gardened, canned and laundered. It was she, not any of the others, who discovered the wild bush heavy with stinging-hot peppers and who cultivated them. She learned rudimentary cooking skills from Sister Roberta and got good enough to take over the kitchen as well as the garden. She attended classes with the Indian girls but formed no attachments to them.

For thirty years she offered her body and her soul to God's Son and His Mother as completely as if she had taken the veil herself. To her of the bleeding heart and bottomless love. To her quae sine tactu pudoris. To the beata viscera Mariae Virginis. To her whose way was narrow but scented with the sweetness of thyme. To Him whose love was so perfectly available it dumbfounded wise men and the damned. He who had become human so we could know Him touch Him see Him in the littlest ways. Become human so His suffering would mirror ours, that His death throes, His doubt, despair, His failure, would speak for and absorb throughout earthtime what we were vulnerable to. And those thirty years of surrender to the living God cracked like a pullet's egg when she met the living man.

It was 1954. People were building houses, fencing and plowing land, some seventeen miles south of Christ the King. They had begun to build a feed store, a grocery store and, to Mary Magna's delight, a pharmacy closer than ninety miles. There she could purchase the bolts of antiseptic cotton for the girls' menstrual periods, the fine needles, the sixty-weight thread that kept them busy mending, mending, the Lydia Pinkham, the StanBack powder, and the aluminum chloride with which she made deodorant.

On one of these trips, when Consolata accompanied Mary Magna in the school's Mercury station wagon, even before they reached the newly cut road it was clear something was happening. Something unbridled was going on under the scalding sun. They could hear loud cheering, and instead of thirty or so energetic people going quietly about the business of making a town, they saw horses galloping off into yards, down the road, and people screaming with laughter. Small girls with red and purple flowers in their hair were jumping up and down. A boy holding for dear life onto a horse's neck was lifted off and declared winner. Young men and boys swung their hats, chased horses and wiped their brimming eyes. As Consolata watched that reckless joy, she heard a faint but insistent Sha sha sha. Sha sha sha. Then a memory of just such skin and just such men, dancing with women in the streets to music beating like an infuriated heart, torsos still, hips making small circles above legs moving so rapidly it was fruitless to decipher how such ease was possible. These men here were not dancing, however; they were laughing, running, calling to each other and to women doubled over in glee. And although they were living here in a hamlet, not in a loud city full of glittering black people, Consolata knew she knew them.

It was some time before Mary Magna could get the pharmacist's attention. Finally he left the crowd and walked them back to his house, where a closed-off part of the front porch served as a shop. He opened the screen door and, politely inclining his head, ushered Mary Magna in. It was while Consolata waited on the steps that she saw him for the first time. Sha sha sha. Sha sha sha. A lean young man astride one horse, leading another. His khaki shirt was soaked with sweat, and at some point he removed his wide flat hat to wipe perspiration from his forehead. His hips were rocking in the saddle, back and forth, back and forth. Sha sha sha. Sha sha sha. Consolata saw his profile, and the wing of a feathered thing, undead, fluttered in her stomach. He rode on past and disappeared into the feedlot. Mary Magna emerged with her purchases, complaining a little about something or other—the price, the quality—and hurried to the station wagon, Consolata, behind her, carrying blue-tissued rolls of surgical cotton. Just as she opened the passenger door he passed again. On foot, running lightly, eager to return to the festive knot of people farther down the road.

Casually, perfunctorily, he looked her way. Consolata looked back and thought she saw hesitation in his eyes if not in his stride. Quickly she ducked into the sun-baked Mercury, where the heat seemed to explain her difficult breathing. She did not see him again for two months of time made unstable by a feathered thing fighting for wingspread. Months of fervent prayer and extra care taken with chores. Months of tension also, because the school had been enjoined to close. Although the endowment of the wealthy woman who founded and funded the order had survived the thirties, it was depleted by the fifties. The good, sweet Indian girls were long gone—snatched away by their mothers and brothers or graduated into a pious life. For three years now the school had been soliciting wards of the state: impudent girls who clearly thought the sisters were hilarious most of the time, sinister the rest of the time. Two had already run away; only four remained. Unless the sisters could persuade the state to send them (and pay for) more wicked, wayward Indian girls, the orders were to prepare for closure and reassignment. The state had wayward girls, all right, since wayward could mean anything from bedwetting to truancy to stuttering in class, but preferred to place them in Protestant schools, where they could understand the clothes if not the religious behavior of the teachers. Catholic churches and schools in Oklahoma were as rare as fish pockets. Which was why the benefactress had bought the mansion in the first place. It was an opportunity to intervene at the heart of the problem: to bring God and language to natives who were assumed to have neither; to alter their diets, their clothes, their minds; to help them despise everything that had once made their lives worthwhile and to offer them instead the privilege of knowing the one and only God and a chance, thereby, for redemption. Mary Magna wrote letter after letter, traveled to Oklahoma City and beyond, hoping to save the school. In that distracted atmosphere, Consolata's fumbling, dropping some things, scorching others, making rushed, unscheduled visits to the chapel, were nuisances to the sisters but not signs of alarm distinguishable from their own. When asked what the matter was or reprimanded for some intolerable lapse, she invented excuses or sulked. Looming in her confusion, daily refreshing her hasty piety, was the fear of being asked to step outside the Convent, to shop in the town again. So she did the yard chores at first light and spent the balance of the day inside, mismanaging her work. None of which helped in the end. He came to her.

On a clear summer day, as she knelt weeding in the garden along with two sullen wards of the state, a male voice behind her said:

"Excuse me, miss."

All he wanted was some black peppers.

He was twenty-nine. She was thirty-nine. And she lost her mind. Completely.

Consolata was not a virgin. One of the reasons she so gratefully accepted Mary Magna's hand, stretching over the litter like a dove's wing, was the dirty pokings her ninth year subjected her to. But never, after the white hand had enclosed her filthy paw, did she know any male or want to, which must have been why being love-struck after thirty celibate years took on an edible quality.

What did he say? Come with me? What they call you? How much for half a peck? Or did he just show up the next day for more of the hot black peppers? Did she walk toward him to get a better look? Or did he move toward her? In any case, with something like amazement, he'd said, "Your eyes are like mint leaves." Had she answered "And yours are like the beginning of the world" aloud, or were these words confined to her head? Did she really drop to her knees and encircle his leg, or was that merely what she was wanting to do?

"I'll return your basket. But it may be late when I do. Is it all right if I disturb you?"

She didn't remember saying anything to that, but her face surely told him what he needed to know, because he was there in the night and she was there too and he took her hand in his. Not a peck basket in sight. Sha sha sha.

Once in his truck, easing down the graveled driveway, the narrow dirt road, and then gaining speed on a wider tarmac one, they did not speak. He drove, it seemed, for the pleasure of the machine: the roar contained, hooded in steel; the sly way it simultaneously parted the near darkness and vaulted into darkness afar—beyond what could be anticipated. They drove for what Consolata believed were hours, no words passing between them. The danger and its necessity focused them, made them calm. She did not know or care where headed or what might happen when they arrived. Speeding toward the unforeseeable, sitting next to him who was darker than the darkness they split, Consolata let the feathers unfold and come unstuck from the walls of a stone-cold womb. Out here where wind was not a help or threat to sunflowers, nor the moon a language of time, of weather, of sowing or harvesting, but a feature of the original world designed for the two of them.

Finally he slowed and turned into a barely passable track, where coyote grass scraped the fenders. In the middle of it he braked and would have taken her in his arms except she was already there.

On the way back they were speechless again. What had been uttered during their lovemaking leaned toward language, gestured its affiliation, but in fact was un-memorable, -controllable or -translatable. Before dawn they pulled away from each other as though, having been arrested, they were each facing prison sentences without parole. As she opened the door and stepped down, he said, "Friday. Noon." Consolata stood there while he backed the truck away. She had not seen him clearly even once during the whole night. But Friday. Noon. They would do it do it do it in daylight. She hugged herself, sank to her knees and doubled over. Her forehead actually tapping the ground as she rocked in a harness of pleasure.

She slipped into the kitchen and pretended to Sister Roberta that she had been in the henhouse.

"Well, then? Where are the eggs?"

"Oh. I forgot the basket."

"Don't go softheaded on me, please."

"No, Sister. I won't."

"Everything is in such disarray."

"Yes, Sister."

"Well, move, then."

"Yes, Sister. Excuse me, Sister."

"Is something funny?"

"No, Sister. Nothing. But . . ."

"But?"

"I . . . What is today?"

"Saint Martha."
"I mean what day of the week."
"Tuesday. Why?"
"Nothing, Sister."
"We need your wits, dear. Not your confusion."
"Yes, Sister."
Consolata snatched a basket and ran out the kitchen door.

Friday. Noon. The sun has hammered everybody back behind stone walls for relief. Everybody but Consolata and, she hopes, the living man. She has no choice but to bear the heat with only a straw hat to protect her from the anvil the sun takes her for. She is standing at the slight turn in the driveway, but in full view of the house. This land is flat as a hoof, open as a baby's mouth. There is nowhere to hide outrageousness. If Sister Roberta or Mary Magna calls to her or asks for an explanation she will invent something—or nothing. She hears his truck before she sees it and when it arrives it passes her by. He does not turn his head, but he signals. His finger lifts from the steering wheel and points farther ahead. Consolata turns right and follows the sound of his tires and then their silence as they touch tarmac. He waits for her on the shoulder of the road.

Inside the truck they look at one another for a long time, seriously, carefully, and then they smile.

He drives to a burned-out farmhouse that sits on a rise of fallow land. Negotiating bluestem and chickweed, he parks behind the black teeth of a broken chimney. Hand in hand, they fight shrub and bramble until they reach a shallow gully. Consolata spots at once what he wants her to see: two fig trees growing into each other. When they are able to speak full sentences, he gazes at her, saying:

"Don't ask me to explain. I can't."
"Nothing to explain."
"I'm trying to get on in my life. A lot of people depend on me."
"I know you're married."
"I aim to stay so."
"I know."

"What else you know?" He puts his forefinger in her navel.

"That I'm way older than you."

He looks up, away from her navel to her eyes, and smiles. "Nobody's older than me."

Consolata laughs.

"Certainly not you," he says. "When's the last time?"

"Before you were born."

"Then you're all mine."

"Oh, yes."

He kisses her lightly, then leans on his elbow. "I've traveled. All over. I've never seen anything like you. How could anything be put together like you? Do you know how beautiful you are? Have you looked at yourself?"

"I'm looking now."

No figs ever appeared on those trees during all the time they met there, but they were grateful for the shade of dusty leaves and the protection of the agonized trunks. The blankets he brought they lay on as much as possible. Later each saw the nicks and bruises the dry creek caused.

Consolata was questioned. She refused to answer; diverted the inquiries into lament. "What's going to happen to me when all this is closed? Nobody has said what's going to happen to me."

"Don't be ridiculous. You know we'll take care of you. Always."

Consolata pouted, pretending to be wild with worry and therefore unreliable. The more assurance she got, the more she insisted upon wandering off, to "be by myself," she said. An urge that struck her mostly on Fridays. Around noon.

When Mary Magna and Sister Roberta left on business in September, Sister Mary Elizabeth and three, now, feckless students continued to pack, clean, study and maintain prayer. Two of the students, Clarissa and Penny, began to grin when they saw Consolata. They were fourteen years old; small-boned girls with beautiful knowing eyes that could go suddenly blank. They lived to get out of that place, and were in fairly good spirits now that the end was coming. Recently they had begun to regard Consolata as a confederate rather than one of the enemy out to ruin their lives. And whispering to each other in a language the sisters had forbidden them to use, they covered for her, did the egg gathering that was Consolata's responsibility. The weeding and washing up too. Sometimes they watched from the schoolroom windows, heads touching, eyes aglow, as the woman they believed old enough to be their grandmother stood in all weather waiting for the Chevrolet truck.

"Does anyone know?" Consolata runs her thumbnail around the living man's nipple.

"Wouldn't be surprised," he answers.

"Your wife?"

"No."

"You told somebody?"

"No."

"Someone saw us?"

"Don't think so."

"Then how could anybody know?"

"I have a twin."

Consolata sits up. "There are two of you?"

"No." He closes his eyes. When he opens them he is looking away. "There's just one of me."

September marched through smearing everything with oil paint: acres of cardamom yellow, burnt orange, miles of sienna, blue ravines both cerulean and midnight, along with heartbreakingly violet skies. When October arrived and gourds were swelling in the places where radishes had been, Mary Magna and Sister Roberta returned, severely irritated by priests, lawyers, clerks and clerics. Their news was no news at all. Everyone's fate was being resolved in Saint Pere, except her own. That decision would come later. Mary Magna's age, seventy-two, was a consideration, but she refused placement in a quiet home. Also there was the upkeep of the property. The title was in the hands of the benefactress' foundation (which was down to its principal now), so the house and land were not exactly church owned; the argument, therefore, was whether it was subject to current and back taxes. But the real question for the assessor was why in a Protestant state a bevy of strange Catholic women with no male mission to control them was entitled to special treatment. Fortunately or unfortunately, no natural resources had so far been discovered on the land, making it impossible for the foundation to unburden it. They could not simply walk off, could they? Mary Magna called everyone together to explain. Another girl had run away, but the last two, Penny and Clarissa, listened in rapt attention as their future—the next four years of it anyway—which had taken shape in some old man in a suit's hands, was presented to them. They bowed their beautiful heads in solemn acquiescence, certain that the help they needed to get out of the clutch of nuns was on the way.

Consolata, however, paid scant attention to Mary Magna's words. She wasn't going anywhere. She would live in the field if she had to, or, better, in the fire-ruined house that had become her mind's home. Three times now she had followed him through it, balancing on buckled floorboards and smelling twelve-year-old smoke. Out there with not even a tree line in view, like a house built on the sand waves of the lonely Sahara, with no one or thing to hinder it, the house had burned freely in the play of wind and its own preen. Had it begun at night, with children asleep? Or was it unoccupied when the flames first seethed? Was the husband sixty acres away, bundling, branding, clearing, sowing? The wife stooped over a washtub in the yard, wisps of hair irritating her forehead? She would have thrown a bucket or two, then, yelling to the children, rushed to collect what she could. Piling everything she could reach, snatch, into the yard. Surely they had a bell, a rusty triangle—something to ring or bang to warn the other of advancing danger. When the husband got there, the smoke would have forced him to cry. But only the smoke, for they were not crying people. He would have worried first about the stock and guided them to safety or set them free, remembering that he had no property insurance. Other than what lay in the yard, all was lost. Even the sunflowers at the northwest corner of the house, near the kitchen, where the wife could see them while stirring hominy.

Consolata ferreted in drawers where field mice had nibbled propane gas receipts. Saw how the wind had smoothed charred furniture to silk. Nether shapes had taken over the space from which humans had fled. A kind of statuary of ash people. A man, eight feet tall, hovered near the fireplace. His legs, sturdy cowboy legs, and the set of his jaw as he faced them answered immediate questions of domain. The finger at the tip of his long black arm pointed left toward sky where a wall had crumbled, demanding quick exit from his premises. Near the pointing man, faintly etched on the ocher wall, was a girl with butterfly wings three feet long. The opposite wall was inhabited by what Consolata thought were fishmen, but the living man said, No, more like Eskimo eyes.

"Eskimo?" she asked, bunching her hair away from her neck. "What's an Eskimo?"

He laughed and, obeying the cowboy's order, pulled her away, over the rubble of the collapsed wall, back to the gully, where they competed with the fig trees for holding on to one another.

Mid-October he skipped a week. A Friday came and Consolata waited for two and a half hours where the dirt road met the tarmac. She would have waited longer, but Penny and Clarissa came and led her away.

He must be dead, she thought, and no one to tell her so. All night she fretted—on her pallet in the pantry or hunched in darkness at the kitchen table. Morning found her watching the world of living things dribbling away with his absence. Her heart, clogged with awfulness, weakened. Her veins seemed to have turned into crinkly cellophane tubes. The heaviness in her chest was gaining weight so fast she was unable to breathe properly. Finally she decided to find out or find him.

Saturday was a busy day in those parts. The once-a-week bus honked her out of the way as she strode down the middle of the county road. Consolata skittered to the shoulder and kept on, her unbraided hair lifting in the breeze of the tailpipe. A few minutes later an oil truck passed her, its driver yelling something through the window. Half an hour later there was a glistening in the distance. A car? A truck? Him? Her heart gurgled and began to seep blood back into her cellophane veins. She dared not let the smile growing in her mouth spread to her face. Nor did she dare stop walking while the vehicle came slowly into view. Yes, dear God, a truck. And one person at the wheel, my Jesus. And now it slowed. Consolata turned to watch it come full stop and to feast on the living man's face.

He leaned out of the window, smiling.

"Want a lift?"

Consolata ran across the road and darted around to the passenger door. By the time she got there it was open. She climbed in, and for some reason—a feminine desire to scold or annihilate twenty-four hours of desperation; to pretend, at least, that the suffering he had caused her required an apology, an explanation to win her forgiveness—some instinct like that preserved her and she did not let her hand slip into his crotch as it wanted to.

He was silent, of course. But it was not the silence of the Friday noon pickups. Then the unspeaking was lush with promise. Easy. Vocal. This silence was barren, a muteness lined with acid. And then she noticed the smell. Not unpleasant, not at all, but not his. Consolata froze; then, not daring to look at his face, she glanced sideways at his feet. He was wearing not the black high-tops but cowboy boots, convincing her that a stranger sat behind the steering wheel, inhabiting the body of him, but not him.

She thought to scream, to throw herself out onto the road. She would fight him if he touched her. She had no time to imagine other options, because they were approaching the dirt road that led to the Convent. She was just about to fling open the door, when the stranger braked and slowed to a standstill. He leaned over, brushing her breasts with his arm, and lifted the door handle. She stepped down quickly and turned to see.

He touched the brim of his Stetson, smiling. "Anytime," he said. "Anytime at all."

She backed away, staring at the exact face of him, repelled by but locked into his eyes, chaste and wide with hatred.

The incident does not halt the fig tree meetings. He comes the next Friday wearing the right shoes and exuding the right smell, and they argue a little.

"What did he do?"

"Nothing. He didn't even ask me where I was going. Just drove me back."

"Good thing he did."

"Why?"

"Did us both a favor."

"No, he didn't. He was . . ."

"What?"

"I don't know."

"What'd he say to you?"

"He said, 'Want a lift?' and then he said, 'Anytime.' Like he'd do it again. I could tell he doesn't like me."

"Probably not. Why should he? You want him to? Like you?"

"No. Oh, no, but."

"But what?"

Consolata sits up straight and looks steadily toward the back of the fire-ruined house. Something brown and furry scurries into what is left of a charred rain barrel.

"You talk to him about me?" she asks.

"Never told him a thing about you."

"Then how did he know I was coming to find you?"

"Maybe he didn't. Maybe he just didn't think you should be walking to town like that."

"He didn't turn the truck around. He was driving north. That's why I thought it was you."

"Look," he says. He squats on his haunches, tossing pebbles. "We have to have a signal. I can't always show up on Fridays. Let's think of something, so you'll know."

They thought of nothing that would work. In the end she told him she would wait the Fridays, but only for an hour. He said, If I'm not on time, I'm not coming at all.

The regularity of their meetings, before his twin showed up, had smoothed her hunger to a blunt blade. Now irregularity knifed it. Even so, twice more he carried her off to the place where fig trees insisted on life. She did not know it then, but the second time was the last.

It is the end of October. He walls a portion of the fire-ruined house with a horse blanket, and they lie on an army-issue bedroll. The pale sky above them is ringed with a darkness coming, which they could not have seen had they looked. So the falling snow that lights her hair and cools his wet back surprises them. Later they speak of their situation. Blocked by weather and circumstance, they talk, mostly, about Where. He mentions a town ninety miles north but corrects himself quickly, because no motel or hotel would take them. She suggests the Convent because of the hiding places in it everywhere. He snorts his displeasure.

"Listen," she whispers. "There is a small room in the cellar. No. Wait, just listen. I will fix it, make it beautiful. With candles. It's cool and dark in the summer, warm as coffee in winter. We'll have a lamp to see each other with, but nobody can see us. We can shout as loud as we want and nobody can hear. Pears are down there and walls of wine. The bottles sleep on their sides, and each one has a name, like Veuve Clicquot or Médoc, and a number: 1-9-1-5 or 1-9-2-6, like prisoners waiting to be freed. Do it," she urges him. "Please do it. Come to my house."

While he considers, her mind races ahead with plans. Plans to cram rosemary into the pillow slips; rinse linen sheets in hot water steeped in cinnamon. They will slake their thirst with the prisoner wine, she tells him. He laughs a low, satisfied laugh and she bites his lip which, in retrospect, was her big mistake.

Consolata did all of it and more. The cellar room sparkled in the light of an eight-holder candelabra from Holland and reeked of ancient herbs. Seckel pears crowded a white bowl. None of which pleased him for he never arrived. Never felt the slide of old linen on his skin, or picked flakes of stick cinnamon from her hair. The two wineglasses she rescued from straw-filled crates and polished to abnormal clarity collected dust particles, then, by November, just before Thanksgiving, an industrious spider moved in.

Penny and Clarissa had washed their hair and sat by the stove, finger-combing it dry. Every now and then one of them would lean and shake a shiny black panel of it closer to the heat. Softly singing forbidden Algonquian lullabies, they watched Consolata just as they always did: her days of excitement, of manic energy; her slow change to nail-biting distraction. They liked her because she was stolen, as they had been, and felt sorry for her too. They regarded her behavior as serious instruction about the limits and possibilities of love and imprisonment, and took the lesson with them for the balance of their lives. Now, however, their instant future claimed priority. Bags packed, plans set, they needed only money.

"Where do you keep the money, Consolata? Please, Consolata. Wednesday they take us to the Correctional. Just a little, Consolata. In the pantry, yes? Well, where? There was one dollar and twenty cents from Monday alone."

Consolata ignored them. "Stop pestering me."

"We helped you, Consolata. Now you must help us. It's not stealing—we worked hard here. Please? Think how hard we worked."

Their voices chanting, soothing, they swayed their hair and looked at her with the glorious eyes of maidens in peril.

The knock on the kitchen door was not loud, but its confidence was unmistakable. Three taps. No more. The girls stilled their hair in their hands. Consolata rose from her chair as if summoned by the sheriff or an angel. In a way it was both, in the shape of a young woman, exhausted, breathing hard but ramrod straight.

"That's some walk," she said. "Please. Let me sit."

Penny and Clarissa disappeared like smoke.

The young woman took the chair Penny had vacated.

"Can I get you something?" asked Consolata.

"Water, would you?"

"Not tea? You look froze."

"Yes. But water first. Then some tea."

Consolata poured water from a pitcher and bent to check the stove fire.

"What's that smell?" asked the visitor. "Sage?"

Consolata nodded. The woman covered her lips with her fingers.

"Does it bother you?"

"It'll pass. Thank you." She drank the water slowly until the glass was empty.

Consolata knew, or thought she did, but asked anyway. "What is it you want?"

"Your help." Her voice was soft, noncommittal. No judgment, no pleading.

"I can't help you."

"You can if you want to."

"What kind of help are you looking for?"

"I can't have this child."

Hot water splashed from the spout to the saucer. Consolata put down the kettle and sopped the water with a towel. She had never seen the woman—girl really, not out of her twenties—but there was no confusion from the moment she stepped inside about who she was. His scent was all over her, or hers was all over him. They had lived together close enough long enough to breathe phlox and Camay soap and tobacco and to exhale it in their wake. That and some other thing: the scent of small children, the lovely aroma of sweet oil, baby powder and a meatless diet. This was a mother here, saying a brute unmotherly thing that rushed at Consolata like a forked tongue. She dodged the tongue, but the toxin behind it shocked her with what she had known but never imagined: she was sharing him with his wife. Now she saw the pictures that represented exactly what that word—sharing— meant.

"I can't help you with that! What's wrong with you?"

"I've had two children in two years. If I have another . . ."

"Why come to me? Why you asking me?"

"Who else?" asked the woman, in her clear, matter-of-fact voice.

The poison spread. Consolata had lost him. Completely. Forever. His wife might not know it, but Consolata remembered his face. Not when she bit his lip, but when she had hummed over the blood she licked from it. He'd sucked air sharply. Said, "Don't ever do that again." But his eyes, first startled, then revolted, had said the rest of what she should have known right away. Clover, cinnamon, soft old linen—who would chance pears and a wall of prisoner wine with a woman bent on eating him like a meal?

"You get on out of here. You didn't come here for that. You came to tell me, show me, what you're like. And you think I'll stop when I know what you're willing to do. Well, I won't."

"No, but he will."

239

"You wouldn't have come here if you thought so. You want to see what I'm like; if I'm pregnant too."

"Listen to me. He can't fail at what he is doing. None of us can. We are making something."

"What do I care about your raggedy little town? Get out. Go on. I have work to do."

Did she walk all the way home? Or was that a lie too? Was her car parked somewhere near? Or if she did walk, did nobody pick her up? Is that why she lost the baby?

Her name was Soane, and when she and Consolata became fast friends, Soane told her she didn't think so. It was the evil in her heart that caused it. Arrogance dripping with self-righteousness, she said. Pretending a sacrifice she had no intention of making taught her not to fool with God's ways. The life she offered as a bargain fell between her legs in a swamp of red fluids and windblown sheets. Their friendship was some time coming. In the meanwhile, after the woman left, Consolata threw a cloth bag of coins at Penny and Clarissa, shouting, "Get out of my face!"

While the light changed and the meals did too, the next few days were one long siege of sorrow, during which Consolata picked through the scraps of her gobble-gobble love. Romance stretched to the breaking point broke, exposing a simple mindless transfer. From Christ, to whom one gave total surrender and then swallowed the idea of His flesh, to a living man. Shame. Shame without blame. Consolata virtually crawled back to the little chapel (wishing fervently that He could be there, glowing red in the dim light). Scuttled back, as women do, as into arms understanding where the body, like a muscle spasm, has no memory of its cringe. No beseeching prayer emerged. No Domine, non sum dignus. She simply bent the knees she had been so happy to open and said, "Dear Lord, I didn't want to eat him. I just wanted to go home."

Mary Magna came into the chapel and, kneeling with her, put an arm around Consolata's shoulder, saying, "At last."

"You don't know," said Consolata.

"I don't need to, child."

"But he, but he." Sha sha sha. Sha sha sha, she wanted to say, meaning, he and I are the same.

"Sh sh sh. Sh sh sh," said Mary Magna. "Never speak of him again."

She might not have agreed so quickly, but as Mary Magna led her out of the chapel into the schoolroom, a sunshot seared her right eye, announcing the beginning of her bat vision, and she began to see best in the dark. Consolata had been spoken to.

Mary Magna spent money she could not afford to take the household on a trip to Middleton, where each of them, but especially Consolata, confessed and attended mass. Clarissa and Penny, models of penitence, urged without success a visit to the Indian and Western Museum advertised on the road. Sister Mary Elizabeth said it was an unwise way to spend post-confessional time. The long ride back was silent except for the *shish* of missal pages turning and occasional humming from the last of the school's clientele.

Soon only Mother and Sister Roberta were left. Sister Mary Elizabeth accepted a teaching post in Indiana. Penny and Clarissa had been taken east and, as was later learned, escaped from the bus one night in Fayetteville, Arkansas. Except for a money order, made out to Consolata and signed with a storybook name, they were never heard from again.

The three women spent the winter waiting, then not waiting, for some alternative to retirement or a "home." The independence the mission was designed for was beginning to feel like abandonment. Meanwhile they took steps to keep up the property and not incur debt the foundation could not meet. Sargeant Person agreed to lease land from them for rough corn and alfalfa. They made sauces and jellies and European bread. Sold eggs, peppers, hot relish and angry barbecue sauce, which they advertised on a square of cardboard covering the faded blue and white name of the school. Most of their customers in 1955 drove trucks between Arkansas and Texas. Ruby citizens seldom stopped to buy anything other than peppers, since they were supreme cooks themselves and made or grew what they wanted. Only in the sixties, when times were fat, did they join the truckers and look upon what they called Convent-bred chickens as superior enough to their own to be worth a journey. Then they would also try a little jalapeño jelly, or a corn relish. Pecan saplings planted in the forties were strong in 1960. The Convent sold the nuts, and when pies from the harvest were made, they went as soon as posted. They made rhubarb pie so delicious it made customers babble, and the barbecue sauce got a heavenly reputation based on the hellfire peppers.

It was an all-right life for Consolata. Better than all right, for Mary Magna had taught her patience as the first order of business. After arranging for her confirmation, she had taken the young Consolata aside and together they would watch coffee brew or sit in silence at the edge of the garden. God's generosity, she said, is nowhere better seen than in the gift of patience. The lesson held Consolata in good stead, and she hardly noticed the things she was losing. The first to go were the rudiments of her first language. Every now and then she found herself speaking and thinking in that in-between place, the valley between the regulations of the first language and the vocabulary of the second. The next thing to disappear was embarrassment. Finally she lost the ability to bear light. By the time Mavis arrived, Sister Roberta had gone into a nursing home and Consolata had nothing on her mind but the care of Mary Magna.

But before that, before the disheveled woman in thong slippers hollered at the edge of the garden, before Mary Magna's illness, still in a state of devotion and light-blindness, and ten years after that summer of hiding in a gully behind a house full of inhospitable ash people, Consolata was tricked into raising the dead.

They were subdued years. Penance attended to but not all-consuming. There was time and mind for everyday things. Consolata learned to manage any and every thing that did not require paper: she perfected the barbecue sauce that drove cattle-country people wild; quarreled with the chickens; gave hateful geese a wide berth; and tended the garden. She and Sister Roberta had agreed to try again for a cow and Consolata was standing in the garden, wondering where to pen it, when sweat began to pour from her neck, her hairline, like rain. So much it clouded the sunglasses she now wore. She removed the glasses to wipe the sweat from her eyes. Through that salty water she saw a shadow moving toward her. When it got close it turned into a small woman. Consolata, overcome with dizziness, tried to hold on to a bean pole, failed and sank to the ground. When she woke, she was sitting in the red chair, the small woman humming while mopping her forehead.

"Talk about luck," she said, and smiled around a wad of chewing gum.

"What's happening to me?" Consolata looked toward the house.

"Change, I expect. Here's your glasses. Bent, though."

Her name was Lone DuPres, she said, and if she had not come for a few peppers, she said, who knew how long Consolata would have lain in the snap beans.

Consolata found herself too weak to stand, so she let her head fall back on the chair's crown and asked for water.

"Uh uh," said Lone. "You already got too much of that. How old are you?"

"Forty-nine. Fifty soon."

"Well, I'm over seventy and I know my stuff. You do as I say, your change will be easier and shorter."

"You don't know that's what this is."

"Bet on it. And it's not just the sweat. You feel something more, don't you?"

"Like what?"

"You'd know it if you had it."

"What's it feel like?"

"You tell me. Some women can't stomach it. Others say it reminds them of, well, you know."

"My throat is parched," said Consolata.

Lone dug around in her bag. "I'll brew you something to help."

"No. The sisters. I mean, they won't like. Won't let you just walk on in and start messing on the stove."

"Oh, they'll be fine."

And they were. Lone gave Consolata a hot drink that tasted of pure salt. When she described her spell and Lone's remedy to Mary

Magna she laughed, saying, "Well, the teacher I am thinks 'baloney.' The woman I am thinks anything that helps, helps. But be very careful." Mary Magna lowered her voice. "I think she practices."

Lone didn't visit often, but when she did she gave Consolata information that made her uneasy. Consolata complained that she did not believe in magic; that the church and everything holy forbade its claims to knowingness and its practice. Lone wasn't aggressive. She simply said, "Sometimes folks need more."

"Never," said Consolata. "In my faith, faith is all I need."

"You need what we all need: earth, air, water. Don't separate God from His elements. He created it all. You stuck on dividing Him from His works. Don't unbalance His world."

Consolata listened halfheartedly. Her curiosity was mild; her religious habits entrenched. Her safety did not lie in the fall of a broom or the droppings of a coyote. Her happiness was not increased or decreased by the sight of a malformed animal. She fancied no conversation with water. Nor did she believe that ordinary folk could or should interfere with natural consequences. The road from Demby, however, was straight as a saw, and a teenager driving it for the first time believed not only that he could drive it blindfolded but that he could drive it in his sleep, which is what Scout Morgan was doing, off and on, as he traveled early one evening the road that passed the Convent. He was fifteen years old, driving his best friend's father's truck (which was nothing compared to the Little Deere his uncle taught him to handle), while his brother, Easter, slept in the truck bed and the best friend slept at his side. They had sneaked off to Red Fork to see the Black Rodeo all their fathers forbade them to attend and had drunk themselves happy with Falstaff beer. During one of Scout's involuntary naps at the wheel, the truck careened off the road and probably would have done no serious damage but for the roadside poles stacked and ready to go as soon as the power crew was empowered to install them. The truck hit the poles and flipped. July Person and Easter were thrown out. Scout was stuck inside, crooked red lines highlighting the black skin of his temple.

Lone, sitting at Consolata's table, sensed rather than heard the accident: the shouts of July and Easter could not have traveled that far. She rose and grabbed Consolata's arm.

"Come on!"

"Where to?"

"Close by, I think."

When they arrived, Easter and July had pulled Scout from the cab and were howling over his dead body. Lone turned to Consolata, saying, "I'm too old now. Can't do it anymore, but you can."

"Lift him?"

"No. Go inside him. Wake him up."

"Inside? How?"

"Step in. Just step on in. Help him, girl!"

Consolata looked at the body and without hesitation removed her glasses and focused on the trickles of red discoloring his hair. She stepped in. Saw the stretch of road he had dreamed through, felt the flip of the truck, the headache, the chest pressure, the unwillingness to breathe. As from a distance she heard Easter and July kicking the truck and moaning. Inside the boy she saw a pinpoint of light receding. Pulling up energy that felt like fear, she stared at it until it widened. Then more, more, so air could come seeping, at first, then rushing rushing in. Although it hurt like the devil to look at it, she concentrated as though the lungs in need were her own.

Scout opened his eyes, groaned and sat up. The women told the unhurt boys to carry him back to the Convent. They hesitated, exchanging looks. Lone shouted, "What the hell is the matter with you all?"

Both were profoundly relieved by Scout's recovery, but, No, m'am, Miss DuPres, they said, we got to get on home. "Let's see if it still runs," said Easter. They righted the truck and found it sound enough to drive. Lone went with them, leaving Consolata half exhilarated by and half ashamed of what she had done. Practiced.

Weeks passed before Lone returned to put her mind at ease about the boy's recovery.

"You gifted. I knew it from the start."

Consolata turned her lips down and crossed herself, whispering,

"Ave Maria, gratia plena." The exhilaration was gone now, and the thing seemed nasty to her. Like devilment. Like evil craft. Something it would mortify her to tell Mary Magna, Jesus or the Virgin. She hadn't known what she was doing; she was under a spell. Lone's spell. And told her so.

"Don't be a fool. God don't make mistakes. Despising His gift, now, that is a mistake. You calling Him a fool, like you?"

"I don't understand anything you're saying," Consolata told her.

"Yes you do. Let your mind grow long and use what God gives you."

"I think He wants me to ignore you."

"Hardhead," said Lone. She hoisted her bag and walked down the driveway to wait in the sun for her ride.

Then Soane came, saying, "Lone DuPres told me what you did. I came to thank you with all my heart."

She looked much the same to Consolata, except that the long hair of 1954, sticky with distress, was cut now. She carried a basket and placed it on the table. "You will be in my prayers forever."

Consolata lifted the napkin. Round sugar cookies were layered between waxed paper. "Mother will like these with her tea," she said. Then, looking at Soane, "Go nice with coffee too."

"I'd love a cup. More than anything."

Consolata placed the sugar cookies on a platter. "Lone thinks—"

"I don't care about that. You gave him back to me."

A gander screamed in the yard, scattering the geese before him.

"I didn't know he belonged to you."

"I know you didn't."

"And it was something I couldn't help doing. I mean it was out of my hands, so to speak."

"I know that too."

"What does he think?"

"He thinks he saved himself."

"Maybe he's right."

"Maybe he is."

"What do you think?"

"That he was lucky to have us both."

Consolata shook crumbs from the basket and folded the napkin neatly inside. They traded that basket back and forth for years.

Other than with Mary Magna, "stepping in" was of no use. There was no call for it. The light Consolata could not bear to approach her own eyes, she endured for the Reverend Mother when she became ill. At first she tried it out of the weakness of devotion turned to panic—nothing seemed to relieve the sick woman—then, angered by helplessness, she assumed an attitude of command. Stepping in to find the pinpoint of light. Manipulating it, widening it, strengthening it. Reviving, even raising, her from time to time. And so intense were the steppings in, Mary Magna glowed like a lamp till her very last breath in Consolata's arms. So she had practiced, and although it was for the benefit of the woman she loved, she knew it was anathema, that Mary Magna would have recoiled in disgust and fury knowing her life was prolonged by evil. That the bliss of that final entrance was being deliberately delayed by one who ought to know better. So Consolata never told her. Yet, however repugnant, the gift did not evaporate. Troubling as it was, yoking the sin of pride to witchcraft, she came to terms with it in a way she persuaded herself would not offend Him or place her soul in peril. It was a question of language. Lone called it "stepping in." Consolata said it was "seeing in." Thus the gift was "in sight." Something God made free to anyone who wanted to develop it. It was devious but it settled the argument between herself and Lone and made it possible for her to accept Lone's remedies for all sorts of ills and to experiment with others while the "in sight" blazed away. The dimmer the visible world, the more dazzling her "in sight" became.

When Mary Magna died, Consolata, fifty-four years old, was orphaned in a way she was not as a street baby and was never as a servant. There was reason the Church cautioned against excessive human love and when Mary Magna left her, Consolata accepted the sympathy of her two friends, the help and murmurs of support from Mavis, the efforts to cheer her from Grace, but her rope to the world had slid from her fingers. She had no identification, no insurance, no family, no work. Facing extinction, waiting to be evicted, wary of God, she felt like a curl of paper—nothing written on it—lying in the corner of an empty closet. They had promised to take care of her always but did not tell her that always was not all ways nor forever. Prisoner wine helped until it didn't and she found herself, full of a drinker's malice, wishing she had the strength to beat the life out of the women free-loading in the house. "God don't make mistakes," Lone had shouted at her. Perhaps not, but He was sometimes overgenerous. Like giving satanic gifts to a drunken, ignorant, penniless woman living in dark-ness unable to rise from a cot to do something useful or die on it and rid the world of her stench. Gray-haired, her eyes drained of what eyes were made for, she imagined how she must appear. Her colorless eyes saw nothing clearly except what took place in the minds of others. Exactly the opposite of that blind season when she rutted in dirt with the living man and thought she was seeing for the first time because she was looking so hard. But she had been spoken to, half cursed, half blessed. He had burned the green away and replaced it with pure sight that damned her if she used it.

Footsteps, then a knock, interrupted her sad, dead-end thoughts.

The girl opened the door.

"Connie?"

"Who else?"

"It's me, Pallas. I called my father again. So. You know. He's meet-ing me in Tulsa. I came to say goodbye."

"I see."

"It's been great. I needed to. Well, it's been forever since I last saw him."

"That long?"

"Can you believe it?"

"Hard to. You've fattened up."

"Yeah. I know."

"What will you do about it?"

"Same as always. Diet."

"I don't mean that. I mean the baby. You're pregnant."

"I am not."

"No?"

"No!"

"Why not?"

"I'm only sixteen!"

"Oh," said Consolata, looking at the moon head floating above a spine, the four little appendages—paws or hands or hooves or feet. Hard to tell at that stage. Pallas could be carrying a lamb, a baby, a jaguar. "Pity," she said as Pallas fled from the room. And "pity" again as she imagined the child's probable life with its silly young mother. She remembered another girl, about the same age, who had come a few years ago—at a very bad time. For seventeen days Consolata had been inside, alone, keeping Mary Magna's breath coming and going, the cool blue light flickering until Mary Magna asked permission to go, bereft though she was of the last sacrament. The second girl, Grace, had arrived in time to hold off the fearful loneliness that dropped the moment the body was removed, letting Consolata sleep. Mavis had just returned with Lourdes water and illegal painkillers. Consolata welcomed the company which distracted her from self-pitying thoughts of eviction, starvation and an uncontrite death. Minus papers or patron she was as vulnerable as she had been at nine when she clung to Mary Magna's hand at the railing of the *Atenas*. Whatever help Lone DuPres or Soane might offer could not include shelter. Not in that town.

Then the girl from Ruby came. A cup of tears just behind her eyes. And something else. She was not anxious, as might have been expected, but revolted by the work of her womb. A revulsion so severe it cut mind from body and saw its flesh-producing flesh as foreign, rebellious, unnatural, diseased. Consolata could not fathom what brought on that repugnance, but there it was. And here it was again in the No! shout of another one: a terror without alloy. With the first one Consolata did what she knew Mary Magna would have done: quieted the girl and advised her to wait her time. Told her that she was welcome to deliver there if she wanted to. Mavis was jubilant, Grace amused. They took the field rent and drove off to shop for the expected newborn, returning with booties and diapers and dolls enough for a kindergarten. The girl, sharp in her refusal to have the midwife attend her, waited quietly sullen for a week or so. Or so Consolata thought. What she did not know until labor began was that the young mother had been hitting her stomach relentlessly. Had Consolata's eyesight been better and had the girl's skin not been black as an ocean lover's night, she would have seen the bruises at once. As it was, she saw swellings and wide areas where the skin showed purple underneath, rather than silver. But the real damage was the mop handle inserted with a rapist's skill—mercilessly, repeatedly—between her legs. With the gusto and intention of a rabid male, she had tried to bash the life out of her life. And, in a way, was triumphantly successful. The five- or six-month baby revolted. Feisty, outraged, rigid with fright, it tried to escape the battering and battered ship that carried it. The blows to its delicate skull, the trouncing its hind parts took. The shudders in its spine. Otherwise there was no hope. Had it not tried to rescue itself, it would break into pieces or drown in its mother's food. So he was born, in a manner of speaking, too soon and fatigued by the flight. But breathing. Sort of. Mavis took over. Grace went to bed. Together Consolata and Mavis cleaned his eyes, stuck their fingers in his throat, clearing it for air, and tried to feed him. It worked for a few days, then he surrendered himself to the company of Merle and Pearl. By that time the mother was gone, having never touched, glanced at, inquired after or named him. Grace called him Che and Consolata did not know to this day where he was buried. Only that she had murmured Agnus Dei, qui tollis peccata mundi: miserere nobis over the three pounds of gallant but defeated life before Mavis, smiling and cooing, carried it away.

Just as well, thought Consolata. Life with that mother would have been hell for Che. Now here was another one screaming No! as if that made it so. Pity.

Reaching for a bottle, Consolata found it empty. She sighed and sat back in the chair. Without wine her thoughts, she knew, would be unbearable: resignation, self-pity, muted rage, disgust and shame glowing like cinders in a dying fire. As she rose to replenish her vice, a grand weariness took her, forcing her back to the seat, tipping her chin on her chest. She slept herself into sobriety. Headachy, sandy-mouthed she woke in quick need of a toilet. On the second floor, she could hear sniffles behind one door, singing behind another. Back down the stairs, she decided to catch a little air and shuffled into the kitchen and out the door. The sun had gone leaving behind a friendlier light. Consolata surveyed the winter-plagued garden. Tomato vines hung limp over fallen fruit, black and smashed in the dirt. Mustards were pale yellow with rot and inattention. A whole spill of melons caved in on themselves near heads of chrysanthemums stricken mud brown. A few chicken feathers were stuck to the low wire fencing protecting the garden from whatever it could. Without human help, gopher holes, termite castles, evidence of rabbit forays and determined crows abounded. The corn scrabble in neatly harvested fields beyond looked forlorn. And the pepper bushes, held on to by the wrinkled fingers of their yield, were rigid with cold. Despite the grains of soil blowing against her legs, Consolata sat down in the faded red chair.

"Non sum dignus," she whispered. "But tell me. Where is the rest of days, the aisle of thyme, the scent of veronica you promised? The cream and honey you said I had earned? The happiness that comes of well-done chores, the serenity duty grants us, the blessings of good works? Was what I did for love of you so terrible?"

Mary Magna had nothing to say. Consolata listened to the refusing silence, more wondering than annoyed by the sky, in plumage now, gold and blue-green, strutting like requited love on the horizon. She was afraid of dying alone, ungrieved in unholy ground, but knew that was precisely what lay before her. How she longed for the good death. "I'll miss You," she told Him. "I really will." The skylight wavered.

A man approached. Medium height, light step, he came right on up the drive. He wore a cowboy hat that hid his features, but Consolata couldn't have seen them anyway. Where he sat on the kitchen steps, framed by the door, a triangle of shadow obscured his face but not his clothes: a green vest over a white shirt, red suspenders hanging low on either side of his tan trousers, shiny black work shoes.

"Who is that?" she asked.

"Come on, girl. You know me." He leaned forward, and she saw that he wore sunglasses—the mirror type that glitter.

"No," she said. "Can't say I do."

"Well, not important. I'm traveling here." There were ten yards between them, but his words licked her cheek.

"You from the town?"

"Uh uh. I'm far country. Got a thing to drink?"

"Look you in the house." Consolata was beginning to slide toward his language like honey oozing from a comb.

"Oh, well," he said, as though that settled it and he would rather go thirsty.

"Just holler," said Consolata. "The girls can bring you something." She felt light, weightless, as though she could move, if she wanted to, without standing up.

"Don't you know me better than that?" the man asked. "I don't want see your girls. I want see you."

Consolata laughed. "You have your glasses much more me."

Suddenly he was next to her without having moved—smiling like he was having (or expecting) such a good time. Consolata laughed again. It seemed so funny, comical really, the way he had flitted over to her from the steps and how he was looking at her—flirtatious, full of secret fun. Not six inches from her face, he removed his tall hat. Fresh, tea-colored hair came tumbling down, cascading over his shoulders and down his back. He took off his glasses then and winked, a slow seductive movement of a lid. His eyes, she saw, were as round and green as new apples.

In candlelight on a bitter January evening, Consolata cleans, washes and washes again two freshly killed hens. They are young, poor layers with pinfeathers difficult to extract. Their hearts, necks, giblets and livers turn slowly in boiling water. She lifts the skin to reach under it, fingering as far as she can. Under the breast, she searches for a pocket close to the wing. Then, holding the breast in her left palm, the fingers of her right tunnel the back skin, gently pushing for the spine. Into all these places—where the skin has been loosened and the membrane separated from the flesh it once protected—she slides butter. Thick. Pale. Slippery.

Pallas wiped her eyes with the heel of her hand and then blew her nose. Now what?

This latest phone call, which she had mentioned to Connie, was not very different from the initial one. Just shorter. But it produced the same frustration as what had passed for conversation with her father last summer.

Jesus Christ where the hell are you? We thought you were dead. Thank God. They found the car but it's bashed to hell on one side and somebody stripped it. You okay? Oh, baby. *Daddy.* Where is he—boy is his ass over. Tell me what happened. Your bitch mother's not making any sense as usual. Did he hurt you? *Daddy, no.* Well, what? Was he alone? We're suing the school, baby. Got them by the short hairs. *It wasn't him. Some boys chased me.* What? *In their truck. They hit my car and forced me off the road. I ran and then—* They rape you? *Daddy!* Hold on sweetheart. Jo Anne get me that detective guy. Tell him I got Pallas. No, she's okay, just get him, will you? Go ahead, baby. *I'm* Where are you? *Will you come and get me Daddy?* Of course I will. Right away. Do you need money? Can you get to an airport, a train station? Just tell me where you'll be. Wait. Maybe you should call the police. The local ones I mean. They can get you to an airport. Tell them to call me. No. You call me from the station. Where are you? Pallas? Where you calling from? Pallas, you there? *Minnesota.* Minnesota? Jesus. I thought you were in New Mexico. What the hell's up there? Bloomington? No, Saint Paul. Are you near Saint Paul, sweetheart? *I'm not near anything, Daddy. It's like country.* Call the police, Pallas. Make them come get you, you hear? *Okay, Daddy.* Then call me from the station. *Okay.* You got that? You're not hurt or anything? *No Daddy.* Good. Okay, now. I'll be right here or Jo Anne will if I go out. Boy what you put me through. But everything's going to be okay now. We'll talk about that asshole when you get back. Okay, now? Call me. We have to talk. Love you, baby.

Talk. Sure. Pallas didn't call anybody—police, Dee Dee, or him—until August. He was furious but wired her traveling money all the same.

If they had laughed behind her back before Carlos, if they had joked at her expense then, it came to her only as pale sensation: a broken gesture upon entering study hall; an eye slide as she turned away from her locker; an unstable smile as she joined a crowded lunch table. She had never been truly popular, but her address and her father's money hid the fact. Now she was an open joke (Pallas Truelove ran off with the jaaa-ni-tor don't you love it?) that no one tried to hide. She was back in that place where final wars are waged, the organized trenches of high school, where shame is the plate-shifting time it takes to walk down the hall, failure is a fumble with the combination lock and loathing is a condom wafer clogging a fountain. Where aside from the exchange of clothes and toys, there are no good intentions. Where smugness reigns, judgments instant, dismissals permanent. And the adults haven't a clue. Only prison could be as blatant and as frightening, for beneath its rules and rituals scratched a life of gnawing violence. Those who came from peaceful well-regulated homes were overtaken by a cruelty that visited them as soon as they entered the gates. Cruelty decked out in juvenile glee.

Pallas tried. But the humiliation wore her down. Milton pumped her about her mother. He had been warned about the consequences of marrying outside his own people, and every warning had come true: Dee Dee was irresponsible, amoral; a slut if the truth be told. Pallas was vague, noncommittal in her answers. He was still pursuing a lawsuit against the school for its lax and endangering environment, not to speak of its criminally inclined employees. But the "victim" of the "abduction" had gone willingly; and the destination of the "across state lines" journey was the "victim's" own mother. How criminal could that be? Was there something going on in the father's home they should know about? Something that made the daughter want to, eager to, escape to her mother? Furthermore, nothing untoward had happened on school grounds—except the repair of the "victim's" car and safe guidance home. Also the "abduction" took place during the holiday when the school was closed. Moreover, the "victim" had not only gone willingly, she had cooperated and deceived to voluntarily accompany a man (an artist, even) who had no priors and whose demeanor and work at the high school was exemplary. Had she been assaulted by him sexually? The "victim" said No, no, no, no. Did he drug her, give her something illegal to smoke? Pallas shook her head no, remembering that it was her mother who did that. Who were these people who hit your car? I don't know. I never saw their faces. I got out of there. Where to? I hitched and some people took me in. Who? Some people. In a church kind of place. In Minnesota? No, Oklahoma. What's the address, phone number? Daddy, give it up. I'm home, okay? Yeah but I don't want to have to worry about you. Don't. Don't.

Pallas didn't feel well. Everything she ate added a pound in spite of the fact that she threw most of it up. Thanksgiving she spent alone, with food Providence had prepared. Christmas she begged relief. Milton said No. You stay right here. Just Chicago, she said, to visit his sister. He agreed, finally, and his executive secretary made the arrangements. Pallas stayed with her aunt till December 30, when she took off (leaving a reassuringly misleading note). At the Tulsa airport, it took two and a half hours to hire a car and driver to take her all the way to the Convent. Just a visit, she said. Just to find out how everybody was, she said. And who, besides herself, she could fool. Nobody apparently. Connie glimpsed in an instant. Now what?

Consolata tilts the fowl and peers into their silver and rose cavities. She tosses in salt and scours it all around, then rubs the outer skin with a cinnamon and butter mixture. Onion is added to the bits of neck meat, hearts and giblets speckling the broth. As soon as the hens are roasted brown enough and tender she sets them aside so they can reclaim their liquids.

Lukewarm and shallow, the tub water rose only to her waist. Gigi liked it deep, hot, heavy with bubbles. The plumbing in the mansion was breaking up: producing colored water, heaving and sometimes failing to rise to the second floor. The well water passed through a wood-fed boiler nobody other than herself was interested in preserving. She was an habitual nuisance, trying to accumulate gallons of piping-hot water from a decrepit system that was worse than ever in winter. Seneca, of course, had helped out, bringing several pails of steamy water from the kitchen stove to the bathroom. For bubbles she poured in grains of Ivory Snow and whipped the water up as best she could, although the result was a disappointing slime. She had asked Seneca to join her in the tub, got the usual refusal, and although she understood why her friend preferred not to be seen naked, Gigi couldn't resist teasing her about the infrequency of her bathing. The bloody toilet tissue she had seen, but the ridges on Seneca's skin had only been felt under the covers. Blunt and obnoxious as she could be, Gigi could not ask her about them. The answer might come too close to the bleeding black boy scene.

She stretched her legs out and lifted her feet to admire them, as she had done many times when she ran them up K.D.'s spine while she lay in the loft and he sat with his naked back to her. She missed him, now and then. His chaotic devotion, full of moods and hurts and yearning and lots and lots of giving in. Well, she had dogged him a bit. Enjoyed his availability and adoration because she had so little experience of either. Mikey. Nobody could call that love. But K.D.'s version didn't stay fun for long. She had teased, insulted or refused him once too often, and he chased her around the house, grabbed her, smacked her. Mavis and Seneca had pulled him off, used kitchen equipment on him and got him out of there—all three of them answering his curses with better ones of their own.

Ah, well. This is a new year, she thought. Nineteen seventy-five. New plans, since the old ones had turned out to be trash. When she finally got the box out of the bathroom tile, she whooped to find it full of certificates. The bank officer was tickled, too, and offered her twenty-five dollars for the pleasure of framing them or putting them in a display case for the amusement of his customers. Not every day you could see documentation of one of the biggest scams in the West. She held out for fifty dollars and stomped out of the bank ordering Mavis to just drive, please.

She would make Seneca leave with her. For good this time. Get back in the fray. Somehow. Somewhere. Her mother was unlocatable; her father on death row. Only a grandfather left, in a spiffy trailer in Alcorn, Mississippi. She had not thought about it too carefully, but now she wondered exactly why she had left. The fray, that is. It wasn't just the bleeding boy or Mikey's trick about the couple making out in the desert or the short guy's advice about clear water and entwined trees. Before Mikey, the point of it all was lost to entertainment and adventure. Provocative demonstrations, pamphlets, bickering, police, squatters, leaders and talking, talking, so much talk. None of it was serious. Gigi lifted soapy hands to reclasp a roller in her hair. Neither a high school nor a college student, no one, not even the other girls, took her seriousness seriously. If she hadn't been able to print, no one would have known she was there. Except Mikey. "Bastards," she said aloud. And then, not knowing which of the bastards infuriated her most, she slapped the awful bathwater, hissing "Shit!" with each stroke. It calmed her after a while, enough for her to lean back in the tub, cover her face and whisper into her dripping wet palms, "No, you stupid, stupid bitch. Because you weren't tough enough. Smart enough. Like with every other goddamn thing you got no staying power. You thought it was going to be fun and that it would work. In a season or two. You thought we were hot lava and when they broke us down into sand, you ran."

Gigi was not the crying type; even now, when she realized she had not approved of herself in a long, long time, her eyes were desert-skull dry.

Consolata is peeling and quartering small brown potatoes. She simmers them in water seasoned with pan juices, bay leaf and sage before arranging them in a skillet where they turn darkly gold. She sprinkles paprika and seeds of blackest pepper over them. "Oh, yes," she says. "Oh, yes."

Best goddamn thing on wheels was how he put it, and Mavis hoped his affection for the ten-year-old Cadillac meant he'd give her a break.

She would never know if he did, but just before his shop closed for the day, the mechanic finished and took fifty labor, thirty-two parts, oil and gas thirteen, so almost all of the cornfield rent money was gone. Not another payment due from Mr. Person for three months. Still, there was enough for regular shopping, plus the paint Connie wanted (for the red chair, she guessed; but white too, so maybe the chicken coop), as well as the ice cream sticks. The twins were fond of them and ate them right away. But the Christmas toys had been untouched, so Mavis had spent the five-hour wait for the tuneup and repairs exchanging the Fisher-Price truck for a Tonka and the Tiny Tina doll for one that spoke. Soon Pearl would be old enough for a Barbie. It was amazing how they changed and grew. They could not hold their heads up when they departed, but when she first heard them in the mansion, they were already toddlers, two years old. Based on their laughter, she could tell precisely. And based on how well integrated they were with the other children who chased about the rooms, she knew how they grew. Now they were school age, six and a half, and Mavis had to think of age-appropriate birthday and Christmas presents.

She had been so lonely for them when she'd traveled back to Maryland in 1970. Watching recess at the school where she had enrolled Sal, Frankie and Billy James, she realized with a shock that Sal would be in junior high now, Billy James in third grade and Frankie in fifth. Still, there was no question in her mind that she would recognize them, although she wasn't sure she would identify herself. It may have been her fingers clawed into the playground fencing or something awry in her face; whatever it was it must have frightened the students because a man came over and asked her questions—none of which she could answer. She hurried away trying to hide and look at the same time. She wanted to get to Peg's house but not be seen by Frank or next-door neighbors. When she found it—the bonneted girl still led the ducks—she wept. The rose of Sharon, so strong and wild and beautiful, had been chopped completely down. Only fear of being recognized kept her from running through the street. With swift and brilliant clarity, she understood that she was not safe out there or any place where

Merle and Pearl were not. And that was before she telephoned Birdie and learned of the warrant.

Mavis had pushed her hair into a dark green tam, bought a pair of dime-store glasses and taken a bus to Washington, D.C., and on to Chicago. There she made the purchases Connie wanted for Mother, took another bus, another and arrived at the bus depot parking lot in Middleton, where she had left the Cadillac. Rushing to get the supplies to Connie and be in the company of her twins, she sped all the way. Nervous, shallow of breath, Mavis skidded up the driveway and braked near a nude Gigi who had already taken up residence in her shelter. For three years they bickered and fought and managed, for Connie's sake, to avoid murder. Mavis believed that it was Gigi's distraction with the man from Ruby that kept either one from picking up a knife. For Mavis would have done it, fought to the end anybody, including that street-tough bitch, who threatened to take her life and leave her children unprotected. So it was with sincere, even extravagant, welcome that she had greeted sweet Seneca. A welcome Gigi shared completely, for when Seneca arrived, she spit out that K.D. person like a grape seed. In the new configuration, Mavis' pride of place was secure. Even the sad little rich girl with the hurt but pretty face had not disturbed it. The twins were happy, and Mavis was still closer to Connie than any of the others. And it was because they were so close, understood each other so well, that Mavis had begun to worry. Not about Connie's nocturnal habits, or her drinking—or her not drinking, in fact, for the familiar fumes had disappeared recently. Something else. The way Connie nodded as though listening to someone near; how she said Uh huh or If you say so, answering questions no one had asked. Also she not only had stopped using sunglasses but was dressed up, sort of, every day, in one of the dresses Soane Morgan used to give her when she was through with them. And on her feet were the shiny nun shoes that once sat on her dresser. But with merry laughter ringing in her own ears, ice cream sticks melting in the dead of winter, she was in a weak position to judge such things. Connie never questioned the reality of the twins and for Mavis, who had no intention of explaining or defending what she knew to be true, that acceptance was central. The night visitor was making fewer and fewer appearances, and while that concerned her, what preoccupied her was how fast Merle and Pearl were growing. And whether she could keep up.

Six yellow apples, wrinkled from winter storage, are cored and floating in water. Raisins are heating in a saucepan of wine. Consolata fills the hollow of each apple with a creamy mixture of egg yolks, honey, pecans and butter, to which she adds, one by one, the wine-swollen raisins. She pours the flavored wine into a pan and plops the apples down in. The sweet, warm fluid moves.

The little streets were narrow and straight, but as soon as she made them they flooded. Sometimes she held toilet tissue to catch the blood, but she liked to let it run too. The trick was to slice at just the right depth. Not too light, or the cut yielded too faint a line of red. Not so deep it rose and gushed over so fast you couldn't see the street. Although she had moved the map from her arms to her thighs, she recognized with pleasure the traces of old roads, avenues that even Norma had been repelled by. One was sometimes enough for months. Then there were times when she did two a day, hardly giving a street time to close before she opened another one. But she was not reckless. Her instruments were clean, her iodine (better than Mercurochrome) plentiful. And she had added aloe cream to her kit.

The habit, begun in one of the foster homes, started as an accident. Before her foster brother—another kid in Mama Greer's house—got her underwear off the first time, a safety pin holding the waist of her jeans together where a metal button used to be opened and scratched her stomach as Harry yanked on them. Once the jeans were tossed away and he got to her panties, the line of blood excited him even more. She did not cry. It did not hurt. When Mama Greer bathed her, she clucked, "Poor baby. Why didn't you tell me?" and Mercurochromed the jagged cut. She was not sure what she should have told: the safety pin scratch or Harry's behavior. So she pin-scratched herself on purpose and showed it to Mama Greer. Because the sympathy she got was diluted, she told her about Harry. "Don't you ever say that again. Do you hear me? Do you? Nothing like that happens here." After a meal of her favorite things, she was placed in another home. Nothing happened for years. Until junior high school, then the eleventh grade. By then she knew that there was something inside her that made boys snatch her and men flash her. If she was drinking Coke with five girls at a dime store counter, she was the one whose nipple got tweaked by a boy on a dare from his sniggering friends. Four girls, or just one, might walk down the street, but when she passed the man sitting with his baby daughter on a park bench, it was then he lifted his penis out and made kissing noises. Refuge with boyfriends was no better. They took her devotion for granted, but if she complained to them about being fondled by friends or strangers their fury was directed at her, so she knew it was something inside that was the matter.

She entered the vice like a censored poet whose suspect lexicon was too supple, too shocking to publish. It thrilled her. It steadied her. Access to this under garment life kept her own eyes dry, inducing a serenity rocked only by crying women, the sight of which touched off a pain so wildly triumphant she would do anything to kill it. She was ten and not cutting sidewalks when Kennedy was killed and the whole world wept in public. But she was fifteen when King was killed one spring and another Kennedy that summer. She called in sick to her baby-sitting job each time and stayed indoors to cut short streets, lanes, alleys into her arms. Her blood work was fairly easy to hide. Like Eddie Turtle, most of her boyfriends did it in the dark. For those who insisted on answers she invented a disease. Sympathy was instant for the scars did look surgical.

The safety available in Connie's house had become less intact when Pallas arrived. She had spent a lot of time trying to cheer and feed her, for when Pallas wasn't eating she was crying or trying not to. The relief that descended when the girl left last August disappeared when she returned in December—prettier, fatter, pretending she had just stopped by for a visit. In a limousine, no less. With three suitcases. It was January now, and her night sniffling could be heard all over the house.

Seneca did another street. An intersection, in fact, for it crossed the one she'd done a moment ago.

The table is set; the food placed. Consolata takes off her apron. With the aristocratic gaze of the blind she sweeps the women's faces and says, "I call myself Consolata Sosa. If you want to be here you do what I say. Eat how I say. Sleep when I say. And I will teach you what you are hungry for."

The women look at each other and then at a person they do not recognize. She has the features of dear Connie, but they are sculpted somehow—higher cheekbones, stronger chin. Had her eyebrows always been that thick, her teeth that pearly white? Her hair shows no gray. Her skin is smooth as a peach. Why is she talking that way? And what is she talking about? they wonder. This sweet, unthreatening old lady who seemed to love each one of them best; who never criticized, who shared everything but needed little or no care; required no emotional investment; who listened; who locked no doors and accepted each as she was. What is she talking about, this ideal parent, friend, companion in whose company they were safe from harm? What is she thinking, this perfect landlord who charged nothing and welcomed anybody; this granny goose who could be confided in or ignored, lied to or suborned; this play mother who could be hugged or walked out on, depending on the whim of the child?

"If you have a place," she continued, "that you should be in and somebody who loves you waiting there, then go. If not stay here and follow me. Someone could want to meet you."

No one left. There were nervous questions, a single burst of frightened giggling, a bit of pouting and simulated outrage, but in no time at all they came to see that they could not leave the one place they were free to leave.

Gradually they lost the days.

· · ·

In the beginning the most important thing was the template. First they had to scrub the cellar floor until its stones were as clean as rocks on a shore. Then they ringed the place with candles. Consolata told each to undress and lie down. In flattering light under Consolata's soft vision they did as they were told. How should we lie? However you feel. They tried arms at the sides, outstretched above the head, crossed over breasts or stomach. Seneca lay on her stomach at first, then changed to her back, hands clasping her shoulders. Pallas lay on her side, knees drawn up. Gigi flung her legs and arms apart, while Mavis struck a floater's pose, arms angled, knees pointing in. When each found the position she could tolerate on the cold, uncompromising floor, Consolata walked around her and painted the body's silhouette. Once the outlines were complete, each was instructed to remain there. Unspeaking. Naked in candlelight.

They wriggled in acute distress but were reluctant to move outside the mold they had chosen. Many times they thought they could not endure another second, but none wished to be the first to give in before those pale watching eyes. Consolata spoke first.

"My child body, hurt and soil, leaps into the arms of a woman who teach me my body is nothing my spirit everything. I agreed her until I met another. My flesh is so hungry for itself it ate him. When he fell away the woman rescue me from my body again. Twice she saves it. When her body sickens I care for it in every way flesh works. I hold it in my arms and between my legs. Clean it, rock it, enter it to keep it breath. After she is dead I can not get past that. My bones on hers the only good thing. Not spirit. Bones. No different from the man. My bones on his the only true thing. So I wondering where is the spirit lost in this? It is true, like bones. It is good, like bones. One sweet, one bitter. Where is it lost? Hear me, listen. Never break them in two. Never put one over the other. Eve is Mary's mother. Mary is the daughter of Eve."

Then, in words clearer than her introductory speech (which none of them understood), she told them of a place where white sidewalks met the sea and fish the color of plums swam alongside children. She spoke of fruit that tasted the way sapphires look and boys using rubies for dice. Of scented cathedrals made of gold where gods and goddesses

sat in the pews with the congregation. Of carnations tall as trees.
Dwarfs with diamonds for teeth. Snakes aroused by poetry and bells.
Then she told them of a woman named Piedade, who sang but never
said a word.

That is how the loud dreaming began. How the stories rose in that
place. Half-tales and the never-dreamed escaped from their lips to soar
high above guttering candles, shifting dust from crates and bottles.
And it was never important to know who said the dream or whether it
had meaning. In spite of or because their bodies ache, they step easily
into the dreamer's tale. They enter the heat in the Cadillac, feel the
smack of cold air in the Higgledy Piggledy. They know their tennis
shoes are unlaced and that a bra strap annoys each time it slips from
the shoulder. The Armour package is sticky. They inhale the perfume
of sleeping infants and feel parent-cozy although they notice one's
head is turned awkwardly. They adjust the sleeping baby head then
refuse, outright refuse, what they know and drive away home. They
climb porch stairs carrying frankfurters and babies and purse in their
arms. Saying, "They don't seem to want to wake up, Sal. Sal? Look
here. They don't seem to want to." They kick their legs underwater,
but not too hard for fear of waking fins or scales also down below. The
male voices saying saying forever saying push their own down their
throats. Saying, saying until there is no breath to scream or contradict.
Each one blinks and gags from tear gas, moves her hand slowly to the
scraped shin, the torn ligament. Runs up and down the halls by day,
sleeps in a ball with the lights on at night. Folds the five hundred dollars in the foot of her sock. Yelps with pain from a stranger's penis and a
mother's rivalry—alluring and corrosive as cocaine.

In loud dreaming, monologue is no different from a shriek; accusations directed to the dead and long gone are undone by murmurs of
love. So, exhausted and enraged, they rise and go to their beds vow-
ing never to submit to that again but knowing full well they will. And
they do.

Life, real and intense, shifted to down there in limited pools of
light, in air smoky from kerosene lamps and candle wax. The tem-
plates drew them like magnets. It was Pallas who insisted they shop for
tubes of paint, sticks of colored chalk. Paint thinner and chamois

cloth. They understood and began to begin. First with natural features: breasts and pudenda, toes, ears and head hair. Seneca duplicated in robin's egg blue one of her more elegant scars, one drop of red at its tip. Later on, when she had the hunger to slice her inner thigh, she chose instead to mark the open body lying on the cellar floor. They spoke to each other about what had been dreamed and what had been drawn. Are you sure she was your sister? Maybe she was your mother. Why? Because a mother might, but no sister would do such a thing. Seneca capped her tube. Gigi drew a heart locket around her body's throat, and when Mavis asked her about it, she said it was a gift from her father which she had thrown into the Gulf of Mexico. Were there pictures inside? asked Pallas. Yeah. Two. Whose? Gigi didn't answer; she simply reinforced the dots marking the locket's chain. Pallas had put a baby in her template's stomach. When asked who the father was, she said nothing but drew next to the baby a woman's face with long eyelashes and a crooked fluffy mouth. They pressed her, but gently, without joking or scorn. Carlos? The boys who drove her into the water? Pallas gave the crooked mouth two long fangs.

January folded. February too. By March, days passed uncut from night as careful etchings of body parts and memorabilia occupied them. Yellow barrettes, red peonies, a green cross on a field of white. A majestic penis pierced with a Cupid's bow. Rose of Sharon petals, Lorna Doones. A bright orange couple making steady love under a childish sun.

With Consolata in charge, like a new and revised Reverend Mother, feeding them bloodless food and water alone to quench their thirst, they altered. They had to be reminded of the moving bodies they wore, so seductive were the alive ones below.

A customer stopping by would have noticed little change. May have wondered why the garden was as yet untilled, or who had scratched SORROW on the Cadillac's trunk. May even have wondered why the old woman who answered the knock did not cover her awful eyes with dark glasses; or what on earth the younger ones had done with their hair. A neighbor would notice more—a sense of surfeit; the charged air of the house, its foreign feel and a markedly different look in the tenants' eyes—sociable and connecting when they spoke to you, otherwise they were still and appraising. But if a friend came by, her initial alarm at the sight of the young women might be muted by their adult manner; how calmly themselves they seemed. And Connie— how straight-backed and handsome she looked. How well that familiar dress became her. As she slid into the driver's seat, a basket with a parcel on top beside her, it would annoy her at first being unable to say exactly what was absent. As she drew closer to home and drove down Central Avenue, her gaze might fall on Sweetie Fleetwood's house, Pat Best's house, or she might notice one of the Poole boys or Menus on his way to Ace's. Then she might realize what was missing: unlike some people in Ruby, the Convent women were no longer haunted. Or hunted either, she might have added. But there she would have been wrong.

LONE

The way was narrow, the turn sharp, but she managed to get the Oldsmobile off the dirt and onto the tarmac without knocking the sign down completely. Earlier, on the way in, with the darkness and the single headlight, Lone couldn't prevent the bumper from scraping it, and now, leaving the Convent, its post leaned and the sign—EARLY MELONES—was about to fall. "Can't spell worth poot," she murmured. The one wrapped in a sheet, most likely. Not much schooling there. But "Early" was correct, and not just the letters. July not over, and the Convent garden had melons already ripe for picking. Like their heads. Smooth outside, sweet inside, but Lord, were they thick. None of them would listen. Said Connie was busy, refused to call her and didn't believe a word Lone said. After driving out there in the middle of the night to tell them, warn them, she watched in help-less fury as they yawned and smiled. Now she had to figure out what else to do, otherwise the melons that got split would be their bald heads.

The night air was hot and the rain she had been smelling was far but still coming, which is what she'd thought two hours ago, when, hoping to harvest mandrake while it was still dry, she padded around the streambank near the Oven. Had she not been, she never would have heard the men or discovered the devilment they were cooking.

Clouds hid the nightsky's best jewelry but the road to Ruby was familiar as a collection plate. She squinted nevertheless, in case some-thing or somebody scampered up ahead—beyond the Oldsmobile's single headlight. It could be possum, raccoon, white-tail deer, or even an angry woman since it was women who walked this road. Only women. Never men. For more than twenty years Lone had watched them. Back and forth, back and forth: crying women, staring women, scowling, lip-biting women or women just plain lost. Out here in a red and gold land cut through now and then with black rock or a swatch of green; out here under skies so star-packed it was disgraceful; out here where the wind handled you like a man, women dragged their sorrow up and down the road between Ruby and the Convent. They were the only pedestrians. Sweetie Fleetwood had walked it, Billie Delia too. And the girl called Seneca. Another called Mavis. Arnette, too, and more than once. And not just these days. They had walked this road from the very first. Soane Morgan, for instance, and once, when she was young, Connie as well. Many of the walkers Lone had seen; others she learned about. But the men never walked the road; they drove it, although sometimes their destination was the same as the women's: Sargeant, K.D., Roger, Menus. And the good Deacon himself a couple of decades back. Well, if she did not get somebody to fix the fan belt and plug the oil pan, she would be walking it too, provided there was anyplace left worth traveling to.

If ever there was a time for speeding, this was it, but the condition of the car precluded that. In 1965 the wipers, the air-conditioning, the radio worked. Now a fierce heater was the only element reminiscent of the Oldsmobile's original power. In 1968, after it had had two owners, Deek and then Soane Morgan, Soane asked her if she could use it. Lone screamed her joy. Finally, at seventy-nine, unlicensed but feisty, she was going to learn to drive and have her own car too. No more hitching up the wagon, no more brakes squealing in her yard at all hours, summoning her to emergencies that weren't or to standbys that turned into crises. She could follow her own mind, check on the mothers when she wished; tool on up to the house in her own car and, most important, leave when she wanted to. But the gift came too late. Just as she became truly auto mobile, nobody wanted her craft. After having infuriated the hooved and terrified the clawed, having churned columns of red dust up and down tractor trails for weeks, she had no place to go. Her patients let her poke and peep, but for the delivery they traveled hours (if they could make it) to the hospital in Demby, for the cool hands of whitemen. Now, at eighty-six, in spite of her never-fail reputation (which was to say she never lost a mother, as Fairy once had), they refused her their swollen bellies, their shrieks and grabbing hands. Laughed at her clean bellybands, her drops of mother's urine. Poured her pepper tea in the toilet. It did not matter that she had curled up on their sofas to rock irritable children, nodded in their kitchens after braiding their daughters' hair, planted herbs in their gardens and given good counsel for the past twenty-five years and for fifty more in Haven before being sent for. No matter she taught them how to comb their breasts to set the milk flowing; what to do with the afterbirth; what direction the knife under the mattress should point. No matter she searched the county to get them the kind of dirt they wanted to eat. No matter she had gotten in the bed with them, pressing the soles of her feet to theirs, helping them push, push! Or massaged their stomachs with sweet oil for hours. No matter at all. She had been good enough to bring them into the world, and when she and Fairy were summoned to continue that work in the new place, Ruby, the mothers sat back in their chairs, spread their knees and breathed with relief. Now that Fairy was dead, leaving one midwife for a population that needed and prided itself on families as large as neighborhoods, the mothers took their wombs away from her. But Lone believed that there was more to it than the fashion for maternity wards. She had delivered the Fleetwood babies and each of the defectives had stained her reputation as if she had *made* the babies, not simply delivered them. The suspicion that she was bad luck and the comforts of the Demby hospital combined to deprive her of the work for which she was trained. One of the mothers told her that she couldn't help loving the week of rest, the serving tray, the thermometer, the blood pressure tests; was crazy about the doze of daytime and the pain pills; but mostly she said she loved how people kept asking her how she felt. None of that was available to her if she delivered at home. There she'd be fixing the family's breakfast the second or third day and worrying about the quality of the cow's milk as well as her own. Others must have felt the same—the luxury of sleep and being away from home, the newborn taken each night for somebody else's care. And the fathers—well, Lone suspected they, too, were happier with closed doors, waiting in the hall, being in a place where other men were in charge instead of some toothless woman gumming gum to keep her gums strong. "Don't mistake the fathers' thanks," Fairy had warned her. "Men scared of us, always will be. To them we're death's hand-maiden standing as between them and the children their wives carry." During those times, Fairy said, the midwife is the interference, the one giving orders, on whose secret skill so much depended, and the dependency irritated them. Especially here in this place where they had come to multiply in peace. Fairy was right as usual, but Lone had another liability. It was said she could read minds, a gift from some-thing that, whatever it was, was not God, and which she had used as early as two, when she positioned herself to be found in the yard when her mother was dead in the bed. Lone denied it; she believed every-body knew what other people were thinking. They just avoided the obvious. Yet she did know something more profound than Morgan memory or Pat Best's history book. She knew what neither memory nor history can say or record: the "trick" of life and its "reason."

In any case, her livelihood over (she had been called on twice in the last eight years), Lone was dependent on the generosity of congre-gations and neighbors. She spent her time gathering medicinal herbs, flitting from one church to another to receive a Helping Hand collec-tion, and surveying the fields, which invited her not because they were open but because they were full of secrets. Like the carful of skeletons she'd found a few months ago. If she had been paying attention to her own mind instead of gossip, she would have investigated the Lenten buzzards as soon as they appeared—two years ago at spring thaw, March of 1974. But because they were seen right when the Morgans and Fleetwoods had announced the wedding, people were confused about whether the marriage was summoning the buzzards or protect-ing the town from them. Now everybody knew they had been attracted to a family feast of people lost in a blizzard. Arkansas plates. Harper Jury's label on some cough medicine. They loved each other, the fam-ily did. Even with the disturbance of birds of prey, you could tell they were embracing as they slept deeper and deeper into that deep cold.

At first she thought Sargeant must have known all about it. He raised corn in those fields. But there was no mistaking the astonishment on his face or on any of the others' when they heard. The problem was whether to notify the law or not. Not, it was decided. Even to bury them would be admitting to something they had no hand in. When some of the men went to look, much of their attention was not on the scene at hand but west on the Convent that loomed in their sight line. She should have known then. Had she been paying attention, first to the buzzards, then to the minds of men, she would not be using up all her Wrigley's and gasoline on a mission she hoped would be her last. Eyesight too dim, joints too stiff—this was no work for a gifted midwife. But God had given her the task, bless His holy heart, and at thirty miles an hour on a hot July night, she knew she was traveling in His time, not outside it. It was He who placed her there; encouraged her to look for the medicine best picked dry at night.

The streambed was dry; the coming rain would remedy that even as it softened the two-legged mandrake root. She had heard light laughter and radio music traveling from the Oven. Young couples courting. At least they were in the open, she thought, not scrambling up into a hayloft or under a blanket in the back of a truck. Then the laughter and the music stopped. Deep male voices gave orders; flashlights cut shafts on bodies, faces, hands and what they carried. Without a murmur, the couples left, but the men didn't. Leaning against the Oven's walls or squatting on their haunches, they clustered in darkness. Lone shrouded her own flashlight with her apron and would have moved invisibly to the rear of Holy Redeemer, where her car was parked, had she not remembered the other events she had ignored or misunderstood: the Lenten buzzards; Apollo's new handgun. She clicked herself back into complete darkness and sat down on the thirsty grass. She had to stop nursing resentment at the townspeople's refusal of her services; stop stealing penny revenge by ignoring what was going on and letting evil have its way. Playing blind was to avoid the language God spoke in. He did not thunder instructions or whisper messages into ears. Oh, no. He was a liberating God. A teacher who taught you how to learn, to see for yourself. His signs were clear, abundantly so, if you stopped steeping in vanity's sour juice and paid attention to His world. He wanted her to hear the men gathered at the Oven to decide and figure out how to run the Convent women off, and if He wanted her to witness that, He must also want her to do something about it. At first she didn't know what was going on, or what to do. But as in the past when she was confused, she closed her eyes and whispered, "Thy will. Thy will." The voices rose then, and she heard as clear as if she had been standing among them what they said to one another and what they meant. What they vocalized and what they did not.

There were nine of them. Some smoked, some sighed, as one by one they began to speak. Much of what they said Lone had heard before, although without the rough scales the words grew as they snaked through the night air. The topic was not new, but it had none of the delight that dressed the theme when delivered from a pulpit. Reverend Cary had captured the subject in a sermon so well received he included a version of it every Sunday.

"What have you given up to live here?" he asked, hitting "up" like a soprano. "What sacrifice do you make *every* day to live here in God's beauty, His bounty, His peace?"

"Tell us, Reverend. Say it."

"I'll tell you what." Reverend Cary chuckled.

"Yes, sir."

"Go ahead, now."

Reverend Cary had lifted his right hand straight in the air and curled it into a fist. Then, one finger at a time, he began to list what the congregation had deprived itself of.

"Television."

The congregation rippled with laughter.

"Disco."

They laughed merrily, louder, shaking their heads.

"Policemen."

They roared with laughter.

"Picture shows, filthy music." He continued with fingers from his left hand. "Wickedness in the streets, theft in the night, murder in the morning. Liquor for lunch and dope for dinner. That's what you have given up."

Each item drew sighs and moans of sorrow. Suffused with gratitude for having refused and escaped the sordid, the cruel, the ungodly, all of the up-to-date evils disguised as pleasure, each member of the congregation could feel his or her heart swell with pity for those who wrestled with those "sacrifices."

But there was no pity here. Here, when the men spoke of the ruination that was upon them—how Ruby was changing in intolerable ways—they did not think to fix it by extending a hand in fellowship or love. They mapped defense instead and honed evidence for its need, till each piece fit an already polished groove. A few did most of the talking, some said little and two said nothing at all, but silent though they were, Lone knew the leadership was twinned.

Remember how they scandalized the wedding? What you say? Uh huh and it was that very same day I caught them kissing on each other in the back of that ratty Cadillac. Very same day, and if that wasn't enough to please the devil, two more was fighting over them in the dirt. Right down in it. Lord, I hate a nasty woman. Sweetie said they tried their best to poison her. I heard that too. Got caught in a snowstorm out that way and took shelter with them. Should have known better. Well, you know Sweetie. Anyway said she heard noises coming from somewhere in that house. Sounded to her like little babies crying. What in God's name little babies doing out there? You asking me? Whatever it is, it ain't natural. Well, it used to house little girls, didn't it? Yeah, I remember. Said it was a school. School for what? What they teaching out there? Sargeant, didn't you find marijuana growing in the middle of your alfalfa? Yep. Sure did. That don't surprise me. All I know is they beat Arnette up some when she went out there to confront them about the lies they told her. She thinks they kept her baby and told her it was stillborn. My wife says they did an abortion on her. You believe it? I don't know, but I wouldn't put it past them. What I do know is how messed up her face was. Aw, man. We can't have this. Roger told me that the Mother—you know, the old white one used to shop here sometimes?—well, he said when she died she weighed less than fifty pounds and shone like sulfur. Jesus! Said the girl he dropped off there was openly flirting with him. That's the one half naked all the time? I knew something was wrong with her from the time she stepped off the bus. How she get a bus to come out here anyway? Guess, why don't you? You think they got powers? I *know* they got powers. Question is whose power is stronger. Why don't they just get on out, leave? Huh! Would you if you had a big old house to live in without having to work for it? Something's going on out there, and I don't like any of it. No men. Kissing on themselves. Babies hid away. Jesus! No telling what else. Look what happened to Billie Delia after she started hanging around out there. Knocked her mama down the stairs and took off for that place like a shoat hunting teat. I hear they drink like fish too. The old woman was always drunk when I saw her and remember the first words out their mouths when they came to the wedding? Anything to drink is what they asked for and when they got a glass of lemonade, they acted like they'd been spit on and walked on out the door. I remember that. Bitches. More like witches. But look here, brother, the bones beat all. I can't believe a whole family died out there without nobody knowing it. They wasn't all that far away, know what I'm saying? Can't nobody tell me they left the road and got themselves lost in a field with a big old house less than two miles away. They would have seen it. Had to. The man would have got out and walked to it, see what I mean? He could reason, couldn't he, and even if he couldn't reason he could see. How you going to miss a house that size out here in land flat as a nail head? You saying they had something to do with it? Listen, nothing ever happened around here like what's going on now. Before those heifers came to town this was a peaceable kingdom. The others before them at least had some religion. These here sluts out there by themselves never step foot in church and I bet you a dollar to a fat nickel they ain't thinking about one either. They don't need men and they don't need God. Can't say they haven't been warned. Asked first and then warned. If they stayed to themselves, that'd be something. But they don't. They meddle. Drawing folks out there like flies to shit and everybody who goes near them is maimed somehow and the mess is seeping back into *our* homes, *our* families. We can't have it, you all. Can't have it at all.

So, Lone thought, the fangs and the tail are somewhere else. Out yonder all slithery in a house full of women. Not women locked safely away from men; but worse, women who chose themselves for company, which is to say not a convent but a coven. Lone shook her head and adjusted her Doublemint. She was listening only halfheartedly to the words, trying to divine the thoughts behind them. Some of it she got right away. Sargeant, she knew, would be nodding at every shred of gossip, chewing on the rag end of truth and wondering aloud why this deliberately beautiful town governed by responsible men couldn't remain so: stable, prosperous, with no talk-back young people. Why would they want to leave and raise families (and customers) else-where? But he would be thinking how much less his outlay would be if he owned the Convent land, and how, if the women are gone from there, he would be in a better position to own it. Everyone knew he had already visited the Convent—to "warn" them, which is to say he offered to buy the place, and when the response was an incomprehen-sible stare, he told the old woman to "think carefully" and that "other things could happen to lower the price." Wisdom Poole would be looking for a reason to explain why he had no control anymore over his brothers and sisters. To explain how it happened that those who used to worship him, listen to him, were now strays trying to be on their own. The shooting last year between Brood and Apollo was over Billie Delia and would be enough reason for him to go gallivanting off for the pleasure of throwing some women in the road. Billie Delia was friendly with those women, made one of his younger brothers drive her out there, and it was after that that the trouble between Apollo and Brood turned dangerous. Neither one had followed Wisdom's orders to never speak to or look at that girl again. The result was biblical—a man lying in wait to slaughter his brother. As for the Fleetwoods, Arnold and Jeff, well, they'd been wanting to blame somebody for Sweetie's children for a long time. Maybe it was the midwife's fault, maybe it was the government's fault, but the midwife could only be disemployed and the government was not accountable, and although Lone had delivered some of Jeff's sick children long before the first woman arrived, they wouldn't let a little thing like that keep them from finding fault anywhere but in their own blood. Or Sweetie's. Menus, well, he'd be ripe for a raid on anybody. Spending those weeks out there drying out, you'd think he'd be grateful. Those women must have witnessed some things, seen some things he didn't want ranging around in anybody's mind in case they fell out of their mouths. Or maybe it was just to erase the shame he felt at having let Harper and the others talk him out of marrying that woman he brought home. That pretty redbone girl they told him was not good enough for him; said she was more like a fast woman than a bride. He let out like he drank because of what Vietnam had done to him, but Lone thought the pretty redbone girl's loss was more to the point. He hadn't had the courage to leave and go on and live with her someplace else. Chose instead both to submit to his father's rule and charge him a neat price for it: undisturbed acceptance of his affliction. Getting rid of some unattached women who had wiped up after him, washed his drawers, removed his vomit, listened to his curses as well as his sobs might convince him for a while that he was truly a man unpolluted by his mother's weakness, worthy of his father's patience and that he was right to let the redbone go. Lone could not count how many times she had sat in New Zion and heard his father, Harper, begin to testify, begin to examine his own sins and end up going on about loose women who could keep you from knowing who, what and where your children are. He'd married a Blackhorse woman, Catherine, and worried her into nervous digestion carrying on about what she was doing and who she was seeing and this and that, and was she properly instructing their daughter, Kate. Kate got married as fast as she could just to get out from under his hand. His first wife, Menus' mother, Martha, must have given him a bad time. So bad he never let their only son forget it. Then there was K.D., the family man. Talking about how strange one of those Convent girls was and how he knew it right away soon as he saw her get off the bus. Ha ha. He's a daddy now of a four-month-old son with all its fingers and toes and who knows maybe a full brain too courtesy of the doctor willing to treat black folks in Demby. So he and Arnette both sniffed their noses at Lone, and however happy Arnette must be now and willing to pass her earlier "mistake" off on the Convent women's tricking her, K.D. would have another grudge. The girl whose name he now scandalized he had stalked for years till she threw him out the door. Take a whole lot of healthy babies to make him forget that. He's a Morgan, after all, and they haven't forgotten a thing since 1755.

Lone understood these private thoughts and some of what Steward's and Deacon's motive might be: neither one put up with what he couldn't control. But she could not have imagined Steward's rancor—his bile at the thought that his grandnephew (maybe?) had surely been hurt or destroyed in that place. It was a floating blister in his bloodstream, which neither shrank nor came to a head. Nor could she have imagined how deep in the meat of his brain stem lay the memory of how close his brother came to breaking up his marriage to Soane. How off the course Deek slid when he was looking in those poison and poisoning eyes. For months the two of them had met secretly, for months Deek was distracted, making mistakes and just suppose the hussy had gotten pregnant? Had a mixed-up child? Steward seethed at the thought of that barely averted betrayal of all they owed and promised the Old Fathers. But a narrowly escaped treason against the fathers' law, the law of continuance and multiplication, was overwhelmed by the permanent threat to his cherished view of himself and his brother. The women in the Convent were for him a flaunting parody of the nineteen Negro ladies of his and his brother's youthful memory and perfect understanding. They were the degradation of that moment they'd shared of sunlit skin and verbena. They, with their mindless giggling, outraged the dulcet tones, the tinkling in the merry and welcoming laughter of the nineteen ladies who, scheduled to live forever in pastel shaded dreams, were now doomed to extinction by this new and obscene breed of female. He could not abide them for sullying his personal history with their streetwalkers' clothes and whores' appetites; mocking and desecrating the vision that carried him and his brother through a war, that imbued their marriages and strengthened their efforts to build a town where the vision could flourish. He would never forgive them that and he would not tolerate this loss of charity.

Nor did Lone know the glacier that was Deacon Morgan's pride. Its hidden bulk, its accretion and unmovability. She knew about his long ago relationship with Consolata. But she could not have fathomed his personal shame or understood how important it was to erase both the shame and the kind of woman he believed was its source. An uncontrollable, gnawing woman who had bitten his lip just to lap the blood it shed; a beautiful, golden-skinned, outside woman with moss-green eyes that tried to trap a man, close him up in a cellar room with liquor to enfeeble him so they could do carnal things, unnatural things in the dark; a Salomé from whom he had escaped just in time or she would have had his head on a dinner plate. That ravenous ground-fucking woman who had not left his life but had weaseled her way into Soane's affections and, he suspected, had plied her with evil potions to make her less loving than she used to be and it was not the eternal grieving for their sons that froze her but the mess she was swallowing still, given to her by the woman whose very name she herself had made into a joke and a travesty of what a woman should be.

Lone didn't, couldn't, know all, but she knew enough and the flashlights had revealed the equipment: handcuffs glinted, rope coiled and she did not have to guess what else they had. Stepping softly, she made her way along the edge of the stream toward her car. "Thy will. Thy will," she whispered, convinced that what she had heard and surmised was no idleness. The men had not come there merely to rehearse. Like boot camp recruits, like invaders preparing for slaughter, they were there to rave, to heat the blood or turn it icicle cold the better to execute the mission. One thing in particular she had quickly understood: the only voice not singing belonged to the one conducting the choir.

"Where is Richard Misner?" Lone didn't bother to say hello. She had knocked on Misner's door, then entered his house, to find it dark and empty. Now she had roused his closest neighbor, Frances Poole DuPres, from her sleep. Frances groaned.

"What in the world is going on with you, Lone?"

"Tell me where Misner is."

"They're gone to Muskogee. Why?"

"They? They who?"

"Reverend Misner and Anna. A conference. What you need him for this time of night?"

"Let me in," said Lone, and stepped past Frances into the living room.

"Come on in the kitchen," said Frances.

"No time. Listen." Lone described the meeting, saying, "A whole passel of menfolk planning something against the Convent. Morgans,

Fleetwoods and Wisdom's there too. They going after those women out there."

"Lord, what kind of mess is this? They're going to scare them off in the middle of the night?"

"Woman, listen to me. Those men got guns with sights on them."

"That doesn't mean anything. I've never seen my brother go anywhere minus his rifle, except church, and even then it's in the car."

"They got rope too, Frannie."

"Rope?"

"Two-inch."

"What're you thinking?"

"We wasting time. Where's Sut?"

"Sleep."

"Wake him."

"I'm not going to disturb my husband for some wild—"

"Wake him, Frannie. I am not a crazy woman and you know it."

The first drops were warm and fat, carrying the scent of white loco and cholla from regions north and west. They smashed into gentian, desert trumpets and slid from chicory leaves. Plump and slippery they rolled like mercury beads over the cracked earth between garden rows. As they sat in kitchen light, Lone, Frances and Sut DuPres could see, even smell, the rainfall, but they could not hear it, so soft, so downy, were the drops.

Sut was unconvinced that Lone's demand to rush out and stop them was called for but he did agree to speak to Reverends Pulliam and Cary in the morning. Lone said morning might be too late and took off in a huff to find somebody who didn't talk to her as if she were a child unable to wake from a nightmare. Anna Flood was gone; she couldn't go to Soane because of Deek; and since K.D. and Arnette had taken the house that Menus used to own, Dovey Morgan wouldn't be in town. She thought about Kate but knew she would not go up against her father. She considered Penelope but dismissed her, since she was not only married to Wisdom, she was Sargeant's daughter. Lone realized that she would have to go out to the ranches and farms, to people she trusted most not to let family relations cloud their minds. Working windshield wipers were an unavailable blessing, so Lone, rolling gum slowly around in her mouth, concentrated on being careful. Driving past the deserted Oven, pleased she had gotten the mayapples in time, she noticed there were no lights at Anna's place or, way back of it, in Deek Morgan's house. Lone squinted to negotiate the few miles of dirt road between Ruby's and the county's. It could be a tricky stretch because the earth was absorbing the rain now, swelling the roots of parched plants and forming rivulets wherever it could. She drove slowly, thinking if this mission was truly God's intention, nothing could stop her. Halfway to Aaron Poole's house the Oldsmobile halted in a roadside ditch.

Around the time Lone DuPres was trying to avoid the Early Melones sign, the men were finalizing details over coffee and something stronger for those who wished. None was a drinker, except Menus, but they did not object to lacing tonight's coffee. Behind Sargeant's barn-like building, where his trade took place, beyond the paddock where he once kept horses, was a shed. In it he repaired tack—a hobby now, no longer a chargeable service—ruminated and avoided the women in his family. A male cozy, it was equipped with a small stove, a freezer, a worktable and chairs, all standing on an unruinable floor. The men had just begun to blow in their cups when the rain started. After a few swallows they joined Sargeant in the yard to move sacks and cover equipment with tarpaulin. When they returned, drenched, to the shed they found themselves lighthearted and suddenly hungry. Sargeant suggested beefsteaks and went in his house to get what was needed to feed the men. Priscilla, his wife, heard him and offered to help, but he sent her back to bed, firmly. The scented rainfall drummed. The atmosphere in the shed was braced, companionable, as the men ate thick steaks prepared the old-fashioned way, fried in a piping hot skillet.

.   .   .

The rain's perfume was stronger north of Ruby, especially at the Convent, where thick white clover and Scotch broom colonized every place but the garden. Mavis and Pallas, aroused from sleep by its aroma, rushed to tell Consolata, Grace and Seneca that the longed for rain had finally come. Gathered in the kitchen door, first they watched, then they stuck out their hands to feel. It was like lotion on their fingers so they entered it and let it pour like balm on their shaved heads and upturned faces. Consolata started it; the rest were quick to join her. There are great rivers in the world and on their banks and the edges of oceans children thrill to water. In places where rain is light the thrill is almost erotic. But those sensations bow to the rapture of holy women dancing in hot sweet rain. They would have laughed, had enchantment not been so deep. If there were any recollections of a recent warning or intimations of harm, the irresistible rain washed them away. Seneca embraced and finally let go of a dark morning in state housing. Grace witnessed the successful cleansing of a white shirt that never should have been stained. Mavis moved in the shudder of rose of Sharon petals tickling her skin. Pallas, delivered of a delicate son, held him close while the rain rinsed away a scary woman on an escalator and all fear of black water. Consolata, fully housed by the god who sought her out in the garden, was the more furious dancer, Mavis the most elegant. Seneca and Grace danced together, then parted to skip through fresh mud. Pallas, smoothing raindrops from her baby's head, swayed like a frond.

Finally out of the ditch, Lone naturally sought out a DuPres. She had been reared in that family, rescued, then taught by one of the daughters. More than that, she knew what they were made of. Pious DuPres, son of Booker DuPres and nephew to the famous Juvenal DuPres, was her first choice. Like the Morgans and Blackhorses, they were pleased to be descendants of men who had governed in statehouses, but unlike them, they were prouder of earlier generations: artisans, gunsmiths, seamstresses, lacemakers, cobblers, ironmongers, masons whose serious work was stolen from them by white immigrants. Their deeper reverence was for the generations that had seen their shops burned and their supplies thrown overboard. Because white immigrants could not trust or survive fair competition, their people had been arrested, threatened, purged and eliminated from skilled labor and craft. But the families held on to what they could and what they had gained from 1755, when the first DuPres carried a white napkin over his arm and a prayer book in his pocket. The belief that steadied them was not grim. Virtue, unexpected goodness, made them smile. Deliberate righteousness lifted their hearts as little else could. They did not always know what it was, but they spent a lot of time trying to find out. Long before Juvenal was elected to the statehouse, supper conversation at a DuPres table focused on the problems each member was having, how each and all could handle or help. And always the turn was on the ethics of a deed, the clarity of motives, whether a behavior advanced His glory and kept His trust. None of the current DuPreses liked or approved of the Convent women, but that was way beside the point. The actions of Brood and Apollo had insulted them; Wisdom Poole was brother to their daughter-in-law, and in his participation in a group intent on hurting women — for whatever reason — they would quickly see the monster's handiwork. And so they did. When Lone told them all she had heard and what she knew, Pious wasted no time. He instructed his wife, Melinda, to get over to the Beauchamps' place; tell Ren and Luther to meet him. He and Lone would get to Deed Sands and Aaron Poole. Melinda said they ought to notify Dovey, but they could not agree on how to do that if Steward was there. Lone didn't know if they had already started for the Convent or were waiting for sunrise but said someone should risk it and inform Dovey, who could, if she wanted to, let Soane know what was going on.

Tired from their night dance but happy, the women return to the house. Drying themselves, they ask Consolata to tell them again about Piedade, while they oil their heads with wintergreen.

"We sat on the shorewalk. She bathed me in emerald water. Her voice made proud women weep in the streets. Coins fell from the fingers of artists and policemen, and the country's greatest chefs begged us to eat their food. Piedade had songs that could still a wave, make it pause in its curl listening to language it had not heard since the sea opened. Shepherds with colored birds on their shoulders came down from mountains to remember their lives in her songs. Travelers refused to board homebound ships while she sang. At night she took the stars out of her hair and wrapped me in its wool. Her breath smelled of pineapple and cashews. . . ."

The women sleep, wake and sleep again with images of parrots, crystal seashells and a singing woman who never spoke. At four in the morning they wake to prepare for the day. One mixes dough while another lights the stove. Others gather vegetables for the noon meal, then set out the breakfast things. The bread, kneaded into mounds, is placed in baking tins to rise.

Sunlight is yearning for brilliance when the men arrive. The stone-washed blue of the sky is hard to break, but by the time the men park behind shin oak and start for the Convent, the sun has cracked through. Glorious blue. The water of the night rises as mist from puddles and flooded crevices in the road's shoulder. When they reach the Convent, they avoid loud gravel crunch by weaving through tall grass and occasional rainbows to the front door. The claws, perhaps, snatch Steward out of the world. Mottled and glistening from rain, they flank the steps. As he mounts between them, he raises his chin and then his rifle and shoots open a door that has never been locked. It slants inward on its hinges. Sun follows him in, splashing the walls of the foyer, where sexualized infants play with one another through flaking paint. Suddenly a woman with the same white skin appears, and all Steward needs to see are her sensual appraising eyes to pull the trigger again. The other men are startled but not deterred from stepping over her. Fondling their weapons, feeling suddenly so young and good they are reminded that guns are more than decoration, intimidation or comfort. They are meant.

Deek gives the orders.

The men separate.

Three women preparing food in the kitchen hear a shot. A pause. Another shot. Cautiously they look through the swinging door. Backed by light from the slanted door, shadows of armed men loom into the hallway. The women race to the game room and close the door, seconds before the men position themselves in the hall. They hear footsteps pass and enter the kitchen they have just left. No windows in the game room—the women are trapped and know it. Minutes pass. Arnold and Jeff Fleetwood leave the kitchen and notice a trace of wintergreen in the air. They open the game room door. An alabaster ashtray slams into Arnold's temple, exhilarating the woman wielding it. She continues to smash until he is down on all fours, while Jeff, taken off guard, aims his gun a tick too late. It flies from his hand when a cue stick cracks his wrist and then, on upswing, rams into his jaw. He raises his arm, first for protection, then to snatch the point of the cue when the frame of Catherine of Siena breaks over his head.

The women run into the hall, but freeze when they see two figures exit the chapel. As they run back to the kitchen, Harper and Menus are close behind. Harper grabs the waist and arm of one. She is a handful, so he doesn't see the skillet swinging into his skull. He falls, dropping his gun. Menus, struggling to handcuff the wrists of another, turns when his father goes down. The stock that drenches his face is so hot he can't yell. He drops to one knee and a woman's hand reaches for the gun spinning on the floor. Hurt, half blinded, he yanks her left ankle. She crashes kicking at his head with her right foot. Behind him a woman aims a butcher knife and plunges it so deep in the shoulder bone she can't remove it for a second strike. She leaves it there and escapes into the yard with the other two, scattering fowl as they go.

Coming from the second floor, Wisdom Poole and Sargeant Person see no one. They enter the schoolroom where light pours through the windows. They search behind desks pushed to the wall even though it is clear nobody, even a child, is small enough to hide there.

Down below under long slow beams of a Black & Decker, Steward, Deek and K.D. observe defilement and violence and perversions beyond imagination. Lovingly drawn filth carpets the stone floor. K.D. fingers his palm cross. Deek taps his shirt pocket where sunglasses are tucked. He had thought he might use them for other purposes, but he wonders if he needs them now to shield from his sight this sea of depravity beckoning below. None dares step on it. More than justified in their expectations, they turn around and climb the stairs. The schoolroom door is wide open; Sargeant and Wisdom motion them in. Bunched at the windows, all five understand: the women are not hiding. They are loose.

Shortly after the men have left Sargeant's place, the citizens of Ruby arrive at the Oven. The rain is slowing. The trash barrel swirls with debris. The stream has crested but doesn't overflow its banks. It seeps underground instead. Rain cascading off the Oven's head meets mud speckled with grout flakes washed away from bricks. The Oven shifts, just slightly, on one side. The impacted ground on which it rests is undermined. In trucks and cars the citizens go to meet the men.

Neither of the sisters needs persuading, for both have known something awful was happening. Dovey asks Soane to drive. Each is silent with loud, rocketing thoughts. Dovey has watched her husband destroy something in himself for thirty years. The more he gained, the less he became. Now he may be ruining everything. Had twenty-five years of rampant success confused him? Did he think that because they lived away from white law they were beyond it? Of course, no one could ask for a more doting husband and as long as she ignored the unknowable parts, their marriage seemed perfect. Still, she misses the little foreclosed house where her Friend visited. Only once since K.D. took it over has he come to her and that was in a dream where he was moving away from her. She called; he turned. Next thing she knew, she was washing his hair. She woke, puzzled, but pleased to see that her hands were wet from the suds.

Soane is chastising herself for not having talked, just talked, to Deek. Told him she knew about Connie; that the loss of their

287

third child was a judgment against her—not him. After Connie saved Scout's life, Soane's resentment against her evaporated and, because the two of them had become fast friends, she believed she had forgiven Deek also. Now she wondered whether her fear of suffocating in air too thin for breathing, her unrelieved mourning for her sons, keeping the ache alive by refusing to read their last letters were ways of punishing him without seeming to. In any case, she was certain that routing the Convent women had something to do with their marriage. Harper, Sargeant and certainly Arnold wouldn't lift a hand to those women if Deek and Steward had not authorized and manipulated them. If only she had talked twenty-two years ago. Just talked.

"What do you think?" Dovey broke the silence.

"I can't."

"They wouldn't hurt them, would they?"

Soane cut off the wipers. There was no need for them now. "No," she answered. "Just scare them. Into leaving, I mean."

"People talk about them all the time, though. Like they were . . . slime."

"They're different is all."

"I know, but that's been enough before."

"These are women, Dovey. Just women."

"Whores, though, and strange too."

"Dovey!"

"That's what Steward says, and if he believes it—"

"I don't care if they're—" Soane couldn't imagine worse. Both became quiet.

"Lone said K.D. is out there."

"He would be."

"You think Mable knows? Or Priscilla?" asks Dovey.

"Doubt it. Hadn't been for Lone, would we?"

"It'll be all right, I guess. Aaron and Pious will stop them. And the Beauchamps. Even Steward won't mess with Luther."

The sisters laughed then, small hopeful laughs, soothing themselves as they sped through glorious dawn air.

· · ·

Consolata wakes. Seconds earlier she thought she heard footsteps descending. She assumed it was Pallas coming to nurse the baby lying beside her. She touches the diaper to see if a change is needed. Something. Something. Consolata goes chill. Opening the door she hears retreating steps too heavy, too many for a woman. She considers whether or not to disturb the baby's sleep. Then, quickly slipping on a dress, blue with a white collar, she decides to leave the child on the cot. She climbs the stairs and sees immediately a shape lying in the foyer. She runs to it and cradles the woman in her arms, smearing her cheek and the left side of her dress with blood. The pulse at the neck is there but not strong; the breathing is shallow. Consolata rubs the fuzz on the woman's head and begins to step in, deep, deeper to find the pinpoint of light. Shots ring from the next room.

Men are firing through the window at three women running through clover and Scotch broom. Consolata enters, bellowing, "No!"

The men turn.

Consolata narrows her gaze against the sun, then lifts it as though distracted by something high above the heads of the men. "You're back," she says, and smiles.

Deacon Morgan needs the sunglasses, but they are nestled in his shirt pocket. He looks at Consolata and sees in her eyes what has been drained from them and from himself as well. There is blood near her lips. It takes his breath away. He lifts his hand to halt his brother's and discovers who, between them, is the stronger man. The bullet enters her forehead.

Dovey is screaming. Soane is staring.

"This dying may take a while." Lone is desperate for Doublemint as she stanches the white woman's wound. She and Ren have carried her to the sofa in the game room. Lone can't hear a heartbeat, and although the neck pulse seems still to be there, too much blood has left this woman with wrists small as a child's.

"Has anybody gone for Roger?" she shouts.

"Yes," somebody shouts back.

The noise outside the room is giving her a headache along with a fierce desire to chew. Lone leaves the woman to see what is being done to salvage a life or two from the mess.

Dovey is weeping on the stairs.

"Dovey, you have to shut up now. I need a thinking woman. Come in here and get some water; try to get that girl in there to drink it." She drags her toward the kitchen where Soane is.

Earlier, Deacon Morgan had carried Consolata into the kitchen, holding her in his arms for the time it took the women to clear the table. He laid her down carefully, as though any rough gesture might hurt her. It was after Consolata was comfortable—Soane's raincoat folded under her head—that his hands trembled. Then he left to help with the wounded men. Menus, unable to get the knife from his shoulder, was whinnying in pain. Harper's head was swelling, but it was Arnold Fleetwood who seemed to be suffering a concussion. And Jeff's broken jaw and cracked wrist needed attention. Other Ruby people, stirred by the first caravan, had arrived, increasing twofold the disorder and the din. Reverend Pulliam removed the knife from Menus' shoulder and had great difficulty trying to get both Jury men and the Fleetwoods to agree to go to the Demby hospital. A message came from Deed Sands' son that Roger's return from Middleton was expected this morning, and soon as he got back his daughter would send him along. Pulliam was finally persuasive and drove the hurt men away.

Male voices continued to boom. Between loud accusations and sullen if quieter defense, under the onslaught of questions and prophecies of doom, it was a half hour or so before anyone thought to ask what had happened to the other women. When Pious did, Sargeant indicated "out there" with a head motion.

"Run off? To the sheriff?"

"Doubt that."

"What, man?"

"They went down. In the grass."

"You all massacred those women? For what?"

"Now we got white law on us as well as damnation!"

"We didn't come here to kill anybody. Look what they did to Menus and Fleet. It was self-defense!"

Aaron Poole looked at K.D. who had offered that explanation.

"You come in their house and don't expect them to fight you?" The contempt in his eyes was clear but not as chilling as Luther's.

"Who had the guns?" asked Luther.

"We all did, but it was Uncle Steward who—"

Steward slapped him full in the mouth, and had it not been for Simon Cary, another massacre might have taken place. "Hold that man!" shouted Reverend Cary and, pointing to K.D., "You in trouble, son."

Pious banged his fist on the wall. "You have already dishonored us. Now you going to destroy us? What manner of evil is in you?" He had been looking at Steward, but now his gaze took in Wisdom, Sargeant and the other two.

"The evil is in this house," said Steward. "Go down in that cellar and see for yourself."

"My brother is lying. This is our doing. Ours alone. And we bear the responsibility."

For the first time in twenty-one years the twins looked each other dead in the eyes.

Meanwhile Soane and Lone DuPres close the two pale eyes but can do nothing about the third one, wet and lidless, in between.

"She said, 'Divine,'" Soane whispers.

"What?" Lone is trying to organize a sheet to cover the body.

"When I went to her. Right after Steward . . . I held her head and she said, 'Divine.' Then something like 'He's divine he's sleeping divine.' Dreaming, I guess."

"Well, she was shot in the head, Soane."

"What do you think she saw?"

"I don't know, but it's a sweet thought even if it was her last."

Dovey comes in, saying, "She's gone."

"You sure?" asks Lone.

"Go look for yourself."

"I will."

The sisters cover Consolata with the sheet.

"I didn't know her as well as you," Dovey says.

"I loved her. As God is my witness I did, but nobody knew her really."

"Why did they do it?"

"They? You mean 'he,' don't you? Steward killed her. Not Deek."

"You make it sound as though it's all his fault."

"I didn't mean to."

"Then what? What did you mean?"

Soane does not know what she means, other than how to locate a sliver of soap to clean away any little taint she can. But it is an exchange that alters their relationship irrevocably.

Bewildered, angry, sad, frightened people pile into cars, making their way back to children, livestock, fields, household chores and uncertainty. How hard they had worked for this place; how far away they once were from the terribleness they have just witnessed. How could so clean and blessed a mission devour itself and become the world they had escaped?

Lone has said she would stay with the bodies until Roger got there. Melinda asks, "How will you get back? Your car is out at our place."

Lone sighs. "Well, the dead don't move. And Roger's got a lot of work to do." As the car pulls away, Lone looks back at the house. "A lot of work."

He had none. When Roger Best got back to Ruby, he didn't even change his clothes. He gunned the motor of the ambulance/hearse and sped to the Convent. Three women were down in the grass, he'd been told. One in the kitchen. Another across the hall. He searched everywhere. Every inch of grass, every patch of Scotch broom. The henhouse. The garden. Every row of corn in the field beyond. Then every room: the chapel, the schoolroom. The game room was empty; the kitchen too—a sheet and a folded raincoat on the table the only sign that a body had been there. Upstairs he looked in both bathrooms, in all eight bedrooms. Again the kitchen, the pantry. Then he went down into the cellar, stepped over the floor paintings. He opened one door that revealed a coal bin. Behind another a small bed and a pair of shiny shoes on the dresser. No bodies. Nothing. Even the Cadillac was gone.

SAVE-MARIE

"This is why we are here: in this single moment of aching sadness—in contemplating the short life and the unacceptable, incomprehensible death of a child—we confirm, defer or lose our faith. Here in the tick tock of this moment, in this place all our questions, all our fear, our outrage, confusion, desolation seem to merge, snatch away the earth and we feel as though we are falling. Here, we might say, it is time to halt, to linger this one time and reject platitudes about sparrows falling under His eye; about the good dying young (this child didn't have a choice about being good); or about death being the only democracy. This is the time to ask the questions that are really on our minds. Who could do this to a child? Who could permit this for a child? And why?"

Sweetie Fleetwood wouldn't discuss it. Her child would not be laid to rest on Steward Morgan's land. It was a brand-new problem: the subject of burial sites had not come up in Ruby for twenty years, and there was astonishment as well as sadness when the task became necessary. When Save-Marie, the youngest of Sweetie and Jeff's children, died, people assumed the rest of them, Noah, Esther and Ming, would quickly follow. The first was given a strong name for a strong son as well as being the name of his great-grandfather. The second was named Esther for the great-grandmother who loved and cared for the first so selflessly. The third had a name Jeff insisted upon—something having to do with the war. This last child's name was a request (or a lament): Save-Marie, and who was to say whether the call had not been answered. Thus the tense discussion of a formal cemetery was

not only because of Sweetie's wishes and the expectation of more
funerals, but out of a sense that, for complicated reasons, the reaper
was no longer barred entry from Ruby. Richard Misner was therefore
presiding over consecrated ground and launching a new institution.
But whether to use the ad hoc cemetery on Steward's ranch—where
Ruby Smith lay—was a question out of the question for Sweetie.
Under the influence of her brother, Luther, and blaming Steward for
the trouble he got her husband and father-in-law into, she said she
would rather do what Roger Best had done (dug a grave on his own
property), and she couldn't care less that twenty-three years had passed
since that quick and poorly attended backyard burial took place.

Most people understood why she was making such a fuss (grief
plus blame was a heady brew) but Pat Best believed that Sweetie's
stubbornness was more calculated. Rejecting a Morgan offer, casting
doubt on Morgan righteousness might squeeze some favors from Morgan pockets. And if Pat's 8-rock theory was correct, Sweetie's vindic-
tiveness put the 8-rocks in the awkward position of deciding to have a
real and formal cemetery in a town full of immortals. Something seis-
mic had happened since July. So here they were, under a soapy sky on
a mild November day, gathered a mile or so beyond the last Ruby
house, which was, of course, Morgan land, but nobody had the heart
to tell Sweetie so. Standing among the crowd surrounding the
bereaved Fleetwoods, Pat regained something close to stability. Earlier, at the funeral service, the absence of a eulogy had made her cry.
Now she was her familiar, dispassionately amused self. At least she
hoped she was dispassionate, and hoped amusement was what she was
feeling. She knew there were other views about her attitude, some of
which Richard Misner had expressed ("Sad. Sad and cold"), but she
was a scholar, not a romantic, and steeled herself against Misner's
graveside words to observe the mourners instead.

He and Anna Flood had returned two days after the assault on the
Convent women, and it took four days for him to learn what had happened. Pat gave him the two editions of the official story: One, that
nine men had gone to talk to and persuade the Convent women to
leave or mend their ways; there had been a fight; the women took
other shapes and disappeared into thin air. And two (the Fleetwood-

Jury version), that five men had gone to evict the women; that four others—the authors—had gone to restrain or stop them; these four were attacked by the women but had succeeded in driving them out, and they took off in their Cadillac; but unfortunately, some of the five had lost their heads and killed the old woman. Pat left Richard to choose for himself which rendition he preferred. What she withheld from him was her own: that nine 8-rocks murdered five harmless women (*a*) because the women were impure (not 8-rock); (*b*) because the women were unholy (fornicators at the least, abortionists at most); and (*c*) because they *could*—which was what being an 8-rock meant to them and was also what the "deal" required.

Richard didn't believe either of the stories rapidly becoming gospel, and spoke to Simon Cary and Senior Pulliam, who clarified other parts of the tale. But because neither had decided on the meaning of the ending and, therefore, had not been able to formulate a credible, sermonizable account of it, they could not assuage Richard's dissatisfaction. It was Lone who provided him with the livid details that several people were quick to discredit, because Lone, they said, was not reliable. Except for her, no one overheard the men at the Oven and who knew what they really said? Like the rest of the witnesses she arrived after the shots were fired; besides, she and Dovey could be wrong about whether the two women in the house were dead or just wounded; and finally, she didn't see anybody outside the house, living or dead.

As for Lone, she became unhinged by the way the story was being retold; how people were changing it to make themselves look good. Other than Deacon Morgan, who had nothing to say, every one of the assaulting men had a different tale and their families and friends (who had been nowhere near the Convent) supported them, enhancing, recasting, inventing misinformation. Although the DuPreses, Beauchamps, Sandses and Pooles backed up her version, even their reputation for precision and integrity could not prevent altered truth from taking hold in other quarters. If there were no victims the story of the crime was play for anybody's tongue. So Lone shut up and kept what she felt certain of folded in her brain: God had given Ruby a second chance. Had made Himself so visible and unarguable a presence that

PARADISE

even the outrageously prideful (like Steward) and the uncorrectably stupid (like his lying nephew) ought to be able to see it. He had actually swept up and received His servants in broad daylight, for goodness' sake! right before their very eyes, for Christ's sake! Since they were accusing her of lying, she decided to keep quiet and watch the hand of God work the disbelievers and the false witnesses. Would they know they'd been spoken to? Or would they drift further from His ways? One thing, for sure: they could see the Oven; they couldn't misread or misspeak that, so they had better hurry up and fix its slide before it was too late—which it might already be, for the young people had changed its words again. No longer were they calling themselves Be the Furrow of His Brow. The graffiti on the hood of the Oven now was "We Are the Furrow of His Brow."

However sharp the divisions about what really took place, Pat knew the big and agreed-upon fact was that everyone who had been there left the premises certain that lawmen would be happily swarming all over town (they'd killed a white woman, after all), arresting virtually all of Ruby's businessmen. When they learned there were no dead to report, transport or bury, relief was so great they began to forget what they'd actually done or seen. Had it not been for Luther Beauchamp—who told the most damning story—and Pious, Deed Sands and Aaron—who corroborated much of Lone's version—the whole thing might have been sanitized out of existence. Yet even they could not bring themselves to report unnatural deaths in a house with no bodies, which might lead to the discovery of natural deaths in an automobile full of bodies. Though not privy to many people's confidence, Pat gathered from talks with her father, with Kate and from deliberate eavesdropping that four months later they were still chewing the problem, asking God for guidance if they were wrong: if white law should, contrary to everything they knew and believed, be permitted to deal with matters heretofore handled among and by them. The difficulties churned and entangled everybody: distribution of blame, prayers for understanding and forgiveness, arrogant self-defense, outright lies, and a host of unanswered questions that Richard Misner kept putting to them. So the funeral came as a pause but not a conclusion.

298

Maybe they were right about this place all along, Pat thought, surveying the townspeople. Maybe Ruby is lucky. No, she corrected herself. Although the evidence of the assault was invisible, the consequences were not. There was Jeff, his arm around his wife, both looking properly sorrowful but slightly majestic too, for Jeff was now sole owner of his father's furniture and appliance store. Arnold, suddenly a very old man with a persistent headache, and enjoying his own bedroom now that Arnette had moved out, stood with bowed head and roaming eyes that traveled everywhere but near the coffin. Sargeant Person looked as smug as ever: he had no landlord expecting a field fee and unless and until the county auditor got interested in a tiny hamlet of quiet, God-fearing black folk, his avarice would go unabated. Harper Jury, uncontrite, was wearing a dark blue suit and a head wound that, like a medal, gave him leave to assume the position of bloodied but unbowed warrior against evil. Menus was the most unfortunate. He had no customers at Anna's anymore, in part because his ruined shoulder restricted his facility with barber tools but also because his drinking had extended itself to many more days of the week. His dissipation was rapidly coming to its own conclusion. Wisdom Poole had the toughest row to hoe. Seventy family members held him accountable (just as they had his brothers, Brood and Apollo) for scandalizing their forefathers' reputations, giving him no peace or status, reprimanding him daily until he fell on his knees and wept before the entire congregation of Holy Redeemer. After testifying, recommitted, renewed and full of remorse, he began tentative conversations with Brood and Apollo. Arnette and K.D. were building a new house on Steward's property. She was pregnant again, and they both hoped to get in a position to make life unpleasant for the Pooles, the DuPreses, the Sandses and the Beauchamps, especially Luther, who took every opportunity to insult K.D. The most interesting development was with the Morgan brothers. Their distinguishing features were eroding: tobacco choices (they gave up cigar and chaw at the same time), shoes, clothes, facial hair. Pat thought they looked more alike than they probably had at birth. But the inside difference was too deep for anyone to miss. Steward, insolent and unapologetic, took K.D. under his wing, concentrating on making the nephew and the sixteen-month-old grandnephew rich (thus the new house), easing K.D. into the bank while waiting for Dovey to come around, which she seemed to be doing, because there was an obvious coolness between her and Soane. The sisters disagreed about what happened at the Convent. Dovey saw Consolata fall but maintained she did not see who pulled the trigger. Soane knew, and needed to know, one thing: it had not been her husband. She had seen his hand moving over to Steward's in a cautioning, preventing gesture. She saw it and she said it, over and over again, to anyone who would listen.

It was Deacon Morgan who had changed the most. It was as though he had looked in his brother's face and did not like himself anymore. To everyone's surprise he had formed a friendship (well, a relationship anyway) with somebody other than Steward, the cause, reason and basis of which were a mystery. Richard Misner wasn't talking, so all anyone knew for certain was the barefoot walk that took place in public.

It was September then and still hot when Deacon Morgan walked toward Central. Chrysanthemums to the right, chrysanthemums to the left of the brick path leading from his imposing white house. He wore his hat, business suit, vest and a clean white shirt. No shoes. No socks. He entered St. John Street, where he had planted trees fifty feet apart, so great was his optimism twenty years earlier. He turned right on Central. It had been at least a decade since the soles of his shoes, let alone his bare feet, had touched that much concrete. Just past Arnold Fleetwood's house, near the corner of St. Luke, a couple said, "Morning, Deek." He lifted his hand in greeting, his eyes straight ahead. Lily Cary helloed from the porch of her house near Cross Mark but he did not turn his head. "Car broke down?" she asked, staring at his feet. At Harper Jury's drugstore, on the corner of Central and St. Matthew, he felt rather than saw watchful eyes traveling alongside him. He didn't turn to see nor did he glance through the window of the Morgan Savings and Loan Bank as he approached St. Peter. At Cross Peter he crossed and made his way to Richard Misner's house. The last time he was here, six years before, he was angry, suspicious but certain he and his brother would prevail. What he felt now was exotic to a twin—an incompleteness, a muffled solitude, which took away appetite, sleep and sound. Since July, other people seemed to him to be speaking in whispers, or shouting from long distances. Soane watched him but, mercifully, did not initiate dangerous dialogue. It was as though she understood that had she done so, what he said to her would draw the life from their life. He might tell her that green springtime had been sapped away; that outside of that loss, she was grand, more beautiful than he believed a woman could be; that her untamable hair framed a face of planes so sharp he wanted to touch; that after she spoke, the smile that followed made the sun look like a fool. He might tell his wife that he thought at first she was speaking to him—"You're back"— but knew now it wasn't so. And that instantly he longed to know what she saw, but Steward, who saw nothing or everything, stopped them dead lest they know another realm.

Earlier that September morning he had bathed and dressed carefully but could not bring himself to cover his feet. He handled the dark socks, the shiny black shoes for a long while, then put them aside.

He knocked on the door and removed his hat when the younger man answered.

"I need to speak to you, Reverend."

"Come on in."

Deacon Morgan had never consulted with or taken into his confidence any man. All of his intimate conversations had been wordless ones with his brother or brandishing ones with male companions. He spoke to his wife in the opaque manner he thought appropriate. None had required him to translate into speech the raw matter he exposed to Reverend Misner. His words came out like ingots pulled from the fire by an apprentice blacksmith—hot, misshapen, resembling themselves only in their glow. He spoke of a wall in Ravenna, Italy, white in the late afternoon sun with wine colored shadows pressing its edge. Of two children on a beach offering him a shell formed like an S—how open their faces, how loud the bells. Of salt water burning his face on a troop ship. Of colored girls in slacks waving from the door of a canning factory. Then he told him of his grandfather who walked barefoot for two hundred miles rather than dance.

Richard listened intently, interrupting once to offer cool water. Although he did not understand what Deacon was talking about, he could see that the man's life was uninhabitable. Deacon began to speak of a woman he had used; how he had turned up his nose at her because her loose and easy ways gave him the license to drop and despise her. That while the adultery preyed on him for a short while (very short), his long remorse was at having become what the Old Fathers cursed: the kind of man who set himself up to judge, rout and even destroy the needy, the defenseless, the different.

"Who is this woman?" Richard asked him.

Deacon did not answer. He ran his finger around the inside of his shirt collar, then started on another story. It seemed his grandfather, Zechariah, was subject to personal taunts as well as newspaper articles describing his malfeasance in office. He was an embarrassment to Negroes and both a threat and a joke to whites. No one, black or white, could or would help him find other work. He was even passed up for a teaching job at a poor country primary school. The Negroes in a position to help were few (the depression of '73 was severe), but they took Zechariah's dignified manner for coldness and his studied speech for arrogance, mockery or both. The family lost the nice house and were living (all nine of them) with a sister's family. Mindy, his wife, found work sewing at home, and the children did odd jobs. Few knew and fewer remembered that Zechariah had a twin, and before he changed his name, they were known as Coffee and Tea. When Coffee got the statehouse job, Tea seemed as pleased as everybody else. And when his brother was thrown out of office, he was equally affronted and humiliated. One day, years later, when he and his twin were walking near a saloon, some whitemen, amused by the double faces, encouraged the brothers to dance. Since the encouragement took the form of a pistol, Tea, quite reasonably, accommodated the whites, even though he was a grown man, older than they were. Coffee took a bullet in his foot instead. From that moment they weren't brothers anymore. Coffee began to plan a new life elsewhere. He contacted other men, other former legislators who had the same misfortune as his—Juvenal DuPres and Drum Blackhorse. They were the three who formed the nucleus of the Old Fathers. Needless to say, Coffee didn't ask Tea to join them on their journey to Oklahoma.

"I always thought Coffee—Big Papa—was wrong," said Deacon Morgan. "Wrong in what he did to his brother. Tea was his twin, after all. Now I'm less sure. I'm thinking Coffee was right because he saw something in Tea that wasn't just going along with some drunken whiteboys. He saw something that shamed him. The way his brother thought about things; the choices he made when up against it. Coffee couldn't take it. Not because he was ashamed of his twin, but because the shame was in himself. It scared him. So he went off and never spoke to his brother again. Not one word. Know what I mean?"

"It must have been hard," said Richard.

"I'm saying he never said another word to him and wouldn't allow anybody else to call his name."

"Lack of words," Richard said. "Lack of forgiveness. Lack of love. To lose a brother is a hard thing. To choose to lose one, well, that's worse than the original shame, wouldn't you say?"

Deacon looked down at his feet for a long time. Richard stayed quiet with him. Finally he raised his head and said:

"I got a long way to go, Reverend."

"You'll make it," said Richard Misner. "No doubt about it."

Richard and Anna doubted the convenient mass disappearance of the victims and, as soon as they got back, went to look for themselves. Other than a sparkling white crib in a bedroom with the word DIVINE taped to the door, and foodstuffs, there was nothing recently lived-in about the place. The chickens were wilding or half eaten by four-footed prowlers. Pepper bushes were in full flower, but the rest of the garden was lost. Sargeant's cornfield the only human touch. Richard barely glanced at the cellar floor. Anna, however, examining it as closely as her lamp permitted, saw the terribleness K.D. reported, but it wasn't the pornography he had seen, nor was it Satan's scrawl. She saw instead the turbulence of females trying to bridle, without being trampled, the monsters that slavered them.

They left the house and stood in the yard.

"Listen," Anna told him. "One of them or maybe more wasn't

dead. Nobody actually looked—they just assumed. Then, between the time folks left and Roger arrived, they got the hell out of there. Taking the killed ones with them. Simple, right?"

"Right," said Misner, but he didn't sound convinced.

"It's been weeks now, and nobody has come around asking questions. They must not have reported it, so why should we?"

"Whose baby was in there? That crib is new."

"I don't know, but it sure wasn't Arnette's."

He said it again, "Right," with the same level of doubt. Then, "I don't like mysteries."

"You're a preacher. Your whole life's belief is a mystery."

"Belief is mysterious; faith is mysterious. But God is not a mystery. We are."

"Oh, Richard," she said as though it was all too much.

He had asked her to marry him. "Will you marry me, Anna?"

"Oh, I don't know."

"Why not?"

"Your fire's too stingy."

"Not when it counts."

She had never expected to be that happy and coming back to Ruby, instead of making the great announcement, they were sorting out what looked like the total collapse of a town.

"Should we take those chickens? They'll all be eaten anyway."

"If you want to," he said.

"I don't. I'll just see if there're any eggs." Anna entered the henhouse wrinkling her nose and stepping through a half inch of chicken litter. She fought a couple of them to get the five eggs that she thought were probably fresh. When she came out, both hands full, she called, "Richard? Got something I can put these in?" At the edge of the garden a faded red chair lay on its side. Beyond was blossom and death. Shriveled tomato plants alongside crops of leafy green reseeding themselves with golden flowers; pink hollyhocks so tall the heads leaned all the way over a trail of bright squash blossoms; lacy tops of carrots browned and lifeless next to straight green spikes of onion. Melons split their readiness showing gums of juicy red. Anna sighed at the mix of neglect and unconquerable growth. The five eggs warm umber in her hands.

Richard came toward her. "This big enough?" He flicked open his handkerchief.

"Maybe. Here, hold them while I see if the peppers are out."

"No," he said. "I'll go." He dropped the handkerchief over the eggs.

It was when he returned, as they stood near the chair, her hands balancing brown eggs and white cloth, his fingers looking doubled with long pepper pods—green, red and plum black—that they saw it. Or sensed it, rather, for there was nothing to see. A door, she said later. "No, a window," he said, laughing. "That's the difference between us. You see a door; I see a window."

Anna laughed too. They expanded on the subject: What did a door mean? what a window? focusing on the sign rather than the event; excited by the invitation rather than the party. They knew it was there. Knew it so well they were transfixed for a long moment before they backed away and ran to the car. The eggs and peppers lay in the rear seat; the air conditioner lifted her collar. And they laughed some more as they drove along, trading pleasant insults about who was a pessimist, who an optimist. Who saw a closed door; who saw a raised window. Anything to avoid reliving the shiver or saying out loud what they were wondering. Whether through a door needing to be opened or a beckoning window already raised, what would happen if you entered? What would be on the other side? What on earth would it be? What on earth?

Reverend Misner had everyone's attention and just a few words more to offer. His glance focused on the culpable men, seven of whom, with some primitive instinct for protection, clustered together, away, it seemed from the other mourners. Sargeant, Harper, Menus, Arnold, Jeff, K.D., Steward. Wisdom was closest to his own family; and Deacon was not there at all. Richard's thoughts about these men were not generous. Whether they be the first or the last, representing the oldest black families or the newest, the best of the tradition or the most pathetic, they had ended up betraying it all. They think they have out-foxed the whiteman when in fact they imitate him. They think they are protecting their wives and children, when in fact they are maiming them. And when the maimed children ask for help, they look else-where for the cause. Born out of an old hatred, one that began when one kind of black man scorned another kind and that kind took the hatred to another level, their selfishness had trashed two hundred years of suffering and triumph in a moment of such pomposity and error and callousness it froze the mind. Unbridled by Scripture, deafened by the roar of its own history, Ruby, it seemed to him, was an unneces-sary failure. How exquisitely human was the wish for permanent hap-piness, and how thin human imagination became trying to achieve it. Soon Ruby will be like any other country town: the young thinking of elsewhere; the old full of regret. The sermons will be eloquent but fewer and fewer will pay attention or connect them to everyday life. How can they hold it together, he wondered, this hard-won heaven defined only by the absence of the unsaved, the unworthy and the strange? Who will protect them from their leaders?

Suddenly Richard Misner knew he would stay. Not only because Anna wanted to, or because Deek Morgan had sought him out for a confession of sorts, but also because there was no better battle to fight, no better place to be than among these outrageously beautiful, flawed and proud people. Besides, mortality may be new to them but birth was not. The future panted at the gate. Roger Best will get his gas sta-tion and the connecting roads will be laid. Outsiders will come and go, come and go and some will want a sandwich and a can of 3.2 beer. So who knows, maybe there will be a diner too. K.D. and Steward will already be discussing TV. It was inappropriate to smile at a funeral, so Misner envisioned the little girl whose destroyed hands he had once been permitted to hold. It helped him recover his line of thought. The questions he had asked in the mourners' stead needed an answer.

"May I suggest those are not the important questions. Or rather those are the questions of anguish but not of intelligence. And God, being intelligence itself, generosity itself, has given us Mind to know

His subtlety. To know His elegance. His purity. To know that 'what is sown is not alive until it dies.'"

The wind picked up a bit but not enough to make anyone uncomfortable. Misner was losing them; they stood before the open grave closed to everything but their own musings. Funeral thoughts were mingled with plans for Thanksgiving, evaluations of their neighbors, the chitty-chat of daily life. Misner repressed a sigh before concluding his remarks with prayer. But when he bowed his head and gazed at the coffin lid he saw the window in the garden, felt it beckon toward another place—neither life nor death—but there, just yonder, shaping thoughts he did not know he had.

"Wait. Wait." He was shouting. "Do you think this was a short, pitiful life bereft of worth because it did not parallel your own? Let me tell you something. The love she received was wide and deep, and the care given her was gentle and unrelenting, and that love and care enveloped her so completely that the dreams, the visions she had, the journeys she took made her life as compelling, as rich, as valuable as any of ours and probably more blessed. It is our own misfortune if we do not know in our long life what she knew every day of her short one: that although life in life is terminal and life after life is everlasting, He is with us always, in life, after it and especially in between, lying in wait for us to know the splendor." He stopped, disturbed by what he had said and how. Then, as if to apologize to the little girl, he spoke softly, directly to her.

"Oh, Save-Marie, your name always sounded like 'Save me.' 'Save me.' Any other messages hiding in your name? I know one that shines out for all to see: there never was a time when you were not saved, Marie. Amen."

His words embarrassed him a little, but on that day, nothing had ever been clearer.

Billie Delia walked slowly away from the other mourners. She had stood with her mother and grandfather and smiled encouragingly at Arnette, but now she wanted to be alone. This was her first funeral, and she thought about it in terms of how expansive it made her grandfather to have his skills needed. More on her mind was the absence of the women she had liked. They had treated her so well, had not embarrassed her with sympathy, had just given her sunny kindness. Looking at her bruised face and swollen eyes, they sliced cucumber for her lids after making her drink a glass of wine. No one insisted on hearing what drove her there, but she could tell they would listen if she wanted them to. The one called Mavis was the nicest and the funniest was Gigi. Billie Delia was perhaps the only one in town who was not puzzled by where the women were or concerned about how they disappeared. She had another question: When will they return? When will they reappear, with blazing eyes, war paint and huge hands to rip up and stomp down this prison calling itself a town? A town that had tried to ruin her grandfather, succeeded in swallowing her mother and almost broken her own self. A backward noplace ruled by men whose power to control was out of control and who had the nerve to say who could live and who not and where; who had seen in lively, free, unarmed females the mutiny of the mares and so got rid of them. She hoped with all her heart that the women were out there, darkly burnished, biding their time, brass-metaling their nails, filing their incisors—but out there. Which is to say she hoped for a miracle. Not so unreasonable a wish since a minimiracle had already occurred: Brood and Apollo had reconciled, agreeing to wait for her to make up her mind. She knew, as they did, that she never could and that the threesome would end only when they did. The Convent women would roar at that. She could see their pointy teeth.

The reprieve took years but it came. Manley Gibson would die in a ward with others like himself rather than strapped to a chair with no kin looking on. It was a good thing. A great thing. He got to go outside and now he was part of the work crew at the lake road. The lake was so blue. The Kentucky Fried Chicken lunch so fine. Maybe he could run. Some joke. A fifty-two-year-old lifer on the run. Where to? To who? He had been in since 1961, leaving behind an eleven-year-old who didn't write anymore, and the only photograph he had of her was when she was thirteen.

Lunchtime was special. They sat near the lake in full sight of the guards but near the water anyway. Manley wiped his hands on the little paper napkins. To his left, near a couple of trees, a young woman spread two blankets on the grass, a radio in between. Manley turned to see what the crew thought of this: a civilian (and a female, too) right in their midst. Armed guards strolled the road above them. None gave sign that they saw her.

She turned on the radio and stood up, revealing a face he'd know anywhere. For the life of him he couldn't help it. "Gigi!" he hissed.

The girl looked his way. Manley, restraining himself, sauntered over to the trees, hoping the guards would think he was taking a leak.

"Am I right? Is it you?"

"Daddy Man?" At least she looked pleased to see him.

"It is you! Goddamn, I knew it. What you doing here? You knew I was reprieved?"

"No, I didn't know nothing about it."

"Well, look here, I don't get out or nothing, but I ain't on the row no more." Manley turned to see if others had noticed them. "Keep your voice down," he whispered. "So what you doing here?" He noticed her clothes for the first time. "You in the army?"

Gigi smiled. "Sort of."

"Sort of? You mean you was?"

"Oh, Daddy Man, anybody can buy this stuff." Gigi laughed.

"Gimme your address, honey. I wanna write and tell you everything. Hear from your mother? Her old man still alive?" He was rushing; the lunch whistle was due to sound any minute.

"I don't have an address yet." Gigi lifted her cap and replaced it.

"No? Well, uh, you write me, okay? Care of the prison. I'll put you on the list tomorrow. I can get two a month—"

The whistle blew. "Two," Manley repeated. Then, "Say, you still got that locket I give you?"

"I got it."

"Ooh, honey, oh, honey, my little girl." He reached out to touch her but stopped, saying, "I gotta go. They'll demerit me. Care of the prison, hear? Two a month." He backed away, still looking at her. "Will I hear from you?"

Gigi straightened her cap. "You will, Daddy Man. You will."

Later, as Manley sat on the bus, he went over every detail of what he had seen of his daughter. Her army cap and fatigue pants— camouflage colors. Heavy army boots, black T-shirt. And now that he thought of it, he could swear she was packing. He looked toward the lake, darkening in a lower but prettier sun.

Gigi took off her clothes. The nights were chilling the lake, making it harder and harder for the sun to warm it the next day. In this part of the lake it was okay to swim nude. This was lake country: viridian water, upright trees and—in places where no boats or fishermen came—a privacy royals would envy. She picked up a towel and dried her hair. Less than an inch had grown, but she loved how wind and water and fingers and toes rippled in it. She opened a bottle of aloe and began to rub her skin. Then, straightening the towel next to her, she looked toward the lake where her companion was just coming ashore.

The fifteenth painting, like the first, needed more. Trying to remember the chin had frustrated Dee Dee in her first attempt, but when she decided to skip the jawline and just shadow the lower part of her daughter's face, she found the eyes all wrong. Canvas fifteen got it better, but still something was missing. The head was fine, but the body, bleak and uninteresting, seemed to need another shape — at the hip or elbow. Never having experienced a compulsion that was not sensual, she was puzzled by the energy she could summon at will to freshen or begin the figure anew. The eyes kept coming up accusatory; the skin tone eluded her; and the hair was invariably a hat.

Dee Dee sat down on the floor, rolling the brush handle in her fingers while she examined the work she had done. With a long puff of air she got up and went into the living room. It was when she had taken the first sip of the margarita that she saw her coming across the yard, a knapsack or something tied to her chest. But she had no hair. No hair at all and a baby's head lay just under her chin. As she came closer, Dee Dee could see two fat legs, round as doughnuts, poking out of the knapsack thing on its mother's chest. She put down the margarita and pressed her face to the picture window. No mistake. It was Pallas. One hand on the knapsack bottom, the other carrying a sword. A sword? The smile on Pallas' face was beatific. And her dress — rose madder and umber — swirled about her ankles with every step. Dee Dee waved and called out her name. Or tried to. While she thought "Pallas," formed it in her mind, it came out different, like "urg," then "neh neh." Something was wrong with her tongue. Pallas was moving quickly but not coming toward the front door. She was moving past the house, to the side. Dee Dee, in a panic, ran into the studio, grabbed the fifteenth canvas and rushed to the patio, holding it up and shouting, "Urg. Urg. Neh!" Pallas turned, narrowed her eyes and paused as if trying to determine where the sound came from, then, failing, continued on her way. Dee Dee stopped, thinking maybe it was someone else. But with or without hair, that was her face, wasn't it? She of all people knew her own daughter's face, didn't she? As well as she knew her own.

Dee Dee saw Pallas a second time. In the guest bedroom (where Carlos—the motherfucker—used to sleep), Pallas was searching under the bed. As Dee Dee watched, not daring to speak in case the glug sound came out of her mouth, Pallas raised up. With a satisfied grunt, she held aloft a pair of shoes she'd left there on her last, and first, visit. Huaraches, but expensive leather ones, not that plastic or straw stuff. Pallas didn't turn; she left through the sliding glass door. Dee Dee followed and saw her get into a beat-up car waiting on the road. Other people were in the car but the sun was setting so Dee Dee couldn't tell if they were men or women. They drove off into a violet so ultra it broke her heart.

Sally Albright, walking north on Calumet, stopped suddenly in front of the plate-glass window of Jennie's Country Inn. She was sure, almost sure, that the woman sitting by herself at a table for four was her mother. Sally moved closer to peep under the woman's straw hat. She couldn't quite see the face but the fingernails, the hands holding the menu were indisputable. She went inside the restaurant. A lady near the cash register said, "May I help you?" Everyplace Sally went now, she gave folks pause. All because of her hair color. "No," she told the lady. "I'm looking for a—Oh, there she is," and, faking assuredness, sauntered over to the table for four. If she was wrong, she'd say, "'Scuse me, I thought you was somebody else." She slipped into a chair and looked closely at the woman's face.

"Mom?"

Mavis looked up. "Oh, my," she said, smiling. "Look at you."

"I wasn't sure, the hat and all, but God, look, it is you."

Mavis laughed.

"Oh, man. I knew it. God, Mom, it's been . . . years!"

"I know. Have you eaten?"

"Yeah. Just finished. I'm on my lunch hour. I work at—"

The waitress raised her order pad. "Have you all decided yet?"

"Yes," said Mavis. "Orange juice, double grits and two eggs over medium."

"Bacon?" asked the waitress.

"No, thanks."

"We got good sausage—link and patty."

"No, thanks. You serve gravy with the biscuits?"

"Sure do. Poured or on the side?"

"On the side, please."

"Sure thing. And you?" She turned to Sally.

"Just coffee."

"Oh, come on," said Mavis. "Have something. My treat."

"I don't want anything."

"You sure?"

"Yeah, I'm sure."

The waitress left. Mavis lined up the place mat and flatware. "That's what I like about this place. They let you choose. Gravy poured or on the side, see?"

"Mom! I don't want to talk about food." Sally felt as though her mother was sliding away, acting like their seeing each other wasn't important.

"Well, you never did have much of an appetite."

"Where've you been?"

"Well, I couldn't come back, could I?"

"You mean that warrant stuff?"

"I mean everything. How about you? You been all right?"

"Mostly. Frankie's fine. Gets all A's. But Billy James ain't so hot."

"Oh. Why?"

"Hangs out with some real scary little shits."

"Oh, no."

"You should go see him, Ma. Talk to him."

"I will."

"Will you?"

"Can I have my lunch first?" Mavis laughed and removed her hat.

"Ma. You cut your hair off." There it was again—that slidey feeling. "It looks nice, though. How you like mine?"

"Cute."

"No it ain't. Thought I'd like blond tips, but I'm tired of it now. Maybe I'll cut mine too."

The waitress arrived and neatly arranged the plates. Mavis salted her grits and swirled the pat of butter on top. She sipped her orange juice and said, "Ooo. Fresh."

It came out in a rush because she felt she had to hurry. If she was going to say anything, she had to hurry. "I was scared all the time, Ma. All the time. Even before the twins. But when you left, it got worse. You don't know. I mean I was scared to fall asleep."

"Taste this, honey." Mavis offered her the glass of juice.

Sally took a quick swallow. "Daddy was—shit, I don't know how you stood it. He'd get drunk and try to bother me, Ma."

"Oh, baby."

"I fought him, though. Told him the next time he passed out I was gonna cut his throat open. Would have, too."

"I'm so sorry," said Mavis. "I didn't know what else to do. You were always stronger than me."

"Did you never think about us?"

"All the time. And I sneaked back to get a peep at you all."

"No shit?" Sally grinned. "Where?"

"At the school, mostly. I was too scared to go by the house."

"You wouldn't know it now. Daddy married a woman who kicks his butt if he don't act right and keep the yard clean and stuff. She packs a gun, too."

Mavis laughed. "Good for her."

"But I moved out. Me and Charmaine got us a place together over on Auburn. She's a—"

"You sure you don't want something? It's really good, Sal."

Sally picked up a fork, slipped it into her mother's plate, scooping up a buttery dollop of grits. When the fork was in her mouth, their eyes met. Sally felt the nicest thing then. Something long and deep and slow and bright.

"You gonna leave again, Ma?"

"I have to, Sal."

"You coming back?"

"Sure."

"But you'll try and talk to Billy James, won't you? And Frankie'd love it. You want my address?"

"I'll talk to Billy and tell Frankie I love him."

"I'm sick and sorry about everything, Ma. I was just so scared all the time."

"Me too."

They were standing outside. The lunch crowd thickened with shoppers and their kids.

"Gimme a hug, baby."

Sally put her arms around her mother's waist and began to cry.

"Uh uh," said Mavis. "None of that, now."

Sally squeezed.

"Ouch," said Mavis, laughing.

"What?"

"Nothing. That side hurts a bit, that's all."

"You okay?"

"I'm perfect, Sal."

"I don't know what you think about me, but I always loved, always, even when."

"I know that, Sal. Know it now anyway." Mavis pushed a shank of black and yellow hair behind her daughter's ear and kissed her cheek. "Count on me, Sal."

"See you again, won't I?"

"Bye, Sal. Bye."

Sally watched her mother disappear into the crowd. She ran her finger under her nose, then held the cheek that had been kissed. Did she give her the address? Where was she going? Did they pay? When did they pay the cashier? Sally touched her eyelids. One minute they were sopping biscuits; the next they were kissing in the street.

Several years ago she had checked out the foster home and saw the mother—a cheerful, no-nonsense woman the kids seemed to like. So, fine. That was it. Fine. She could go on with her life. And did. Until

1966, when her gaze was drawn to girls with huge chocolate eyes. Seneca would be older now, thirteen years old, but she checked with Mrs. Greer to see if she had kept in touch.

"Who are you, again?"

"Her cousin, Jean."

"Well, she was only here for a short while—a few months really."

"Do you know where . . . ?"

"No, honey. I don't know a thing."

After that she was unexpectedly distracted in malls, theater ticket lines, buses. In 1968 she was certain she spotted her at a Little Richard concert, but the press of the crowd prevented a closer look. Jean was discreet about this subversive search. Jack didn't know she'd had a child before (at fourteen), and it was after marriage, when she had his child, that she began the search for the eyes. The sightings came at such odd moments and in such strange places—once she believed the girl climbing out the back of a pickup truck was her daughter—that when she finally bumped into her, in 1976, she wanted to call an ambulance. Jean and Jack were crossing the stadium parking lot under blazing klieg lights. A girl was standing in front of a car, blood running from her hands. Jean saw the blood first and then the chocolate eyes.

"Seneca!" she screamed, and ran toward her. As she approached she was intercepted by another girl, who, holding a bottle of beer and a cloth, began to clean away the blood.

"Seneca?" Jean shouted over the second girl's head.

"Yes?"

"What happened? It's me!"

"Some glass," said the second girl. "She fell on some glass. I'm taking care of her."

"Jean! Come on!" Jack was several cars down. "Where the hell are you?"

"Coming. Just a minute, okay?"

The girl wiping Seneca's hands looked up from time to time to frown at Jean. "Any glass get in?" she asked Seneca.

Seneca stroked her palms, first one, then the other. "No. I don't think so."

"Jean! Traffic's gonna be hell, babe."

"Don't you remember me?"

Seneca looked up, the bright lights turning her eyes black. "Should I? From where?"

"On Woodlawn. We used to live in those apartments on Wood-lawn."

Seneca shook her head. "I lived on Beacon. Next to the play-ground."

"But your name is Seneca, right?"

"Yes."

"Well, I'm Jean."

"Lady, your old man's calling you." The girlfriend wrung out the cloth and poured the rest of the beer over Seneca's hands.

"Ow," Seneca said to her friend. "It burns." She waved her hands in the air.

"Guess I made a mistake," said Jean. "I thought you were someone I knew from Woodlawn."

Seneca smiled. "That's okay. Everybody makes mistakes."

The friend said, "It's fine now. Look."

Seneca and Jean both looked. Her hands were clean, no blood. Just a few lines that might or might not leave marks.

"Great!"

"Let's go."

"Well, bye."

"Jean!"

"Bye."

Gunning the gas pedal while watching his rearview mirror, Jack said, "Who was that?"

"Some girl I thought I knew from before. When I lived in those apartments on Woodlawn. The housing project there."

"What housing project?"

"On Woodlawn."

"Never any projects on Woodlawn," said Jack. "That was Beacon. Torn down now, but it was never on Woodlawn. Beacon is where it was. Right next to the old playground."

"You sure about that?"

"Sure I'm sure. You losing it, woman."

PARADISE

. . .

In ocean hush a woman black as firewood is singing. Next to her is a younger woman whose head rests on the singing woman's lap. Ruined fingers troll the tea brown hair. All the colors of seashells—wheat, roses, pearl—fuse in the younger woman's face. Her emerald eyes adore the black face framed in cerulean blue. Around them on the beach, sea trash gleams. Discarded bottle caps sparkle near a broken sandal. A small dead radio plays the quiet surf.

There is nothing to beat this solace which is what Piedade's song is about, although the words evoke memories neither one has ever had: of reaching age in the company of the other; of speech shared and divided bread smoking from the fire; the unambivalent bliss of going home to be at home—the ease of coming back to love begun.

When the ocean heaves sending rhythms of water ashore, Piedade looks to see what has come. Another ship, perhaps, but different, heading to port, crew and passengers, lost and saved, atremble, for they have been disconsolate for some time. Now they will rest before shouldering the endless work they were created to do down here in paradise.

A Note About the Author

Toni Morrison is Robert F. Goheen Professor at Princeton University. She has written six previous novels, and has received the National Book Critics Circle Award and the Pulitzer Prize. She won the Nobel Prize for Literature in 1993.

A Note on the Type

The text of this book was set in Electra, a typeface designed by W. A. Dwiggins (1880–1956). This face cannot be classified as either modern or old style. It is not based on any historical model, nor does it echo any particular period or style. It avoids the extreme contrasts between thick and thin elements that mark most modern faces, and it attempts to give a feeling of fluidity, power, and speed.

Composed by North Market Street Graphics,
Lancaster, Pennsylvania
Printed and bound by R. R. Donnelley & Sons,
Harrisonburg, Virginia
Designed by Virginia Tan